The Portion
of Labor

The Portion of Labor

MARY E. WILKINS FREEMAN

ÆGYPAN PRESS

this text from the edition published in 1901 by Harper & Brothers
of New York.

The Portion of Labor
A publication of
ÆGYPAN PRESS

www.aegypan.com

To Henry Mills Alden

Chapter I

On the west side of Ellen's father's house was a file of Norway spruce trees, standing with a sharp pointing of dark boughs towards the north, which gave them an air of expectancy of progress.

Every morning Ellen, whose bedroom faced that way, looked out with a firm belief that she would see them on the other side of the stone wall, advanced several paces towards their native land. She had no doubt of their ability to do so; their roots, projecting in fibrous sprawls from their trunks, were their feet, and she pictured them advancing with wide trailings, and rustlings as of green draperies, and a loudening of that dreamy cry of theirs which was to her imagination a cry of homesickness reminiscent of their old life in the White north. When Ellen had first heard the name Norway spruce, 'way back in her childhood — so far back, though she was only seven and a half now, that it seemed to her like a memory from another life — she had asked her mother to show her Norway on the map, and her strange convictions concerning the trees had seized her. When her mother said that they had come from that northernmost land of Europe, Ellen, to whose childhood all truth was naked and literal, immediately conceived to herself those veritable trees advancing over the frozen seas around the pole, and down through the vast regions which were painted blue on her map, straight to her father's west yard. There they stood and sang the songs of their own country, with a melancholy sweetness of absence and longing, and were forever thinking to return. Ellen felt always a thrill of happy surprise when she saw them still there of a morning, for she felt that she would miss them sorely when they were gone. She said nothing of all this to her mother; it was one of the secrets of the soul which created her individuality and made her a spiritual birth. She was also silent about her belief concerning the cherry trees in the east yard. There were three of them, giants of their kind, which filled the east yard every spring as with mountains of white bloom, breathing wide gusts of honey sweetness, and humming with bees. Ellen believed that these trees had once stood in the Garden of Eden, but she never expected to find them missing from the east yard of a morning, for she remembered the angel with the flaming sword, and she knew how one branch of the eastern-most tree happened to be blasted as if by fire. And she thought that these trees were happy, and never sighed to the wind as the dark evergreens did, because they had still the same blossoms and the same fruit that they had in Eden, and so did not fairly know that they were not there still. Sometimes Ellen, sitting underneath them on a low rib of rock on a May morning, used to fancy with success that she and the trees were together in that first garden which she had read about in the Bible.

Sometimes, after one of these successful imaginings, when Ellen's mother called her into the house she would stare at her little daughter uneasily, and give her a spoonful of a bitter spring medicine which she had brewed herself. When Ellen's father, Andrew Brewster, came home from the shop, she would speak to him aside as he was washing his hands at the kitchen sink, and tell him that it seemed to her that Ellen looked kind of "pindlin'." Then Andrew, before he sat down at the dinner-table, would take Ellen's face in his two moist hands, look at her with anxiety thinly veiled by facetiousness, rub his rough, dark cheek against her soft, white one until he had reddened it, then laugh, and tell her she looked like a bo'sn. Ellen never quite knew what her father meant by bo'sn, but she understood that it signified something very rosy and hearty indeed.

Ellen's father always picked out for her the choicest and tenderest bits of the humble dishes, and his keen eyes were more watchful of her plate than of his own. Always after Ellen's mother had said to her father that she thought Ellen looked pindling he was late about coming home from the shop, and would turn in at the gate laden with paper parcels. Then Ellen would find an orange or some other delicacy beside her plate at supper. Ellen's aunt Eva, her mother's younger sister, who lived with them, would look askance at the tidbit with open sarcasm. "You jest spoil that young one, Fanny," she would say to her sister.

"You can do jest as you are a mind to with your own young ones when you get them, but you can let mine alone. It's none of your business what her father and me give her to eat; you don't buy it," Ellen's mother would retort. There was the utmost frankness of speech between the two sisters. Neither could have been in the slightest doubt as to what the other thought of her, for it was openly proclaimed to her a dozen times a day, and the conclusion was never complimentary. Ellen learned very early to form her own opinions of character from her own intuition, otherwise she would have held her aunt and mother in somewhat slighting estimation, and she loved them both dearly. They were head-strong, violent-tempered women, but she had an instinct for the staple qualities below that surface turbulence, which was lashed higher by every gust of opposition. These two loud, contending voices, which filled the house before and after shop-hours — for Eva worked in the shop with her brother-in-law — with a duet of discords instead of harmonies, meant no more to Ellen than the wrangle of the robins in the cherry trees. She supposed that two sisters always conversed in that way. She never knew why her father, after a fiery but ineffectual attempt to quell the feminine tumult, would send her across the east yard to her grandmother Brewster's, and seat himself on the east doorstep in summer, or go down to the store in the winter. She would sit at the window in her grandmother's sitting room, eating peacefully the slice of pound-cake or cookie with which she was always regaled, and listen to the scolding voices across the yard as she might have listened to any outside disturbance. She was never sucked into the whirlpool of wrath which seemed to gyrate perpetually in her home, and wondered at her grandmother Brewster's impatient exclamations concerning the poor child, and her poor boy, and that it was a shame and a disgrace, when now and then a louder explosion of wrath struck her ears.

Ellen's grandmother — Mrs. Zelotes Brewster, as she was called, though her husband Zelotes had been dead for many years — was an aristocrat by virtue of inborn prejudices and convictions, in despite of circumstances. The neighbors said that Mrs. Zelotes Brewster had always been high-feeling, and had held up her head with the best. It would have been nearer the truth to say that she held up her head above the best. No one seeing the erect old woman, in her draperies of the finest black goods to be bought in the city, could estimate in what heights of thin upper air of spiritual consequence her head was elevated. She had always a clear sight of the head-tops of any throng in which she found herself, and queens or duchesses would have been no exception. She would never have failed to find some stool of superior possessions or traits upon which to raise herself, and look down upon crown and coronet. When she read in the papers about the marriage of a New York belle to an English duke, she reflected that the duke could be by no means as fine a figure of a man as Zelotes had been, and as her son Andrew was, although both her husband and son had got all their education in the town schools, and had worked in shoe-shops all their lives. She could have looked at a palace or a castle, and have remained true to the splendors of her little one-story-and-a-half house with a best parlor and sitting room, and a shed kitchen for use in hot weather.

She would not for one instant have been swerved from utmost admiration and faith in her set of white-and-gold wedding china by the contemplation of Copeland and Royal Sèvres. She would have pitted her hair-cloth furniture of the ugliest period of household art against all the Chippendales and First Empire pieces in existence.

As Mrs. Zelotes had never seen any household possessions to equal her own, let alone to surpass them, she was of the same mind with regard to her husband and his family, herself and her family, her son and little granddaughter. She never saw any gowns and shawls which compared with hers in fineness and richness; she never tasted a morsel of cookery which was not as sawdust when she reflected upon her own; and all that humiliated her in the least, or caused her to feel in the least dissatisfied, was her son's wife and her family and antecedents.

Mrs. Zelotes Brewster had considered that her son Andrew was marrying immeasurably beneath him when he married Fanny Loud, of Loudville. Loudville was a humble, an almost disreputably humble, suburb of the little provincial city. The Louds from whom the locality took its name were never held in much repute, being considered of a stratum decidedly below the ordinary social one of the city. When Andrew told his mother that he was to marry a Loud, she declared that she would not go to his wedding, nor receive the girl at her house, and she kept her word. When one day Andrew brought his sweetheart to his home to call, trusting to her pretty face and graceful though rather sharp manner to win his mother's heart, he found her entrenched in the kitchen, and absolutely indifferent to the charms of his Fanny in her stylish, albeit somewhat tawdry, finery, though she had peeped to good purpose from her parlor window, which commanded the road, before she fled kitchenward.

Mrs. Zelotes was beating eggs with as firm an impetus as if she were heaving up earth-works to strengthen her own pride when her son thrust his timid face into the kitchen. "Mother, Fanny's in the parlor," he said, beseechingly.

"Let her set there, then, if she wants to," said his mother, and that was all she would say.

Very soon Fanny went home on her lover's arm, freeing her mind with no uncertain voice on the way, though she was on the public road, and within hearing of sharp ears in open windows. Fanny had a pride as fierce as Mrs. Zelotes Brewster's, though it was not so well sustained, and she would then and there have refused to marry Andrew had she not loved him with all her passionate and ill-regulated heart. But she never forgave her mother-in-law for the slight she had put upon her that day, and the slights which she put upon her later. She would have refused to live next door to Mrs. Zelotes had not Andrew owned the land and been in a measure forced to build there. Every time she had flaunted out of her new house-door in her wedding finery she had an uncomfortable feeling of defiance under a fire of hostile eyes in the next house. She kept her own windows upon that side as clear and bright as diamonds, and her curtains in the stiffest, snowy slants, lest her terrible mother-in-law should have occasion to impeach her housekeeping, she being a notable housewife. The habits of the Louds of Loudville were considered shiftless in the extreme, and poor Fanny had heard an insinuation of Mrs. Zelotes to that effect.

The elder Mrs. Brewster's knowledge of her son's house and his wife was limited to the view from her west windows, but there was half-truce when little Ellen was born. Mrs. Brewster, who considered that no woman could be obtained with such a fine knowledge of nursing as she possessed, and who had, moreover, a regard for her poor boy's pocketbook, appeared for the first time in his doorway, and opened her heart to her son's child, if not to his wife, whom she began to tolerate.

However, the two women had almost a hand-to-hand encounter over little Ellen's cradle, the elder Mrs. Brewster judging that it was for her good to be rocked to sleep, the younger not. Little Ellen herself, however, turned the balance that time in favor of her grandmother, since she cried every time the gentle, swaying motion was hushed, and absolutely refused to go to sleep, and her mother from the first held every course which seemed to contribute to her pleasure and comfort as a sacred duty. At last it came to pass that the two women met only upon that small neutral ground of love, and upon all other territory were sworn foes. Especially was Mrs. Zelotes wroth when Eva Loud, after the death of her father, one of the most worthless and shiftless of the Louds of Loudville, came to live with her married sister. She spoke openly to Fanny concerning her opinion of another woman's coming to live on poor Andrew, and paid no heed to the assertions that Eva would work and pay her way.

Mrs. Zelotes, although she acknowledged it no social degradation for a man to work in a shoe-factory, regarded a woman who worked therein as having hopelessly forfeited her caste. Eva Loud had worked in a shop ever since she was fourteen, and had tagged the grimy and leathery procession of Louds, who worked in shoe-factories when they worked at all, in a short skirt with her hair in a strong black pigtail. There was a kind of bold grace and showy beauty about this Eva Loud which added to Mrs. Zelotes's scorn and dislike.

"She walks off to work in the shop as proud as if she was going to a party," she said, and she fairly trembled with anger when she saw the girl set out with her son in the morning. She would have considered it much more according to the eternal fitness of things had her son Andrew been attending a queen whom he would have dropped at her palace on the way. She writhed inwardly whenever little Ellen spoke of her aunt Eva, and would have forbidden her to do so had she dared.

"To think of that child associating with a shop-girl!" she said to Mrs. Pointdexter. Mrs. Pointdexter was her particular friend, whom she regarded with loving tolerance of superiority, though she had been the daughter of a former clergyman of the town, and had wedded another, and might presumably have been accounted herself of a somewhat higher estate. The gentle and dependent clergyman's widow, when she came back to her native city after the death of her husband, found herself all at once in a pleasant little valley of humiliation at the feet of her old friend, and was contented to abide there. "Perhaps your son's sister-in-law will marry and go away," she said, consolingly, to Mrs. Zelotes, who indeed lived in that hope. But Eva remained at her sister's, and, though she had admirers in plenty, did not marry, and the dissension grew.

It was an odd thing that, however the sisters quarreled, the minute Andrew tried to take sides with his wife and assail Eva in his turn, Fanny turned and defended her. "I am not going to desert all the sister I have got in the world," she said. "If you want me to leave, say so, and I will go, but I shall never turn Eva out of doors. I would rather go with her and work in the shop." Then the next moment the wrangle would recommence, and the harsh trebles of wrath would swell high. Andrew could not appreciate this savageness of race loyalty in the face of anger and dissension, and his brain reeled with the apparent inconsistency of the thing.

"Sometimes I think they are both crazy," he used to tell his mother, who sympathized with him after a covertly triumphant fashion. She never said, "I told you so," but the thought was evident on her face, and her son saw it there.

However, he said not a word against his wife, except by implication. Though she and her sister were making his home unbearable, he still loved her, and, even if he did not, he had something of his mother's pride.

However, at last, when Ellen was almost eight years old, matters came suddenly to a climax one evening in November. The two sisters were having a fiercer dispute than usual. Eva was taking her sister to task for cutting over a dress of hers for Ellen, Fanny claiming that she had given her permission to do so, and Eva denying it. The child sat listening in her little chair with a look of dawning intelligence of wrath and wicked temper in her face, because she was herself in a manner the cause of the dissension. Suddenly Andrew Brewster, with a fiery outburst of inconsequent masculine wrath with the whole situation, essayed to cut the Gordian knot. He grabbed the little dress of bright woolen stuff, which lay partly made upon the table, and crammed it into the stove, and a reek of burning wool filled the room. Then both women turned upon him with a combination of anger to which his wrath was wildfire.

Andrew caught up little Ellen, who was beginning to look scared, wrapped the first thing he could seize around her, and fairly fled across the yard to his mother's. Then he sat down and wept like a boy, and his pride left him at last. "Oh, mother," he sobbed, "if it were not for the child, I would go away, for my home is a hell!"

Mrs. Zelotes stood clasping little Ellen, who clung to her, trembling. "Well, come over here with me," she said, "you and Ellen."

"Live here in the next house!" said Andrew. "Do you suppose Fanny would have the child living under her very eyes in the next house? No, there is no way out of the misery — no way; but if it was not for the child, I would go!"

Andrew burst out in such wild sobs that his mother released Ellen and ran to him; and the child, trembling and crying with a curious softness, as of fear at being heard, ran out of the house and back to her home. "Oh, mother," she cried, breaking in upon the dialogue of anger which was still going on there with her little tremulous flute — "oh, mother, father is crying!"

"I don't care," answered her mother, fiercely, her temper causing her to lose sight of the child's agitation. "I don't care. If it wasn't for you, I would leave him. I wouldn't live as I am doing. I would leave everybody. I am tired of this awful life. Oh, if it wasn't for you, Ellen, I would leave everybody and start fresh!"

"You can leave *me* whenever you want to," said Eva, her handsome face burning red with wrath, and she went out of the room, which was suffocating with the fumes of the burning wool, tossing her black head, all banged and coiled in the latest fashion.

Of late years Fanny had sunk her personal vanity further and further in that for her child. She brushed her own hair back hard from her temples, and candidly revealed all her unyouthful lines, and dwelt fondly upon the arrangement of little Ellen's locks, which were of a fine, pale yellow, as clear as the color of amber.

She never recut her skirts or her sleeves, but she studied anxiously all the slightest changes in children's fashions. After her sister had left the room with a loud bang of the door, she sat for a moment gazing straight ahead, her face working, then she burst into such a passion of hysterical

wailing as the child had never heard. Ellen, watching her mother with
eyes so frightened and full of horror that there was no room for childish
love and pity in them, grew very pale. She had left the door by which
she had entered open; she gazed one moment at her mother, then she
turned and slipped out of the room, and, opening the outer door softly,
though her mother would not have heard nor noticed, went out of the
house.

Then she ran as fast as she could down the frozen road, a little, dark
figure, passing as rapidly as the shadow of a cloud between the earth
and the full moon.

Chapter II

*T*he greatest complexity in the world attends the motive-power of
any action. Infinite perspectives of mental mirrors reflect the whys of
all doing. An adult with long practice in analytic introspection soon
becomes bewildered when he strives to evolve the primary and fundamental reasons for his deeds; a child so striving would be lost in
unexpected depths; but a child never strives. A child obeys unquestioningly and absolutely its own spiritual impellings without a backward
glance at them.

Little Ellen Brewster ran down the road that November night, and
did not know then, and never knew afterwards, why she ran. Loving
renunciation was surging high in her childish heart, giving an indication
of tidal possibilities for the future, and there was also a bitter, angry
hurt of slighted dependency and affection. Had she not heard them say,
her own mother and father say, that they would be better off and happier
with her out of the way, and she their dearest loved and most carefully
cherished possession in the whole world? It is a cruel fall for an apple
of the eye to the ground, for its law of gravitation is of the soul, and its
fall shocks the infinite. Little Ellen felt herself sorely hurt by her fall

from such fair heights; she was pierced by the sharp thorns of selfish interests which flourish below all the heavenward windows of life.

Afterwards, when her mother and father tried to make her tell them why she ran away, she could not say; the answer was beyond her own power.

There was no snow on the ground, but the earth was frozen in great ribs after a late thaw. Ellen ran painfully between the ridges which a long line of ice-wagons had made with their heavy wheels earlier in the day. When the spaces between the ridges were too narrow for her little feet, she ran along the crests, and that was precarious. She fell once and bruised one of her delicate knees, then she fell again, and struck the knee on the same place. It hurt her, and she caught her breath with a gasp of pain. She pulled up her little frock and touched her hand to her knee, and felt it wet, then she whimpered on the lonely road, and, curiously enough, there was pity for her mother as well as for herself in her solitary grieving. "Mother would feel pretty bad if she knew how I was hurt, enough to make it bleed," she murmured, between her soft sobs. Ellen did not dare cry loudly, from a certain unvoiced fear which she had of shocking the stillness of the night, and also from a delicate sense of personal dignity, and a dislike of violent manifestations of feeling which had strengthened with her growth in the midst of the turbulent atmosphere of her home. Ellen had the softest childish voice, and she never screamed or shouted when excited. Instead of catching the motion of the wind, she still lay before it, like some slender-stemmed flower. If Ellen had made much outcry with the hurt in her heart and the smart of her knee, she might have been heard, for the locality was thickly settled, though not in the business portion of the little city. The houses, set prosperously in the midst of shaven lawns — for this was a thrifty and emulative place, and democracy held up its head confidently — were built closely along the road, though that was lonely and deserted at that hour. It was the hour between half-past six and half-past seven, when people were lingering at their supper-tables, and had not yet started upon their evening pursuits. The lights shone for the most part from the rear windows of the houses, and there was a vague compound odor of tea and bread and beefsteak in the air. Poor Ellen had not had her supper; the wrangle at home had dismissed it from everybody's mind. She felt more pitiful towards her mother and herself when she smelt the food and reflected upon that. To think of her going away without any supper, all alone in the dark night! There was no moon, and the solemn brilliancy of the stars made her think with a shiver of awe of the Old Testament and the possibility of the Day of Judgment. Suppose it should come, and she all alone out in the night, in the midst of all those worlds and the great White Throne, without her mother? Ellen's grandmother, who was of a stanch orthodox breed, and was, moreover, anxious to counteract any possible detriment as to religious training from contact with the degenerate Louds of Loudville, had established a strict course of Bible study for her granddaughter at a very early age. All celestial phenomena were in consequence transposed into a Biblical key for the child, and she regarded the heavens swarming with golden stars as a Hebrew child of a thousand years ago might have done.

She was glad when she came within the radius of a street light from time to time; they were stationed at wide intervals in that neighborhood. Soon, however, she reached the factories, when all mystery and awe, and vague terrors of what beside herself might be near unrevealed beneath the mighty brooding of the night, were over. She was, as it were, in the mid-current of the conditions of her own life and times, and the material force of it swept away all symbolisms and unstable drift, and left only the bare rocks and shores of existence. Always when the child had been taken by one of her elders past the factories, humming like gigantic hives, with their windows alert with eager eyes of toil, glancing out at her over bench and machine, Ellen had seen her secretly cherished imaginings recede into a night of distance like stars, and she had felt her little footing upon the earth with a shock, and had clung more closely to the leading hand of love. "That's where your poor father works," her grandmother would say. "Maybe you'll have to work there some day," her aunt Eva had said once; and her mother, who had been with her also, had cried out sharply as if she had been stung, "I guess that little delicate thing ain't never goin' to work in a shoe-shop, Eva Loud." And her aunt Eva had laughed, and declared with emphasis that she guessed there was no need to worry yet awhile.

"She never shall, while I live," her mother had cried; and then Eva, coming to her sister's aid against her own suggestion, had declared, with a vehemence which frightened Ellen, that she would burn the shop down herself first.

As for Ellen's father, he never at that time dwelt upon the child's future as much as his wife did, having a masculine sense of the instability of houses of air which prevented him from entering them without a shivering of walls and roof into naught but star-mediums by his down-rightness of vision. "Oh, let the child be, can't you, Fanny?" he said, when his wife speculated whether Ellen would be or do this or that when she should be a woman. He resented the conception of the woman which would swallow up, like some metaphysical sorceress, his fair little child. So when he now and then led Ellen past the factories it was never with the slightest surmise as to any connection which she might have with them beyond the present one. "There's the shop where father works," he would tell Ellen, with a tender sense of his own importance in his child's eyes, and he was as proud as Punch when Ellen was able to point with her tiny pink finger at the window where father worked. "That's where father works and earns money to buy nice things for little Ellen," Andrew would repeat, beaming at her with divine foolishness, and Ellen looked at the roaring, vibrating building as she might have looked at the wheels of progress. She realized that her father was very great and smart to work in a place like that, and earn money — so much of it. Ellen often heard her mother remark with pride how much money Andrew earned.

Tonight, when Ellen passed in her strange flight, the factories were still, though they were yet blazing with light. The gigantic buildings, after a style of architecture as simple as a child's block house, and adapted to as primitive an end, loomed up beside the road like windowed shells enclosing massive concretenesses of golden light. They looked entirely vacant except for light, for the workmen had all gone home, and there were only the keepers in the buildings. There were three of them, representing three different firms, rival firms, grouped curiously close together, but Lloyd's was much the largest. Andrew and Eva worked in Lloyd's.

She was near the last factory when she met a man hastening along with bent shoulders, of intent, middle-aged progress. After he had passed her with a careless glance at the small, swift figure, she smelt coffee. He was carrying home a pound for his breakfast supply. That suddenly made her cry, though she did not know why. That familiar odor of home and the wontedness of life made her isolation on her little atom of the unusual more pitiful. The man turned round sharply when she sobbed. "Hullo! what's the matter, sis?" he called back, in a pleasant, hoarse voice. Ellen did not answer; she fled as if she had wings on her feet. The man had many children of his own, and was accustomed to their turbulence over trifles. He kept on, thinking that there was a sulky child who had been sent on an errand against her will, that it was not late, and she was safe enough on that road. He resumed his calculation as to whether his income would admit of a new coal-stove that winter. He was a workman in a factory, with one accumulative interest in life — coal-stoves. He bought and traded and swapped coal-stoves every winter with keenest enthusiasm. Now he had one in his mind which he had just viewed in a window with the rapture of an artist. It had a little nickel statuette on the top, and that quite crowded Ellen out of his mind, which had but narrow accommodations.

So Ellen kept on unmolested, though her heart was beating loud with fright. When she came into the brilliantly lighted stretch of Main Street, which was the business center of the city, her childish mind was partly diverted from herself. Ellen had not been down town many times of an evening, and always in hand of her hurrying father or mother. Now she had run away and cut loose from all restrictions of time; there was an eternity for observation before her, with no call indoors in prospect. She stopped at the first bright shop window, and suddenly the exultation of freedom was over the child. She tasted the sweets of rebellion and disobedience. She had stood before that window once before of an evening, and her aunt Eva had been with her, and one of her young men friends had come up behind, and they had gone on, the child dragging backward at her aunt's hand. Now she could stand as long as she wished, and stare and stare, and drink in everything which her childish imagination craved, and that was much. The imagination of a child is often like a voracious maw, seizing upon all that comes within reach, and producing spiritual indigestions and assimilations almost endless in their effects upon the growth. This window before which Ellen stood was that of a market: a great expanse of plate-glass framing a crude study in the clearest color tones. It takes a child or an artist to see a picture without the intrusion of its second dimension of sordid use and the gross reflection of humanity.

Ellen looked at the great shelf laid upon with flesh and vegetables and fruits with the careless precision of a kaleidoscope, and did not for one instant connect anything thereon with the ends of physical appetite, though she had not had her supper. What had a meal of beefsteak and potatoes and squash served on the little white-laid table at home to do with those great golden globes which made one end of the window like the remove from a mine, those satin-smooth spheres, those cuts as of red and white marble? She had eaten apples, but these were as the apples of the gods, lying in a heap of opulence, with a precious light-spot like a ruby on every outward side. The turnips affected her imagination like ivory carvings: she did not recognize them for turnips at all. She never afterwards believed them to be turnips; and as for cabbages, they were green inflorescences of majestic bloom. There is one position from which all common things can be seen with reflections of preciousness, and Ellen had insensibly taken it. The window and the shop behind were illuminated with the yellow glare of gas, but the glass was filmed here and there with frost, which tempered it as with a veil. In the background rosy-faced men in white frocks were moving to and fro, customers were passing in and out, but they were all glorified to the child. She did not see them as butchers, and as men and women selling and buying dinners.

However, all at once everything was spoiled, for her fairy castle of illusion or a higher reality was demolished, and that not by any blow of practicality, but by pity and sentiment. Ellen was a woman-child, and suddenly she struck the rock upon which women so often wreck or effect harbor, whichever it may be. All at once she looked up from the dazzling mosaic of the window and saw the dead partridges and grouse hanging in their rumpled brown mottle of plumage, and the dead rabbits, long and stark, with their fur pointed with frost, hanging in a piteous headlong company, and all her delight and wonder vanished, and she came down to the hard actualities of things. "Oh, the poor birds!" she cried out in her heart. "Oh, the poor birds, and the poor bunnies!"

Just at that moment, when the sudden rush of compassion and indignation had swollen her heart to the size of a woman's, and given it the aches of one, when her eyes were so dilated with the sight of helpless injury and death that they reflected the mystery of it and lost the outlook of childhood, when her pretty baby mouth was curved like an inverted bow of love with the impulse of tears, Cynthia Lennox came up the street and stopped short when she reached her.

Suddenly Ellen felt someone pressing close to her, and, looking up, saw a woman, only middle-aged, but whom she thought very old, because her hair was white, standing looking at her very keenly with clear, light-blue eyes under a high, pale forehead, from which the grey hair was combed uncompromisingly back. The woman had been a beauty once, of a delicate, nervous type, and had a certain beauty now, a something which had endured like the fineness of texture of a web when its glow of color has faded. Her black garments draped her with sober richness, and there was a gleam of dark fur when the wind caught her cloak. A small tuft of ostrich plumes nodded from her bonnet. Ellen smelt flowers vaguely, and looked at the lady's hand, but she did not carry any.

"Whose little girl are you?" Cynthia Lennox asked, softly, and Ellen did not answer. "Can't you tell me whose little girl you are?" Cynthia Lennox asked again. Ellen did not speak, but there was the swift flicker of a thought over her face which told her name as plainly as language if the woman had possessed the skill to interpret it.

"Ellen Brewster — Ellen Brewster is my name," Ellen said to herself very hard, and that was how she endured the reproach of her own silence.

The woman looked at her with surprise and admiration that were fairly passionate. Ellen was a beautiful child, with a face like a white flower. People had always turned to look after her, she was so charming, and had caused her mothers heart to swell with pride. "The way everybody we met has stared after that child today!" she would whisper her husband when she brought Ellen home from some little expedition; then the two would look at the little one's face with the one holy vanity of the world. Ellen wore tonight the little white shawl which her father had caught up when he carried her over to her grandmother's. She held it tightly together under her chin with one tiny hand, and her face looked out from between the soft folds with the absolute purity of curve and color of a pearl.

"Oh, you darling!" said the woman, suddenly; "you darling!" and Ellen shrank away from her. "Don't be afraid, dear," said Cynthia Lennox. "Don't be afraid, only tell me who you are. What is your name, dear?" But Ellen remained silent; only, as she shrank aloof, her eyes grew wild and bright with startled tears, and her sweet baby mouth quivered piteously. She wanted to run, but the habit of obedience was so strong upon her little mind that she feared to do so. This strange woman seemed to have gotten her in some invisible leash.

"Tell me what your name is, darling," said the woman, but she might as well have importuned a flower. Ellen was proof against all commands in that direction. She suddenly felt the furry sweep of the lady's cloak against her cheek, and a nervous, tender arm drawing her close, though she strove feebly to resist. "You are cold, you have nothing on but this little white shawl, and perhaps you are hungry. What were you looking in this window for? Tell me, dear, where is your mother? She did not send you on an errand, such a little girl as you are, so late on such a cold night, with no more on than this?"

A tone of indignation crept into the lady's voice.

"No, mother didn't send me," Ellen said, speaking for the first time.

"Then did you run away, dear?" Ellen was silent. "Oh, if you did, darling, you must tell me where you live, what your father's name is, and I will take you home. Tell me, dear. If it is far, I will get a carriage, and you shall ride home. Tell me, dear."

There was an utmost sweetness of maternal persuasion in Cynthia Lennox's voice; Ellen was swayed by it as a child might have been swayed by the magic pipe of the Pied Piper of Hamelin. She half yielded to her leading motion, then she remembered. "No," she cried out, with a sob of utter desolation. "No, no."

"Why not, dear?"

"They don't want; they don't want. No, no!"

"They don't want you? Your own father and mother don't want you? Darling, what is the matter?" But Ellen was dumb again. She stood sobbing, with a painful restraint, and pulling futilely from the lady's persuasive hand. But it ended in the mastery of the child. Suddenly Cynthia Lennox gathered her up in her arms under her great fur-lined cloak, and carried her a little farther down the street, then across it to a dwelling-house, one of the very few which had withstood the march of business blocks on this crowded main street of the provincial city. A few people looked curiously at the lady carrying such a heavy, weeping child, but she met no one whom she knew, and the others looked indifferently away after a second backward stare. Cynthia Lennox was one to bear herself with such dignity over all jolts of circumstances that she might almost convince others of her own exemption from them. Her mental bearing disproved the evidence of the senses, and she could have committed a crime with such consummate self-poise and grace as to have held a crowd in abeyance with utter distrust of their own eyes before such unquestioning confidence in the sovereignty of the situation. Cynthia Lennox had always had her own way except in one respect, and that experience had come to her lately.

Though she was such a slender woman, she seemed to have great strength in her arms, and she bore Ellen easily and as if she had been used to such a burden. She wrapped her cloak closely around the child.

"Don't be afraid, darling," she kept whispering. Ellen panted in bewilderment, and a terror which was half assuaged by something like fascination.

She was conscious of a soft smother of camphor, in which the fur-lined cloak had lain through the summer, and of that flower odor, which was violets, though she did not know it. Only the wild American scentless ones had come in little Ellen's way so far.

She felt herself carried up steps, then a door was thrown open, and a warm breath of air came in her face, and the cloak was tossed back, and she was set softly on the floor. The hall in which she stood seemed very bright; she blinked and rubbed her eyes.

The lady stood over her, laughing gently, and when the child looked up at her, seemed much younger than she had at first, very young in spite of her white hair. There was a soft red on her cheek; her lips looked full and triumphant with smiles; her eyes were like stars. An emotion of her youth which had never become dulled by satisfaction had suddenly blossomed out on her face, and transformed it. An unassuaged longing may serve to preserve youth as well as an undestroyed illusion; indeed, the two are one. Cynthia Lennox looked at the child as if she had been a young mother, and she her first-born; triumph over the future, and daring for all odds, and perfect faith in the kingdom of joy were in her look. Had she nursed one child like Ellen to womanhood, and tasted the bitter in the cup, she would not have been capable of

that look, and would have been as old as her years. She threw off her
cloak and took off her bonnet, and the light struck her hair and made
it look like silver. A brooch in the laces at her throat shone with a
thousand hues, and as Ellen gazed at it she felt curiously dull and dizzy.
She did not resist at all when the lady removed her little white shawl,
but stared at her with the look of some small and helpless thing in too
large a grasp of destiny to admit of a struggle. "Oh, you darling!"
Cynthia Lennox said, and stooped and kissed her, and half carried her
into a great, warm, dazzling room, with light reflected in long lines of
gold from picture-frames on the wall, and now and then startling patches
of lurid color blazing forth unmeaningly from the dark incline of their
canvases, with gleams of crystal and shadows of bronze in settings of
fretted ebony, with long swayings of rich draperies at doors and windows, a red light of fire in a grate, and two white lights, one of piano
keys, the other of a flying marble figure in a corner, outlined clearly
against dusky red. The light in this room was very dim. It was all beyond
Ellen's imagination. The White North where the Norway spruces lived
would not have seemed as strange to her as this. Neither would Blue-
beard's Castle, nor the House that Jack Built, nor the Palace of King
Solomon, nor the tent in which lived little Joseph in his coat of many
colors, nor even the Garden of Eden, nor Noah's Ark. Her imagination
had not prepared her for a room like this. She had formed her ideas of
rooms upon her grandmother's and her mother's and the neighbors'
best parlors, with their glories of crushed plush and gilt and onyx and
cheap lace and picture-throws and lambrequins. This room was such a
heterodoxy against her creed of civilization that it did not look beautiful
to her as much as strange and bewildering, and when she was bidden to
sit down in a little inlaid precious chair she put down her tiny hand
and reflected, with a sense of strengthening of her household faith, that
her grandmother had beautiful, smooth, shiny hair-cloth.

Cynthia Lennox pulled the chair close to the fire, and bade her hold
out her little feet to the blaze to warm them well. "I am afraid you are
chilled, darling," she said, and looked at her sitting there in her dainty
little red cashmere frock, with her spread of baby-yellow hair over her
shoulders. Then Ellen thought that the lady was younger than her
mother; but her mother had borne her and nursed her, and suffered and
eaten of the tree of knowledge, and tasted the bitter after the sweet; and
this other woman was but as a child in the garden, though she was fairly
old. But along with Ellen's conviction of the lady's youth had come a
conviction of her power, and she yielded to her unquestioningly. Whenever she came near her she gazed with dilating eyes upon the blazing
circle of diamonds at her throat.

When she was bidden, she followed the lady into the dining room, where the glitter of glass and silver and the soft gleam of precious china made her think for a little while that she must be in a store. She had never seen anything like this except in a store, when she had been with her mother to buy a lamp-chimney. So she decided this to be a store, but she said nothing. She did not speak at all, but she ate her biscuits, and slice of breast of chicken, and sponge-cake, and drank her milk.

She had her milk in a little silver cup which seemed as if it might have belonged to another child; she also sat in a small high-chair, which made it seem as if another child had lived or visited in the house. Ellen became singularly possessed with this sense of the presence of a child, and when the door opened she would look around for her to enter, but it was always an old black woman with a face of imperturbable bronze, which caused her to huddle closer into her chair when she drew near.

There were not many colored people in the city, and Ellen had never seen any except at Long Beach, where she had sometimes gone to have a shore dinner with her mother and Aunt Eva. Then she always used to shrink when the black waiter drew near, and her mother and aunt would be convulsed with furtive mirth. "See the little gump," her mother would say in the tenderest tone, and look about to see if others at the other tables saw how cunning she was — what a charming little goose to be afraid of a colored waiter.

Ellen saw nobody except the lady and the black woman, but she was still sure that there was a child in the house, and after supper, when she was taken upstairs to bed, she peeped through every open door with the expectation of seeing her.

But she was so weary and sleepy that her curiosity and capacity for any other emotion was blunted. She had become simply a little, tired, sleepy animal. She let herself be undressed; she was not even moved to much self-pity when the lady discovered the cruel bruise on her delicate knee, and kissed it, and dressed it with a healing salve. She was put into a little nightgown which she knew dreamily belonged to that other child, and was laid in a little bedstead which she noted to be made of gold, with floating lace over the head.

She sleepily noted, too, that there were flowers on the walls, and more floating lace over the bureau. This room did not look so strange to her as the others; she had somehow from the treasures of her fancy provided the family of big bears and little bears with a similar one. Then, too, one of the neighbors, Mrs. George Crocker, had read many articles in women's papers relative to the beautifying of homes, and had furnished a wonderful chamber with old soap-boxes and rolls of Japanese paper which was a sort of a cousin many times removed of this. When she was in bed the lady kissed her, and called her darling, and bade her sleep well, and not be afraid, she was in the next room, and could hear if she spoke. Then she stood looking at her, and Ellen thought that she must be younger than Minnie Swensen, who lived on her street, and wore a yellow pigtail, and went to the high-school. Then she closed her heavy eyes, and forgot to cry about her poor father and mother; still, there was, after all, a hurt about them down in her childish heart, though a great wave of new circumstances had rolled on her shore and submerged for the time her memory and her love, even, she was so feeble and young.

She slept very soundly, and awoke only once, about two o'clock in the morning. Then a passing lantern flashed into the chamber into her eyes, and woke her up, but she only sighed and stretched drowsily, then turned her little body over with a luxurious roll and went to sleep again.

It was poor Andrew Brewster's lantern which flashed in her eyes, for he was out with a posse of police and sympathizing neighbors and friends searching for his lost little girl. He was frantic, and when he came under the gas-lights from time to time the men that saw him shuddered; they would not have known him, for almost the farthest agony of which he was capable had changed his face.

Chapter III

*B*y the next morning all the city was in a commotion over little Ellen's disappearance. Woods on the outskirts were being searched, ponds were being dragged, posters with a stare of dreadful meaning in large characters of black and white were being pasted all over the fences and available barns, and already three of the local editors had been to the Brewster house to obtain particulars and photographs of the missing child for reproduction in the city papers.

The first train from Boston brought two reporters representing great dailies.

Fanny Brewster, white-cheeked, with the rasped redness of tears around her eyes and mouth, clad in her blue calico wrapper, received them in her best parlor. Eva had made a fire in the best parlor stove early that morning. "Folks will be comin' in all day, I expect," said she, speaking with nervous catches of her breath. Ever since the child had been missed, Eva's anxiety had driven her from point to point of unrest as with a stinging lash. She had pelted bareheaded down the road and up the road; she had invaded all the neighbors' houses, insisting upon looking through their farthest and most unlikely closets; she had even penetrated to the woods, and joined wild-eyed the groups of peering workers on the shore of the nearest pond. That she could not endure long, so she had rushed home to her sister, who was either pacing her sitting room with inarticulate murmurs and wails of distress in the sympathizing ears of several of the neighboring women, or else was staring with haggard eyes of fearful hope from a window. When she looked from the eastern window she could see her mother-in-law, Mrs. Zelotes Brewster, at an opposite one, sitting immovable, with her Bible in her lap, prayer in her heart, and an eye of grim holding to faith upon the road for the fulfillment of promise. She felt all her muscles stiffen with anger when she saw the wild eyes of the child's mother at the other window. "It is all her fault," she said to herself — "all her fault — hers and that bold trollop of a sister of hers." When she saw Eva run down the road, with her black hair rising like a mane to the morning wind, she was an embodiment of an imprecatory psalm. When, later on, she saw the three editors coming — Mr. Walsey, of *The Spy*, and Mr. Jones, of *The Observer*, and young Joe Bemis, of *The Star*, on his bicycle — she watched jealously to see if they were admitted. When Fanny's head disappeared from the eastern window she knew that Eva had let them in and Fanny was receiving them in the parlor. "She will tell them all about the words they had last night, that made the dear child run away," she thought. "All the town will know what doings there are in our family." Mrs. Zelotes made up her mind to a course of action. Each editor was granted a long audience with Fanny and Eva, who entertained them with hysterical solemnity and displayed Ellen's photographs in the red plush album, from the last, taken in her best white frock, to one when she was three weeks old, and seeming weakly and not likely to live. This had been taken by a photographer summoned to the house at great expense. "Her father has never spared expense for Ellen," said Fanny, with an outburst of grief. "That's so," said Eva. "I'll testify to that. Andrew Brewster never thought anything was too good for that young one." Then she burst out with a sob louder than her sister's. Eva had usually a coarsely well-kempt appearance, her heavy black hair being securely twisted, and her neck ribbons tied with smart jerks of neatness; but today her hair was still in the fringy braids of yesterday, and her cotton blouse humped untidily in the back. Her face was red and her lips swollen; she looked like a very bacchante of sorrow, and as if she had been on some mad orgy of grief.

Mr. Walsey, of *The Spy,* who had formerly conducted a paper in a college town and was not accustomed to the feminine possibilities of manufacturing localities, felt almost afraid of her. He had never seen a woman of that sort, and thought vaguely of the French Revolution and fish-wives when she gave vent to her distress over the loss of the child. He fairly jumped when she cut short a question of his with a volley of self-recriminatory truths, accompanied with fierce gesturing. He stood back involuntarily out of reach of those powerful, waving arms. "Do I know of any reason for the child to run away?" shrieked Eva, in a voice shrilly hideous with emotion, now and then breaking into hoarseness with the strain of tears. "I guess I know why, I guess I do, and I wish I had been six foot underground before I did what I did. It was all my fault, every bit of it. When I got home, and found that Fan had been making that precious young one a dress out of my old blue one, I pitched into her for it, and she gave it back to me, and then we jawed, and kept it up, till Andrew, he grabbed the dress and flung it into the fire, and did just right, too, and took Ellen and run over to old lady Brewster's with her; then Ellen, she see him cryin', and it scared her 'most to death, poor little thing, and she heard him say that if it wasn't for her he'd quit, and then she come runnin' home to her mother and me, and her mother said the same thing, and then that poor young one, she thought she wa'n't wanted nowheres, and she run. She always was as easy to hurt as a baby robin; it didn't take nothing to set her all of a flutter and a twitter; and now she's just flown out of the nest. Oh my God, I wish my tongue had been torn out by the roots before I'd said a word about her blessed little dress; I wish Fan had cut up every old rag I've got; I'd go dressed in fig-leaves before I'd had it happen. Oh! oh! oh!"

Young Joe Bemis, of *The Star,* was the first to leave, whirling madly and precariously down the street on his wheel, which was dizzily tall in those days. Mrs. Zelotes, hailing him from her open window, might as well have hailed the wind. Her family dissensions were well aired in *The Star* next morning, and she always kept the cutting at the bottom of a little rosewood work-box where she stored away divers small treasures, and never looked at the box without a swift dart of pain as from a hidden sting and the consciousness as of the presence of some noxious insect caged therein.

Mrs. Zelotes was more successful in arresting the progress of the other editors, and (standing at the window, her Bible on the little table at her side) flatly contradicted all that had been told them by her daughter-in-law and her sister. "The Louds always give way, no matter what comes up. You can always tell what kind of a family anybody comes from by the way they take things when anything comes across them. You can't depend on anything she says this morning. My son did not marry just as I wished; everybody knows that; the Louds weren't equal to our family, and everybody knows it, and I have never made any secret as to how I felt, but we have always got along well enough. The Brewsters are not quarrelsome; they never have been. There were no words whatever last night to make my granddaughter run away. Eva and Fanny are all wrong about it. Ellen has been stolen; I know it as well as if I had seen it. A strange-looking woman came to the door yesterday afternoon; she was the tallest woman I ever saw, and she took the widest steps; she measured her dress skirt every step she took, and she spoke gruff. I said then I knew she was a man dressed up. Ellen was playing out in the yard, and she saw the child as she went out, and I see her stoop and look at her real sharp, and my blood run kind of cold then, and I called Ellen away as quick as I could; and the woman, she turned round and gave me a look that I won't ever forget as long as I live. My belief is that that woman was laying in wait when Ellen was going across the yard home from here last night, and she has got her safe somewhere till a reward is offered. Or maybe she wants to keep her, Ellen is such a beautiful child. You needn't put in your papers that my grandchild run away because of quarreling in our family, because she didn't. Eva and Fanny don't know what they are talking about, they are so wrought up; and, coming from the family they do, they don't know how to control themselves and show any sense. I feel it as much as they do, but I have been sitting here all the morning; I know I can't do anything to help, and I am working a good deal harder, waiting, than they are, rushing from pillar to post and taking on, and I'm doing more good. I shall be the only one fit to do anything when they find the poor child. I've got blankets warming by the fire, and my tea-kettle on, and I'm going to be the one to depend on when she's brought home." Mrs. Zelotes gave a glance of defiant faith from the window down the road as she spoke. Then she settled back in her chair and resumed her Bible, and dismissed the tall and forbidding woman whom she had summoned to save the honor of her family resolutely from her conscience. The editors of The Spy and The Observer had a row of ingratiating photographs of little Ellen from three weeks to seven years of age; and their opinions as to the cause of her disappearance, while fully agreeing in all points of sensationalism with those of young Bemis, of *The Star*, differed in detail.

Young Bemis read about the mysterious kidnapper, and wondered, and the demand for *The Star* was chiefly among the immediate neighbors of the Brewsters. Both *The Observer* and *The Spy* doubled their circulation in one day, and every face on the night cars was hidden behind poor little Ellen's baby countenances and the fairy-story of the witch-woman who had lured her away. Mothers kept their children carefully indoors that evening, and pulled down curtains, fearful lest She look in the windows and be tempted. Mrs. Zelotes also waylaid both of the Boston reporters, but with results upon which she had not counted. One presented her story and Fanny's and Eva's with impartial justice; the other kept wholly to the latter version, with the addition of a shrewd theory of his own, deduced from the circumstances which had a parallel in actual history, and boldly stated that the child had probably committed suicide on account of family troubles. Poor Fanny and Eva both saw that, when night was falling and Ellen had not been found. Eva rushed out and secured the paper from the newsboy, and the two sisters gasped over the startling column together.

"It's a lie! oh, Fanny, it's a lie!" cried Eva. "She never would; oh, she never would! That little thing, just because she heard you and me scoldin', and you said that to her, that if it wasn't for her you'd go away. She never would."

"Go away?" sobbed Fanny — "go away? I wouldn't go away from hell if she was there. I would burn; I would hear the clankin' of chains, and groans, and screeches, and devils whisperin' in my ears what I had done wrong, for all eternity, before I'd go where they were playin' harps in heaven, if she was there. I'd like it better, I would. And I'd stay here if I had twenty sisters I didn't get along with, and be happier than I would be anywhere else on earth, if she was here. But she couldn't have done it. She didn't know how. It's awful to put such things into papers."

Eva jumped up with a fierce gesture, ran to the stove, and crammed the paper in. "There!" said she; "I wish I could serve all the papers in the country the same way. I do, and I'd like to put all the editors in after 'em. I'd like to put 'em in the stove with their own papers for kindlin's." Suddenly Eva turned with a swish of skirts, and was out of the room and pounding upstairs, shaking the little house with every step. When she returned she bore over her arm her best dress — a cherished blue silk, ornate with ribbons and cheap lace. "Where's that pattern?" she asked her sister.

"She wouldn't ever do such a thing," moaned Fanny.

"Where's that pattern?"

"What pattern?" Fanny said, faintly.

"That little dress pattern. Her little dress pattern, the one you cut over my dress for her by."

"In the bureau drawer in my room. Oh, she wouldn't."

Eva went into the bedroom, returned with the pattern, got the scissors from Fanny's work-basket, and threw her best silk dress in a rustling heap upon the table.

Fanny stopped moaning and looked at her with wretched wonder. "What be you goin' to do?"

"Do?" cried Eva, fiercely — "do? I'm goin' to cut this dress over for her."

"You ain't."

"Yes, I be. If I drove her away from home, scoldin' because you cut over that other old thing of mine for her, I'm goin' to make up for it now. I'm goin' to give her my best blue silk, that I paid a dollar and a half a yard for, and ain't worn three times. Yes, I be. She's goin' to have a dress cut out of it, an' she's comin' back to wear it, too. You'll see she is comin' home to wear it."

Eva cut wildly into the silk with mad slashes of her gleaming shears, while two neighboring women, who had just come into the room, stared aghast, and even Fanny was partly diverted from her sorrow.

"She's crazy," whispered one of the women, backing away as she spoke.

"Oh, Eva, don't; don't do so," pleaded Fanny, tremulously.

"I be," said Eva, and she cut recklessly up the front breadth.

"You ain't cutting it right," said the other neighbor, who was skillful in such matters, and never fully moved from her own household grooves by any excitement. "If you are a-goin' to cut it at all, you had better cut it right."

"I don't care how I cut it," returned Eva, thrusting the woman away. "Oh, I don't care how I cut it; I want to waste it. I will waste it."

The other neighbor backed entirely out of the room, then turned and fled across the yard, her calico wrapper blowing wildly and lashing about her slender legs, to her own house, the doors of which she locked. Presently the other woman followed her, stepping with the ponderous leisure which results from vastness of body and philosophy of mind. The autumn wind, swirling in impetuous gusts, had little effect upon her broadside of woolen shawl. She had not come out on that raw evening with nothing upon her head. She shook the kitchen door of her friend, and smiled with calm reassurance when it was cautiously set ajar to disclose a wide-eyed and open-mouthed face of terror. "Who is it?"

"It's me. What have you got your door locked for?"

"I think that Eva Loud is raving crazy. I'm afraid of her."

"Lord! you ain't no reason to be 'fraid of her. She ain't crazy. She's only lettin' the birds that fly over your an' my heads settle down to roost. You and me, both of us, if we was situated jest as she is, might think of doin' jest what she's a-doin', but we won't neither of us do it. We'd let our best dresses hang in the closet, safe and sound, while we cut them up in our souls; but Eva, she's different."

"Well, I don't care. I believe she's crazy, and I'm going to keep my doors locked. How do you know she hasn't killed Ellen and put her in the well?"

"Stuff! Now you're lettin' your birds roost, Hattie Monroe."

"I read something that wasn't any worse than that in the paper the other day. I should think they would look in the well. Have Mrs. Jones and Miss Cross gone home?"

"No; they are over there. There's poor Andrew coming now; I wonder if he has heard anything?"

Both women eyed hesitatingly poor Andrew Brewster's dejected figure creeping up the road in the dark.

"You holler and ask him," said the woman in the door.

"I hate to, for I know by his looks he ain't heard anything of her. I know he's jest comin' home to rest a minute, so he can start again. I know he ain't eat a thing since last night. Well, Maria has got some coffee all made, and a nice little piece of steak ready to cook."

"You holler and ask him."

"What is the use? Just see the way he walks; I know without askin'."

However, as Andrew neared his house he involuntarily quickened his pace, and his head and shoulders became suddenly alert. It had occurred to him that possibly Fanny and Eva might have had some news of Ellen during his absence. Possibly she might have come home even.

Then he was hailed by the stout woman standing at the door of the next house. "Heard anything yet, Andrew?"

Andrew shook his head, and looked with despairing eyes at the windows where he used to see Ellen's little face. She had not come, then, for these women would have known it. He entered the house, and Fanny greeted him with a tremulous cry. "Have you heard anything; oh, have you heard anything, Andrew?"

Eva sprang forward and clutched him by the arm.

"Have you?"

Andrew shook his head, and moved her hand from his arm, and pushed past her roughly.

Fanny stood in his way, and threw her arms around him with a wild, sobbing cry, but he pushed her away also with sternness, and went to the kitchen sink to wash his hands. The four women — his wife, her sister, and the two neighbors — stood staring at him; his face was terrible as he dipped the water from the pail on the sink corner, and the terribleness of it was accentuated by the homely and everyday nature of his action.

They all stared, then Fanny burst out with a loud and desperate wail. "He won't speak to me, he pushes me away, when it is our child that's lost — his as well as mine. He hasn't any feelings for me that bore her. He only thinks of himself. Oh, oh, my own husband pushes me away."

Andrew went on washing his hands and his ghastly face, and made no reply. He had actually at that moment not the slightest sympathy with his wife. All his other outlets of affection were choked by his concern for his lost child; and as for pity, he kept reflecting, with a cold cruelty, that it served her right — it served both her and her sister right. Had not they driven the child away between them?

He would not eat the supper which the neighbors had prepared for him; finally he went across the yard to his mother's. It seemed to him at that time that his mother could enter into his state of mind better than anyone else.

When he went out, Fanny called after him, frantically, "Oh, Andrew, you ain't going to leave me?"

When he made no response, she gazed for a second at his retreating back, then her temper came to her aid. She caught her sister's arm, and pulled her away out of the kitchen. "Come with me," she said, hoarsely. "I've got nobody but you. My own husband leaves me when he is in such awful trouble, and goes to that old woman, that has always hated me, for comfort."

The sisters went into Fanny's bedroom, and sat down on the edge of the bed, with their arms round each other. "Oh, Fanny!" sobbed Eva; "poor, poor Fanny! if Andrew turns against you, I will stand by you as long as I live. I will work my fingers to the bone to support you and Ellen. I will never get married. I will stay and work for you and her. And I will never get mad with you again as long as I live, Fanny. Oh, it was all my fault, every bit my fault, but, but —" Eva's voice broke; suddenly she clasped her sister tighter, and then she went down on her knees beside the bed, and hid her tangled head in her lap. "Oh, Fanny," she sobbed out miserably, "there ain't much excuse for me, but there's a little. When Jim Tenny stopped goin' with me last summer, my heart 'most broke. I don't care if you do know it. That's what made me so much worse than I used to be. Oh, my heart 'most broke, Fanny! He's treated me awful, but I can't get over it; and now little Ellen's gone, and I drove her away!"

Fanny bent over her sister, and pressed her head close to her bosom. "Don't you feel so bad, Eva," said she. "You wasn't anymore to blame than I was, and we'll stand by each other as long as we live."

"I'll work my fingers to the bone for you and Ellen, and I'll never get married," said Eva again.

Chapter IV

*E*llen Brewster was two nights and a day at Cynthia Lennox's, and no one discovered it. All day the searching-parties passed the house. Once Ellen was at the window, and one of the men looked up and saw her, and since his solicitude for the lost child filled his heart with responsiveness towards all childhood, he waved his hand and nodded, and bade another man look at that handsome little kid in the window.

"Guess she's about Ellen's size," said the other.

"Shouldn't wonder if she looked something like her," said the first.

"Answers the description well enough," said the other, "same light hair."

Both of the men waved their hands to Ellen as they passed on, but she shrank back afraid. That was about ten o'clock of the morning of the day after Miss Lennox had taken her into her house. She had waked at dawn with a full realization of the situation. She remembered perfectly all that had happened. She was a child for whom there were very few half-lights of life, and no spiritual twilights connected her sleeping and waking hours. She opened her eyes and looked around the room, and remembered how she had run away and how her mother was not there, and she remembered the strange lady with that same odd combination of terror and attraction and docility with which she had regarded her the night before. It was a very cold morning, and there was a delicate film of frost on the windows between the sweeps of the muslin curtains, and the morning sun gave it a rosy glow and a crusting sparkle as of diamonds. The sight of the frost had broken poor Andrew Brewster's heart when he saw it, and reflected how it might have meant death to his little tender child out under the blighting fall of it, like a little house-flower.

Ellen lay winking at it when Cynthia Lennox came into the room and leaned over her. The child cast a timid glance up at the tall, slender figure clad in a dressing gown of quilted crimson silk which dazzled her eyes, accustomed as she was to morning wrappers of dark-blue cotton at ninety-eight cents apiece; and she was filled with undefined apprehensions of splendor and opulence which might overwhelm her simple grasp of life and cause her to lose all her old standards of value.

She had always thought her mother's wrappers very beautiful, but now look at this! Cynthia's face, too, in the dim, rosy light, looked very fair to the child, who had no discernment for those ravages of time of which adults either acquit themselves or by which they measure their own. She did not see the faded color of the woman's face at all; she did not see the spreading marks around mouth and eyes, or the faint parallels of care on the temples; she saw only that which her unbiased childish vision had ever sought in a human face, love and kindness, and tender admiration of herself; and her conviction of its beauty was complete. But at the same time a bitter and piteous jealousy for her mother and home, and all that she had ever loved and believed in, came over her. What right had this strange woman, dressed in a silk dress like that, to be leaning over her in the morning, and looking at her like that — to be leaning over her in the morning instead of her own mother, and looking at her in that way, when she was not her mother? She shrank away towards the other side of the bed with that nestling motion which is the natural one of all young and gentle children even towards vacancy, but suddenly Cynthia was leaning close over her, and she was conscious again of that soft smother of violets, and Cynthia's arms were embracing all her delicate little body with tenderest violence, folding her against the soft red silk over her bosom, and kissing her little, blushing cheeks with the lightest and carefulest kisses, as though she were a butterfly which she feared to harm with her adoring touch.

"Oh, you darling, you precious darling!" whispered Cynthia. "Don't be afraid, darling; don't be afraid, precious; you are very safe; don't be afraid. You shall have such a little, white, new-laid egg for your breakfast, and some slices of toast, such a beautiful brown, and some honey. Do you love honey, sweet? And some chocolate, all in a little pink-and-gold cup which you shall have for your very own."

"I want my mother!" Ellen cried out suddenly, with an exceedingly bitter and terrified and indignant cry.

"There, there, darling!" Cynthia whispered; "there is a beautiful red-and-green parrot downstairs in a great cage that shines like gold, and you shall have him for your own, and he can talk. You shall have him for your very own, sweetheart. Oh, you darling! you darling!"

Ellen felt herself overborne and conquered by this tide of love, which compelled like her mother's, though this woman was not her mother, and her revolt of loyalty was subdued for the time. After all, whether we like it or not, love is somewhat of an impersonal quality to all children, and perhaps to their elders, and it may be in such wise that the goddess is evident.

She did not shrink from Cynthia anymore then, but suffered her to lift her out of bed as if she were a baby and set her on a white fur rug, into which her feet sank, to her astonishment. Her mother had only drawn-in rugs, which Ellen had watched her make. She was a little afraid of the fur rug.

Ellen was very small, and seemed much younger than she was by reason of her baby silence and her little clinging ways. Then, too, she had always been so petted at home, and through never going to school had not been in contact with other children. Often the bloom of childhood is soonest rubbed off by friction with its own kind. Diamond cut diamond holds good in many cases.

Cynthia did not think she was more than six years old, and never dreamed of allowing her to dress herself, and indeed the child had always been largely assisted in so doing. Cynthia washed her and dressed her, and curled her hair, and led her downstairs into the dining room of the night before, which Ellen still regarded with wise eyes as the store. Then she sat in the tall chair which must have been vacated by that mysterious other child, and had her breakfast, eating her new-laid egg, which the black woman broke for her, while she leaned delicately away as far as she could with a timid shrug of her little shoulder, and sipping her chocolate out of the beautiful pink-and-gold cup. That, however, Ellen decided within herself was not nearly as pretty as one with "A Gift of Friendship" on it in gilt letters which her grandmother kept on the whatnot in her best parlor. This had been given to her aunt Ellen, who died when she was a young girl, and was to be hers when she grew up. She did not care as much for the egg and toast either as for the griddle-cakes and maple syrup at home. All through breakfast Cynthia talked to her, and in such manner as the child had never heard. That fine voice, full of sweetest modulations and cadences, which used the language with the precision of a musician, was as different from the voices at home with their guttural slurs and maimed terminals as the song of a spring robin from the scream of the parrot which Ellen could hear in some distant room. And what Cynthia said was as different from ordinary conversation to the child as a fairy tale, being interspersed with terms of endearment which her mother and grandmother would have considered high-flown, and have been shamefaced in employing, and full of a whimsical playfulness which had an undertone of pathos in it. Cynthia was not still for a minute, and seemed to feel that much of her power lay in her speech and voice, like some enchantress who cast her spell by means of her silver tongue. Nobody knew how she dreaded that outcry of Ellen's, "I want my mother!" It gave her the sensations of a murderess, even while she persisted in her crime. So she talked, diverting the child's mind from its natural channel by sheer force of eloquence. She told a story about the parrot, which caused Ellen's eyes to widen with thoughtful wonder; she promised her treasures and pleasures which made her mouth twitch into smiles in spite of herself; but with all her efforts, when after breakfast they went into another room, Ellen broke out again, "I want my mother!"

Cynthia turned white and struggled with herself for a moment, then she spoke. That which she was doing of the nature of a crime was in reality more foreign to her nature than virtue, and her instinct was to return to her narrow and straight way in spite of its cramping of love and natural longings. "Who is your mother, darling?" she asked. "And what is your name?"

But Ellen was silent, except for that one cry, "I want my mother!" The persistency of the child, in spite of her youth and her distress, was almost invulnerable. She came of a stiff-necked family on one side at least, and sometimes stiff-neckedness is more pronounced in a child than in an adult, in whom it may be tempered by experience and policy. "I want my mother! I want my mother!" Ellen repeated in her gentle wail as plaintively inconsequent as the note of a bird, and would say no more.

Then Cynthia displayed the parrot, but a parrot was too fine and fierce a bird for Ellen. She would have preferred him as a subject for her imagination, which could not be harmed by his beak and claws, and she liked Cynthia's story about him better than the gorgeous actuality of the bird himself. She shrank back from that shrieking splendor, clinging with strong talons to his cage wires, against which he pressed cruelly his red breast and beat his gold-green wings, and through which he thrust his hooked beak, and glared with his yellow eyes.

Ellen fairly sobbed at last when the parrot thrust out a wicked and deceiving claw towards her, and said something in his unearthly shriek which seemed to have a distinct reference to her, and fired at her a volley of harsh "How do's" and "Good-mornings," and "Good-nights," and "Polly want a cracker's," then finished with a wild shriek of laughter, her note of human grief making a curious chord with the bird's of inhuman mirth. "I want my mother!" she panted out, and wept, and would not be comforted. Then Cynthia took her away from the parrot and produced the doll. Then truly did the sentiment of emulative motherhood in her childish breast console her for the time for her need of her own mother. Such a doll as that she had never seen, not even in the store-windows at Christmas-time. Still, she had very fine dolls for a little girl whose relatives were not wealthy, but this doll was like a princess, and nearly as large as Ellen.

Ellen held out her arms for this ravishing creature in a French gown, looked into its countenance of unflinching infantile grace and amiability and innocence, and her fickle heart betrayed her, and she laughed with delight, and the tension of anxiety relaxed in her face.

"Where is her mother?" she asked of Cynthia, having a very firm belief in the little girl-motherhood of dolls. She could not imagine a doll without her little mother, and even in the cases of the store-dolls, she wondered how their mothers could let them be sold, and mothered by other little girls, however poor they might be. But she never doubted that her own dolls were her very own children even if they had been bought in a store. So now she asked Cynthia with an indescribably pitying innocence, "Where is her mother?"

Cynthia laughed and looked adoringly at the child with the doll in her arms. "She has no mother but you," said she. "She is yours, but once she belonged to a dear little boy, who used to live with me."

Ellen stared thoughtfully: she had never seen a little boy with a doll. The lady seemed to read her thought, for she laughed again.

"This little boy had curls, and he wore dresses like a little girl, and he was just as pretty as a little girl, and he loved to play with dolls like a little girl," said she.

"Where is he?" asked Ellen, in a small, gentle voice. "Don't he want her now?"

"No, darling," said Cynthia; "he is not here; he has been gone away two years, and he had left off his baby curls and his dresses, and stopped playing with her for a year before that." Cynthia sighed and drew down her mouth, and Ellen looked at her lovingly and wonderingly.

"Be you his mother?" she asked, piteously; then, before Cynthia could answer, her own lip quivered and she sobbed out again, even while she hugged her doll-child to her bosom, "I want my mother! I want my mother!"

All that day the struggle went on. Cynthia Lennox, leading her little guest, who always bore the doll, traversed the fine old house in search of distraction, for the heart of the child was sore for its mother, and success was always intermittent. The music-box played, the pictures were explained, and even old trunks of laid-away treasures ransacked. Cynthia took her through the hothouses and gave her all the flowers she liked to pick, to still that longing cry of hers. Cynthia Lennox had fine hothouses kept by an old colored man, the husband of her black cook. Her establishment was very small; her one other maid she had sent away early that morning to make a visit with a sick sister in another town. The old colored couple had lived in her family since she was born, and would have been silent had she stolen a whole family of children. Ellen caught a glimpse of a bent, dark figure at one end of the pink-house as they entered; he glanced up at her with no appearance of surprise, only a broad, welcoming expansion of his whole face, which caused her to shrink; then he shuffled out in response to an order of his mistress.

Ellen stared at the pinks, swarming as airily as butterflies in motley tints of palest rose to deepest carmine over the blue-green jungle of their stems; she sniffed the warm, moist, perfumed atmosphere; she followed Cynthia down the long perspective of bloom, then she said again that she wanted her mother; and Cynthia led her into the rose-house, then into one where the grapes hung low overhead and the air was as sweet and strong as wine, but even there Ellen wanted her mother.

But it was not until the next morning when she was eating her breakfast that the climax came. Then the door-bell rang, and presently Cynthia was summoned into another room. She kissed Ellen, and bade her go on with her breakfast and she would return shortly; but before she had quite left the room a man stood unexpectedly in the door-way, a man who looked younger than Cynthia. He had a fair mustache, a high forehead scowling over near-sighted blue eyes, and stood with a careless slouch of shoulders in a grey coat.

"Good-morning," he began. Then he stopped short when he saw Ellen in her tall chair staring shyly around at him through her soft golden mist of hair. "What child is that?" he demanded; but Cynthia with a sharp cry sprang to him, and fairly pulled him out of the room, and closed the door.

Then Ellen heard voices rising higher and higher, and Cynthia say, in a voice of shrill passion: "I cannot, Lyman. I cannot give her up. You don't know what I have suffered since George married and took little Robert away. I can't let this child go."

Then came the man's voice, hoarse with excitement: "But, Cynthia, you must; you are mad. Think what this means. Why, if people know what you have done, kept this child, while all this search has been going on, and made no effort to find out who she was —"

"I did ask her, and she would not tell me," Cynthia said, miserably.

"Good Lord! what of that? That is nothing but a subterfuge. You must have seen in the papers —"

"I have not looked at a paper since she came."

"Of course you have not. You were afraid to. Why, good God! Cynthia Lennox, I don't know but you will stand in danger of lynching if people ever find this out, that you have taken in this child and kept her in this way — I don't know what people will do."

Ellen waited for no more; she rose softly, she gathered up her great doll which sat in a little chair near by, she gathered up her pink-and-gold cup which had been given her, and the pinks which had been brought from the hothouse the day before, which Cynthia had arranged in a vase beside her plate, then she stole very softly out of the side door, and out of the house, and ran down the street as fast as her little feet could carry her.

Chapter V

*T*hat morning, after the street in front of Lloyd's factory had been cleared of the flocking employés with their little dinner-boxes, and the great broadside of the front windows had been set with faces of the workers, a distracted figure came past. A young fellow at a window of the cutting-room noticed her first. "Look at that, Jim Tenny," said he, with a shove of an elbow towards his next neighbor.

"Get out, will ye?" growled Jim Tenny, but he looked.

Then three girls from the stitching-room came crowding up behind with furtively tender pressings of round arms against the shoulders of the young men. "We come in here to see if that was Eva Loud," said one, a sharp-faced, alert girl, not pretty, but a favorite among the male employés, to the constant wonder of the other girls.

"Yes, it's her fast enough," rejoined another, a sweet-faced blonde with an exaggeratedly fashionable coiffure and a noticeable smartness in the tie of her neck-ribbon and the set of her cotton waist. "Just look at the poor thing's hair. Only see how frowsly it is, and she has come out without her hat."

"Well, I don't wonder," said the third girl, who was elderly and whose complexion was tanned and weather-beaten almost to the color of the leather upon which she worked. Yet through this seamed and discolored face, with thin greyish hair drawn back tightly from the temples, one could discern, as through a transparent mask, a past prettiness and an exceeding gentleness and faithfulness. "If my sister's little Helen was to be lost I shouldn't know whether my hat was on or not," said she. "I believe I should go raving mad."

"You wouldn't have to slave as you have done supportin' it ever since your sister's husband died," said the pretty girl. "Only look how Eva's waist bags in the back and she ain't got any belt on. I wouldn't come out lookin' so."

"I should die if I didn't have something to work for. That's the difference between being a worker and a slave," said the other girl, simply. "Poor Eva!"

"Well, it was a pretty young one," said the first girl.

"Looks to me as if Eva Loud's skirt was comin' off," said the pretty girl. She pressed close to Jim Tenny with a familiar air of proprietorship as she spoke, but the young man did not seem to heed her. He was looking over his bench at the figure on the street below, and his heavy black eyebrows were scowling, and his mouth set.

Jim Tenny was handsome after a swarthy and grimy fashion, for the tint of the leather seemed to have become absorbed into his skin. His black mustache bristled roughly, but his face was freer than usual from his black beard-stubble, because the day before had been Sunday and he had shaved. His black right hand with its squat discolored nails grasped his cutting-knife with a hard clutch, his left held the piece of leather firmly in place, while he stared out with that angry and anxious scowl at Eva, who had paused on the street below, and was staring up at the windows, as if she meditated a wild search in the factory for the lost child. There was a curious likeness between the two faces; people had been accustomed to say that Eva Loud and her gentleman looked more like brother and sister than a courting couple, and there was, moreover, a curious spirit of comradeship between the two. It asserted itself now with the young man, in opposition to the more purely sexual attraction of the pretty girl who was leaning against him, and for whom he had deserted Eva.

After all, friendship and good comradeship are a steadier force than love, if not as overwhelming, and it may be that tortoise of the emotions which outruns the hare.

"Well, for my part, I think a good deal more of Eva Loud than if she had come out all frizzed and ruffled — shows her heart is in the right place," said the man who had spoken first. He spoke with a guttural drawl, and kept on with his work, but there was a meaning in his words for the pretty girl, who had coquetted with him before taking up with Jim Tenny.

"That is so," said another man at Jim Tenny's right. "She is right to come out as she has done when she is so anxious for the child." This man was a fair-haired Swede, and he spoke English with a curious and careful precision, very different from the hurried, slurring intonations of the other men. He had been taught the language by a philanthropic young lady, a college graduate, in whose father's family he had lived when he first came to America, and in consequence he spoke like a gentleman and had some considerable difficulty in understanding his companions.

"Eva Loud has had a damned hard time, take it all together," spoke out another man, looking over is bench at the girl on the street. He was small and thin and wiry, a mass of brown-coated muscles under his loose-hanging gingham shirt. He plied feverishly his cutting-knife with his lean, hairy hands as he spoke. He was accounted one of the best and swiftest cutters in Lloyd's, and he worked unceasingly, for he had an invalid wife and four children to support. Now and then he had to stop to cough, then he worked faster.

"That's so," said the first man.

"Yes, that is so," said the Swede, with a nod of his fair head.

"And now to lose this young one that she set her life by," said the first girl, with an evident point of malice in her tone, and a covert look at the pretty girl at Jim Tenny's side. Jim Tenny paled under his grime; the hand which held the knife clinched.

"What do you s'pose has become of the young one?" said the first girl. "There's a good many out from the shop huntin' this mornin', ain't there?"

"Fifty," said the first man, laconically.

"You three were out all day yesterday, wa'n't you?"

"Yes, Jim and Carl and me were out till after midnight."

"Well, I wonder whether the poor little young one is alive? Don't seem as if she could be — but —"

"Look there! look there!" screamed the elderly girl suddenly. "Look at *there!*" She began to dance, she laughed, she sobbed, she waved her lean hands frantically out of the window, leaning far over the bench. "Look at there!" she kept crying. Then she turned and ran out of the room, with the other girls and half the cutting-room after her.

"Damn it, she's got the child!" said the thin man. He kept on working, his dark, sinewy hands flying over the sheets of leather, but the tears ran down his cheeks. Lloyd's emptied itself into the street, and surrounded Eva Loud and Ellen, who, running aimlessly, had come straight to her aunt. Jim Tenny was first.

Eva stood clasping the child, who was too frightened to cry, and was breathing in hushed gasps, her face hidden on her aunt's broad bosom. Eva had caught her up at the first sight of her, and now she stood clasping her fiercely, and looking at them all as if she thought they wanted to rob her of the child. Even when a great cheer went up from the crowd, and was echoed by another from the factory, with an accompaniment of waving bare, leather-stained arms and hands, that expression of desperate defiance instead of the joy of recovery did not leave her face, not until she saw Jim Tenny's face working with repressed emotion and met his eyes full of the memory of old comradeship. Then her bold heart and her pride all melted and she burst out in a great wail before them all.

"Oh, Jim!" she cried out. "Oh, Jim, I lost you, and then I thought I'd lost her! Oh, Jim!"

Then there was a chorus of feminine sobs, for Eva's wild weeping had precipitated the ready sympathy of half the girls present. The men started a cheer to cover a certain chivalrous shamefacedness which was upon them at the sight of the girl's grief, and another cheer from the factory echoed it. Then came another sound, the great steam-whistle of Lloyd's; then the whistles of the other neighboring factories responded, and people began to swarm out of them, and the windows to fill with eager faces. Jim Tenny grasped Eva's arm with a grasp like a vise. "Come this way," said he, sharply. "Come this way, Eva."

"Oh, Jim! oh, Jim!" Eva sobbed again; but she followed him, little Ellen's golden fleece tossing over her shoulder.

"She's got her; she's got her!" shouted the people.

Then the leather-stained hands gyrated, the cheers went up, and again the whistles blew.

Jim Tenny, with his hand on Eva's arm, pushed his way through the crowd.

"Where you goin', Jim?" asked the pretty girl at his elbow, but he pushed past her roughly, and did not seem to hear. Eva's face was all inflamed and convulsed with sobs, but she did not dream of covering it — she was full of the holy shamelessness of grief and joy. "Let me see

her! let me see her! Oh, the dear little thing, only look at her! Where
have you been, precious? Are you hungry? Oh, Nellie, she is hungry, I
know! She looks thin. Run over to the bakery and buy her some cookies,
quick! Are you cold? Give her this sacque. Only look at her! Kate, only
look at her! Are you hurt, darling? Has anybody hurt you? If anybody
has, he shall be hung! Oh, you darling! Only see her, 'Liza."

But Jim Tenny, his mouth set, his black brows scowling, his hard
grasp on Eva's arm, pushed straight through the gathering crowd until
they came to Clarkson's stables at the rear of Lloyd's, where he kept his
horse and buggy — for he lived at a distance from his work, and drove
over every morning. He pointed to a chair which a hostler had occupied,
tilted against the wall, for a morning smoke, after the horses were fed
and watered, and which he had vacated to join the jubilant crowd. "Sit
down there," he said to Eva. Then he hailed a staring man coming out
of the office. "Here, help me in with my horse, quick!" said he.

The man stared still, with slowly rising indignation. He was portly
and middle-aged, the senior partner of the firm, who seldom touched
his own horses of late years, and had a son at Harvard. "What's to pay?
What do you mean? Anybody sick?" he asked.

"Help me into the buggy with my horse!" shouted Jim Tenny. "I tell
you the child is found, and I've got to take it home to its folks."

"Don't they know yet? Is that it?"

"Yes, I tell you." Jim was backing out his horse as he spoke.

Mr. Clarkson seized a harness and threw the collar over the horse's
head, while Jim ran out the buggy. When Mr. Clarkson lifted Eva and
Ellen into the buggy he gave the child's head a pat. "God bless it!" he
said, and his voice broke.

The horse was restive. Jim took a leap into the buggy at Eva's side,
and they were out with a dash and a swift rattle. The crowd parted before
them, and cheer after cheer went up. The whistles sounded again. Then
all the city bells rang out. They were signaling the other searchers that
the child was found. Jim and Eva and Ellen made a progress of triumph
down the street. The crowd pursued them with cheers of rejoicing; doors
and windows flew open; the house-yards were full of people. Jim drove
as fast as he could, scowling hard to hide his tenderness and pity. Eva
sat by his side, weeping in her terrible candor of grief and joy, and
Ellen's golden locks tossed on her shoulder.

Chapter VI

*A*s Jim Tenny, with Eva Loud and the child, drove down the road towards the Brewster house, his horse and buggy became the nucleus of a gathering procession, shouting and exclaiming, with voices all tuned to one key of passionate sympathy. There were even many women of the poorer class who had no sense of indecency in following the utmost lead of their tender emotions. Some of them bore children of their own in their arms, and were telling them with passionate croonings to look at the other little girl in the carriage who had been lost, and gone away a whole day and two nights from her mother. They often called out fondly to Ellen and Eva, and ordered Jim to wait a moment that they might look at the poor darling. But Jim drove on as fast as he was able, though he had sometimes to rein his horse sharply to avoid riding down some lean racing boys, who would now and then shoot ahead of him with loud whoops of triumph. Once as he drove he laid one hand caressingly over Eva's. "Poor girl!" he said, hoarsely and shamefacedly, and Eva sobbed loudly. When Jim reached Mrs. Zelotes Brewster's house there was a swift displacement of lights and shadows in a window, a door flew open, and the gaunt old woman was at the wheel.

"Stop!" she cried. "Stop! Bring her in here to me! Let me have her! Give her to me; I have got everything ready! Come, Ellen — come to grandmother!"

Then there was a mad rush from the opposite direction, and the child's mother was there, reaching into the buggy with fierce arms of love and longing. "Give her to me!" she shrieked out. "Give me my baby, Eva Loud! Oh, Ellen, where have you been?"

Fanny Brewster dragged her child from her sister's arms so forcibly that she seemed fairly to fly over the wheel. Then she strained her to her hungry bosom, covering her with kisses, wetting her soft face and yellow hair with tears.

"My baby, mother's darling, mother's baby!" she gasped out with great pants of satisfied love; but another pair of lean, wiry old arms stole around the child's slender body.

"Give her to me!" demanded Mrs. Zelotes Brewster. "She is my son's child, and I have a right to her! You will kill her, goin' on so over her. Give her to me! I have everything all ready in my house to take care of her. Give her to me, Fanny Loud!"

"Keep your hands off her!" cried Fanny. "She's my own baby, and nobody's goin' to take her away from me, I guess."

"Give her to me this minute!" said Mrs. Zelotes Brewster. "You'll kill her, goin' on so. You're frightenin' her to death. Give her to me this minute!"

Ellen, meanwhile, that little tender blossom tossed helplessly by contending waves of love, was weeping and trembling with joy at the feel of her mother's arms and with awe and terror at this tempest of passion which she had evoked.

"Give her to me!" demanded Mrs. Zelotes Brewster.

The crowd who had followed stood gaping with working faces. The mothers wept over their own children. Eva stood at her sister's elbow, with a hand on one of the child's, which was laid over Fanny's shoulder. Jim Tenny had his face hidden on his horse's neck.

"Give her to me!" said Mrs. Zelotes again. "Give her to me, I say! I am her own grandmother!"

"And I am her own mother!" called out Fanny, with a great master-note of love and triumph and defiance. "I'm her own mother, and I've got her, and nobody but God shall take her from me again." The tears streamed down her cheeks; she kissed the child with pale, parted lips. She was at once pathetic and terrible. She was human love and selfishness incarnate.

Mrs. Zelotes Brewster stared at her, and her face changed suddenly and softened. She turned and went back into her own house. Her grey head appeared a second beside her window, then sank out of sight. She was kneeling there with her Bible at her side, a sudden sweet humility of thankfulness rising from her whole spirit like a perfume, when Fanny, with Eva following, still clinging to the child's little hand over her sister's shoulder, went across the yard to her own house to tell her husband. The others followed, and stood about outside, listening with curiosity sanctified by intensest sympathy. One nervous-faced boy leaped on the slant of the bulkhead to peer in a window of the sitting room, and when his mother pulled him back forcibly, rubbed his grimy little knuckles across his eyes, and a dark smooch appeared on his nose and cheeks. He was a young boy, very small and thin for his age. He whispered to his mother and she nodded, and he darted off in the direction of his own home.

Andrew Brewster had just come home after an all-night's search, and he was in his bedroom in the bitter sleep of utter exhaustion and despair. Suddenly his heart had failed him and his brain had reeled. He had begun to feel dazed, to forget for a minute what he was looking for. He had made incoherent replies to the men with him, and finally one, after a whispered consultation with the others, had said: "Look at here, Andrew, old fellow; you'd better go home and rest a bit. We'll look all the harder while you're gone, and maybe she'll be found when you wake up."

"Who will be found?" Andrew asked, with a dazed look. He reeled as if he were drunk.

"Ain't had anything, has he?" one of the men whispered.

"Not a drop to my knowledge."

Andrew's lips trembled perceptibly; his forehead was knitted with vacuous perplexity; his eyes reflected blanks of unreason; his whole body had an effect of weak settling and subsidence. The man who worked next to him in the cutting-room at Lloyd's, and had searched at his side indefatigably from the first, stole a tender hand under his shoulder. "Come along with me, old man," he said, and Andrew obeyed.

When Fanny and Eva came in with the child, he lay prostrate on the bed, and scarcely seemed to breathe. A great qualm of fear shot over Fanny for a second. His father had died of heart-disease.

"Is he — dead?" she gasped to Eva.

"No, of course he ain't," said Eva. "He's asleep; he's wore out. Andrew, Andrew, Andrew, wake up! She's found, Andrew; Ellen's found." But Andrew did not stir.

"He is!" gasped Fanny, again.

"No, he ain't. Andrew, Andrew Brewster, wake up, wake up! Ellen's here! She's found!"

Fanny put Ellen down, and bent over Andrew and listened. "No, I can hear him breathe," she cried. Then she kissed him, and leaned her mouth close to his ear. "Andrew!" she said, in a voice which Eva and Ellen had never heard before. "Andrew, poor old man, wake up; she's found! Our child is found!"

When Andrew still did not wake, but only stirred, and moaned faintly, Fanny lifted Ellen onto the bed. "Kiss poor father, and wake him," she told her.

Ellen, whose blue eyes were big with fright and wonder, whose lips were quivering, and whose little body was vibrating with the strain of her nerves, laid her soft cheek against her father's rough, pale one, and stole a little arm under his neck. "Father, wake up!" she called out in her little, trembling, sweet voice, and that reached Andrew Brewster in the depths of his own physical inertness. He opened his eyes and looked at the child, and the light came into them, and then the sound of his sobbing filled the house and reached the people out in the yard, and an echo arose from them. Gradually the crowd dispersed. Jim Tenny, before he drove away, went to the door and spoke to Eva.

"Anything I can do?" he asked, with a curious, tender roughness. He did not look at her as he spoke.

"No; thank you, Jim," replied Eva.

Suddenly the young man reached out a hand and stroked her rough hair. "Well, take care of yourself, old girl," he said.

Eva went to her sister as Jim went out of the yard. Ellen was in the sitting room with her father, and Fanny had gone to the kitchen to heat some milk for the child, whom she firmly believed to have had nothing to eat during her absence.

"Fanny," said Eva.

"Well?" said Fanny. "I can't stop; I must get some milk for her; she must be 'most starved."

Fanny turned and looked at Eva, who cast down her eyes before her in a very shamefacedness of happiness and contrition.

"Why, what is it?" repeated Fanny, staring at her.

"I've got Jim back, I guess, as well as Ellen," said Eva, "and I'm going to be a good woman."

After all the crowd of people outside had gone, the little nervous boy raced into the Brewster yard with a tin cup of chestnuts in his hand. He knocked at the side door, and when Fanny opened it he thrust them upon her. "They're for her!" he blurted out, and was gone, racing like a deer.

"Don't you want the cup back?" Fanny shouted after him.

"No, ma'am," he called back, and that, although his mother had charged him to bring back the cup or he would get a scolding.

Chapter VII

*E*llen had clung fast all the time to her doll, her bunch of pinks, and her cup and saucer; or, rather, she had guarded them jealously. "Where did you get all these things?" her aunt Eva had asked her, amazedly, when she first caught sight of her, and then had not waited for an answer in her wild excitement of joy at the recovery of the child. The great, smiling wax doll had ridden between Jim and Eva in the buggy, Eva had held the pink cup and saucer with a kind of mechanical carefulness, and Ellen herself clutched the pinks in one little hand, though she crushed them against her aunt's bosom as she sat in her lap. Ellen's grandmother and aunt had glanced at these treasures with momentary astonishment, and so had her mother, but curiosity was in abeyance for both of them for the time; rapture at the sight of the beloved child at whose loss they had suffered such agonies was the one emotion of their souls. But later investigation was to follow.

When Ellen did not seem to care for her hot milk liberally sweetened in her own mug, and griddle-cakes with plenty of syrup, her mother looked at her, and her eyes of love sharpened with inquiry. "Ain't you hungry?" she said. Ellen shook her head. She was sitting at the table in the dining room, and her father, mother, and aunt were all hovering about her, watching her. Some of the neighbor women were also in the room, staring with a sort of deprecating tenderness of curiosity.

"Do you feel sick?" Ellen's father inquired, anxiously.

"You don't feel sick, do you?" repeated her mother.

Ellen shook her head.

Just then Mrs. Zelotes Brewster came in with her black-and-white-checked shawl pinned around her gaunt old face, which had in it a strange softness and sweetness, which made Fanny look at her again, after the first glance, and not know why.

"We've got our blessing back again, mother," said her son Andrew, in a broken voice.

"But she won't eat her breakfast, now mother has gone and cooked it for her, so nice, too," said Fanny, in a tone of confidence which she had never before used towards Mrs. Zelotes.

"You don't feel sick, do you, Ellen?" asked her grandmother.

Ellen shook her head. "No, ma'am," said she.

"She says she don't feel sick, and she ain't hungry," Andrew said, anxiously.

"I wonder if she would eat one of my new doughnuts. I've got some real nice ones," said a neighbor — the stout woman from the next house, whose breadth of body seemed to symbolize a corresponding spiritual breadth of motherliness, as she stood there looking at the child who had been lost and was found.

"Don't you want one of Aunty Wetherhed's nice doughnuts?" asked Fanny.

"No; I thank you," replied Ellen. Eva started suddenly with an air of mysterious purpose, opened a door, ran down cellar, and returned with a tumbler of jelly, but Ellen shook her head even at that.

"Have you had your breakfast?" said Fanny.

Then Ellen was utterly quiet. She did not speak; she made no sign or motion. She sat still, looking straight before her.

"Don't you hear, Ellen?" said Andrew. "Have you had your breakfast this morning?"

"Tell Auntie Eva if you have had your breakfast," Eva said.

Mrs. Zelotes Brewster spoke with more authority, and she went further.

"Tell grandmother if you have had your breakfast, and where you had it," said she.

But Ellen was dumb and motionless. They all looked at one another. "Tell Aunty Wetherhed: that's a good girl," said the stout woman.

"Where are those things she had when I first saw her?" asked Mrs. Zelotes, suddenly. Eva went into the sitting room, and fetched them out — the bunch of pinks, the cup and saucer, and the doll. Ellen's eyes gave a quick look of love and delight at the doll.

"She had these, luggin' along in her little arms, when I first caught sight of her comin'," said Eva.

"Where did you get them, Ellen?" asked Fanny. "Who gave them to you?"

Ellen was silent, with all their inquiring eyes fixed upon her face like a compelling battery. "Where have you been, Ellen, all the time you have been gone?" asked Mrs. Zelotes. "Now you have got back safe, you must tell us where you have been."

Andrew stooped his head down to the child's, and rubbed his rough cheek against her soft one, with his old facetious caress. "Tell father where you've been," he whispered. Ellen gave him a little piteous glance, and her lip quivered, but she did not speak.

"Where do you s'pose she got them?" whispered one neighbor to another.

"I can't imagine; that's a beautiful doll."

"Ain't it? It must have cost a lot. I know, because my Hattie had one her aunt gave her last Christmas; that one cost a dollar and ninety-eight cents, and it didn't begin to compare with this. That's a handsome cup and saucer, too."

"Yes, but you can get real handsome cups and saucers to Crosby's for twenty-five cents. I don't think so much of that."

"Them pinks must have come from a greenhouse."

"Yes, they must."

"Well, there's lots of greenhouses in the city besides the florists. That don't help much." Then the first woman inclined her lips closely to the other woman's ear and whispered, causing the other to start back. "No, I can't believe she would," said she.

"She came from those Louds on her mother's side," whispered the first woman, guardedly, with dark emphasis.

"Ellen," said Fanny, suddenly, and almost sharply, "you didn't take those things in any way you hadn't ought to, did you? Tell mother."

"Fanny!" cried Andrew.

"If she did, it's the first time a Brewster ever stole," said Mrs. Zelotes. Her face was no longer strange with unwonted sweetness as she looked at Fanny.

Andrew put his face down to Ellen's again. "Father knows she didn't steal the things; never mind," he whispered.

Suddenly the stout woman made a soft, ponderous rush out of the room and the house. She passed the window with oscillating swiftness.

"Where's Miss Wetherhed gone?" said one woman to another.

"She's thought of somethin'."

"Maybe she left her bread in the oven."

"No, she's thought of somethin'."

A very old lady, who had been sitting in a rocking-chair on the other side of the room, rose trembling and came to Ellen and leaned over her, looking at her with small, black, bright eyes through gold-rimmed spectacles. The old woman was deaf, and her voice was shrill and high-pitched to reach her own consciousness. "What did such a good little girl as you be run away from father and mother for?" she piped, going back to first principles and the root of the whole matter, since she had heard nothing of the discussion which had been going on about her, and had supposed it to deal with them.

Ellen gasped. Suddenly all her first woe returned upon her recollection. She turned innocent, accusing eyes upon her father's loving face, then her mother's and aunt's. "You said — you said — you —" she stammered out, but then her father and mother were both down upon their knees before her in her chair embracing her, and Eva, too, seized her little hands. "You mustn't ever think of what you heard father and mother say, Ellen," Andrew said, solemnly. "You must forget all about it. Father and mother were both very wrong and wicked —"

"And Aunt Eva, too," sobbed Eva.

"And they didn't mean what they said," continued Andrew. "You are the greatest blessing in this whole world to father and mother; you're all they have got. You don't know what father and mother have been through, thinking you were lost and they might never see their little girl again. Now you mustn't ever think of what they said again."

"And you won't ever hear them say it again, Ellen," Fanny Brewster said, with a noble humbling of herself before her child.

"No, you won't," said Eva.

"Mother is goin' to try to do better, and have more patience, and not let you hear such talk anymore," said Fanny, kissing Ellen passionately, and rising with Andrew's arm around her.

"I'm going to try, too, Ellen," said Eva.

The stout woman came padding softly and heavily into the room, and there was a bright-blue silken gleam in her hand. She waved a whole yard of silk of the most brilliant blue before Ellen's dazzled eyes. "There!" said she, triumphantly, "if you will tell Aunty Wetherhed where you've been, and all about it, she'll give you all this beautiful silk to make a new dress for your new dolly."

Ellen looked in the woman's face, she looked at the blue silk, and she looked at the doll, but she was silent.

"Only think what a beautiful dress it will make!" said a woman.

"And see how pretty it goes with the dolly's light hair," said Fanny.

"Ellen," whispered Andrew, "you tell father, and he'll buy you a whole pound of candy down to the store."

"I shouldn't wonder if I could find something to make your dolly a cloak," said a woman.

"And I'll make her a beautiful little bonnet, if you'll tell," said another.

"Only think, a whole pound of candy!" said Andrew.

"I'll buy you a gold ring," Eva cried out — "a gold ring with a little blue stone in it."

"And you shall go to ride with mother on the cars tomorrow," said Fanny.

"Father will get you some oranges, too," said Andrew.

But Ellen sat silent and unmoved by all that sweet bribery, a little martyr to something within herself, a sense of honor, love for the lady who had concealed her, and upon whom her confession might bring some dire penalty; or perhaps she was strengthened in her silence by something less worthy — possibly that stiff-neckedness which had descended to her from a long line of Puritans upon her father's side. At all events she was silent, and opposed successfully her one little new will to the onslaught of all those older and more experienced ones before her, though nobody knew at what cost of agony to herself. She had always been a singularly docile and obedient child; this was the first persistent disobedience of her whole life, and it reacted upon herself with a cruel spiritual hurt. She sat clasping the great doll, the pinks, and the pink cup and saucer before her on the table — a lone little weak child, opposing her single individuality against so many, and to her own hurt and horror and self-condemnation, and she did not weaken; but all at once her head drooped on one side, and her father caught her.

"There! you can all stop tormentin' this blessed child!" he cried. "Ellen, Ellen, look at Father! Oh, mother, look here; she's fainted dead away!"

"Fanny!"

When Ellen came to herself she was on the bed in her mother's room, and her aunt Eva was putting some of her beautiful cologne on her head, and her mother was trying to make her drink water, and her grandmother had a glass of her currant wine, and they were calling to her with voices of far-off love, as if from another world.

And after that she was questioned no more about her mysterious journey.

"Wherever she has been, she has got no harm," said Mrs. Zelotes Brewster, "and there's no use in trying to drive a child, when it comes of our family. She's got some notion in her head, and you've got to leave her alone to get over it. She's got back safe and sound, and that's the main thing."

"I wish I knew where she got those things," Fanny said. Looseness of principle as to property rights was not as strange to her imagination as to that of her mother-in-law.

For a long time afterwards she passed consciously and uneasily by cups and saucers in stores, and would not look their way lest she should see the counterpart of Ellen's, which was Sèvres, and worth more than the whole counterful, had she only known it, and she hurried past the florists who displayed pinks in their windows. The doll was evidently not new, and she had not the same anxiety with regard to that.

No one was allowed to ask Ellen further questions that day, not even the reporters, who went away quite baffled by this infantile pertinacity in silence, and were forced to draw upon their imaginations, with results varying from realistic horrors to Alice in Wonderland. Ellen was kissed and cuddled by some women and young girls, but not many were allowed to see her. The doctor had been called in after her fainting-fit, and pronounced it as his opinion that she was a very nervous child, and had been under a severe strain, and he would not answer for the result if she were to be further excited.

"Let her have her own way: if she wants to talk, let her, and if she wants to be silent, let her alone. She is as delicate as that cup," said the doctor, looking at the shell-like thing which Ellen had brought home, with some curiosity.

Chapter VIII

*T*hat evening Lyman Risley came to see Cynthia. He looked at her anxiously and scrutinizingly when he entered the room, and did not respond to her salutation.

"Well, I have seen the child," he said, in a hushed voice, with a look towards the door as he seated himself before the fire and spread out his hands towards the blaze. He looked nervous and chilly.

"How did she look?" asked Cynthia.

"Why in the name of common-sense, Cynthia," he said, abruptly, without noticing her query, "if you had to give that child china for a souvenir, didn't you give her something besides Royal Sèvres?" Lyman Risley undoubtedly looked younger than Cynthia, but his manner even more than his looks gave him the appearance of comparative youth. There was in it a vehemence and impetuosity almost like that of a boy. Cynthia, with her strained nervous intensity, seemed very much older.

"Why not?" said she.

"Why not? Well, it is fortunate for you that those people have a knowledge for the most part of the fundamental properties of the drama of life, such as bread-and-butter, and a table from which to eat it, and a knife with which to cut it, and a bed in which to sleep, and a stove and coal, and so on, and so on, and that the artistic accessories, such as Royal Sèvres, which is no better than common crockery for the honest purpose of holding the tea for the solace of the thirsty mouth of labor, is beneath their attention."

"How does the child look, Lyman?" asked Cynthia Lennox. She was leaning back in a great crimson-covered chair before the fire, a long, slender, graceful shape, in a clinging white silk gown which was a favorite of hers for house wear. The light in the room was subdued, coming mostly through crimson shades, and the faint, worn lines on Cynthia's face did not show; it looked, with her soft crown of grey hair, like a cameo against the crimson background of the chair. The man beside her looked at her with that impatience of his masculine estate and his superior youth, and yet with the adoration which nothing could conquer. He had passed two-thirds of his life, metaphorically, at this woman's feet, and had formed a habit of admiration and lovership which no facts nor developments could ever alter. He was frowning, he replied with a certain sharpness, and yet he leaned towards her as he spoke, and his eyes followed her long, graceful lines and noted the clear delicacy of her features against the crimson background. "How the child looked — how the child looked; Cynthia, you do not realize what you did. You have not the faintest realization of what it means for a woman to keep a lost child hidden away as you did, when its parents and half the city were hunting for it. I tell you I did not know what the consequences might be to you if it were found out. There is wild blood in a city like this, and even the staid old New England stream is capable of erratic currents. I tell you I have had a day of dreadful anxiety, and it was worse because I had to be guarded. I dared scarcely speak to anyone about the matter. I have listened on street corners; I have made errands to newspaper offices. I meant to get you away if — Well, never mind — I tell you, you do not realize what you did, Cynthia."

Cynthia glanced at him without moving her head, then she looked away, her face quivering slightly, more as if from a reflection of his agitation than from her own. "You say you saw her," she said.

"This afternoon," the man went on, "I got fairly desperate. I resolved to go to the fountain-head for information, and take my chances. So down I went to Maple Street, where the Brewsters live, and I rang the front-door bell, and the child's aunt, a handsome, breathless kind of creature, came and ushered me into the best parlor, and went into the next room — the sitting room — to call the others. I caught sight of enough women for a woman's club in the sitting room. Then Andrew Brewster came in, and I offered my legal services out of friendly interest in the case, and in that way I found out what I wanted to. Cynthia, that child has not told."

Cynthia raised herself and sat straight, and her face flashed like a white flame. "Were they harsh to her?" she demanded. "Were they cruel? Did they question her, and were they harsh and cruel because she would not tell? Why did you not tell them yourself? Why did you not, Lyman Risley? Why did you not tell the whole story rather than have that child blamed? Well, I will go myself. I will go this minute. They shall not blame that darling. What do you think I care for myself? Let them lynch me if they want to. I will go this minute!" Cynthia sprang to her feet, but Risley, with a hoarse shout under his breath, caught hold of her and forced her back.

"For God's sake, sit down, Cynthia!" he said. "Didn't you hear the door-bell? Somebody is coming."

The door-bell had in fact rung, and Cynthia had not noticed it. She lay back in her chair as the door opened, and Mrs. Norman Lloyd entered. "Good-evening, Cynthia," she said, beamingly. "I thought I would stop a few minutes on my way to meeting. I'm rather early. No, don't get up," as Cynthia rose. "Don't get up; I can only stay a minute. Never mind about giving me a chair, Mr. Risley — thank you. Yes, this is a real comfortable chair." Mrs. Lloyd, seated where the firelight played over her wide sweep of rich skirts, and her velvet fur-trimmed cloak and plumed bonnet, beamed upon them with an expansive benevolence and kindliness. She was a large, handsome, florid woman. Her greyish-brown hair was carefully crimped, and looped back from her fat, pink cheeks, a fine shell-and-gold comb surmounted her smooth French twist, and held her bonnet in place. She unfastened her cloak, and a diamond brooch at her throat caught the light and blazed red like a ruby. She was the wife of Norman Lloyd, the largest shoe-manufacturer in the place. There was between her and Cynthia a sort of relationship by marriage. Norman Lloyd's brother George had married Cynthia's sister, who had died ten years before, and of whose little son, Robert, Cynthia had had the charge. Now George, who was a lawyer in St. Louis, had married again. Mrs. Norman had sympathized openly with Cynthia when the child was taken from Cynthia at his father's second marriage. "I call it a shame," she had said, "giving that child to a perfect stranger to bring up, and I don't see any need of George's marrying again, anyway. I don't know what I should do if I thought Norman would marry again if I died. I think one husband and one wife is enough for any man or woman if they believe in the resurrection. It has always seemed to me that the answer to that awful question in the New Testament, as to whose wife that woman who had so many husbands would be in the other world, meant that people who had done so much marrying on earth would have to be old maids and old bachelors in heaven. George ought to be ashamed of himself, and Cynthia ought to keep that child."

Ever since she had been very solicitously friendly towards Cynthia, who had always imperceptibly held herself aloof from her, owing to a difference in degree. Cynthia had no prejudices of mind, but many of nerves, and this woman was distinctly not of her sort, though she had a certain liking for her. Every time she was brought in contact with her she had a painful sense of a grating adjustment as of points of meeting which did not dovetail as they should. Norman Lloyd represented one of the old families of the city, distinguished by large possessions and college training, and he was the first of his race to engage in trade. His wife came from a vastly different stock, being the daughter of a shoe-manufacturer herself, and the granddaughter of a cobbler who had tapped his neighbor's shoes in his little shop in the L of his humble cottage house. Mrs. Norman Lloyd was innocently unconscious of any reason for concealing the fact, and was fond, when driving out to take the air in her fine carriage, of pointing out to any stranger who happened to be with her the house where her grandfather cobbled shoes and laid the foundation of the family fortune. "That all came from that little shop of my grandfather," she would say, pointing proudly at Lloyd's great factory, which was not far from the old cottage. "Mr. Lloyd didn't have much of anything when I married him, but I had considerable, and Mr. Lloyd went into the factory, and he has been blessed, and the property has increased until it has come to this." Mrs. Lloyd's chief pride was in the very facts which others deprecated. When she considered the many-windowed pile of Lloyd's, and that her husband was the recognized head and authority over all those throngs of grimy men, walking with the stoop of daily labor, carrying their little dinner-boxes with mechanical clutches of leather-tanned fingers, she used to send up a prayer for humility, lest evil and downfall of pride come to her. She was a pious woman, a member of the First Baptist Church, and active in charitable work. Mrs. Norman Lloyd adored her husband, and her estimate of him was almost ludicrously different from that of the grimy men who flocked to his factory, she seeing a most kindly spirited and amiable man, devoting himself to the best interests of his employés, and striving ever for their benefit rather than his own, and the others

seeing an aristocrat by birth and training, who was in trade because of
shrewd business instincts and a longing for wealth and power, but who
despised, and felt himself wholly superior to, the means by which it was
acquired.

"We ain't anything but the rounds of the ladder for Norman Lloyd
to climb by, and he only sees and feels us with the soles of his patent-
leathers," one of the turbulent spirits in his factory said. Mrs. Norman
Lloyd would not have believed her ears had she heard him.

Mrs. Lloyd had not sat long before Cynthia's fire that evening before
she opened on the subject of the lost child. "Oh, Cynthia, have you
heard —" she began, but Risley cut her short.

"About that little girl who ran away?" he said. "Yes, we have; we were
just talking about her."

"Did you ever hear anything like it?" said Mrs. Lloyd. "They say they
can't find out where she's been. She won't tell. Don't you believe
somebody has threatened her if she does?"

Cynthia raised herself and began to speak, but a slight, almost
imperceptible gesture from the man beside her stopped her.

"What did you say, Cynthia?"

"There is no accounting for children's freaks," said Risley, shortly
and harshly. Mrs. Lloyd was not thin-skinned; such a current of exuber-
ant cordiality emanated from her own nature that she was not very
susceptible to any counter-force. Now, however, she felt vaguely and
wonderingly, as a child might have done, that for some reason Lyman
Risley was rude to her, and she had a sense of bewildered injury. Mrs.
Lloyd was always, moreover, somewhat anxious as to the relations
between Cynthia and Lyman Risley. She heard a deal of talk about it
first and last; and while she had no word of unkind comment herself,
yet she felt at times uneasy. "Folks do talk about Cynthia and Lyman
Risley keeping company so long," she told her husband; "it's as much
as twenty years. It does seem as if they ought to get married, don't you
think so, Norman? Do you suppose it is because the property was left
that way — for you know Lyman hasn't got anything besides what he
earns — or do you suppose it is because Cynthia doesn't want to marry
him? I guess it is that. Cynthia never seemed to me as if she would ever
care enough about any man to marry him. I guess that's it; but I do
think she ought to stop his coming there quite so much, especially when
people know that about her property."

Cynthia's property was hers on condition that her husband took her
name if she married, otherwise it was forfeited to her sister's child.
"Catch a Risley ever taking his wife's name!" said Mrs. Lloyd. "Of course
Cynthia would be willing to give up the money if she loved him, but I

don't believe she does. It seems as if Lyman Risley ought to see it would be better for him not to go there so much if they weren't going to be married."

So it happened when Risley caught up her question to Cynthia in that peremptory fashion, Mrs. Lloyd felt in addition to the present cause some which had gone before for her grievance. She addressed herself thereafter entirely and pointedly to Cynthia. "Did you ever see that little girl, Cynthia?" said she.

"Yes," replied Cynthia, in a voice so strange that the other woman stared wonderingly at her.

"Ain't you feeling well, Cynthia?" she asked.

"Very well, thank you," said Cynthia.

"When did you see her?" asked Mrs. Lloyd. Cynthia opened her mouth as if to speak, then she glanced at Risley, whose eyes held her, and laughed instead — a strange, nervous laugh. Happily, Mrs. Lloyd did not wait for her answer. She had her own important information to impart. She had in reality stopped for that purpose. "Well, I have seen her," she said. "I met her in front of Crosby's one day last summer. And she was so sweet-looking I stopped and spoke to her — I couldn't help it. She had beautiful eyes, and the softest light curls, and she was dressed so pretty, and the flowers on her hat were nice. The embroidery on her dress was very fine, too. Usually, you know, those people don't care about the fineness, as long as it is wide, and showy, and bright-colored. I asked her what her name was, and she answered just as pretty, and her mother told me how old she was. Her mother was a handsome woman, though she had an up-and-coming kind of way with her. But she seemed real pleased to have me notice the child. Where do you suppose she was all that time, Cynthia?"

"She was in some safe place, undoubtedly," said Risley, and again Mrs. Lloyd felt that she was snubbed, though not seeing how nor why, and again she rebelled with that soft and gentle persistency in her own course which was the only rebellion of which she was capable.

"Where do you suppose she was, Cynthia?" said she.

"I think some woman must have seen her, and coaxed her in and kept her, she was such a pretty child," said Cynthia, defiantly and desperately. But the other woman looked at her in wonder.

"Oh, Cynthia, I can't believe that," said she. "It don't seem as if any woman could be so bad as that when the child's mother was in such agony over her." And then she added, "I can't believe it, because it seems to me that if any woman was bad enough to do that, she couldn't have given her up at all, she was such a beautiful child." Mrs. Norman Lloyd had no children of her own, and was given to gazing with eyes of gentle

envy at pretty, rosy little girls, frilled with white embroidery like white
pinks, dancing along in leading hands of maternal love. "It don't seem
to me I could ever have given her up, if I had once been bad enough to
steal her," she said. "What put such an idea into your head, Cynthia?"

When the church-bell clanged out just then Lyman Risley had never
been so thankful in his life. Mrs. Lloyd rose promptly, for she had to
lead the meeting, that being the custom among the sisters in her church.
"Well," said she, "I am thankful she is found, anyway; I couldn't have
slept a wink that night if I had known she was lost, the dear little thing.
Good-night, Cynthia; don't come to the door. Good-night, Mr. Risley.
Come and see me, Cynthia — do, dear."

When Mrs. Norman Lloyd was gone, Risley looked at Cynthia with
a long breath of relief, but she turned to him with seemingly no
appreciation of it, and repeated her declaration which Mrs. Lloyd's
coming had interrupted: "Lyman, I am going there tonight — this
minute. Will you go with me? No, you must not go with me. I am
going!" She sprang to her feet.

"Sit down, Cynthia," said Risley. "I tell you they were not harsh to
her. You don't seem to consider that they love the child — possibly better
than you can — and would not in the nature of things be harsh to her
under such circumstances. Sit down and hear the rest of it."

"But they will be harsh by-and-by, after the first joy of finding her is
over," said Cynthia. "I will go and tell them the first thing in the
morning, Lyman."

"You will do nothing so foolish. They are not only not insisting upon
her telling her secret, but announced to me their determination not to
do so in the future. I wish you could have seen that man's face when
he told me what a delicate, nervous little thing his child was, and the
doctor said she must not be fretted if she had taken a notion not to tell;
and I wish you could have seen the mother and the aunt, and the
grandmother, Mrs. Zelotes Brewster. They would all give each other and
themselves up to be torn of wild beasts first. It is easy to see where the
child got her extraordinary strength of will. They took me out in the
sitting room, and there was a wild flurry of feminine skirts before me.
I had previously overheard myself announced as Lawyer Risley by the
aunt, and the response from various voices that they were 'goin' if he
was comin' out in the sittin' room.' It always made them nervous to see
lawyers. Well, I followed the parents and the grandmother and the aunt
out. I dared not refuse when they suggested it, and I hoped desperately
that the child would not remember me from that one scared glance she
gave at me this morning. But there she sat in her little chair, holding
the doll you gave her, and she looked up at me when I entered, and I

have never in the whole course of my existence seen such an expression upon the face of a child. Remember me? Indeed she did, and she promised me with the faithfulest, stanchest eyes of a woman set in a child's head that she would not tell; that I need not fear for one minute; that the lady who had given her the doll was quite safe. She knew, and she must have heard what I said to you this morning. She is the most wonderful child I have ever seen."

Cynthia had sank back in her chair. Lyman Risley put his cigar back between his lips; Cynthia was quite still, her delicate profile towards him.

"I assure you there is not the slightest danger of their troubling the child because of her silence, and you would do an exceedingly foolish thing, and its consequences would react not upon yourself only, but — upon others, were you to confess the truth to them," he said after a little. "You must think of others — of your friends, and of your sister's boy, whose loss led you into this. This would — well, it would get into the papers, Cynthia."

"Do you think that the doll continued to please her?" asked Cynthia.

"Cynthia, I want you to promise," said her friend, persistently.

"Very well, I will promise, if you will promise to let me know the minute you hear that they are treating her harshly because of her silence."

Suddenly Cynthia turned her face upon him. "Lyman," said she, "do you think that I could do anything for her —"

"Do anything for her?" he repeated, vaguely.

"Yes; they cannot have money. They must be poor: the father works in the factory. Would they allow me —"

The lawyer laughed. "Cynthia," he said, "you do not realize that pride finds its native element in all strata of society, and riches are comparative. Let me inform you that these Brewsters, of whom this child sprung, claim as high places in the synagogue as any of your Lennoxes and Risleys, and, what is more, they believe themselves there. They have seen the tops of their neighbors' heads as often as you or I. The mere fact of familiarity with shoe-knives and leather, and hand-skill instead of brain-skill, makes no difference with such inherent confidence of importance as theirs. The Louds, on the other side — the handsome aunt is a Loud — are rather below caste, but they make up for it with defiance. And as for riches, I would have you know that the Brewsters are as rich in their own estimation as you in yours; that they have possessions which entirely meet their needs and their æsthetic longings; that not only does Andrew Brewster earn exceedingly good wages in the shop, and is able to provide plenty of nourishing food and good clothes, but even by-and-by, if he prospers and is prudent, something rather extra in the way of education — perhaps a piano. I would have you know that there is a Rogers group on a little marble-topped table in the front window, and a table in the side window with a worked spread, on which reposes a red plush photograph album; that there is also a set of fine parlor furniture, with various devices in the way of silken and lace scarves over the corners and backs of the chairs and sofa, and that there is a tapestry carpet; that in the sitting room is a fine crushed-plush couch, and a multiplicity of rocking-chairs; that there is a complete dining-set in the next room, the door of which stood open, and even a side-board with red napkins, and a fine display of glass, every whit as elegant in their estimation as your cut glass in yours. The child's father owns his house and land free of encumbrance. He told me so in the course of his artless boasting as to what he might some day be able to do for the precious little creature of his own flesh and blood; and the grandmother owns her comfortable place next door, and she herself was dressed in black silk, and I will swear the lace on her cap was real, and she wore a great brooch containing hair of the departed, and it was set in pearl. What are you going to do in the face of opulence like this, Cynthia?"

Cynthia did not speak; her face looked as still as if it were carved in ivory.

"Cynthia," said the man, in a harsh voice, "I did not dream you were so broken up over losing that little boy of your sister's, poor girl."

Cynthia still said nothing, but a tear rolled down her cheek. Lyman Risley saw it, then he looked straight ahead, scowling over his cigar. He seemed suddenly to realize in this woman whom he loved something anomalous, yet lovely — a beauty, as it were, of deformity, an overdevelopment in one direction, though a direction of utter grace and sweetness, like the lip of an orchid.

Why should she break her heart over a child whom she had never seen before, and have no love and pity for the man who had laid his best at her feet so long?

He saw at a flash the sweet yet monstrous imperfection of her, and he loved her better for it.

Chapter IX

*A*fter Ellen's experience in running away, she dreamed her dreams with a difference. The breath of human passion had stained the pure crystal of her childish imagination; she peopled all her air-castles, and sounds of wailing farewells floated from the White North of her fancy after the procession of the evergreen trees in the west yard, and the cherry trees on the east had found out that they were not in the Garden of Eden. In those days Ellen grew taller and thinner, and the cherubic roundness of her face lengthened into a sweet wistfulness of wonder and pleading, as of one who would look farther, since she heard sounds and saw signs in her sky which indicated more beyond. Andrew and Fanny watched her more anxiously than ever, and decided not to send her to school before spring, though all the neighbors exclaimed at their tardiness in so doing. "She'll be two years back of my Hattie gettin' into the high-school," said one woman, bluntly, to Fanny, who retorted, angrily,

"I don't care if she's ten years behind, if she don't lose her health."

"You wait and see if she's two years behind!" exclaimed Eva, who had just returned from the shop, and had entered the room bringing a fresh breath of December air, her cheeks glowing, her black eyes shining.

Eva was so handsome in those days that she fairly forced admiration, even from those of her own sex whose delicacy of taste she offended. She had a parcel in her hand, which she had bought at a store on her way home, for she was getting ready to be married to Jim Tenny. "I tell you there don't nobody know what that young one can do," continued Eva, with a radiant nod of triumph. "There ain't many grown-up folks round here that can read like her, and she's studied geography, and she knows her multiplication-table, and she can spell better than some that's been through the high-school. You jest wait till Ellen gets started on her schoolin' — she won't stay in the grammar-school long, I can tell you that. She'll go ahead of some that's got a start now and think they're 'most there." Eva pulled off her hat, and the coarse black curls on her forehead sprang up like released wire. She nodded emphatically with a good-humored combativeness at the visiting woman and at her sister.

"I hope your cheeks are red enough," said Fanny, looking at her with grateful admiration.

The visiting woman sniffed covertly, and a retort which seemed to her exceedingly witty was loud in her own consciousness. "Them that likes beets and pinies is welcome to them," she thought, but she did not speak. "Well," said she, "folks must do as they think best about their own children. I have always thought a good deal of an education myself. I was brought up that way." She looked with eyes that were fairly cruel at Eva Loud and Fanny, who had been a Loud, who had both stopped going to school at a very early age.

Then the rich red flamed over Eva's forehead and neck as well as her cheeks. There was nothing covert about her, she would drag an ambushed enemy forth into the open field even at the risk of damaging disclosures regarding herself.

"Why don't you say jest what you mean, right out, Jennie Stebbins?" she demanded. "You are hintin' that Fanny and me never had no education, and twittin' us with it."

"It wa'n't our fault," said Fanny, no less angrily.

"No, it wa'n't our fault," assented Eva. "We had to quit school. Folks can live with empty heads, but they can't with empty stomachs. It had to be one or the other. If you want to twit us with bein' poor, you can, Jennie Stebbins."

"I haven't said anything," said Mrs. Stebbins, with a scared and injured air. "I'd like to know what you're making all this fuss about? I don't know. What did I say?"

"If I'd said anything mean, I wouldn't turn tail an' run, I'd stick to it about one minute and a half, if it killed me," said Eva, scornfully.

"You know what you was hintin' at, jest as well as we do," said Fanny; "but it ain't so true as you and some other folks may think, I can tell you that. If Eva and me didn't go to school as long as some, we have always read every chance we could get."

"That's so," said Eva, emphatically. "I guess we've read enough sight more than some folks that has had a good deal more chance to read. Fanny and me have taken books out of the library full as much as any of the neighbors, I rather guess."

"We've read every single thing that Mrs. Southworth has ever written," said Fanny, "and that's sayin' considerable."

"And all Pansy's and Rider Haggard's," declared Eva, with triumph.

"And every one of The Duchess and Marie Corelli, and Sir Walter Scott, and George Macdonald, and Laura Jean Libbey, and Charles Reade, and more, besides, than I can think of."

"Fanny has read 'most all Tennyson," said Eva, with loyal admiration; "she likes poetry, but I don't very well. She has read most all Tennyson and Longfellow, and we've both read *Queechee*, and *St. Elmo*, and *Jane Eyre*."

"And we've read the Bible through," said Fanny, "because we read in a paper once that that was a complete education. We made up our minds we'd read it through, and we did, though it took us quite a while."

"And we take *Zion's Herald*, and *The Rowe Gazette*, and *The Youth's Companion*," said Eva.

"And we've both of us learned Ellen geography and spellin' and 'rithmetic, till we know most as much as she does," said Fanny.

"That's so," said Fanny. "I snum, I believe I could get into the high-school myself, if I wasn't goin' to git married," said Eva, with a gay laugh. She was so happy in those days that her power of continued resentment was small. The tide of her own bliss returned upon her full consciousness and overflowed, and crested, as with glory, all petty annoyances.

The visiting woman took up her work, and rose to go with a slightly abashed air, though her small brown eyes were still blanks of impregnable defense. "Well, I dunno what I've said to stir you both so," she remarked again. "If I've said anythin' that riled you, I'm sorry, I'm sure. As I said before, folks must do as they are a mind to with their own children. If they see fit to keep 'em home from school until they're women grown, and if they think it's best not to punish 'em when they run away, why they must. I ain't got no right to say anythin', and I ain't."

"You —" began Fanny, and then she stopped short, and Eva began arranging her hair before the glass. "The wind blew so comin' home," she said, "that my hair is all out." The visiting woman stared with a motion of adjustive bewilderment, as one might before a sudden change of wind, then she looked, as a shadowy motion disturbed the even light of the room and little Ellen passed the window. She knew at once, for she had heard the gossip, that the ready tongues of recrimination were hushed because of the child, and then Ellen entered.

The winter afternoon was waning and the light was low; the child's face, with its clear fairness, seemed to gleam out in the room like a lamp with a pale luminosity of its own.

The three women, the mother, and aunt, and the visiting neighbor, all looked at her, and Ellen smiled up at them as innocently sweet as a flower. There was that in Ellen's smile and regard at that time which no woman could resist. Suddenly the visiting neighbor laid a finger softly under her chin and tilted up her little face towards the light. Then she said with that unconscious poetry of bereavement which sees a likeness in all fair things of earth to the face of the lost treasure, "I do believe she looks like my first little girl that died."

After the visiting woman had gone, Fanny and Eva calling after her to come again, they looked at each other, then at Ellen. "That little girl that died favored the Stebbinses, and was dark as an Injun," said Fanny, "no more like Ellen —"

"That's so," acquiesced Eva; "I remember that young one. Lookin' like Ellen — I'd like to see the child that did look like her; there ain't none round these parts. I wish you could have seen folks stare at her when I took her down street yesterday. One woman said, 'Ain't she pretty as a picture,' so loud I heard it, but Ellen didn't seem to."

"Sometimes I wonder if we'll make her proud," Fanny said, in a hushed voice, with a look of admiration that savored of worship at Ellen.

"She don't ever seem to notice," said Eva, with a hushed response. Indeed, Ellen had seemed to pay no attention whatever to their remarks, whether from an innate humility and lack of self-consciousness, or because she was so accustomed to adulation that it had become as the breath of her nostrils, to be taken no more account of. She had seated herself in her favorite place in a rocking-chair at a west window, with her chin resting on the sill, and her eyes staring into the great out-of-doors, full of winds and skies and trees and her own imaginings.

She would sit so, motionless, for hours at a time, and sometimes her mother would rouse her almost roughly. "What be you thinkin' about, settin' there so still?" she would ask, with eyes of vague anxiety fixed upon her, but Ellen could never answer.

Though it was getting late, it did not seem dark as early as usual, since there was a full moon and there was snow on the ground which gave forth a pale light in a wide surface of reflection. However, the moon was behind clouds, for it was beginning to snow again quite heavily, and the white flakes drove in whirlwinds past the street-lamp on the corner of the street. Now and then a tramping and muffled figure came into the radius of light, then passed into the white gloom beyond.

Fanny was preparing supper, and the light from the dining room shone in where Ellen sat, but the sitting room was not lighted. Ellen began to smell the fragrance of tea and toast, and there was a reflection of the dining room table and lamp outside pictured vividly against the white sheet of storm.

Ellen knew better, but it amused her to think that her home was out-of-doors as well as under her father's and mother's roof. Eva passed her with her hands full of kindlings. She was going to make a fire in the parlor-stove, for Jim Tenny was coming that evening. She laid a tender hand on Ellen's head as she passed, and smoothed her hair. Ellen had a sort of acquiescent wonder over her aunt Eva in those days. She heard people say Eva was getting ready to be married, and speculated. "What is getting ready to be married?" she asked Eva.

"Why, getting your clothes made, you little ninny," Eva answered.

The next day Ellen had watched her mother at work upon a new little frock for herself for some time before she spoke.

"Mother," she said.

"Yes, child."

"Mother, you are making that new dress for me, ain't you?"

"Of course I am; why?"

"And you made me a new coat last week?"

"Why, you know I did, Ellen; what do you mean?"

"And you are going to make me a petticoat and put that pretty lace on it?"

"You know I am, Ellen Brewster, what be you drivin' at?"

"Be I a-gettin' ready to be married, mother?" asked Ellen, with the strangest look of wonder and awe and anticipation.

Fanny had told this saying of the child's to everybody, and that evening when Jim Tenny came he caught up Ellen and gave her a toss to the ceiling, a trick of his which filled Ellen with a sort of fearful delight, the delight of helplessness in the hands of strength, and the titillation of evanescent risk.

"So you are gettin' ready to be married, are you?" Jim Tenny said, with a great laugh, looking at her soberly, with big black eyes. Jim Tenny was a handsome fellow, and much larger and stronger than her father. Ellen liked him; he often brought candies in his pocket for her, and they were great friends, but she could never understand why he stayed in the parlor all alone with her aunt Eva, instead of in the sitting room with the others.

Ellen had looked back at him as soberly. "Mother says I ain't," she replied, "but —"

"But what?"

"I am getting most as many new clothes as Aunt Eva, and she is."

"And you think maybe you are gettin' ready to be married, after all, hey?"

"I think maybe mother wants to surprise me," Ellen said.

Jim Tenny had all of a sudden shaken convulsively as if with mirth, but his face remained perfectly sober.

That evening after the parlor door was closed upon Jim and Eva, Ellen wondered what they were laughing at.

Tonight when she saw Eva enter the room, a lighted lamp illuminating her face fairly reckless with happiness, to light the fire in the courting-stove as her sister facetiously called it, she thought to herself that Jim Tenny was coming, that they would be shut up in there all alone as usual, and then she looked out at the storm and the night again, and the little home picture thrown against it. Then she saw her father coming into the yard with his arms full of parcels, and she was out of her chair and at the kitchen door to meet him.

Andrew had brought as usual some dainties for his darling. He watched Ellen unwrap the various parcels, not smiling as usual, but with a curious knitting of his forehead and pitiful compression of mouth. When she had finished and ran into the other room to show a great orange to her aunt, he drew a heavy sigh that was almost a groan. His wife coming in from the kitchen with a dish heard him, and looked at him with quick anxiety, though she spoke in a merry, rallying way.

"For the land sake, Andrew Brewster, what be you groanin' that way for?" she cried out.

Andrew's tense face did not relax; he strove to push past her without a word, but Fanny stood before him. "Now, look at here, Andrew," said she, "you ain't goin' to walk off with a face like that, unless I know what the matter is. Are you sick?"

"No, I ain't sick, Fanny," Andrew said; then in a low voice, "Let me go, I will tell you by-and-by."

"No, Andrew, you have got to tell me now. I'm goin' to know whatever has happened."

"Wait till after supper, Fanny."

"No, I can't wait. Look here, Andrew, you are my husband, and there ain't no trouble that can come to you in this world that I can't bear, except not knowin'. You've got to tell me what the matter is."

"Well, keep quiet till after supper, then," said Andrew. Then suddenly he leaned his face close to her and whispered with a hiss of tragedy, "Lloyd's shut down."

Fanny recoiled and looked at him.

"When?"

"The foreman gave notice tonight."

"For how long? Did he say?"

"Oh, till business got better — same old story. Unless I'm mistaken, Lloyd's will be shut down all winter."

"Well, it ain't so bad for us as for some," said Fanny. Both pride and a wish to cheer her husband induced her to say that. She did not like to think that, after the fine marriage she had made, she needed to be as distressed at a temporary loss of employment as others. Then, too, that look of overhanging melancholy in Andrew's face alarmed her; she felt that she must drive it away at any cost.

"Seems to me it's bad enough for anybody," said Andrew, morosely.

"Now, Andrew, you know it ain't. Here we own the house clear, and we've got that money in the savings-bank, and all that's your mother's is yours in the end. Of course we ain't always thinkin' of that, and I'm sure I hope she'll outlive me, but it's so. You know we shan't starve if you don't have work."

"We shall starve in the end, and you know I've been —" Andrew stopped suddenly as he heard Ellen and his sister-in-law coming. He shook his head at his wife with a warning motion that she should keep silence.

"Don't Eva know?" she whispered.

"No, she came out early. Do for Heaven's sake keep quiet till after supper."

Eva was sharp-eyed, and all through supper she watched Andrew, and the lines of melancholy on his face, which did not disappear even when he forced conversation.

"What in creation ails you, Andrew?" she burst out, finally. "You look like a walking funeral."

Andrew made no reply, and Fanny volunteered an answer. "He's all tired out," she said; "he's got a little cold. Eat some more of the stew, Andrew; it'll do you good, it's nice and hot."

"You can't cheat me," said Eva. "There's something to pay." She took a mouthful, then she stared at Andrew, with a sudden pallor. "It ain't anythin' about Jim, is it?" she gasped out. "Because if it is, there's no use in your waitin' to tell me, you might as well have it over at once. You won't make it any easier for me, I can tell you that."

"No, it ain't anything about Jim, in the way you mean, Eva," her sister said, soothingly. "Eat your supper and don't worry."

"What do you mean by that? Jim ain't sick?"

"No, I tell you; don't be a goose, Eva."

"He ain't been anywhere with —"

"Do keep still, Eva!" Fanny cried, impatiently. "If I didn't have anymore faith than that in a man, I'd give him up. I don't think you're fair to Jim. Of course he ain't been with that girl, when he's goin' to marry you next month."

"I'm just as fair to Jim as he deserves," Eva said, simply. "I think just as much of him, but what a man's done once he may do again, and I can't help it if I think of it, and he shouldn't be surprised. He's brought it on himself. I've got as much faith in him as anybody can have, seein' as he's a man. Well, if it ain't that, Andrew Brewster, what is it?"

"Now, you let him alone till after supper, Eva," Fanny said. "Do let him have a little peace."

"Well, I'll get it out of him afterwards," Eva said.

As soon as she got up from the table she pushed him into the sitting room. "Now, out with it," said she. Ellen, who had followed them, stood looking at them both, her lips parted, her eyes full of half-alarmed curiosity.

"Lloyd's has shut down, if you want to know," Andrew said, shortly.

"Oh my God!" cried Eva. Andrew shrank from her impatiently. She made that ejaculation because she was a Loud, and had an off-streak in her blood. Not one of Andrew's pure New England stock would have so expressed herself. He sat down beside the lamp and took up the evening paper. Eva stood looking at him a minute. She was quite pale, she was weighing consequences. Then she went out to her sister. "Well, you know what's happened, Fan, I s'pose," she said.

"Yes, I'm awful sorry, but I tell Andrew it ain't so bad for us as for some; we shan't starve."

"I don't know as I care much whether I starve or not," said Eva. "It's goin' to make me put off my weddin'; and if I do put it off, Jim and me will never get married at all; I feel it in my bones."

"Why, what should you have to put it off for?" asked Fanny.

"Why? I should think you'd know why without askin'. Ain't I spent every dollar I have saved up on my weddin' fixin's, and Jim, he's got his mother on his hands, and she's been sick, and he ain't saved up anything. If you s'pose I'm goin' to marry him and make him any worse off than he is now you're mistaken."

"Well, mebbe Jim can work somewhere else, and mebbe Lloyd's won't be shut up long," Fanny said, consolingly. "I wouldn't give up so, if I was you."

"I might jest as well," Eva returned. "It's no use, Jim and me will never get married." Eva's face was curiously set; she was not in the least loud nor violent as was usually the case when she was in trouble, her voice was quite low, and she spoke slowly.

Fanny looked anxiously at her. "It ain't as though you hadn't a roof to cover you," she said, "for you've got mine and Andrew's as long as we have one ourselves."

"Do you think I'd live on Andrew long?" demanded Eva.

"You won't have to. Jim will get work in a week or two, and you'll get married. Don't act so. I declare, I'm ashamed of you, Eva Loud. I thought you had more sense, to give up discouraged at no more than this. I don't see why you jump way ahead into trouble before you get to it."

"I've got to it, and I can feel the steam of it in my face," Eva said, with unconscious imagery. Then she lit a lamp, and went upstairs to change her dress before Jim Tenny arrived.

It was snowing hard. Ellen sat in her place by the window and watched the flakes drive past the radiance of the street-lamp on the corner, and past the reflection of the warm, bright room. Now she could see, since the light was in the room where she sat, her father beside the table reading his paper, and shadowy images of all the familiar things projecting themselves like a mirage of home into the night and storm. Ellen could see, even without turning round, that her father looked very sober, and did not seem to be much interested in his paper, and a vague sense of calamity oppressed her. She did not know just what might be involved in Lloyd's shutting down, but she saw that her father and aunt were disturbed, and her imaginings were half eclipsed by a shadow of material things. Ellen dearly loved this early evening hour when she could stare out into the mystery of the night, herself sheltered under the wing of home, and the fancies which her childish brain wove were as a garment of spirit for the future; but tonight she did not dream so much as she wondered and reflected. Pretty soon Ellen saw a man's figure plodding through the fast-gathering snow, and heard her aunt Eva make a soft, heavy rush down the front stairs, and she knew the man was Jim Tenny, and her aunt had been watching for him. Ellen wondered why she had watched up in her cold room, why she had not sat downstairs where it was warm, and let Jim ring the door-bell. Ellen liked Jim Tenny, but there was often that in her aunt's eyes regarding him which made Ellen look past him and above him to see if there was another man there. Ellen heard the fire crackling in the parlor-stove, and saw the light shining under the parlor threshold, and heard the soft hum of voices. Her mother, having finished washing up the supper dishes, came in presently and seated herself beside the lamp with her needle-work.

"You don't feel any wind comin' in the window?" she said, anxiously, to Ellen.

"No, ma'am," replied Ellen.

Andrew looked up quickly. "You're sure you don't?" he said.

"No, sir."

Ellen watched her mother sewing out in the snowy yard, then a dark shadow came between the reflection and the window, then another. Two men treading in the snow in even file, one in the other's foot-tracks, came into the yard.

"Somebody's comin'," said Ellen, as a knock, came on the side door.

"Did you see who 'twas?" Fanny asked, starting up.

"Two men."

"It's somebody to see you, Andrew," Fanny said, and Andrew tossed his paper on the table and went to the door.

When the door was opened Ellen heard a man cough.

"I should think anybody was crazy to come out such a night as this, coughin' that way," murmured Fanny. "I do believe it's Joe Atkins; sounds like his cough." Then Andrew entered with the two men stamping and shaking themselves.

"Here's Joseph Atkins and Nahum Beals," Andrew said, in his melancholy voice, all unstirred by the usual warmth of greeting. The two men bowed stiffly.

"Good-evenin'," Fanny said, and rose and pushed forward the rocking-chair in which she had been seated to Joseph Atkins, who was a consumptive man with an invalid wife, and worked next Andrew in Lloyd's.

"Keep your settin', keep your settin'," he returned in his quick, nervous way, as if his very words were money for dire need, and sat himself down in a straight chair far from the fire. The other man, Nahum Beals, was very young. He seated himself next to Joseph, and the two side by side looked with gloomy significance at Andrew and Fanny. Then Joseph Atkins burst out suddenly in a rattling volley of coughs.

"You hadn't ought to come out such a night as this, I'm afraid, Mr. Atkins," said Fanny.

"He's been out jest as bad weather as this all winter," said the young man, Nahum Beals, in an unexpectedly deep voice. "The workers of this world can't afford to take no account of weather. It's for the rich folks to look out betwixt their lace curtains and see if it looks lowery, so they shan't git their gold harnesses and their shiny carriages, an' their silks an' velvets an' ostrich feathers wet. The poor folks that it's life and death to have to go out whether or no, no matter if they've got an extra suit of clothes or not. They've got to go out through the drenchin' rain and the snowdrifts, to earn money so that the rich folks can have them gold-plated harnesses and them silks and velvets. Joe's been out all winter in weather as bad as this, after he's been standin' all day in a shop as hot as hell, drenched with sweat. One more time won't make much difference."

"It would be 'nough sight better for me if it did," said Joseph Atkins, chokingly, and still with that same seeming of hurry.

Fanny had gone out to the dining room, and now she returned stirring some whiskey and molasses in a cup.

"Here," said she, "you take this, Mr. Atkins; it's real good for a cough. Andrew cured a cold with it last month."

"Mine ain't a cold, and it can't be cured in this world, but it's better for me, I guess," said Joe Atkins, chokingly, but he took the cup.

"Now, you hadn't ought to talk so," Fanny said. "You had ought to think of your wife and children."

"My life is insured," said Joseph Atkins.

"We ain't got no money and no jewelry, and no silver to leave them we love — all we've got to leave 'em is the price of our own lives," said Nahum Beals.

"I wish I had got my life insured," Andrew said.

"Don't talk so, Andrew," Fanny cried, with a shudder.

"My life is insured for two thousand dollars," Joe Atkins said, with an odd sort of pride. "I had it done three years ago. My lungs was sound as anybody's then, but that very next summer I worked up under that tin roof, and came out as wet as if I'd been dipped in the river, into an east wind, and got a chill. It was the only time I ever struck luck — to get insured before that happened. Nobody'd look at me now, and I dunno what they'd do. I ain't laid up a cent, I've had so much sickness in my family."

"If you hadn't worked that summer in the annex under that tin roof, you'd be as well as you ever was now," said Nahum Beals.

"I worked there 'longside of you that summer," said Andrew to Joe, with bitter reminiscence. "We used to strip like a gang of convicts, and we stood in pools of sweat. It was that awful hot summer, and the room had only that one row of windows facing the east, and the wind never that way."

"Not till I came out of the shop that night I took the chill," said Joe.

Suddenly the young man, Nahum Beals, hit his knees a sounding slap, which made Ellen, furtively and timidly attentive at her window, jump. "It seems sometimes as if the Almighty himself was in league with 'em," he shouted out, "but I tell you it won't last, it won't last."

"I don't see much sign of any change for the better," Andrew said, gloomily.

"I tell you, sir, it won't last," repeated Nahum Beals. "I tell you, the Lord only raises 'em up higher and higher that He may dash 'em lower when the time comes. The same earth is beneath the high places of this life, and the lowly ones, and the law that governs 'em is the same, and — the higher the place the longer the fall, and the longer the fall the sorer the hurt." Nahum Beals sprang to his feet with a strange abandon of self-consciousness and a fiery impetus for one of his New England blood. He had a delicate, nervous face, like a woman's, his blue eyes gleamed like blue flames under his overhang of white forehead, he shook his head as if it were maned like a lion, and, though he wore his thin, fair hair short, one could seem to see it flung back in glistening lines. He spread his hands as if he were addressing an audience, and as he did so the parlor door opened and Jim Tenny and Eva stood there, listening.

"I tell you, sir," shouted Nahum Beals, "the time will come when you will all thank God that you belong to the poor and down-trodden of this earth, and not to the rich and great — the time will come. There's knives to sharpen today, and wood for scaffolds as plenty as in the days of the French Revolution, and the hand that marks the time of day on the clock of men's patience with wrong and oppression has near gone round to the same hour and minute."

Andrew Brewster looked at him, with a curious expression half of disgust, half of sympathy. His sense of dignity in the face of adversity inherited from his New England race was shocked; he was not one to be blindly swayed by another's fervor even when his own wrongs were in question. He would not have made a good follower in a revolution, nor a leader. He would simply have found his own place of fixed principle and abided there. Then, too, he had a judicial mind which could combine the elements of counsels for and against his own cause.

"Now, look at here," he said, slowly, "I ain't goin' to say I don't think we ain't in a hard place, and that there's somethin' wrong that's to blame for it, but I dunno but you go most too far, Nahum; or, rather, I dunno as you go far enough. I dunno but we've got to dig down past the poor and the rich, farther into the everlastin' foundations of things to get at what's the trouble."

Jim Tenny, standing in the parlor doorway, with an arm around Eva's waist, broke in suddenly with a defiant laugh. "I don't care nothin' about the everlastin' foundations of things, and I don't care a darn about the rich and the poor," he proclaimed. "I'm willin' to leave that to lecturers and dynamiters, and let 'em settle it if they can. I don't grudge the rich nothin', and I ain't goin' to call the Almighty to account for givin' somebody else the biggest piece of pie; mebbe it would give me the stomach-ache. All I'm concerned about is Lloyd's shut-down."

"That's so," said Eva.

"I tell you, sir, it ain't the facts of the case, but the reason for the facts, which we must think of," maintained Nahum Beals.

"I don't care a darn for the facts nor the reasons," said Jim Tenny; "all I care about is I'm out of work maybe till spring, with my mother dependent on me, and not a cent laid up, I've been so darned careless, and here's Eva says she won't marry me till I get work."

"I won't," said Eva, who was very pale, except for burning spots on her cheeks.

"She's afraid she won't get frostin' on her cake, and silk dresses, I expect," Jim Tenny said, and laughed, but his laugh was very bitter.

"Jim Tenny, you know better than that," Eva cried, sharply. "I won't stand that."

Jim Tenny, with a quick motion, unwound his arm from Eva's waist and stripped up his sleeve. "There, look at that, will you," he cried out, shaking his lean, muscular arm at them; "look at that muscle, and me tellin' her that I could earn a livin' for her, and she afraid. I can dig if I can't make shoes. I guess there's work in this world for them that's willin', and don't pick and choose."

"There ain't," declared Nahum, shortly.

"You can't dig when the ground's froze hard," Eva said, with literal meaning.

"Then I'll take a pickaxe," cried Jim.

"You can dig, but who's goin' to pay you for the diggin'?" demanded Nahum Beals.

"The idea of a girl's bein' afraid I wa'n't enough of a man to support a wife with an arm like that," said Jim Tenny, "as if I couldn't dig for her, or fight for her."

"The fightin' has got to come first in order to get the diggin', and the pay for it," said Nahum.

"Now, look at here," Andrew Brewster broke in, "you know I'm in as bad a box as you, and I come home tonight feelin' as if I didn't care whether I lived or died; but if it's true what McGrath said tonight, we've got to use common-sense in lookin' at things even if it goes against us. If what McGrath said was true, that Lloyd's losing money keeping on, I dunno how we can expect him or any other man to do that."

"Why not he lose money as well as we?" demanded Nahum, fiercely.

"'Cause we ain't got none to lose," cried Jim Tenny, with a hard laugh, and Eva and Fanny echoed him hysterically.

Nahum took no notice of the interruption. Tragedy, to his comprehension, never verged on comedy. One could imagine his face of intense melancholy and denunciation relaxed with laughter no more than that of the stern prophet of righteous retribution whose name he bore.

"Why shouldn't Norman Lloyd lose money?" he demanded again. "Why shouldn't he lose his fine house as well as I my poor little home? Why shouldn't he lose his purple and fine linen as well as Jim his chances of happiness? Why shouldn't he lose his diamond shirt-studs, and his carriage and horses, as well as Joe his life?"

"Well, he earned his money, I suppose," Andrew said, slowly, "and I suppose it's for him to say what he'll do with it."

"Earned his money? He didn't earn his money," cried Nahum Beals. "We earned it, every dollar of it, by the sweat of our brows, and it's for us, not him, to say what shall be done with it. Well, the time will come, I tell ye, the time will come."

"We shan't see it," said Joe Atkins.

"It may come sooner than you think," said Nahum. Then Nahum Beals, with a sudden access of bitterness, broke in. "Look at Norman Lloyd," he cried, "havin' that great house, and horses and carriages, and dressin' like a dude, and his wife rustlin' in silks so you can hear her comin' a mile off, and shinin' like a jeweler's window — look at 'em all — all the factory bosses — livin' like princes on the money we've earned for 'em; and look at their relations, and look at the rich folks that ain't never earned a cent, that's had money left 'em. Go right up and down the Main Street, here in this city. See the Lloyds and the Maguires and the Marshalls and the Risleys and the Lennoxes —"

"There ain't none of the Lennoxes left except that one woman," said Andrew.

"Well, look at her. There she is without chick or child, rollin' in riches, and Norman Lloyd's her own brother-in-law. Why don't she give him a little money to run the factory this winter, so you and me won't have to lose everythin'?"

"I suppose she's got a right to do as she pleases with her own," said Andrew.

"I tell you she ain't," shouted Nahum. "She ain't the one to say, 'It's the Lord, and He's said it.' Cynthia Lennox and all the women like her are the oppressors of the poor. They are accursed in the sight of the Lord, as were those women we read about in the Old Testament, with their mantles and crisping-pins. Their low voices and their silk sweeps and their shrinkin' from touchin' shoulders with their fellow-beings in a crowd don't alter matters a mite."

"Now, Nahum," cried Jim Tenny, with one of his sudden turns of base when his sense of humor was touched, "you don't mean to say that you want Cynthia Lennox to give you her money?"

"I'd die, and see her dead, before I'd touch a dollar of her money!" cried Nahum — "before I'd touch a dollar of her money or anything that was bought with her money, her money or any other rich person's. I want what I earn. I don't want a gift with a curse on it. Let her keep her fine things. She and her kind are responsible for all the misery of the poor on the face of the earth."

"Seems to me you're reasonin' in a circle, Nahum," Andrew said, good-humoredly.

"Look here, Andrew, if you're on the side of the rich, why don't you say so?" cried Eva.

"He ain't," returned Fanny — "you know better, Eva Loud."

"No, I ain't," declared Andrew. "You all of you know I'm with the class I belong to; I ain't a toady to no rich folks; I don't think no more of 'em than you do, and I don't want any favors of 'em — all I want is pay for my honest work, and that's an even swap, and I ain't beholden, but I want to look at things fair and square. I don't want to be carried away because I'm out of work, though, God knows, it's hard enough."

"I don't know what's goin' to become of us," said Joseph Atkins — then he coughed.

"I don't," Jim Tenny said, bitterly.

"And God knows I don't," cried Eva, and she sat down in the nearest chair, flung up her hands before her face, and wept.

Then Fanny spoke to Ellen, who had been sitting very still and attentive, her eyes growing larger, her cheeks redder with excitement. Fanny had often glanced uneasily at her, and wished to send her to bed, but she was in the habit of warming Ellen's little chamber at the head of the stairs by leaving open the sitting room door for a while before she went to it, and she was afraid of cooling the room too much for Joseph Atkins, and had not ventured to interrupt the conversation. Now, seeing the child's fevered face, she made up her mind. "Come, Ellen, it's your bedtime," she said, and Ellen rose reluctantly, and, kissing her father, she went to her aunt Eva, who caught at her convulsively and kissed her, and sobbed against her cheek. "Oh, oh!" she wailed, "you precious little thing, you precious little thing, I don't know what's goin' to become of us all."

"Don't, Eva," said Fanny, sharply; "can't you see she's all wrought up? She hadn't ought to have heard all this talk."

Andrew looked anxiously at his wife, rose, and caught up Ellen in his arms with a hug of fervent and protective love. "Don't you worry, father's darlin'," he whispered. "Don't you worry about anythin' you have heard. Father will always have enough to take care of you with."

Jim Tenny, when Andrew set the child down, caught her up again with a sounding kiss. "Don't you let your big ears ache, you little pitcher," said he, with a gay laugh. "Little doll-babies like you haven't anythin' to worry about if Lloyd's shut down every day in the year."

"They're the very ones whom it concerns," said Nahum Beals, when Ellen and her mother had gone upstairs.

"Well, I wouldn't have had that little nervous thing hear all this, if I'd thought," Andrew said, anxiously.

Joseph Atkins, whom Fanny had stationed in a sheltered corner near the stove when she opened the door, peered around at Andrew.

"Seems as if she was too young to get much sense of it," he remarked. "My Maria, that's her age, wouldn't."

"Ellen hears everything and makes her own sense of it," said Andrew, "and the Lord only knows what she's made of this. I hope she won't fret over it."

"I wish my tongue had been cut off before I said anything before her," cried Eva. "I know just what that child is. She'll find out what a hard world she's in soon enough, anyway, and I don't want to be the one to open her eyes ahead of time."

Ellen went to bed quietly, and her mother did not think she had paid much attention to what had been going on, and said so when she went downstairs after Ellen had been kissed and tucked in bed and the lamp put out. "I guess she didn't mind much about it, after all," she said to Andrew. "I guess the room was pretty warm, and that was what made her cheeks so red."

But Ellen, after her mother left her, turned her little head towards the wall and wept softly, lest someone hear her, but nonetheless bitterly that she had no right conception of the cause of her grief. There was over her childish soul the awful shadow of the labor and poverty of the world. She knew naught of the substance behind the shadow, but the darkness terrified her all the more, and she cried and cried as if her heart would break. Then she, with a sudden resolution, born she could not have told of what strange understanding and misunderstanding of what she had heard that evening, slipped out of bed, groped about until she found her cherished doll, sitting in her little chair in the corner. She was accustomed to take the doll to bed with her, and had undressed her for that purpose early in the evening, but she had climbed into bed and left her sitting in the corner.

"Don't you want your dolly?" her mother had asked.

"No, ma'am; I guess I don't want her tonight," Ellen had replied, with a little break in her voice. Now, when she reached the doll, she gathered her up in her little arms, and groped her way with her into the closet. She hugged the doll, and kissed her wildly, then she shook her. "You have been naughty," she whispered — "yes, you have, dreadful naughty. No, don't you talk to me; you have been naughty. What right had you to be livin' with rich folks, and wearin' such fine things, when other children don't have anything. What right had that little boy that was your mother before I was, and that rich lady that gave you to me? They had ought to be put in the closet, too. God had ought to put them all in the closet, the way I'm goin' to put you. Don't you say a word; you needn't cry; you've been dreadful naughty."

Ellen set the doll, face to the wall, in the corner of the closet, and left her there. Then she crept back into bed, and lay there crying over her precious baby shivering in her thin nightgown all alone in the dark closet. But she was firm in keeping her there, since, with that strange, involuntary grasp of symbolism which has always been maintained by the baby-fingers of humanity for the satisfying of needs beyond resources and the solving of problems outside knowledge, she had a conviction that she was, in such fashion, righting wrong and punishing evil. But she wept over the poor doll until she fell asleep.

Chapter X

*W*hen Ellen woke the next morning she had a curious feeling, as if she were blinded by the glare of many hitherto unsuspected windows opening into the greatness outside the little world, just large enough to contain them, in which she had dwelt all her life with her parents, her aunt, her grandmother, and her doll. She tried to adjust herself to her old point of view with her simple childish recognition of the most primitive facts as a basis for dreams, but she remembered what Mr. Atkins, who coughed so dreadfully, had said the night before; she remembered what the young man with the bulging forehead, who frightened her terribly, had said; she remembered the gloomy look in her father's face, the misery in her aunt Eva's; and she remembered her doll in the closet — and either everything was different or had a different light upon it. In reality Ellen's evening in the sound and sight of that current of rebellion against the odds of life which has taken the poor off their foot hold of understanding since the beginning of the world had aged her. She had lost something out of her childhood. She dreaded to go downstairs; she had a feeling of shamefacedness struggling within her; she was afraid that her father and mother would look at her sharply, then look again, and ask her what the matter was, and she would not

know what to say. When she went down, and backed about for her
mother to fasten her little frock as was her wont, she was careful to keep
her face turned away; but Fanny caught her up and kissed her in her
usual way, and then her aunt Eva sung out to know if she wanted to go
on a sleigh-ride, and had she seen the snow; and then her father came
in and that look of last night had gone from his face, and Ellen was her
old self again until she was alone by herself and remembered.

Fanny and Andrew and Eva had agreed to say nothing before the
child about the shutting-up of Lloyd's, and their troubles in consequence. "She heard too much last night," Andrew said; "there's no use
in her botherin' her little head with it. I guess that baby won't suffer."

"She's jest the child to fret herself most to pieces thinkin' we were
awful poor, and she would starve or somethin'," Fanny said.

"Well, she shan't be worried if I can help it, no matter what happens
to me," Eva said.

After breakfast that morning Eva went to work on a little dress of
Ellen's. When Fanny told her not to spend her time over that, when she
had so much sewing of her own to do, Eva replied with a gay, hard
laugh, that she guessed she'd wait and finish her weddin'-fix when she
was goin' to be married.

"Eva Loud, you ain't goin' to be so silly as to put off your weddin',"
Fanny cried out.

"I dunno as I've put it off; I dunno as I want to get married, anyhow,"
Eva said, still laughing. "I dunno, but I'd rather be old maid aunt to
Ellen."

"Eva Loud," cried her sister; "do you know what you are doin'?"

"Pretty well, I reckon," said Eva.

"Do you know that if you put off Jim Tenny, and he not likin' it, ten
chances to one Aggie Bemis will get hold of him again?"

"Well," said Eva, "let her. I won't have been the one to drag him into
misery, anyhow."

"Well, if you can feel that way," Fanny returned, looking at her sister
with a sort of mixed admiration and pity.

"I can. I tell you what 'tis, Fanny. When I look at Jim, handsome and
head up in the air, and think how he'd look all bowed down, hair turnin'
grey, and not carin' whether he's shaved and has on a clean shirt or not,
'cause he's got loaded down with debt, and the grocery-man and the
butcher after him, and no work, and me and the children draggin' him
down, I can bear anything. If another girl wants to do it, she must,
though I'd like to kill her when I think of it. I can't do it, because — I
think too much of him."

"He might lose his work after he was married, you know."

"Well, I suppose we'd have to run the risk of that; but I'm goin' to start fair or not at all."

"Well, maybe he'll get work," Fanny said.

"He won't," said Eva. She began to sing "Nancy Lee" over Ellen's dress.

After breakfast Ellen begged a piece of old brown calico of her mother. "Why, of course you can have it, child," said her mother; "but what on earth do you want it for? I was goin' to put it in the rag-bag."

"I want to make my dolly a dress."

"Why, that ain't fit for your dolly's dress. Only think how queer that beautiful doll would look in a dress made of that. Why, you ain't thought anything but silk and satin was good enough for her."

"I'll give you a piece of my new blue silk to make your doll a dress," said Eva.

But Ellen persisted. When the doll came out of her closet of vicarious penance she was arrayed like a very scullion among dolls, in the remnant of the dress in which Fanny Brewster had done her house-work all summer.

"There," Ellen told the doll, when her mother did not hear "you look more like the way you ought to, and you ought to be happy, and not ever think you wish you had your silk dress on. Think of all the poor children who never have any silk dresses, or any dresses at all — nothing except their cloth bodies in the coldest weather. You ought to be thankful to have this." For all which good advice and philosophy the little mother of the doll would often look at the discarded beauty of the wardrobe, with tears in her eyes and fondest pity in her heart; but she never flinched. When the young man Nahum Beals came in, as he often did of an evening, and raised his voice in fierce denunciation against the luxury and extravagance of the rich, Ellen would listen and consider that he would undoubtedly approve of what she had done, did he know, and would allow that she had made her small effort towards righting things.

"Only think what Mr. Beals would say if he saw you in your silk dress; why, I don't know but he would throw you out of the window," she told her doll once.

Ellen did not feel any difference in her way of living after her father was out of work. "She ain't goin' to be stented in one single thing; remember that," Andrew told Fanny, with angry emphasis. "That little, delicate thing is goin' to have everything she needs, if I spend every cent I've saved and mortgage the place."

"Oh, you'll get work before it comes to that," Fanny said, consolingly.

"Whether I do or not, it shan't make any difference," declared Andrew. "I'm goin' to hire a horse and sleigh and take her sleigh-ridin' this afternoon. It'll be good, and she's been talkin' about a sleigh-ride ever since snow flew."

"She could do without that," Fanny said, doubtfully.

"Well, she ain't goin' to."

So it happened that the very day after Lloyd's had shut down, when every man out of employment felt poorer than he did later when he had grown accustomed to the sensation of no money coming in, Andrew Brewster hired a horse and double sleigh, and took Ellen, her mother, grandmother, and aunt out sleigh-riding. Ellen sat on the back seat of the sleigh, full of that radiant happiness felt by a child whose pleasures have not been repeated often enough for satiety. The sleigh slid over the blue levels of snow followed by long creaks like wakes of sound, when the livery-stable horse shook his head proudly and set his bells in a flurry. Ellen drew a long breath of rapture. These unaccustomed sounds held harmonies of happiness which would echo through her future, for no one can estimate the immortality of some little delight of a child. In all her life, Ellen never forgot that sleigh-ride. It was a very cold day, and the virgin snow did not melt at all; the wind blew a soft, steady pressure from the west, and its wings were evident from the glistening crystals which were lifted and borne along. The trees held their shining boughs against the blue of the sky, and burned and blazed here and there as with lamps of diamonds. The child looked at them, and they lit her soul. Her little face, between the swan's-down puffs of her hood, deepened in color like a rose; her blue eyes shone; she laughed and dimpled silently; she was in too much bliss to speak. The others kept looking at her, then at one another. Fanny nudged her mother-in-law, behind the child's back, and the two women exchanged glances of confidential pride. Andrew and Eva kept glancing around at her, and asking if she were having a good time. Eva was smartly dressed in her best hat, gay with bows and red wings bristling as sharply as the headdress of an Indian chief in the old pictures. She had a red coat, and a long fur boa wound around her throat; the clear crimson of her cheeks, her great black eyes, and her heavy black braids were so striking that people whom they met looked long at her. Eva talked fast to Andrew, and laughed often and loudly.

Whenever that strident laugh of hers rang out, Mrs. Zelotes Brewster, on the seat behind, moved her be-shawled shoulders with a shivering hunch of disgust. "Can't you tell that girl not to laugh so loud when we're out ridin'," she said to her son that evening; "I saw folks lookin'."

"Oh, never mind, mother," Andrew said; "the poor girl's got a good deal on her mind."

"I suppose you mean that Tinny feller," said Mrs. Zelotes, alluding to something which had happened that afternoon in the course of the sleigh-ride.

The sleighing that day was excellent, for there had been an ice coating on the road before, and the last not very heavy snowfall had been just enough. The Brewsters passed and met many others: young men out with their sweethearts, whole families drawn by the sober old horse as old as the grown-up children; rakish young men driving stable teams, leaning forward with long circles of whip over the horses' backs, leaving the scent of cigars behind them; and often, too, two young ladies in dainty turnouts; and sometimes two girls or four girls from Lloyd's, who had clubbed together and hired a sleigh, taking reckless advantage of their enforced vacation.

"There's Daisy and Hat Sears, and — and there's Nell White and Eaat Ryoce in the team behind," Eva said.

"I should think they better be savin' their money if Lloyd's has shut up," said Mrs. Zelotes, severely.

"We ain't savin' ours, or Andrew ain't," Eva retorted, with a laugh.

"It's different with us," said Mrs. Zelotes, proudly, "though I shouldn't think it was right for Andrew to hire a team every day."

"Sometimes I think folks might just as well have a little as they're goin' along, for half the time they never seem to get there," Eva said, with another hard laugh at her own wit; and just then she saw something which made her turn deathly white, and catch her breath with a gasp in spite of herself, though that was all. She held up her head like a queen and turned her handsome white face full towards Jim Tenny and the girl for whom he had jilted her before, as they drove past, and bowed and smiled in a fashion which made the red flame up over the young man's swarthy cheek, and the pretty girl at his side shrink a little and avert her tousled fair head with a nervous giggle.

Mrs. Zelotes Brewster twisted herself about and looked after them. "There's John Tibbets and his wife in that sleigh; he's thrown out of work as well as you, Andrew," said Fanny, hastily. "See that feather in her bonnet blow; it's standin' up straight." But Fanny's manœuvre to turn the attention of her mother-in-law was of no avail, for nothing short of sudden death could interpose an effectual barrier between Mrs. Zelotes Brewster's tongue and mind set with the purpose of speech. "Was that the Tinny fellow?" she demanded.

"Yes; I guess so. I didn't notice in particular," Fanny replied, in a low voice. Then she added, pointing to an advancing sleigh. "Good land, there's that Smith girl. They said she wasn't able to ride out. Seems to me she's taken a queer day for it."

"Was that that Tinny fellow?" Mrs. Zelotes asked again. She leaned forward and gave Eva a hard nudge on her red-coated elbow.

"Yes, it was," Eva answered, calmly.

"Who was that girl with him?"

"It was Aggie Bemis."

Mrs. Zelotes gave a sniff, then she settled back, studying Eva's back with a sort of reflective curiosity. Presently she fumbled under the sleigh cushion for an extra shawl which she had brought, and handed it up to Eva. "Don't you want this extra shawl?" she asked, while Fanny stared at her wonderingly. Mrs. Zelotes's civilities towards her sister had been few and far between.

"No, thank you," Eva replied, with a start.

"Hadn't you better? It must be pretty cold sitting up there. You must take all the wind. You can wrap this shawl all around your face and ears, and I don't want it."

"No, thank you; I'm plenty warm," Eva replied. She swallowed hard, and set her mouth hard. There was something about this kindness of her old disapprover which touched her deeply, and moved her to weakness more than had the sight of her recreant love with another girl. Fanny saw the little quiver pass over her sister's face, and leaned over and whispered.

"I shouldn't be a mite surprised if that girl asked Jim to take her. It would be just like her."

"It don't make any odds whether she did or not," returned Eva, with no affectation of secrecy. "I don't care which way 'twas." She sat up straighter than ever, and some men in a passing sleigh turned to look after her.

"I s'pose she don't think my shawl looks genteel enough to wear," Mrs. Zelotes said to Fanny; "but she's dreadful silly."

They drove through the main street of the city and passed Cynthia Lennox's house. Ellen looked at it with the guilt of secrecy. She thought she saw the lady's head at a front window, and the front door opened and Cynthia came down the walk with a rich sweep of black draperies, and the soft sable toss of plumes. "There's Cynthia Lennox," said Fanny. "She's a handsome-lookin' woman, ain't she?"

"She's most as old as Andrew, but you'd never suspect it," said Mrs. Zelotes. She had used to have a fancy that Andrew and Cynthia might make a match. She had seen no reason to the contrary, and she always looked at Cynthia with a curious sense of injury and resentment when she thought of what might have been.

As Cynthia Lennox swept down the walk today, the old lady said, sharply:

"I don't see why she should walk any prouder than anybody else. I don't know why she should, if she's right-minded. The Lennoxes wasn't any grander than the Brewsters way back, if they have got a little more money of late years. Cynthia's grandfather, old Squire Lennox, used to keep the store, and live in one side of it, and her mother's father, Calvin Goodenough, kept the tavern. I dunno as she has so much to be proud of, though she's handsome enough, and shows her bringin' up, as folks can't that ain't had it." Fanny winced a little; her bringing up was a sore subject with her.

"Well, folks can't help their bringin' up," she retorted, sharply.

"There's Lloyd's team," Andrew said, quickly, partly to avert the impending tongue-clash between his wife and mother.

He reined his horse to one side at a respectful distance, and Norman H. Lloyd, with his wife at his side, swept by in his fine sleigh, streaming on the wind with black fur tails, his pair of bays stepping high to the music of their arches of bells. The Brewsters eyed Norman Lloyd's Russian coat with the wide sable collar turned up around his proud, clear-cut face, the fur-gauntleted hands which held the lines and the whip, for Mr. Lloyd preferred to drive his own blooded pair, both from a love of horseflesh and a greater confidence in his own guidance than in that of other people. Mr. Lloyd was no coward, but he would have confided to no man his sensations had he sat behind those furnaces of fiery motion with other hands than his own upon the lines.

"I should think Mis' Lloyd would be afraid to ride with such horses," said Mrs. Zelotes, as they leaped aside in passing; then she bowed and smiled with eager pleasure, and yet with perfect self-respect. She felt herself every whit as good as Mrs. Norman Lloyd, and her handsome Paisley shawl and velvet bonnet as genteel as the other woman's sealskins and floating plumes. Mrs. Lloyd loomed up like a vast figure of richness enveloped in her bulky winter wraps; her face was superb with health and enjoyment and good-humor. Her cheeks were a deep crimson in the cold wind; she smiled radiantly all the time as if at life itself. She had no thought of fear behind those prancing bays which seemed so frightful to Mrs. Zelotes, used to the steadiest stable team a few times during the year, and driven with a wary eye to railroad crossings and a sense of one's mortality in the midst of life strong upon her. Mrs. Norman Lloyd had never any doubt when her husband held the lines. She would have smiled behind ostriches and zebras. To her mind Norman Lloyd was, as it were, impregnable to all combinations of alien strength or circumstances. When she bowed on passing the Brewsters, she did not move her fixed smile until she caught sight of Ellen. Then emotion broke through the even radiance of her face. She moved her head with a flurry of nods; she waved her hand; she even kissed it to her.

"Bow to Mis' Lloyd, Ellen," said her grandmother; and Ellen ducked her head solemnly. She remembered what she had heard the night before, and the sleigh swept by, Mrs. Lloyd's rosy face smiling back over the black fringe of dancing tails. Eva had shot a swift glance of utmost rancor at the Lloyds, then sat stiff and upright until they passed.

"I wouldn't ask Ellen to bow to that woman," said she, fiercely, between her teeth. "I hate the whole tribe."

No one heard her except Andrew, and he shook the lines over the steady stable horse, and said, "G'lang!" hoarsely.

Mrs. Norman Lloyd, in the other sleigh, had turned to her husband with somewhat timid and deprecating enthusiasm. "Ain't she a sweet little girl?" said she.

"What little girl?" Lloyd asked, abstractedly. He had not looked at the Brewsters at all.

"That little Ellen Brewster who ran away and was gone most three days a little while ago. She was in that sleigh we just passed. She is just the sweetest child I ever laid eyes on," and Norman Lloyd smiled vaguely and coldly, and cast a glance over his sable-clad shoulders to see how far behind the team whose approaching bells he heard might be.

"I suppose her father and aunt are out of work on account of the closing of the factory," remarked Mrs. Lloyd, and a shadow of reflection came over her radiant face.

"Yes, I believe they worked there," Lloyd replied, shaking loose the reins and speeding the horses, that he might not be overtaken. In a few minutes they reached the factory neighborhood. There were three factories: two of them on opposite sides of the road, humming with labor, and puffing with jets of steam at different points; Lloyd's, beyond, was as large as both those standing hushed with windows blank in the afternoon sunshine.

"I suppose the poor men feel pretty badly at being thrown out of work," Mrs. Lloyd said, looking up at the windows as she slipped past in her nest of furs.

"They feel so badly that I have seen a round dozen since we started out taking advantage of their liberty to have a sleigh-ride with livery teams at a good round price," Lloyd replied, with languid emphasis. He never spoke with any force of argument to his wife, nor indeed to anyone else, in justification of his actions. His reasons for action were in most cases self-evolved and entirely self-regulated. He had said not a word to anyone, not even to his foreman, of his purpose to close the factory until it was quite fixed; he had asked no advice, explained to no one the course of reasoning which led to his doing so. Rowe was a city of strikes, but there had never been a strike at Lloyd's because he had abandoned the situation in every case before the clouds of rebellion were near enough for the storm to break. When Briggs and McGuire, the rival manufacturers at his right and left, had resorted to cut prices when business was dull, as a refuge from closing up, Lloyd closed with no attempt at compromise.

"I suppose they need a little recreation," Mrs. Lloyd observed, thinking of the little girl's face peeping out between her mother and grandmother in the sleigh they had just passed.

"Their little recreation is on about the same scale for them as my hiring a special railroad train every day in the week to go to Boston would be for me," returned Lloyd, setting his handsome face ahead at the track.

"It does seem dreadful foolish," said his wife, "when they are out of work, and maybe won't earn anymore money to support their families all winter —" Mrs. Lloyd hesitated a minute. "I wonder," said she, "if they feel sort of desperate, and think they won't have enough for their families, anyway — that is, enough to feed them, and they might as well get a little good time out of it to remember by-and-by when there ain't enough bread-and-butter. I dunno but we might do something like that, if we were in their places — don't you, Norman?"

"No, I do not," replied Lloyd; "and that is the reason why you and I are not in their places."

Mrs. Lloyd put her sealskin muff before her face as they turned a windy corner, and reflected that her husband was much wiser than she, and that the world couldn't be regulated by women's hearts, pleasant as it would be for the world and the women, since the final outcome would doubtless be destruction.

Mrs. Norman Lloyd was an eminent survival of the purest and oldest-fashioned femininity, a very woman of St. Paul, except that she did not keep silence in the sanctuary.

Just after they had turned the corner they passed an outlying grocery store much frequented as a lounging-place by idle men. There was a row of them on the wooden platform (backed against the wall), cold as it was, watching the sleighs pass, and two or three knots gathered together for the purposes of confabulation. Nearly all of them were employés of Lloyd's, and they had met at that unseasonable hour on that bitter day, drifting together unconsciously as towards a common nucleus of trouble, to talk over the situation.

When these men, huddled up in their shabby great-coats, with caps pulled over shaggy brows and sullenly flashing eyes, saw the Lloyds approaching, the rumble of conversation suddenly ceased. They all stood staring when their employer passed. Only one man, Nahum Beals, looked fairly at Lloyd's face with a denouncing flash of eyes.

To this man Lloyd, recognizing him and some of the others as his employés, bowed. Nahum Beals stood glaring at him in accusing silence, and his head was as immovable as if carved in stone. The other men, with their averted eyes, made a curious, motionless tableau of futile and dumb resistance to power which might have been carved with truth on the face of the rock from the beginning of the earth.

Chapter XI

*T*he closing of Lloyd's marked, in some inscrutable way, the close of the first period of Ellen Brewster's childhood. Looking back in later years, she always felt her retrospective thought strike a barrier there, beyond which her images of the past were confused. Yet it was difficult to tell why it was so, for after the first the child could, it seemed, have realized no difference in her life. Now and then she heard some of that conversation characterized at once by the confidence of wrong and injustice, and the logical doubt of it, by solid reasoning which, if followed far enough, refuted itself, by keen and unanswerable argument, and the wildest and most futile enthusiasm. But she had gained nothing except the conviction of the great wrongs of the poor of this earth and the awful tyranny of the rich, of the everlasting moaning of Lazarus at the gates and the cry for water later on from the depths of the rich man's hell. Somehow that last never comforted Ellen; she had no conception of the joy of the injured party over righteous retribution. She pitied the rich man and Lazarus impartially, yet all the time a spirit of fierce partisanship with these poor men was strengthening with her growth, their eloquence over their wrongs stirred her soul, and set her feet outside her childhood. Still, as before said, there was no tangible difference in her daily life. The little petted treasure of the Brewsters had all her small luxuries, sweets, and cushions of life, as well after as before the closing of Lloyd's. And the preparations for her aunt's wedding went on also. The sight of her lover sleigh-riding with her rival that afternoon had been too much for the resolution of Eva Loud's undisciplined nature. She had herself gone to Jim Tenny's house that evening, and called him to account, to learn that he had seriously taken her resolution not to marry at present to proceed from a fear that he would not provide properly for her, and that he had in this state of indignation been easily led by the sight of Aggie Bemis's pretty face in her front door, as he drove by, to stop. She had told Jim that she would marry him as she had agreed if he looked at matters in that way, and had passed Aggie Bemis's window leaning on Jim's arm with a side stare of triumph.

"Be you goin' to get married next month after what you said this mornin'?" her sister asked, half joyfully, half anxiously.

"Yes, I be," was all Eva replied, and Fanny stared at her; she was so purely normal in her inconsistency as to seem almost the other thing.

The preparations for the wedding went on, but Eva never seemed as happy as she had done before the closing of Lloyd's. Jim Tenny could get no more work, and neither could Andrew.

Fanny lamented that the shop had closed at that time of year, for she had planned a Christmas tree of unprecedented splendor for Ellen, but Mrs. Zelotes was to be depended upon as usual, and Andrew told his wife to make no difference. "That little thing ain't goin' to be cheated nohow," he said one night after Ellen had gone to bed and his visiting companions of the cutting-room had happened in.

"I know my children won't get much," Joseph Atkins said, coughing as he spoke; "they wouldn't if Lloyd's hadn't shut down. I never see the time when I could afford to make any account of Christmas, much as ever I could manage a turkey Thanksgiving day."

"The poor that the Lord died for can't afford to keep his birthday; it is the rich that he's going to cast into outer darkness, that keep it for their own ends, and it's a blasphemy and a mockery," proclaimed Nahum Beals. He was very excited that night, and would often spring to his feet and stride across the room. There was another man there that night, a cousin of Joseph Atkins, John Sargent by name. He had recently moved to Rowe, since he had obtained work at McGuire's, "had accepted a position in the finishing-room of Mr. H. S. McGuire's factory in the city of Rowe," as the item in the local paper put it. He was a young man, younger than his cousin, but he looked older. He had a handsome face, under the most complete control as to its muscles. When he laughed he gave the impression of the fixedness of merriment of a mask.

He looked keenly at Nahum Beals with that immovable laugh on his face, and spoke with perfectly good-natured sarcasm. "All very well for the string-pieces of the bridge from oppression to freedom," he said, "but you need some common-sense for the ties, or you'll slump."

"What do you mean?"

"We ain't in the Old Testament, but the nineteenth century, and those old prophets, if they were alive today, would have to step down out of their flaming chariots and hang their mantles on the bushes, and instead of standing on mountaintops and tellin' their enemies what rats they were, and how they would get what they deserved later on, they would have to tell their enemies what they wanted them to do to better matters, and make them do it."

"Instead of standing by your own strike in Greenboro, you quit and come here to work in McGuire's the minute you got a chance," said Nahum Beals, sullenly, and Sargent responded, with his unrelaxing laugh, "I left enough strikers for the situation in Greenboro; don't you worry about me."

"I think he done quite right to quit the strike if he got a chance to work," Joseph Atkins interposed. "Folks have got to look out for themselves, labor reform or no labor reform."

"That's the corner-stone of labor reform, seems to me," said Andrew.

"Seems to me sometimes you talk like a damned scab," cried Nahum Beals, fiercely, red spots flickering in his thin cheeks. Andrew looked at him, and spoke with slow wrath. "Look here, Nahum Beals," he said, "you're in my house, but I ain't goin' to stand no such talk as that, I can tell you."

John Sargent laid a pacifically detaining hand on Nahum Beals's arm as he strode past him. "Oh, Lord, stop rampagin' up and down like a wildcat," he said. "What good do you think you're doin' tearin' and shoutin' and insultin' people? He ain't talkin' like a scab, he's only talkin' a tie to your string-piece."

"That's so," said Joseph Atkins. Sargent boarded with him, and the board money was a godsend to him, now he was out of work. John Sargent had fixed his own price, and it was an unheard-of one for such simple fare as he had. His weekly dollars kept the whole poor family in food. But John Sargent was a bachelor, and earning remarkably good wages, and Joseph Atkins's ailing wife, whom illness and privation had made unnaturally grasping and ungrateful, told her cronies that it wasn't as if he couldn't afford it.

Upstairs little Ellen lay in her bed, her doll in her arms, listening to the low rumble of masculine voices in the room below. Her mother had gone out, and there were only the men there. They were smoking, and the odor of their pipes floated up into Ellen's chamber through the door-cracks. She thought how her grandmother Brewster would sniff when she came in next day. She could hear her saying, "Well, for my part, if those men couldn't smoke their old pipes somewhere else besides in my sittin' room, I wouldn't have 'em in the house." But that reflection did not trouble Ellen very long, and she had never been disturbed herself by the odor of the pipes. She thought of them insensibly as the usual atmosphere when men were gathered together in any place except the church. She knew that they were talking about that old trouble, and Nahum Beals's voice of high wrath made her shrink; but, after all, she was removed from it all that night into a little prospective paradise of her own, which, as is the case in childhood, seemed to overgild her own future and all the troubles of the world. Christmas was only a week distant, she was to have a tree, and the very next evening her mother had promised to take her down-town and show her the beautiful, lighted Christmas shops. She wondered, listening to that rumble of discontent below, why grown-up men and women ever fretted when they were at liberty to go down-town every evening when they chose and look at the lighted shops, for she could still picture pure delight for others without envy or bitterness.

The next day the child was radiant; she danced rather than walked; she could not speak without a smile; she could eat nothing, for her happiness was so purely spiritual that desires of the flesh were in abeyance. Her heart beat fast; the constantly recurring memory of what was about to happen fairly overwhelmed her as with waves of delight.

"If you don't eat your supper you can't go, and that's all there is about it," her mother told her when they were seated at the table, and Ellen sat dreaming before her toast and peach preserve.

"You must eat your supper, Ellen," Andrew said, anxiously. Andrew had on his other coat, and he had shaved, and was going too, as was Mrs. Zelotes Brewster.

"She ain't eat a thing all day, she's so excited about goin'," Fanny said. "Now, Ellen, you must eat your supper, or you can't go — you'll be sick."

And Ellen ate her supper, though exceeding joy as well as exceeding woe can make food lose its savor, and toast and preserves were as ashes on her tongue when the very fragrance of coming happiness was in her soul.

When, finally, in hand of her mother, while Andrew walked behind with her grandmother, she went towards the lights of the town, she had a feeling as of wings on her feet. However, she walked soberly enough with wide eyes of amazement and delight at everything — the long, silver track of the snowy road under the light of the full moon, the slants of the house roofs sparkling with crusts of crystals, the lighted windows set with house plants, for the dwellers in the outskirts of Rowe loved house plants, and their front windows bloomed with the emulative splendor of geraniums from fall to spring. She saw behind them glimpses of lives and some doings as real as her own, but mysterious under the locks of other personalities, and therefore as full of possibilities of preciousness as the sheet of morning dew over a neighbor's yard; she had often believed she saw diamonds sparkle in that, though never in her own. She had proved it otherwise too often. So Ellen, seeing through a window a little girl of her own age in a red frock, straightway believed it to be satin of the richest quality, and, seeing through another window a tea-table spread, had no doubt that the tin teapot was silver. A girl with a crown of yellow braids pulled down a curtain, and she thought her as beautiful as an angel; but of all this she said nothing at all, only walked soberly on, holding fast to her mother's hand.

When they were halfway to the shops, a door of a white house close to the road flew open and shut again with a bang, there was a scurry and grating slide on the front walk, then the gate was thrown back, and a boy dashed through with a wild whoop, just escaping contact with Mrs. Zelotes Brewster. "You'd better be careful," said she, sharply. "It ain't the thing for boys to come tearin' out of yards in the evenin' without seein' where they are goin'."

The boy cast an abashed glance at her. The street-lamp shone full on his face, which was round and reddened by the frosty winds, with an aimlessly grinning mouth of uncertain youth, and black eyes with a bold and cheerful outlook on the unknown. He was only ten, but he was large for his age. Ellen, when he looked from her grandmother back at her, thought him almost a man, and then she saw that he was the boy who had brought the chestnuts to her the night when she had returned from her runaway excursion. The boy recognized her at the same moment, and his mouth seemed to gape wider, and a moist red overspread his face down to his swathing woolen scarf. Then he gave another whoop significant of the extreme of nervous abashedness and the incipient defiance of his masculine estate, there was a flourish of heels, followed by a swift glimmering slide of steel, and he was off trailing his sled.

"That's that Joy boy that brought Ellen the chestnuts that time," Fanny said. "Do you remember him, Ellen?"

"Yes, ma'am," replied Ellen. The look of the boy in her face had bewildered and confused her, without her knowing the why of it. It was as if she had spelled a word in her reading-book whose meaning she could not grasp.

"I don't care who he is," said Mrs. Zelotes, "he ain't no business racin' out of gates that way, and his folks hadn't ought to let a boy no older than that out alone of nights."

They kept on, and the boy apparently left them far behind in his career of youthful exuberance, until they came to the factories. Andrew looked up at the windows of Lloyd's, dark except for a faint glimmer in a basement window from the lamp of the solitary watchman, and drew a heavy sigh.

"It ain't as bad for you as it is for some," his mother said, sharply, and then she jumped aside, catching her son's arm as the boy sprang out of a covering shadow under the wall of Lloyd's and dashed before them with another wild whoop and another glance of defiant bashfulness at Ellen.

"My land! it's that boy again," cried Mrs. Zelotes. "Here, you boy! — boy! What's your name?"

"His name is Granville Joy," Ellen replied, unexpectedly.

"Why, how did you know, child?" her grandmother asked. "Seems to me he's got a highfalutin' name enough. Here you, Granville — if that's your name — don't you know any better than to —" But the boy was gone, his sled creaking on the hard snow at his heels, and a faint whoop sounded from the distance.

"I guess if I had the bringin' up of that boy there wouldn't be such doin's," said Mrs. Zelotes, severely. "His mother's a pretty woman, but I don't believe she's got much force. She wouldn't have given him such a name if she had."

"She named him after the town she came from," said Fanny. "She told me once. She's a real smart woman, and she makes that boy stand around."

"She must; it looks as if he was standin' round pretty lively jest now," said Mrs. Zelotes. "Namin' of a boy after a town! They'd better wait and name a town after the boy if he amounts to anything."

"His mother told me he was goin' into the first grammar-school next year," said Fanny.

"I pity the teacher," said Mrs. Zelotes, and then she recoiled, for the boy made another dart from behind a lamp-post, crossed their path, and was off again.

"My land!" gasped Mrs. Zelotes, "you speak to him, Andrew." But Andrew laughed. "Might as well speak to a whirlwind," said he. "He ain't doin' any harm, mother; it's only his boyish antics. For Heaven's sake, let him enjoy himself while he can, it won't be long before the

grind-mill in there will get hold of him, and then he'll be sober enough
to suit anybody," and Andrew pointed at Lloyd's as he spoke.

"Boys can be boys," said Mrs. Zelotes, severely, "and they can have a
good time, but they can behave themselves."

None of them looking after that flying and whooping figure ahead
had the slightest idea of the true situation. They did not know that the
boy was confused by the fires, nonetheless ardent that they were so
innocent, of a first love for Ellen; that, ever since he had seen her little,
fair face on her aunt's shoulder the day when she was found, it had been
even closer to his heart than his sled and his jackstones and his ball,
and his hope of pudding for dinner. They did not know that he had
toiled at the wood-pile of a Saturday, and run errands after school, to
earn money to buy Christmas presents for his mother and Ellen; that
he had at that very minute in his purse in the bottom of his pocket the
sum of eighty-nine cents, mostly in coppers, since his wage was generally
payable in that coin, and his pocket sagged arduously therefrom. They
did not know that he was even then bound upon an errand to the grocery
store for a bag of flour to be brought home on his sled, and would
thereby swell his exchequer by another cent. They did not know what
dawning chords of love, and knowledge of love, that wild whoop
expressed; and the boy dodged and darted and hid, and appeared before
them all the way to the busy main street of Rowe; and, after they had
entered the great store where the finest Christmas display was held, he
stood before the window staring at Ellen vanishing in a brilliant vista,
and whooped now and then, regardless of public opinion.

Ellen, when once she was inside the store, forgot everything else. She
clung more tightly to her mother's hand, as one will cling to any wonted
stay of love in the midst of strangeness, even of joy, and she saw
everything with eyes which photographed it upon her very soul. At first
she had an impression of a dazzling incoherence of splendor, of a blare
as of thousands of musical instruments all sounding different notes of
delight, of a weaving pattern of colors, too intricate to master, of a
mingled odor of paint and varnish, and pine and hemlock boughs, and
then she spelled out the letters of the details. She looked at those
counters set with the miniature paraphernalia of household life which
give the first sweet taste of domesticity and housekeeping joys to a little
girl.

There were the sets of dolls' furniture, and the dolls, dishes, and there
was a counter with dolls' cooking-stoves and ranges bristling with the
most delightful realism of pots and pans, at which she gazed so fixedly
and breathlessly that she looked almost stupid. Her elders watched half
in delight, half with pain, that they could not purchase everything at

which she looked. Mrs. Zelotes bought some things surreptitiously, hiding the parcels under her shawl. Andrew, whispering to a salesman, asked the price of a great cooking-stove at which Ellen looked long. When he heard the amount he sighed. Fanny touched his arm comfortingly. "There would be no sense in your buying that, if you had all the money in creation," she said, in a hushed voice. "There's a twenty-five-cent one that's good enough. I'm going to buy that for her tomorrow. She'll never know the difference." But Andrew Brewster, nevertheless, went through the great, dazzling shop with his heart full of bitterness. It seemed to him monstrous and incredible that he had a child as beautiful and altogether wonderful as that, and could not buy the whole stock for her if she wanted it. He had never in his whole life wanted anything for himself that he could not have, enough to give him pain, but he wanted for his child with a longing that was a passion. Her little desires seemed to him the most important and sacred needs in the whole world. He watched her with pity and admiration, and shame at his own impotence of love to give her all.

But Ellen knew nothing of it. She was radiant. She never thought of wanting all those treasures further than she already had them. She gazed at the wonders in that department where the toy animals were kept, and which resembled a miniature menagerie, the silence broken by the mooing of cows, the braying of donkeys, the whistle of canaries, and the roars of mock-lions when their powers were invoked by the attendants, and her ears drank in that discordant Bable of tiny mimicry like music. There was no spirit of criticism in her. She was utterly pleased with everything.

When her grandmother held up a toy-horse and said the fore-legs were too long, Ellen wondered what she meant. To her mind it was more like a horse than any real one she had ever seen.

As she gazed at the decorations, the wreaths, the gauze, the tinsel, and paper angels, suspended by invisible wires over the counters, and all glittering and shining and twinkling with light, a strong whiff of evergreen fragrance came to her, and the aroma of fir-balsam, and it was to her the very breath of all the mysterious joy and hitherto untasted festivity of this earth into which she had come. She felt deep in her childish soul the sense of a promise of happiness in the future, of which this was a foretaste. When she went into the department where the dolls dwelt, she fairly turned pale. They swung, and sat, and lay, and stood, as in angelic ranks, all smiling between shining fluffs of hair. It was a chorus of smiles, and made the child's heart fairly leap. She felt as if all the dolls were smiling at her. She clung fast to her mother's hand, and hid her face against her skirt.

"Why, what is the matter, Ellen?" Fanny asked. Ellen looked up, and smiled timidly and confusedly, then at the dazzle of waxen faces and golden locks above skirts of delicate pink and blue and white, like flower petals.

"You never saw so many dolls together before, did you, Ellen?" said Andrew; then he added, wistfully, "There ain't one of 'em any bigger and prettier than your own doll, be they, Ellen?" And that, although he had never recovered from his uneasiness about that mysterious doll.

Ellen had not seen Cynthia Lennox since that morning several weeks ago when she had run away from her, except one glimpse when she was sleigh-riding. Now all at once, when they had stopped to look at some wonderful doll-houses, she saw her face to face. Ellen had been gazing with rapture at a great doll-house completely furnished, and Andrew had made one of his miserable side inquiries as to its price, and Fanny had said, quite loud, "Lord, Andrew, you might just as well ask the price of the store! You know such a thing as that is out of the question for any child unless her father is rich as Norman Lloyd," and Ellen, who had not noticed what they were saying, looked up, when a faint breath of violets smote her sense with a quick memory, and there was the strange lady who had taken her into her house and kept her and given her the doll, the strange lady whom the gentleman said might be punished for keeping her if people were to know.

Cynthia Lennox went pale when, without knowing what was going to happen, she looked down and saw suddenly the child's innocent face looking into hers. She stood wavering in her trailing, fur-lined, and softly whispering draperies, so marked and set aside by her grace and elegance and countenance of superiority and proud calm that people turned to look after her more than after many a young beauty, and did not, for a second, know what to say or do. She had no mind to shrink from a recognition of the child; she had no fear of the result, but there was a distinct shrinking at a scene with that flashing-eyed and heavy-browed mother of the child in such a place as that. She would undoubt-edly speak very loud. She expected the volley of recrimination in a high treble which would follow the announcement in that sweet little flute which she remembered so well.

"Mamma, that is the lady who kept me, and would not let me go home."

But Ellen, after a second's innocent and startled regard, turned away with no more recognition than if she had been a stranger. She turned her little back to her, and looked at the doll-house. A great flush flamed over Cynthia Lennox's face, and a qualm of mortal shame. She took an impetuous glide forward, and was just about to speak and tell the truth, whatever the consequences, and not be outdone in magnanimity by that child, when a young girl with a sickly but impudent and pretty face jostled her rudely. The utter pertness of her ignorant youth knew no respect for even the rich Miss Cynthia Lennox. "Here's your parcel, lady," she said, in her rough young voice, its shrillness modified by hoarseness from too much shouting for cash boys during this busy season, and she thrust, with her absent eyes upon a gentleman coming towards her, a parcel into Cynthia's hands. Somehow the touch of that parcel seemed to bring Cynthia to her senses. It was a Kodak which she had been purchasing for the little boy who had lived with her, and whom it had almost broken her heart to lose. She remembered what her friend Lyman Risley had said, that it might make trouble for others besides herself. She took her parcel with that involuntary meekness which the proudest learn before the matchless audacity of youthful ignorance when it fairly asserts itself, and passed out of the store to her waiting carriage. Ellen saw her.

"That was Cynthia Lennox, wasn't it?" Fanny said, with something like awe. "Wasn't that an elegant cloak she had on? I guess it was Russian sable."

"I don't care if it was, it ain't a mite handsomer than my cape lined with squirrel," said Mrs. Zelotes.

Ellen looked intently at a game on the counter. It was ten o'clock when Ellen went home. She had been into all the principal stores which were decorated for Christmas. Her brain resembled a kaleidoscope as she hurried along at her mother's hand. Every thought seemed to whirl the disk, and new and more dazzling combinations appeared, but the principle which underlay the whole was that of the mystery of festivity and joy upon the face of the earth, of which this Christmas wealth was the key.

The Brewsters had scarcely reached the factory neighborhood when there was a swift bound ahead of them and the familiar whoop.

"There's that boy again," said Mrs. Zelotes.

She made various remonstrances, and even Andrew, when the boy had passed his own home in his persistent dogging of them, called out to him, as did Fanny, but he was too far ahead to hear. The boy followed them quite to their gate, proceeding with wild spurts and dashes from shadow to shadow, and at last reappeared from behind one of the evergreen trees in the west yard, springing out of its long shadow with strange effect. He darted close to Ellen as she passed in the gate, crammed something into her hand, and was gone. Andrew could not catch him, though he ran after him. "He ran like a rabbit," he said, coming breathlessly into the house, where they were looking at the treasure the boy had thrust upon Ellen. It was a marvel of a patent top, which the boy had long desired to own. He had spent all his money on it, and his mother was cheated of her Christmas present, but he had given, and Ellen had received, her first token of love.

Chapter XII

*T*he next spring Ellen went to school. When a child who has reigned in undisputed sovereignty at home is thrust among other children at school, one of two things happens: either she is scorned and rebelled against, and her little crown of superiority rolled in the dust of the common playground, or she extends the territories of her empire. Ellen extended hers, though involuntarily, for there was no conscious thirst for power in her.

On her first morning at school, she seated herself at her desk and looked forth from the golden cloud of her curls, her eyes full of innocent contemplation, her mouth corners gravely drooping. She knew one little girl who sat not far from her. The little girl's name was Floretta Vining. Floretta was built on the scale of a fairy, with tiny, fine, waxen features, a little tossing mane of flaxen hair, eyes a most lovely and perfect blue, with no more depth in them than in the blue of china, and an expression of the sweetest and most innocent inanity and irresponsibility. Nobody ever expected anything of this little Floretta Vining. She was always a negative success. She smiled around from the foot of her curving class, and never had her lessons, but she never disobeyed the rules, except that of punctuality.

Floretta was late at school. She came daintily up the aisle, two cheap bangles on one wrist slipping over a slim hand, and tinkling. Floretta's mother had a taste for the cheaply decorative. There was an abundance of coarse lace on Floretta's frock, and she wore a superfluous sash which was not too fresh. Floretta toed out excessively, her slender little feet pointing out sharply, almost at right angles with each other, and Ellen admired her for that. She watched her coming, planting each foot as carefully and precisely as a bird, her lace frills flouncing up and down, her bangles jingling, and thought how very pretty she was.

Ellen felt herself very loving towards the teacher and Floretta Vining. Floretta leaned forward as soon as she was seated and gazed at her with astonishment, and that deepening of amiability and general sweetness which one can imagine in the face of a doll after persistent scrutiny. Ellen smiled decorously, for she was not sure how much smiling was permissible in school. When she smiled guardedly at Floretta, she was conscious of another face regarding her, twisted slightly over a shabby little shoulder covered with an ignominious blue stuff, spotted and faded. This little girl's wisp of brown braid was tied with a shoestring, and she looked poorer than any other child in the school, but she had an honest light in her eyes, and Ellen considered her to be rather more beautiful than Floretta.

She was Maria Atkins, Joseph Atkins's second child. Ellen sat with her book before her, and the strange, new atmosphere of the school-room stole over her senses. It was not altogether pleasant, although it was considered that the ventilation was after the most approved modern system. She perceived a strong odor of peppermints, and Floretta Vining was waving ostentatiously a coarse little pocket-handkerchief scented with New-mown Hay. There was also a strong effusion of stale dinners and storm-beaten woolen garments, but there was, after all, that savor of festivity which Ellen was apt to discover in the new. She looked over her book with utter content. In a line with her, on the boys' side, there appeared a covertly peeping face under a thatch of light hair, and Ellen, influenced insensibly by the boy's shyly worshipful eyes, looked and saw Granville Joy. She remembered the Christmas top, and blushed very pink without knowing why, and flirted all her curls towards the boys' side.

Ellen, from having so little acquaintance with boys, had had no very well-defined sentiments towards them, but now, on being set apart with her feminine element, and separated so definitely by the middle aisle of the school-room, she began to experience sensations both of shyness and exclusiveness. She did not think the boys, in their coarse clothes, with their cropped heads, half as pretty as the girls.

The teacher coming down the aisle laid a caressing hand on Ellen's curls, and the child looked up at her with that confidence which is exquisite flattery.

After she had passed, Ellen heard a subtle whisper somewhere at her back; it was half audible, but its meaning was entirely plain. It signified utmost scorn and satirical contempt. It was fine-pointed and far-reaching. A number looked around. It was as expressive as a whole sentence, and, being as concentrated, was fairly explosive with meaning.

"H'm, ain't you pretty? Ain't you dreadful pretty, little dolly-pinky-rosy. H'm, teacher's partial. Ain't you pretty? Ain't you stuck up? H'm."

Ellen, not being used to the school vernacular, did not fairly apprehend all this, and least of all that it was directed towards herself. She cast a startled look around, then turned to her book. She leaned back in her seat and held her book before her face with both hands, and began to read, spelling out the words noiselessly. All at once, she felt a fine prick on her head, and threw back one hand and turned quickly. The little girl behind was engrossed in study, and all Ellen could see was the parting in her thick black hair, for her head was supported by her two hands, her elbows were resting on her desk, and she was whispering the boundaries of the State of Massachusetts.

Ellen turned back to her reading-book, and recommenced studying with the painful faithfulness of the new student; then came again that small, fine, exasperating prick, and she thrust her face around quickly to see that same faithfully intent little girl.

Ellen rubbed her head doubtfully, and tried to fix her attention again upon her book, but presently it came again; a prick so small and fine that it strained consciousness; an infinitesimal point of torture, and this time Ellen, turning with a swift flirt of her head, caught the culprit. It was that faithful little girl, who held a black-headed belt-pin in her hand; she had been carefully separating one hair at a time from Ellen's golden curls, and tweaking it out.

Ellen looked at her with a singular expression compounded of bewilderment, of injury, of resentment, of alarm, and of a readiness to accept it all as a somewhat peculiar advance towards good-fellowship and a merry understanding. But the expression on that dark, somewhat grimy little face, looking out at her from a jungle of coarse, black locks, was fairly impish, almost malicious. There was not merriment in it so much as jibing; instead of that soft regard and worshipful admiration which Ellen was accustomed to find in new eyes, there was resentful envy.

Then Ellen shrank, and bristled with defiance at the same time, for she had the spirit of both the Brewsters and the Louds in her, in spite of her delicacy of organization. She was a fine instrument, capable of chords of tragedy as well as angelic strains. She saw that the little girl who was treating her so was dressed very poorly, that her dress was not only shabby, but actually dirty; that she, as well as the other girl whom she noticed, had her braid tied with an old shoestring, and that a curious smell of leather pervaded her. Ellen continued to regard the little girl, then suddenly she felt a hand on her shoulder, and the teacher, Miss Rebecca Mitchell, was looking down at her. "What is the trouble?" asked Miss Mitchell. That look of half-wondering admiration to which Ellen was accustomed was in the teacher's eyes, and Ellen again thought her beautiful.

One of the first, though a scarcely acknowledged principle of beauty, is that of reflection of the fairness of the observer. Ellen being as innocently self-seeking for love and admiration as any young thing for its natural sustenance, was quick to recognize it, though she did not understand that what she saw was herself in the teacher's eyes, and not the teacher. She gazed up in that roseate face with the wide mouth set in an inverted bow of smile, curtained, as it were, with smoothly crinkled auburn hair clearly outlined against the cheeks, at the palpitating curve of shiny black-silk bosom, adorned with a festoon of heavy gold watch-chain, and thought that here was love, and beauty, and richness, and elegance, and great wisdom, calling for reverence but no fear. She answered not one word to the teacher's question, but continued to gaze at her with that look of wide-eyed and contemplative regard.

"What is the trouble, Ellen?" repeated Miss Mitchell. "Why were you looking around so?" Ellen said nothing. The little girl behind had her head bent over her book so low that the sulky curves of her mouth did not show. The teacher turned to her — "Abby Atkins," said she, "what were you doing?"

Abby Atkins did not raise her studious head. She did not seem to hear.

"Abby Atkins," said the teacher, sharply, "answer me. What were you doing?" Then the little girl answered, with a sulky note, half growl, half whimper, like some helpless but indomitable little trapped animal, "Nothin'."

"Ellen," said the teacher, and her voice changed indescribably. "What was she doing?" Ellen did not answer. She looked up in the teacher's face, then cast down her eyes and sat there, her little hands folded in tightly clinched fists in her lap, her mouth a pink line of resistance. "Ellen," repeated the teacher, and she tried to make her voice sharp, but in spite of herself it was caressing. Her heart had gone out to the child the moment she had seen her enter the school-room. She was as helpless before her as before a lover. She was wild to catch her up and caress her instead of pestering her with questions. "Ellen, you must answer me," she said, but Ellen sat still.

Half the scholars were on their feet, reaching and craning their necks. The teacher turned on them, and there was no lack of sharpness in her tone. "Sit down this moment, every one of you," she called. "Abby

Atkins, if there is anymore disturbance, I shall know what is at the root of the matter. If I see you turning around again, Ellen, I shall insist upon knowing why." Then the teacher placed a caressing hand upon Ellen's yellow head, and passed down the aisle to her desk.

Ellen had no more trouble during the session. Abby Atkins was commendably quiet and studious, and when called out to recitation made the best one in her class. She was really brilliant in a defiant, reluctant fashion. However, though she did not again disturb Ellen's curls, she glowered at her with furtive but unrelaxed hostility over her book. Especially a blue ribbon which confined Ellen's curls in a beautiful bow fired her eyes of animosity. She looked hard at it, then she pulled her black braid over her shoulder and felt of the hard shoestring knot, and frowned with an ugly frown of envy and bitterest injury, and asked herself the world-wide and world-old question as to the why of inequality, and, though it was based on such trivialities as blue ribbons and shoestrings, it was nonetheless vital to her mind. She would have loved, have gloried, to pull off that blue ribbon, put it on her own black braid, and tie up those yellow curls with her own shoestring with a vicious yank of security. But all the time it was not so much because she wanted the ribbon as because she did not wish to be slighted in the distribution of things. Abby Atkins cared no more for personal ornament than a wildcat, but she wanted her just allotment of the booty of the world. So at recess she watched her chance. Ellen was surrounded by an admiring circle of big girls, gushing with affection. "Oh, you dear little thing," they said. "Only look at her beautiful curls. Give me a kiss, won't you, darling?" Little reverent fingers twined Ellen's golden curls, red apples were thrust forward for her to take bites, sticky morsels of candy were forced secretly into her hands. Abby Atkins stood aloof. "You mean little thing," one of the big girls said suddenly, catching hold of her thin shoulder and shaking her — "you mean little thing, I saw you."

"So did I," said another big girl, "and I was a good mind to tell on you."

"Yes, you had better look out, and not plague that dear little thing," said the other.

"You ought to be ashamed of yourself," chimed in still another big girl. "Only look how pretty she is, the little darling — the idea of your tormenting her. You deserve a good, hard whipping, Abby Atkins."

This big girl was herself a beauty and wore a fine and precise blue-ribbon bow, and Abby Atkins looked at her with a scowl of hatred.

"She's an ugly little thing," said the big girls among themselves as they went edging gently and imperceptibly away towards a knot of big boys, and then Abby Atkins's chance had come. She advanced with a spring upon Ellen Brewster, and she pulled that blue ribbon off her head so cruelly and fiercely that she pulled out some of the golden hairs with it and threw it on the ground, and stamped on it. Then she seized Ellen by the shoulders and proceeded to shake her for wearing a blue ribbon when she herself wore a shoestring, but she reckoned without Ellen. One would as soon have expected to meet fight in a little child angel as in this Ellen Brewster, but she did not come of her ancestors for nothing.

Although she was so daintily built that she looked smaller, she was in reality larger than the other girl, and as she straightened herself in her wrath she seemed a head taller and proportionately broad. She tossed her yellow head, and her face took on an expression of noble courage and indignation, but she never said a word. She simply took Abby Atkins by the arms and lifted her off her feet and seated her on the ground. Then she picked up her blue ribbon, and walked off, and Abby scrambled to her feet and looked after her with a vanquished but untamed air. Nobody had seen what happened except Abby's younger sister Maria and Granville Joy. Granville pressed stealthily close to Ellen as she marched away and whispered, his face blazing, his voice full of confidence and congratulation, "Say, if she'd been a boy, I'd licked her for you, and you wouldn't hev had to tech her yourself;" and Maria walked up and eyes her prostrate but defiantly glaring sister — "I ain't sorry one mite, Abby Atkins," she declared — "so there."

"You go 'long," returned Abby, struggling to her feet, and shaking her small skirts energetically.

"Your dress is jest as wet as if you'd set down in a puddle, and you'll catch it when you get home," Maria said, pitilessly.

"I ain't afraid."

"What made you touch her, anyhow; she hadn't done nothin'?"

"If you want to wear shoestrings when other folks wear ribbons, you can," said Abby Atkins. She walked away, switching, with unabated dignity in the midst of defeat, the draggled tail of her poor little dress. She had gone down like a cat; she was not in the least hurt except in her sense of justice; that was jarred to a still greater lack of equilibrium. She felt as if she had been floored by Providence in conjunction with a blue bow, and her very soul rose in futile rebellion. But, curiously enough, her personal ire against Ellen vanished.

At the afternoon recess she gave Ellen the sound half of an old red Baldwin apple which she had brought for luncheon, and watched her bite into it, which Ellen did readily, for she was not a child to cherish enmity, with an odd triumph. "The other half ain't fit to eat, it's all wormy," said Abby Atkins, flinging it away as she spoke.

"Then you ought to have kept this," Ellen cried out, holding towards her the half, minus one little bite. But Abby Atkins shook her head forcibly. "That was why I gave it to you," said she. "Say, didn't you never have to tie up your hair with a shoestring?" Ellen shook her head, looking at her wonderingly. Then with a sudden impulse she tore off the blue ribbon from her curls. "Say, you take it," she said, "my mother won't care. I'd just as lief wear the shoestring, honest."

"I don't want your blue ribbon," Abby returned, stoutly; "a shoestring is a good deal better to tie the hair with. I don't want your blue ribbon; I don't want no blue ribbon unless it's mine."

"It would be yours if I give it to you," Ellen declared, with blue eyes of astonishment and consternation upon this very strange little girl.

"No, it wouldn't," maintained Abby Atkins.

But it ended in the two girls, with that wonderful and inexplicable adjustment of childhood into one groove after harsh grating on different levels, walking off together with arms around each other's waist, and after school began Ellen often felt a soft, catlike pat on her head, and turned round with a loving glance at Abby Atkins.

Ellen talked more about Abby Atkins than any other of the children when she got home, and while her mother looked at it all easily, her grandmother was doubtful. "There's others that I should rather have Ellen thick with," said she. "I ain't nothin' against the Atkinses, but they can't have been as well brought up as some, they have had so little to do with, and their mother's been ailin' so long."

"Ellen may as well begin as she can hold out, and be intimate with them that will be intimate with her," Eva said, rather bitterly. Eva was married by this time, and living with Jim and his mother. She wore in those days an expression of bitterly defiant triumph and happiness, as of one who has wrested his sweet from fate under the ban of the law, and is determined to get the flavor of it though the skies fall. "I suppose I did wrong marrying Jim," she often told her sister, "but I can't help it."

"Maybe Jim will get work before long," her sister would say, consolingly.

"I have about given up," Eva would reply. "I guess Jim will have to roost on a flour-barrel at Munsey's store the rest of his days; but as long as he belongs to me, it don't make so much difference."

Eva had taken up an agency for a cosmetic which was manufactured by a woman in Rowe. She had one window of the north parlor in the Tenny cottage, which had been given up to her when she married Jim, filled with the little pink boxes containing the "Fairy Cream," and a great sign, but the trade languished. Both Eva and Jim had tried in vain to obtain employment in factories in other towns.

Lloyd's had not reopened, although it was April, and Andrew was drawing on his savings. Fanny had surreptitiously answered an advertisement purporting to give instructions to women as to the earning of large sums of money at home, and was engaged with a stock of glass and paints which she hurriedly swept out of sight when anyone's shadow passed the window, and later she found herself to be the victim of a small swindling conspiracy, and lost the dollar which she had invested. But Ellen knew nothing of all this. She lacked none of her accustomed necessaries nor luxuries, and with her school a new life full of keen, new savors or relish began for her. There were also new affections in it.

Ellen was as yet too young, and too confident in love, to have new affections plunge her into anything but a delightful sort of anti-blossom tumult. There was no suspense, no doubt, no jealousy, only utter acquiescence of single-heartedness, admiration, and trust. She thought Abby Atkins and Floretta Vining lovely and dependable; she parted from them at night without a pang, and looked forward blissfully to the meeting next morning. She also had sentiments equally peaceful and pronounced, though instinctively more secret, towards Granville Joy. She used to glance over towards the boys' side and meet his side-long eyes without so much a quickening of her pulses as a quickening of her imagination.

"I know who your beau is," Floretta Vining, who was in advance of her years, said to her once, and Ellen looked at her with half-stupid wonder.

"His first name begins with a G and his last with a J," Floretta tittered, and Ellen continued to look at her with the faintest suspicion of a blush, because she had a feminine instinct that a blush was in order, not because she knew of any reason for it.

"He is," said Floretta, with another exceedingly foolish giggle. "My, you are as red as a beet."

"I ain't old enough to have a beau," Ellen said, her soft cheeks becoming redder, and her baby face all in a tremor.

"Yes, you be," Floretta said, with authority, "because you are so pretty, and have got such pretty curls. Ben Simonds said the other day you were the prettiest girl in school."

"Then do you think he is my beau, too?" asked Ellen, innocently. But Floretta frowned, and tittered, and hesitated.

"He said except one," she faltered out, finally.

"Well, who was that?" asked Ellen.

"How do I know?" pouted Floretta. "Mebbe it was me, though I don't think I'm so very pretty."

"Then Ben Simonds is your beau," said Ellen, reflectively.

"Yes, I guess he is," admitted Floretta.

That night, amid much wonder and tender ridicule, Ellen told her mother and Aunt Eva, and her father, that Ben Simonds was Floretta's beau, and Granville Joy was hers. But Andrew laughed doubtfully.

"I don't want that little thing to get such ideas into her head yet a while," he told Fanny afterwards, but she only laughed at him, seeing nothing but the childish play of the thing; but he, being a man, saw deeper.

However, Ellen's fondest new love was not for any of her little mates, but for her school-teacher. To her the child's heart went out in worship. All through the spring she offered her violets — violets gathered laboriously after school in the meadow back of her grandmother's house. She used to skip from hillock to hillock of marsh grass with wary steps, lest she might slip and wet her feet in the meadow ooze and incur her mother's displeasure, for Fanny, in spite of her worship of the child, could speak with no uncertain voice. She pulled up handfuls of the flowers, gleaming blue in the dark-green hollows. Later she carried roses from the choice bush in the yard, and, later, pears from her grandmother's tree. She used to watch for Miss Mitchell at her gate and run to meet her, and seize her hand and walk at her side, blushing with delight. Miss Mitchell lived not far from Ellen, in a tidy white house with a handsome smoke tree on one side of the front walk and a willow with upside-down branches on the other. Miss Mitchell had been born and brought up in this house, but she had been teaching school in a distant town ever since Ellen's day, so they had never been acquainted before she went to school. Miss Mitchell lived alone with her mother, who was an old friend of Mrs. Zelotes. Ellen privately thought her rather better-looking than her own grandmother, though her admiration was based upon wholly sentimental reasons. Old Mrs. Mitchell might have earned more money in a museum of freaks than her daughter in a district school. She was a mountain of rotundity, a conjunction of palpitating spheres, but the soul that dwelt in this painfully ponderous body was as mellow with affection and kindliness as a ripe pear, and the voice that proceeded from her ever-smiling lips was a hoarse and dovelike coo of love. Ellen at first started a little aghast at this gigantic fleshliness, this general slough and slump of outline, this insistency of repellent curves, and then the old woman spoke and thrust out a great, soft hand, and the heart of the child overleaped her artistic sense and her reason, and she thought old Mrs. Mitchell beautiful. Mrs. Mitchell never failed to regale her with a superior sort of cookie, and often with a covert peppermint, and that although the Mitchells were not well off. The old place was mortgaged, and Miss Mitchell had hard work to pay the interest. Ellen had the vaguest ideas about the mortgage, and was half inclined to think it might be a disfiguring patch in the plastering of the sitting room, which hung down in an unsightly fashion with a disclosure of hairy edges, and threatened danger to the heads underneath.

Often of a Saturday afternoon Ellen went to visit Miss Mitchell and her mother, and really preferred them to friends of her own age. Miss Mitchell had a store of superannuated paper dolls which dated from her own childhood. Their quaint costumes, and old-fashioned coiffures, and simpers were of overwhelming interest to Ellen. Even at that early age she had a perception of the advantages of an atmosphere to art, and even to the affections. Without understanding it, she loved those obsolete paper-dolls and those women of former generations better because they gave her breathing-scope for her imagination. She could love Abby Atkins and Floretta Vining at one bite, as it were, and that was the end of it, but she could sit and ponder and dream over Miss Mitchell and her mother, and see whole vistas of them in receding mirrors of affection.

As for the teacher and her mother, they simply adored the child — as indeed everybody did. She continued at her first school for a year, which was one of the hardest financially ever experienced in Rowe. Norman Lloyd during all that time did not reopen his factory, and in the autumn two others shut down. The streets were full of the discontented ranks of impotent labor, and all the public buildings were props for the weary shoulders of the unemployed. On pleasant days the sunny sides of the vacant factories, especially, furnished settings for lines of scowling faces of misery.

This atmosphere affected Ellen more than anyone realized, since the personal bearing of it was kept from her. She did not know that her father was drawing upon his precious savings for daily needs, she did not know how her aunt Eva and her uncle Jim were getting into greater difficulties every day, but she was too sensitive not to be aware of disturbances which were not in direct contact with herself. She never forgot what she had overheard that night Lloyd's had shut down; it was always like a blot upon the face of her happy consciousness of life. She often overheard, as then, those loud, dissenting voices of her father and his friends in the sitting room, after she had gone to bed; and then, too, Abby Atkins, who was not spared any knowledge of hardship, told her a good deal. "It's awful the way them rich folks treat us," said Abby

Atkins. "They own the shops and everything, and take all the money, and let our folks do all the work. It's awful. But then," continued Abby Atkins, comfortingly, "your father has got money saved in the bank, and he owns his house, so you can get along if he don't have work. My father ain't got any, and he's got the old-fashioned consumption, and he coughs, and it takes money for his medicine. Then mother's sick a good deal too, and has to have medicine. We have to have more medicine than most anything else, and we hardly ever have any pie or cake, and it's all the fault of them rich folks." Abby Atkins wound up with a tragic climax and a fierce roll of her black eyes.

That evening Ellen went in to see her grandmother, and was presented with some cookies, which she did not eat.

"Why don't you eat them?" Mrs. Zelotes asked.

"Can I have them to do just what I want to with?" asked Ellen.

"What on earth do you want to do with a cookie except eat it?" Ellen blushed; she had a shamed-faced feeling before a contemplated generosity.

"What do you want to do with them except eat them?" her grandmother asked, severely.

"Abby Atkins don't have any cookies 'cause her father's out of work," said Ellen, abashedly.

"Did that Atkins girl ask you to bring her cookies?"

"No, ma'am."

"You can do jest what you are a mind to with 'em," Mrs. Zelotes said, abruptly.

Ellen never knew why her grandmother insisted upon her drinking a little glass of very nice and very spicy cordial before she went home, but the truth was, that Mrs. Zelotes thought the child so angelic in this disposition to give up the cookies which she loved to her little friend that she was straightway alarmed and thought her too good to live.

The next day she told Fanny, and said to her, with her old face stern with anxiety, that the child was lookin' real pindlin', and Ellen had to take bitters for a month afterwards because she gave the cookies to Abby Atkins.

Chapter XIII

*I*n all growth there is emulation and striving for precedence between the spiritual and the physical, and this very emulation may determine the rate of progression of the whole. Sometimes the one, sometimes the other, may be in advance, but all the time the tendency is towards the distant goal. Sometimes the two keep abreast, and then there is the greatest harmony in speed. In Ellen Brewster at twelve and fifteen the spiritual outstripped the physical, as is often the case. Her eyes grew intense and hollow with reflection under knitting brows, her thin shoulders stooped like those of a sage bent with study and contemplation. She was slender to emaciation; her clothes hung loosely over her form, which seemed as sexless as a lily-stem; indeed, her body seemed only made for the head, which was flowerlike and charming, but almost painful in its delicacy, and with such weight of innocent pondering upon the unknown conditions of things in which she found herself. At times, of course, there were ebullitions of youthful spirit, and the child was as inconsequent as a kitten. At those times she was neither child nor woman; she was an anomalous thing made up not so much of actualities as of instincts. She romped with her mates as unseen and uncomprehended of herself as any young animal, but the flame of her striving spirit made everything full of unread meaning.

Ellen was accounted a most remarkable scholar. She had left Miss Mitchell's school, and was in one of a higher grade. At fifteen she entered the high-school and had a master.

Andrew was growing old fast in those days, though not so old as to years. Though he was far from old, his hair was grey, his back bent. He moved with a weary shuffle. The men in the shop began to eye him furtively. "Andrew Brewster will get fired next," they said. "The boss ain't no use for men with the first snap gone." Indeed, Andrew was constantly given jobs of lower grades, which did not pay so well. Whenever the force was reduced on account of dullness in trade, Andrew was one of the first to be laid aside on waiting orders in the regular army of toil. On one of these occasions, in the spring after Ellen was fifteen, his first fit of recklessness seized him. One night, after loafing a week, he came home with fever spots in his cheeks and a curiously bright, strained look in his eyes. Fanny gazed sharply at him across the supper-table. Finally she laid down her knife and fork, rested her elbows on the table, and fixed her eyes commandingly upon him. "Andrew Brewster, what is the matter?" said she. Ellen turned her flowerlike face towards her father, who took a swallow of tea without saying a word, though he shuffled his feet uneasily. "Andrew, you answer me," repeated Fanny.

"There ain't anything the matter," answered Andrew, with a strange sullenness for him.

"There is, too. Now, Andrew Brewster, I ain't goin' to be put off. I know you're on the shelf on account of hard times, so it ain't that. It's something new. Now I want to know what it is."

"It ain't anything."

"Yes, it is. Andrew, you ought to tell me. You know I ain't afraid to bear anything that you have to bear, and Ellen is getting old enough now, so she can understand, and she can't always be spared. She'd better get a little knowledge of hardships while she has us to help her bear 'em."

"This ain't a hardship, and there ain't anything to spare, Ellen," said Andrew; and he laughed with a hilarity totally unlike him.

That was all Fanny could get out of him, but she was half reassured. She told Eva that she didn't believe but he had been buying some Christmas present that he knew was extravagant for Ellen, and was afraid to tell her because he knew she would scold. But Andrew had not been buying Christmas presents, but speculating in mining stocks. He had resisted the temptation long. Year in and year out he had heard the talk right and left in the shop, on the street, and at the store of an evening. "I'll give you a point," he had heard one say to another during a discussion as to prices and dividends. He had heard it all described as a short cross-cut over the fields of hard labor to wealth and comfort, and he had kept his face straight ahead in his narrow track of caution and hereditary instincts until then. "The savings bank is good enough for me," he used to say; "that's where my father kept his money. I don't know anything about your stocks. I'd rather have a little and have it safe." The men could not reason him out of his position, not even when Billy Monroe made fifteen hundred dollars on a Colorado mine which had cost him fifteen cents per share, and left the shop, and drove a fast horse in a Goddard buggy.

It was even reported that fifteen hundred was fifteen thousand, but Andrew was proof against this brilliant loadstar of success, though many of his mates followed it afar, just before the shares dropped below par.

Jim Tenny went with the rest. "Tell you what 'tis, Andrew, old man," he said, clapping Andrew on the shoulder as they were going out of the shop one night, "you'd better go in too."

"The savings-bank is good enough for me," said Andrew, with his gentle doggedness.

"You can buy a trotter," urged Jim.

"I never was much on trotters," replied Andrew.

"I ain't going to walk home many times more, you bet," Jim said to Eva when he got home, and then he bent back her tensely set face and kissed it. Eva was crocheting hoods for fifteen cents apiece for a neighboring woman who was a padrone on a small scale, having taken a large order from a dealer for which she realized twenty cents apiece, and employed all the women in the neighborhood to do the work.

"Why not?" said she.

"Oh," said Jim, gaily, "I've bought some of that 'Golden Hope' mining stock. Billy Monroe has just made fifteen thousand on it, and I'll make as much in a week or two."

"Oh, Jim, you ain't taken all the money out of the bank?"

"Don't you worry, old girl," replied Jim. "I guess you'll find I can take care of you yet."

But the stock went down, and Jim's little venture with it.

"Guess you were about right, old man," he said to Andrew.

Andrew was rather looked up to for his superior caution and sagacity. He was continually congratulated upon it. "Savings-banks are good enough for me," he kept repeating. But that was four years ago, and now his turn had come; the contagion of speculation had struck him at last. That was the way with Lloyd's failing employés.

Andrew kept his stock certificate in a little, tin, trunk-shaped box which had belonged to his father. It had a key and a tiny padlock, and he had always stored in it the deed of his house, his savings-bank book, and his insurance policy. He carried the key in his pocket. Fanny never opened the box, or had any curiosity about it, believing that she was acquainted with its contents; but now when, on coming unexpectedly into the bedroom — the box was always kept at the head of the bed — she heard a rattle of papers, and caught Andrew locking the box with a confused air, she began to suspect something. She began to look hard at the box, to take it up and shake it when her husband was away. Fanny was crocheting hoods as well as Eva. Ellen wished to learn, but her mother would not allow that. "You've got enough to do to study your lessons," she said. Andrew watched his wife crochet with ill-concealed impatience.

"I ain't goin' to have you do that long," he said — "workin' at that rate for no more money. That Mrs. William Pendergrass that lets out these hoods is as bad as any factory boss in the country."

"Well, she got the chance," said Fanny, "and they won't let out the work except that way; they can get it done so much cheaper."

"Well, you shan't have it, anyhow," said Andrew, smiling mysteriously.

"Why, you ain't goin' to work again, be you, Andrew?"

"You wait."

"Well, don't you talk the way poor Jim did. Eva wasn't going to crochet anymore hoods, and now Jim's out of work again. Eva told me yesterday that she didn't know where the money was comin' from. Jim's mother owns the place, and it ain't worth much, anyhow, and they can't take it from her in her lifetime, even if she was willing to let it go. Eva said she was goin' to try again for work herself in the shop. She thought maybe there might be some kind of a job she could get. Don't you talk like Jim did about his good-for-nothin' mining stock. I've been glad enough that you had sense enough to keep what little we had where 'twas safe."

"Ain't it most time for Ellen to be comin' home?" asked Andrew, to turn the conversation, as he felt somewhat guilty and uncomfortable, though his eyes were jubilant. He had very little doubt about the success of his venture. As it is with a man who yields to love for the first time in his life, it was with Andrew in his tardy subjection to the hazards of fortune. He was a much more devoted slave than those who had long wooed her. He had always taken nothing but the principal newspaper published in Rowe, but now he subscribed to a Boston paper, the one which had the fullest financial column, though Fanny exclaimed at his extravagance.

Along in midsummer, in the midst of Ellen's vacation, the mining stock dropped fast a point or more a day. Andrew's heart began to sink, though he was far from losing hope. He used to talk it over with the men who advised him to buy, and come home fortified.

All he had to do was to be patient; the fall meant nothing wrong with the mine, only the wrangle of speculators. "It's like a football, first on one side, and then on the other," said the man, "but the football's there all the same, and if it's that you want, you're all right."

One night when Nahum Beals and Atkins and John Sargent were in, Andrew repeated this wisdom, concealing the fact of its personal application. He was anxious to have some confirmation.

"I suppose it's about so," he said.

Then John Sargent spoke up. "No, it is not so," he said — "that is, not in many cases. There isn't any football — that's the trouble. There's nothing but the money; a lot of fools have paid for it when it never existed out of their imagination."

"About so," said Nahum Beals. Andrew and Atkins exchanged glances. Atkins was at once sympathizing and triumphant.

"Lots of those things appear to be doing well, and to be all right," said Andrew, uneasily. "The directors keep saying that they are in a prosperous condition, even if the stock drops." He almost betrayed himself.

John Sargent laughed that curious, inflexible laugh of his. "Lord, I know all about that," said he. "I had some once. First one thing and then another came up to hinder the working of the mine and the payments of dividends. First there wasn't any water, an unprecedented dry season in those parts, oldest inhabitants for evidence. Then there was too much water, no way to mine except they employed professional divers, everything under water. Then the transportation was to pay; then, when that was remedied, the ore didn't come out in shape to transport in the rough and had to be worked up on the premises, and new mills had to be built and new machinery put in, and a few little Irish dividends were collected for that. Then when they got the mills up and the machinery in, they struck another kind of ore that ought to be trans- ported; then there came a landslide and carried half the road into a cañon. So it went on, one thing and another. If ever that darned mine had got into working order, right kind of ore, water enough and not too much, roads and machinery all right, and everything swimming, the Day of Judgment would have come."

"Did you ever get anything out of it?" inquired Andrew.

"Anything out of it?" repeated the other. "Yes, I got enough worldly wisdom never to buy anymore mining stock, after I had paid assessments on it for two years and the whole thing went to pieces."

"It may come up yet," said Andrew.

"There's nothing to come up," said John Sargent. He had been away from Rowe a year, but had just returned, and was again boarding with Atkins, and all the family lived on his board money. Andrew and Nahum Beals were smoking pipes. Andrew gently, like a philosopher, who smokes that he may dream; Nahum with furious jets and frequent removals of his pipe for scowling speeches. John Sargent did not smoke at all. He had left off cigars first, then even his pipe. He gave the money which he saved thereby to Mrs. Atkins as a bonus on his board money.

The lamp burned dimly in the blue fog of tobacco smoke, and the windows where the curtains were not drawn were blanks of silvery

moonlight. Ellen sat on the doorstep outside and heard the talk. She
did not understand it, nor take much interest in it. Their minds were
fixed upon the way of living, and hers upon life itself. She could bring
her simplicity to bear upon the world-old question of riches and poverty
and labor, but this temporal adjunct of stocks and markets was as yet
beyond her. Her mother had gone to her aunt Eva's and she sat alone
out in the wide mystery of the summer night, watching the lovely shift
of radiance and shadows, as she might have watched the play of a
kaleidoscope, seeing the beauty of the new combinations, and seeing
without comprehending the unit which governed them all. The night
was full of cries of insistent life and growth, of birds and insects, of calls
of children, and now and then the faraway roar of railroad trains. It was
nearly midsummer. The year was almost at its height, but had not passed
it. Growth and bloom was still in the ascendant, and had not yet attained
that maturity of perfection beyond which is the slope of death.

Everywhere about her were the revolutions of those unseen wheels of
nature whose immortal trend is towards the completion of time, and
whose momentum can overlap the grave; and the child was within them
and swept onward with the perfecting flowers, and the ripening fruit,
and the insects which were feeling their wings; and all unconsciously,
in a moment as it were, she unfolded a little farther towards her own
heyday of bloom. Suddenly from those heights of the primitive and the
eternal upon which a child starts and where she still lingered she saw
her future before her, shining with new lights, and a wonderful conviction of bliss to come was over her. It was that conviction which comes
at times to all unconquered souls, and which has the very essence of
truth in it, since it overleaps the darkness of life that lies between them
and that bliss. Suddenly Ellen felt that she was born to great happiness,
and all that was to come was towards that end. Her heart beat loud in
her ears. There was a whippoorwill calling in some trees to the left; the
moon was dim under a golden dapple of clouds. She could not feel her
hands or her feet; she seemed to feel nothing except her soul.

Then she heard, loud and sweet and clear, a boy's whistle, one of the
popular tunes of the day. It came nearer and nearer, and it was in the
same key with the child's thoughts and dreams. Then she saw a slender
figure dark against the moonlight stop at a fence, and she jumped up
and ran towards it with no hesitation through the dewy grass; and it
was the boy, Granville Joy. He stood looking at her. He had a handsome,
eager face, and Ellen looked at him, her lips parted, her face like a lily
in the white light.

"Hulloo," said the boy.

"Hulloo," Ellen responded, faintly.

Granville extended one rough, brown, boyish hand over the fence, and Ellen laid her little, soft hand in it. He pulled her gently close, then Ellen lifted her face, and the boy bent his, and the two kissed each other over the fence. Then the boy went on down the street, but he did not whistle, and Ellen went back to the doorstep, and, looking about to be sure that none of the men in the sitting room saw, pulled off one little shoe and drew forth a sprig of southernwood, or boy's-love, which was crushed under her foot.

That day Floretta Vining had told her that if she would put a sprig of boy's-love in her shoe, the very first boy she met would be the one she was going to marry; and Ellen, who was passing from one grade of school to another, had tried it.

Chapter XIV

The high-school master was a distant relative of the Lloyd's, through whom he had obtained the position. One evening when he was taking tea with them at Cynthia Lennox's, he spoke of Ellen. "I have one really remarkable scholar," he said, with a curious air of self-gratulation, as if he were principally responsible for it; "her name is Brewster — Ellen Brewster."

"Good land! That must be the child that ran away five or six years ago, and all the town up in arms over it," said Mrs. Norman Lloyd. "Don't you remember, Cynthia?"

"Yes," replied Cynthia, and continued pouring tea. Cynthia was very little changed. In some faces time seems to engrave lines delicately, once for all, and then lay by. She was rather more charming now than when one had looked at her with any expectancy of youth, since there was now no sense of disappointment.

"I remember that," said Norman Lloyd. "The child would never tell where she had been. A curious case."

"Well," said the school-master, "leaving that childish episode out of the question, she has a really remarkable mind. If she were a boy, I should advise a thorough education and a profession. I should as it is, if her family were able to bear the expense. She has that intuitive order of mind which is wonderful enough, though not, after all, so rare in a girl; but in addition she has the logical, which, according to my experience, is almost unknown in a woman. She ought to have an education."

"But," said Risley, "what is the use of educating that unfortunate child?"

"What do you mean?"

"What I say. What is the use? There she is in her sphere of life, the daughter of a factory operative, in all probability in after-years to be the wife of one and the mother of others. Nothing but a rich marriage can save her, and that she is not likely to make. Milk-maids are more likely to make rich marriages than factory girls; there is a certain savor of romance about milk, and the dewy meadows, and the breath of kine, but a shoe factory is brutally realistic and illusionary. Now, why do you want to increase the poor child's horizon farther than her little feet can carry her? Fit her to be a good female soldier in the ranks of labor, to be a good wife and mother to the makers of shoes, to wash and iron their uniforms of toil, to cook well the food which affords them the requisite nourishment to make shoes, to appreciate book-lore, which is a pleasure and a profit to the makers of shoes; possibly in the non-event of marriage she will make shoes herself. The system of education in our schools is all wrong. It is both senseless and futile. Look at the children filing past to school, and look at their fathers, and their mothers too, filing past to the factory. Look at their present, and look at their future. And look at the trash taught them in their text-books — trash from its utter dissociation with their lives. You might as well teach a Zulu lace-work, instead of the use of the assagai."

"Now look here, Mr. Risley," said the school-master, his face flushing, "is not — I beg your pardon, of course — this view of yours a little narrow and ultra-conservative? You do not want to establish a permanent factory-operative class in this country, do you? That is what your theory would ultimately tend towards. Ought not these children be given their chance to rise in the ranks; ought they to be condemned to tread in the same path as their fathers?"

"I would have those little paths which intersect every unoccupied field in this locality worn by the feet of these men and their children after them unto the third and fourth generation," said Risley. "If not, where is our skilled labor?"

"Oh, Mr. Risley," said Mrs. Lloyd, anxiously, "you wouldn't want all those dear little children to work as hard as their fathers, and not do any better, would you?"

"If they don't, who is going to make our shoes, dear Mrs. Lloyd?" asked Risley.

Mrs. Lloyd and the school-master stared at him, and Lloyd laughed his low, almost mirthless laugh.

"Don't you know, Edward," he said, "that Mr. Risley is not in earnest, and speaks with the deadly intent of an anarchist with a bomb in his bag? He is the most out-and-out radical in the country. If there were a strike, and I did not yield to the demands of the oppressed, and imported foreign labor, I don't know that my life would be safe from him."

"Then you do approve of a higher education?" asked the school-master, while Mrs. Lloyd stared from one to the other in bewilderment.

"Yes, if we and our posterity have to go barefoot," said Risley, laughing out with a sudden undertone of seriousness.

"I suppose everybody could get accustomed to going barefoot after a while," said Mrs. Lloyd. "Do you suppose that dear little thing was barefooted when she ran away, Cynthia?"

Risley answered as if he had been addressed. "I can vouch for the fact that she was not, Mrs. Lloyd," he said. "They would sooner have walked on red-hot plowshares themselves than let her."

"Her father is getting quite an old man," Norman Lloyd said, with no apparent relevancy, as if he were talking to himself.

All the time Cynthia Lennox had been quietly sitting at the head of the table. When the rest of the company had gone, and she and Risley were alone, seated in the drawing room before the parlor fire, for it was a chilly day, she turned her fair, worn face towards him on the crimson velvet of her chair. "Do you know why I did not speak and tell them where the child was that time?" she asked.

"Because of your own good sense?"

"No; because of you."

He looked at her adoringly. She was older than he, her beauty rather recorded than still evident on her face; she had been to him from the first like a fair, forbidden flower behind a wall of prohibition, but nothing could alter his habit of loving her.

"Yes," said she. "It was more on your account than on my own; confession would be good for the soul. The secret has always rankled in my pride. I would much rather defy opinion than fly before it. But I know that you would mind. However, there was another reason."

"What?"

She hesitated a little and colored, even laughed a little, embarrassed laugh which was foreign to her. "Well, Lyman," said she, finally, "one reason why I did not speak was that I see my way clear to making up to that child and her parents for any wrong which I may have done them by causing them a few hours' anxiety. When she has finished the high-school I mean to send her to college."

Chapter XV

*W*hen Ellen was about sixteen, in her second year at the high-school, her own family never looked at her without a slight shock of wonder, as before the unexpected. Her mates, being themselves in the transition state, received her unquestioningly as a fellow-traveler, and colored like themselves with the new lights of the journey. But Ellen's father and mother and grandmother never ceased regarding her with astonishment and admiration and something like alarm. While they regarded Ellen with the utmost pride, they still privately regretted this perfection of bloom which was the forerunner of independence of the parent stalk — at least, Andrew did. Andrew had grown older and more careworn; his mine had not yet paid any dividends, but he had scattering jobs of work, and with his wife's assistance had managed to rub along, and his secret was still safe.

One day in February there was a half-holiday. Lloyd's was shut for the rest of the day, for his brother in St. Louis was dead, and had been brought to Rowe to be buried, and his funeral was at two o'clock.

"Goin' to the funeral, old man?" one of Andrew's fellow-workmen had asked, jostling him as he went out of the shop at noon. Before Andrew could answer, another voice broke in fiercely. It belonged to Joseph Atkins, who was ghastly that day.

"I ain't goin' to no funerals," he said; "guess they won't shut up shop for mine." Then he coughed. His daughter Abby, who had been working in the factory for some time then, pressed close behind her father, and the expression in her face was an echo of his.

"When I strike, that's what I'm going to strike for — to have the shop shut up the day of my funeral," said she; and the remark had a ghastly flippancy, contradicted by her intense manner. A laugh went around, and a young fellow with a handsome, unshaven face caught her by the arm.

"You'd better strike to have the shop shut up the day you're married," said he; but Abby flung away from him.

"I'll thank you to let me alone, Tom Hardy," she said, with a snap; and the men laughed harder.

Abby was attractive to men in spite of her smallness and leanness and incisiveness of manner. She was called mighty smart and dry, which was the shop synonym for witty, and her favors, possibly because she never granted them, were accounted valuable. Abby Atkins had more admirers than many a girl who was prettier and presumably more winning in every way, and could have married twice to their once. But Abby had no wish for a lover. "I've got all I can do to earn my own living and the living of them that belong to me," said she.

That afternoon Andrew Brewster stayed at home. After dinner Eva Tenny and her little girl came in, and Ellen went down street on an errand.

Mrs. Zelotes Brewster was crossing her yard to her son's house when she saw Ellen passing, and paused to gaze at her with that superb pride which pertains to self and is yet superior to it. It was the idealized pride of her own youth. When she proceeded again against the February gusts, it was with an unconscious aping of her granddaughter's freedom of gait. Mrs. Zelotes wore an old red cashmere scarf crossed over her bosom; she held up her black skirts in front, and they trailed pointedly in the rear; she also stood well back on her heels, and when she paused in the windswept yard presented a curious likeness to an old robin pausing for reconnoiter. Fanny and Eva Tenny in the next house saw her coming.

"Look at her holding up her dress in front and letting it drag in the back," said Eva. "It always seemed to me there was somethin' wrong about any woman that held up her dress in front and let it drag behind."

Eva retained all the coarse beauty of her youth, but lines of unalterable hardness were fixed on her forehead and at her mouth corners, and the fierce flush in her cheeks was as set as paint. Her beauty had endured the siege; no guns of mishaps could affect it, but that charm of evanescence which awakens tenderness was gone. Jim Tenny's affection seemed to be waning, and Eva looked at herself in the glass even when bedecked with tawdry finery, and owned that she did not wonder. She strained up her hair into the latest perkiness of twist, and crimped it, and curled her feathers, and tied her ribbons not as much in hope as in a stern determination to do her part towards the furbishing of her faded star of attraction. "Jim don't act as if he thought so much of me, an' I dun'no' as I wonder," she told her sister.

Fanny looked at her critically. "You mean you ain't so good-lookin' as you used to be?" said she.

Eva nodded.

"Well, if that is all men care for us," said Fanny.

"It ain't," said Eva, "only it's the key to it. It's like losin' the key and not bein' able to get in the door in consequence."

"It wa'n't my husband's key," said Fanny, with a glance at her own face, faded as to feature and bloom, but intensified as to love and daily duty, like that of a dog sharpened to one faithfulness of existence.

"Andrew ain't Jim," said Eva, shortly.

"I know he ain't," Fanny assented, with emphasis.

"But I wouldn't swap off my husband for a dozen of yours," said Eva.

"Well, I wouldn't swap off mine for a thousand of yours," returned Fanny, sharply; and there might have been one of the old-time tussles between the sisters had not Eva's violent, half-bitter sense of humor averted it. She broke into a hard laugh.

"Good Lord," she said, "I dun'no' as I should want a thousand like Jim. Seems to me it would be considerable care."

Fanny began to speak, but checked herself. She had heard rumors regarding Jim Tenny of late and had flown fiercely with denial at the woman who told her, and had not repeated them to her sister.

She was thinking how she had heard that Jim had been seen driving in Wenham with Aggie Morse several times lately. Aggie Morse had been Aggie Bemis, Jim's old sweetheart. She had married a well-to-do merchant in Wenham, who died six months before and left her with considerable property. It was her own smart little turn-out in which she had been seen with Jim.

Eva was working in the shop, and Jim had been out of employment for nearly a year, and living on his wife. There was a demand for girls and not for men just then, so Jim loafed. His old mother cared for the house as well as she was able, and Eva did the rest nights and mornings. At first Jim had tried to help about the house-work, but Eva had interfered.

"It ain't a man's work," said she. "Your mother can leave the hard part of it till I get home." Eva used to put the money she earned surreptitiously into her husband's pockets that he might not feel his manly pride injured, but she defeated her own ends by her very solicitude. Jim Tenny began to reason that his wife saw his shame and ignominious helplessness, else she would not have been so anxious to cover it. The stoop of discouragement which Eva used to fear for his shoulders did not come, but, instead, something worse — the defiant set-back of recklessness. He took his wife's earnings and despised himself. Whenever he paid a bill, he was sure the men in the store said, the minute his back was turned, "It's his wife's money that paid for that." He took to loafing on sunny corners, and eying the passers-by with the blank impudence of regard of those outside the current of life. When his wife passed by on her way from the shop he nodded to her as if she were a stranger, and presently followed her home at a distance. He would not be seen on the street with her if he could avoid it. If by any chance when he was standing on his corner of idleness his little girl came past, he melted away imperceptibly. He could not bear it that the child should see him standing there in that company of futility and openly avowed inadequacy. The child was a keen-eyed, slender little girl, resembling neither father nor mother, but looking rather like her paternal grandmother, who was a fair, attenuated woman, with an intelligence which had sharpened on herself for want of anything more legitimate, and worn her out by the unnatural friction. The little Amabel, for Eva had been romantic in the naming of her child, was an old-fashioned-looking child in spite of Eva's careful decoration of the little figure in the best childish finery which she could muster.

Little Amabel was reading a child's book at another window. When Mrs. Zelotes entered she eyed her with the sharpness and inscrutable conclusions therefrom of a kitten, then turned a leaf in her book.

When Mrs. Zelotes had greeted her daughter-in-law and Eva, she looked with disapproval at Amabel.

"When I was a little girl I should have been punished if I hadn't got up and curtsied and said good-afternoon when company came in," she remarked, severely.

Amabel was not a favorite outside of her own family. People used to stare aghast at her unexpected questions and demands delivered in a shrill clarion as from some summit of childish wisdom, and they said she was a queer child. She yielded always to command from utter helplessness, but the why of obedience was strongly alert within her. The child might have been in some subtle and uncanny fashion the offspring of her age and generation instead of her natural parents, she was so unlike either of them, and so much a product of the times, with her meekness and slavishness of weakness and futility, and her unquenchable and unconquerable vitality of dissent.

Ellen adored the little Amabel. Presently, when she returned from her errand down-town, she cried out with delight when she saw her; and the child ran to meet her, and clung to her, with her flaxen head snuggled close to her cheek. Ellen caught the child up, seated herself, and sat cuddling her as she used to cuddle her doll.

"You dear little thing!" she murmured, "you dear little thing! You did come to see Ellen, didn't you?" And the child gazed up in the young girl's face with a rapt expression. Nothing can express the admiration, which is almost as unquestionable as worship, of a very little girl for a big one. Amabel loved her mother with a rather unusual intensity for a child, but Ellen was what she herself would be when she was grown up. Through Ellen her love of self and her ambition budded into blossom. Ellen could do nothing wrong because she did what she herself would do when she was grown. She never questioned Ellen for her reasons.

Mrs. Zelotes kept looking at the two, with pride in Ellen and disapproval of her caresses of the child. "Seems to me you might speak to your own folks as well as to have no eyes for anybody but that child," she said, finally.

"Why, grandma, I spoke to you just a little while ago," returned Ellen. "You know I saw you just a few minutes before I went down-town." Ellen straightened the child on her knees, and began to try to twist her soft, straight flaxen locks into curls. Andrew lounged in from the kitchen and sat down and regarded Ellen fondly. The girl's cheeks were a splendid color from her walk in the cold wind, her hair around her temples caught the light from the window, and seemed to wreathe her head with a yellow flame. She tossed the child about with lithe young arms, whose every motion suggested reserves of tender strength. Ellen was more beautiful than she had ever been before, and yet something was gone from her face, though only temporarily, since the lines for the vanished meaning was still there. All the introspection and dreaminess and poetry of her face were gone, for the girl was, for the time, overbalanced on the physical side of her life. The joy of existence for itself alone was intoxicating her. The innocent frivolities of her sex had seized her too, and the instincts which had not yet reached her brain nor gone farther than her bounding pulses of youth. "Ellen is getting real fond of dress," Fanny often said to Andrew. He only laughed at that. "Well, pretty birds like pretty feathers, and no wonder," said he. But he did not laugh when Fanny added that Ellen seemed to think more about the boys than she used to. There was scarcely a boy in the high-school who was not Ellen's admirer. It was a curious happening in those days when Ellen was herself in much less degree the stuff of which dreams are made than she had been and would be thereafter, that she was the object of so many. Every morning when she entered the school-room she was reflected in a glorious multiple of ideals in no one could tell how many boyish hearts. Floretta Vining began to imitate her, and kept close to Ellen with supremest diplomacy, that she might thereby catch some of the crumbs of attention which fell from Ellen's full table. Often when some happy boy had secured a short monopoly of Ellen, his rival took up with Floretta, and she was content, being one of those purely feminine things who have no pride when the sweets of life are concerned. Floretta dressed her hair like Ellen's, and tied her neck-ribbons the same way; she held her head like her, she talked like her, except when the two girls were absolutely alone; then she sometimes relapsed suddenly, to Ellen's bewilderment, into her own ways, and her blue eyes took on an expression as near animosity as her ingratiating politic nature could admit.

Ellen did not affiliate as much with Floretta as with Maria Atkins. Abby had gone to work in the shop, and so Ellen did not see so much of her. Maria was not as much a favorite with the boys as she had been since they had passed and not yet returned to that stage when feminine comradeship satisfies; so Ellen used to confide in her with a surety of sympathy and no contention. Once, when the girls were sleeping together, Ellen made a stupendous revelation to Maria, having first bound her to inviolable secrecy. "I love a boy," said she, holding Maria's little arm tightly.

"I know who," said Maria, with a hushed voice.

"He kissed me once, and then I knew it," said Ellen.

"Well, I guess he loves you," said Maria. Ellen shivered and drew a fluttering sigh of assent. Then the two girls lay in each other's arms, looking at the moonlight which streamed in through the window. God knew in what realms of pure romance, and of passion so sublimated by innocence that no tinge of earthliness remained, the two wandered in their dreams.

At last, that afternoon in February, Ellen put down little Amabel and got out her needle-work. She was making a lace neck-tie for her own adornment. She showed it to her grandmother at her mother's command. "It's real pretty," said Mrs. Zelotes. "Ellen takes after the Brewsters; they were always handy with their needles."

"Can uncle sew?" asked little Amabel, suddenly, from her corner, in a tone big with wonder.

Eva and the others chuckled, but Mrs. Zelotes eyed the child severely. "Little girls shouldn't ask silly questions," said she.

Andrew passed his hand with a rough caress over the small flaxen head. "Uncle Andrew can't sew anything but shoes," said he.

Little Amabel's question had aroused in Mrs. Zelotes a carping spirit even against Ellen. Presently she turned to her. "I heard something about you," said she. "I want to know if it is true. I heard that you were walking home from school with that Joy boy one day last week." Ellen looked at her grandmother without flinching, though the pink was over her face and neck.

"Yes'm, I did," said she.

"Well, I think it's about time it was put a stop to," said Mrs. Zelotes. "That Joy boy!"

Then Fanny lost her temper. "I can manage my own daughter, Grandma Brewster," said she, "and I'll thank you to attend to your own affairs."

"You don't seem to know enough to manage her," retorted Mrs. Zelotes, "if you let her go traipsin' round with that Joy boy."

The warfare waged high for a time. Andrew withdrew to the kitchen. Ellen took little Amabel up in her own chamber and showed her her beautiful doll, which looked not a day older, so carefully had she been cherished, than when she first had her. Ellen felt both resentment and shame, and also a fierce dawning of partisanship towards Granville Joy. "Why should my grandmother speak of him so scornfully?" she asked herself. "He is a real good boy."

That night was very cold, a night full of fierce white glitter of frost and moonlight, and raging with a turbulence of winds. Ellen lay awake listening to them. Presently between the whistle of the wind she heard another, a familiar pipe from a boyish throat. She sprang out of bed and peeped from her window, and there was a dark, slight figure out in the yard, and he was looking up at her window, whistling. Shame, and mirth, and also exultation, which overpowered them both, stirred within the child's breast. She had read of things like this. Here was her boy lover coming out this bitter night just for the sake of looking up at her window. She adored him for it. Then she heard a window raised with a violent rasp across the yard, and saw her grandmother's nightcapped head thrust forth. She heard her shrill, imperious voice call out quite distinctly, "Boy, who be you?"

The lovelorn whistler ceased his pipe, and evidently, had he consulted his own discretion, would have shown a pair of flying heels, but he walked bravely up to the window and the nightcapped head and replied. Ellen could not hear what he said, but she distinguished plainly enough her grandmother's concluding remarks.

"Go home," cried Mrs. Zelotes; "go home just as fast as you can and go to bed. Go home!" Mrs. Zelotes made a violent shooting motion with her hands and her white head as if he were a cat, and Granville Joy obeyed. However, Ellen heard his brave, retreating whistle far down the road. She went back to bed, and lay awake with a fervor of young love roused into a flame by opposition swelling high in her heart. But the next afternoon, after school, Ellen, to Granville Joy's great bliss and astonishment, insinuated herself, through the crowd of out-going scholars, close to him, and presently, had he not been so incredulous, for he was a modest boy, he would have said it was by no volition of his own that he found himself walking down the street with her. And when they reached his house, which was only halfway to her own, she looked at him with such a wistful surprise as he motioned to leave her that he could not mistake it, and he walked on at her side quite to her own house. Granville Joy was a gentle boy, young for his age, which was a year more than Ellen's. He had a face as gentle as a girl's, and really beautiful. Women all loved him, and the schoolgirls raised an admiring treble chorus in his praise whenever his name was spoken. He was saved from effeminacy by nervous impulses which passed for sustained manly daring. "He once licked a boy a third bigger than he was, and you needn't call him sissy," one girl said once to a decrying friend. Today, as the boy and girl neared Mrs. Zelotes's house, Granville was conscious of an inward shrinking before the remembrance of the terrible old lady. He expected every minute to hear the grating upward slide of the window and that old voice, which had in it a terrible intimidation of feminine will. Granville had a mother as gentle as himself, and a woman with the strength of her own conviction upon her filled him with awe as of something anomalous. He wondered uneasily what he should do if the old lady were to hail him and call him to an account again, whether it would be a more manly course to face her, or obey, since she was Ellen's grandmother. He kept an uneasy eye upon the house, and presently, when he saw the stern old face at the window, he quailed a little. But Ellen for the first time in her life took his arm, and the two marched past under the fire of Mrs. Zelotes's gaze. Ellen had retaliated, not nobly, but as naturally under the conditions of her life at that time as the branch of a tree blows east before the west wind.

Chapter XVI

*E*llen, when she graduated, was openly pronounced the flower of her class. Not a girl equaled her, not a boy surpassed her. When Ellen came home one night about two months before her graduation, and announced that she was to have the valedictory, such a light of pure joy flashed over her mother's face that she looked ten years younger.

"Well, I guess your father will be pleased enough," she said. She was hard at work, finishing women's wrappers of cheap cotton. The hood industry had failed some time before, since the hoods had gone out of fashion. The same woman had taken a contract to supply a large firm with wrappers, and employed many in the neighborhood, paying them the smallest possible prices. This woman was a usurer on a scale so pitiful and petty that it almost condoned usury. Sometimes a man on discovering the miserable pittance for which his wife toiled during every minute which she could snatch from her household duties and the care of her children, would inveigh against it. "That woman is cheating you," he would say, to be met with the argument that she herself was only making ten cents on a wrapper. Looked at in that light, the wretched profit of the workers did not seem so out of proportion. It was usury in a nutshell, so infinitesimal as almost to escape detection. Fanny worked every minute which she could secure on these wrappers — the ungainly, slatternly home-gear of other poor women. There was an air of dejected femininity and slipshod drudgery about every fold of one of them when it was hung up finished. Fanny used to keep them on a row of hooks in her bedroom until a dozen were completed, when she carried them to her employer, and Ellen used to look at them with a sense of depression. She imagined worn, patient faces of the sisters of poverty above the limp collars, and poor, veinous hands dangling from the clumsy sleeves.

Fanny would never allow Ellen to assist her in this work, though she begged hard to do so. "Wait till you get out of school," said she. "You've got enough to do while you are in school."

When Ellen told her about the valedictory, Fanny was so overjoyed that she lost sight of her work, and sewed in the sleeves wrong. "There, only see what you have made me do!" she cried, laughing with delight at her own folly. "Only see, you have made me sew in both these sleeves wrong. You are a great child. Another time you had better keep away with your valedictories till I get my wrapper finished." Ellen looked up from the book which she had taken.

"Let me rip them out for you, mother," she said.

"No, you keep on with your study — it won't take me but a minute. I don't know what your father will say. It is a great honor to be chosen to write the valedictory out of that big class. I guess your father will be pleased."

"I hope I can write a good one," said Ellen.

"Well, if you can't, I'd give up my beat," said the mother, looking at her with enthusiasm, and speaking with scornful chiding. "Why don't you go over and tell your grandmother Brewster? She'll be tickled 'most to death."

Ellen had not been gone long when Andrew came home, coming into the yard, bent as if beneath some invisible burden of toil. Just then he had work, but not in Lloyd's. He had grown too old for Lloyd's, and had been discharged long ago.

He had so far been able to conceal from Fanny the fact that he had withdrawn all his little savings to invest in that mining stock. The stock had not yet come up, as he had expected. He very seldom had a circular reporting progress nowadays. When he did have one in the post office his heart used to stand still until he had torn open the envelope and read it. It was uniformly not so hopeful as formerly, while speciously apologetic. Andrew still had faith, although his heart was sick with its long deferring. He could not actually believe that all his savings were gone, sunken out of sight forever in this awful shaft of miscalculation and misfortune. What he dreaded most was that Fanny should find out, as she would have to were he long out of employment.

Andrew, when he entered the house on his return from work, had come to open a door into the room where his wife was, with a deprecating and apologetic air. He gained confidence when, after a few minutes, the sore subject had not been broached.

Tonight, as usual, when he came into the sitting room where Fanny was sewing it was with a sidelong glance of uneasy deprecation towards her, and an attempt to speak easily, as if he had nothing on his mind.

"Pretty warm day," he began, but his wife cut him short. She faced around towards him beaming, her work — a pink wrapper — slid from her lap to the floor.

"What do you think, Andrew?" she said. "What do you s'pose has happened? Guess." Andrew laughed gratefully, and with the greatest alacrity. Surely this was nothing about mining-stocks, unless, indeed, she had heard, and the stocks had gone up, but that seemed to much like the millennium. He dismissed that from his mind before it entered. He stood before her in his worn clothes. He always wore a collar and a black tie, and his haggard face was carefully shaven. Andrew was punctiliously neat, on Ellen's account. He was always thinking, suppose he should meet Ellen coming home from school, with some young ladies whose fathers were rich and did not have to work in the shop, how mortified she might feel if he looked shabby and unkempt.

"Guess, Andrew," she said.

"What is it?" said Andrew.

"Oh, you guess."

"I don't see what it can be, Fanny."

"Well, Ellen has got the valedictory. What's the matter with you? Be you deaf? Ellen has got the valedictory out of all them girls and boys."

"She has, has she?" said Andrew. He dropped into a chair and looked at his wife. There was something about the intense interchange of confidence of delight between these two faces of father and mother which had almost the unrestraint of lunacy. Andrew's jaw fairly dropped with his smile, which was a silent laugh rather than a smile; his eyes were wild with delight. "She has, has she?" he kept repeating.

"Yes, she has," said Fanny. She tossed her head with an incomparable pride; she coughed a little, affected cough. "I s'pose you know what a compliment it is?" said she. "It means that she's smarter than all them boys and girls — the smartest one in her whole class."

"Yes, I s'pose it does," said Andrew. "So she has got it! Well!"

"There she comes now," said Fanny, "and Grandma Brewster."

Andrew borrowed money to buy a gold watch and chain for a graduating gift for his daughter. He would scarcely have essayed anything quite so magnificent, but Fanny innocently tempted him. The two had been sitting in the door in the cool of the evening, one day in June, about two weeks before the graduation, and had just watched Ellen's light muslin skirts flutter out of sight. She had gone down-town to purchase some ribbon for her graduating dress — she and Floretta Vining, who had come over to accompany her. "I feel kind of anxious to have her have something pretty when she graduates," Fanny said, speaking as if she were feeling her way into a mind of opposition. Neither she nor Andrew had ever owned a watch, and the scheme seemed to her breathless with magnificence.

"Yes, she ought to have something pretty," agreed Andrew.

"I don't want her to feel ashamed when she sees the other girls' presents," said Fanny.

"That's so," assented Andrew.

"Well," said Fanny, "I've been thinkin' —"

"What?"

"Well, I've been thinkin' that — of course your mother is goin' to give her the dress, and that's all, of course, and it's a real handsome present. I ain't sayin' a word against that; but there ain't anybody else to give her much except us. Poor Eva 'd like to, but she can't; it takes all she earns, since Jim's out of work, and I don't know what she's goin' to do. So that leaves nobody but us, and I've been thinkin' — I dun'no' what you'll say, Andrew, but I've been thinkin' — s'pose you took a little money out of the bank, and — got Ellen — a watch." Fanny spoke the last word in a faint whisper. She actually turned pale in the darkness.

"A watch?" repeated Andrew.

"Yes, a watch. I've always wanted Ellen to have a gold watch and chain. I've always thought she could, and so she could if you hadn't been out of work so much."

"Yes, she could," said Andrew — "a watch and mebbe a piano. I thought I'd be back in Lloyd's before now. Well, mebbe I shall before long. They say there's better times comin' by fall."

"Well, Ellen will be graduated by that time," said Fanny, "and she ought to have the watch now if she's ever goin' to. She'll never think so much of it. Floretta Vining is goin' to have a watch, too. Mrs. Cross says her mother told her so; said Mr. Vining had it all bought — a real handsome one. I don't believe Sam Vining can afford to buy a gold watch. I don't believe it is all gold, for my part. They ain't got as much as we have, if Sam has had work steadier. I don't believe it's gold. I don't want Ellen to have a watch at all unless it's a real good one. It seems to me you'd better take a little money out and buy her one, Andrew."

"Well, I'll see," said Andrew. He had a terrible sense of guilt before Fanny. Suppose she knew that there was no money at all in the bank to take out?

"Well, I'll buy her one if you say so," said he, in a curious, slow, stern voice. In his heart was a fierce rising of rebellion, that he, hard-working and frugal and self-denying all his life, should be denied the privilege of buying a present for his darling without resorting to deception, and even almost robbery. He did not at that minute blame himself in the least for his misadventure with his mining stock. Had not the same relentless Providence driven him to that also? His weary spirit took for the first time a poise of utter self-righteousness in opposition to this

Providence, and he blasphemed in his inner closet of self, before the face of the Lord, as he comprehended it.

"Well, I have a sort of set my heart on it," said Fanny.

"She shall have the watch," repeated Andrew, and his voice was fairly defiant.

After Fanny had gone into the house and lighted her lamp, and resumed work on her wrapper, Andrew still sat on the step in the cool evening. There was a full moon, and great masses of shadows seemed to float and hover and alight on the earth with a gigantic brooding as of birds. The trees seemed redoubled in size from the soft indetermination of the moonlight which confused shadow and light, and deceived the eye as with soft loomings out of false distances. There was a tall pine, grown from a sapling since Ellen's childhood, and that looked more like a column of mist than a tree, but the Norway spruces clove the air sharply like silhouettes in ink, and outlined their dark profiles clearly against the silver radiance.

To Andrew, looking at it all, came the feeling of a traveler who passes all scenes whether of joy or woe, being himself in his passing the one thing which remains, and somehow he got from it an enormous comfort.

"We're all travelin' along," he said aloud, in a strained, solemn voice.

"What did you say, Andrew?" Fanny called from the open window.

"Nothin'," replied Andrew.

Chapter XVII

*E*llen had always had objective points, as it were, in her life, and she always would have, no matter how long she lived. She came to places where she stopped mentally, for retrospection and forethought, wherefrom she could seem to obtain a view of that which lay behind, and of the path which was set for her feet in advance. She saw the tracked and the trackless. Once, going with Abby Atkins and Floretta in search of early spring flowers, Ellen had lingered and let them go out of sight, and had sat down on a springing mat of wintergreen leaves under the windy outstretch of a great pine, and had remained there quite deaf to shrill halloos. She had sat there with eyes of inward scrutiny like an Eastern sage's, motionless as on a rock of thought, while her daily life eddied around her. Ellen, sitting there, had said to herself: "This I will always remember. No matter how long I live, where I am, and what happens to me, I will always remember how I was a child, and sat here this morning in spring under the pine tree, looking backward and forward. I will never forget."

When, finally, Abby and Floretta had run back, and spied her there, they had stared half frightened. "You ain't sick, are you, Ellen?" asked Abby, anxiously.

"What are you sitting there for?" asked Floretta.

Ellen had replied that she was not sick, and had risen and run on, looking for flowers, but the flowers for her bloomed always against a background of the past, and nodded with forward flings of fragrance into the future; for the other children, who were wholly of their own day and generation, they bloomed in the simple light of their own desire of possession. They picked only flowers, but Ellen picked thoughts, and they kept casting bewildered side-glances at her, for the look which had come into her eyes as she sat beneath the pine tree lingered.

It was as if a rose had a second of self-consciousness between the bud and the blossom; a bird between its mother's brooding and the song. She had caught sight of the innermost processes of things, of her wheels of life.

Ellen waked up on that June morning, and the old sensation of a pause before advance was upon her, and the strange solemnity which was almost a terror, from the feeble clutching of her mind at the comprehension of infinity. She looked at the morning sunlight coming between the white slants of her curtains, an airy flutter of her new dress from the closet, her valedictory, tied with a white satin ribbon, on the stand, and she saw quite plainly all which had led up to this, and to her, Ellen Brewster; and she saw also the inevitableness of its passing, the precious valedictory being laid away and buried beneath a pile of future ones; she saw the crowd of future valedictorians advancing like a flock of white doves in their white gowns, when hers was worn out, and its beauty gone, pressing forward, dimming her to her own vision. She saw how she would come to look calmly and coldly upon all that filled her with such joy and excitement today; how the savor of the moment would pass from her tongue, and she said to herself that she would always remember this moment.

Then suddenly — since she had in herself an impetus of motion which nothing, not even reflection, could long check — she saw quite plainly a light beyond, after all this should have passed, and the leaping power of her spirit to gain it. And then, since she was healthy, and given only at wide intervals to these Eastern lapses of consciousness from the present, she was back in her day, and alive to all its importance as a part of time.

She felt the bounding elation of tossing on the crest of her wave of success, and the full rainbow glory of it dazzled her eyes. She was first in her class, she was valedictorian, she had a beautiful dress, she was young, she was first. It is a poor spirit, and one incapable of courage in defeat, who feels not triumph in victory. Ellen was triumphant and confident. She had faith in herself and the love and approbation of everybody.

When she was seated with her class on the stage in the city hall, where the graduating exercises were held, she saw herself just as she looked, and it was with a satisfaction which had nothing weakly in its vein, and smiled radiantly and innocently at herself as seen in this mirror of love and appreciation of all who knew her.

When the band stopped playing, and Ellen, who as valedictorian came last as the crown and capsheaf of it all, stepped forward from the semicircle of white-clad girls and seriously abashed boys, there was a subdued murmur and then a hush all over the hall. Andrew and Fanny and the grandmother, seated directly in front of the stage — for they had come early to secure good seats — heard whispers of admiration on every side. It was admiration with no dissent — such jealous ears as theirs could not be deceived. Fanny's face was blazing with the sweet shame of pride in her child; Andrew was pale; the grandmother sat as if petrified, with a proud toss of her head. They looked straight ahead; they dared not encounter each other's eyes, for they were more self-conscious than Ellen. They felt the attention of the whole assembly upon them. Andrew was conscious of feeling ill and faint. His own joy seemed to overwhelm him. He forgot his stocks, he forgot his borrowed money, he forgot Lloyd's; he was perfectly happy at the sight of that beautiful young creature of his own heart, who was preferred before all others in the sight of the whole city. In truth, there was about Ellen a majesty and nobility of youth and innocence and beauty which overawed. The other girls of the class were as young and as pretty, but none of them had that indescribable quality which seemed to raise her above them all. Ellen still kept her blond fairness, but there was nothing of the doll-like which often characterizes the blond type. Although she was small, Ellen's color had the firmness and unwavering of tinted marble; she carried her crown of yellow braids as if it had been gold; she moved and looked and spoke with decision. The violent and intense temperament which she had inherited from two sides of her family had crystallized in her to something more forcible, but also more impressive. However, she was, after all, only a young girl, scarcely more than a child, whatever her principle of underlying character might be, and when she stood there before them all — all her townspeople who represented her world, the human shore upon which her own little individuality beat — when she saw those attentive faces, row upon row, all fixed upon her, she felt her heart pound against her side; she had no sensation of the roll of paper in her hand; an awful terror as of suddenly discovered depths came over her, as the wild clapping of hands to which her appearance had given rise died away. Ellen stood still, holding the valedictory as if it had been a stick. A little wondering murmur began to be heard. Andrew felt as if he were dying. Fanny gripped his arm hard. Mrs. Zelotes had the look of one about to spring. Ellen had the terrible sensation which has in it a nightmare of inability to move, allied with the intensest consciousness. She knew that she was to read her valedictory, she knew that she must raise that white-ribboned roll and read, or else be disgraced forever, and yet she was powerless. But suddenly some compelling glance seemed to arouse her from this lock of nerve and muscle; she raised her eyes, and Cynthia Lennox, on the farther side of the hall, was gazing full at her with an indescribable gaze of passion and help and command. Her own mother's look could not have influenced her. Ellen raised her valedictory, bowed, and began to read. Andrew looked so pale that people nudged one another to look at him. Mrs. Zelotes settled back, relaxing stiffly from her fierce attitude. Fanny wiped her forehead with a cheap lace-bordered handkerchief. There was a stifled sob farther back, that came from Eva Tenny, who sat back on account of a break across the shoulders in the back of her silk dress. Amabel, anæmic and eager in a little, tawdry, cheap muslin frock, sat beside her, with worshipful eyes on Ellen. "What ailed her?" she whispered, hitting her mother with a sharp little elbow. "Hush up!" whispered Eva, angrily, surreptitiously wiping her eyes. In front, directly in her line of vision, sat the woman of whom she was jealous — the young widow, who had been Aggie Bemis, arrayed in a handsome India silk and a flower-laden hat. Eva's hat was trimmed with a draggled feather and a bunch of roses which she had tried to color with aniline dye. When she got home that night she tore the feather out of the hat and flung it across the room. She wished to do it that afternoon every time she looked at the other woman's roses against the smooth knot of her brown hair, and that repressed impulse, with her alarm at Ellen's silence, had made her almost hysterical. When

Ellen's clear young voice rose and filled the hall she calmed herself.
Ellen had not folded back her first page with a flutter of the white satin
ribbons before people began to sit straight and stare at each other
incredulously. The subject of the valedictory, as well as those of the
other essays, had been allotted, and Ellen's had been "Equality," and
she had written a most revolutionary valedictory. Ellen had written with
a sort of poetic fire, and, crude as it all was, she might have had the
inspiration of a Shelley or a Chatterton as she stood there, raising her
fearless young front over the marshaling of her sentiments on the
smooth sheets of foolscap. Her voice, once started, rang out clear and
full. She had hesitated at nothing, she flung all castes into a common
heap of equality with her strong young arms, and she set them all on
one level of the synagogue. She forced the employer and his employé
to one bench of service in the grand system of things; she gave the
laborer, and the laborer only, the reward of labor. As Ellen went on
reading calmly, with the steadfastness of one promulgating principles,
not the excitement of one carried away by enthusiasm, she began to be
interrupted by applause, but she read on, never wavering, her clear voice
overcoming everything. She was quite innocently throwing her wordy
bomb to the agitation of public sentiment. She had no thought of such
an effect. She was stating what she believed to be facts with her youthful
dogmatism. She had no fear lest the facts strike too hard. The school-
master's face grew long with dismay; he sat pulling his mustache in a
fashion he had when disturbed. He glanced uneasily now and then at
Mr. Lloyd, and at another leading manufacturer who was present. The
other manufacturer sat quite stolid and unsmiling beside a fidgeting
wife, who presently arose and swept out with a loud rustle of silks. She
looked back once and beckoned angrily to her husband, but he did not
stir. He was on the school-board. The school-master trembled when he
saw that imperturbable face of storing recollection before him. Mr.
Lloyd leaned towards Lyman Risley, who sat beside him and whispered
and laughed. It was quite evident that he did not consider the flight of
this little fledgling in the face of things seriously. But even he, as Ellen's
clearly delivered sentiments grew more and more defined — almost
anarchistic — became a little grave in spite of the absurd incongruity
between them and the girlish lips. Once he looked in some wonder at
the school-teacher as much as to say, "Why did you permit this?" and
the young man pulled his mustache harder.

When Ellen finished and made her bow, such a storm of applause
arose as had never before been heard at a high-school exhibition. The
audience was for the most part composed of factory employés and their
families, as most of the graduates were of that class of the community.

Many of them were of foreign blood, people who had come to the country expecting the state of things advocated in Ellen's valedictory, and had remained more or less sullen and dissenting at the non-fulfillment of their expectation. One tall Swede, with a lurid flashing of blue eyes under a thick, blond thatch, led the renewed charges of applause. Red spots came on his cheeks, gaunt with high cheekbones; his cold Northern blood was up. He stood upreared against a background of the crowd under the balcony; he stamped when the applause died low; then it swelled again and again like great waves. The Swede brandished his long arms, he shouted, others echoed him. Even the women hallooed in a frenzy of applause, they clapped their hands, they stood up in their seats. Only a few sat silent and contemptuous through all the enthusiasm. Thomas Briggs, the manufacturer, was one of them. He sat like a rock, his great, red, imperturbable face of dissent fixed straight ahead. Mrs. Lloyd clapped wildly, on account of the girl who had read the valedictory. She had slept through the greater part of it, for it was very warm, and the heat always made her drowsy. She kept leaning towards Cynthia as she clapped, and asking in a loud whisper if she wasn't sweet. Cynthia did not applaud, but her delicate face was pale with emotion. Lyman Risley, beside her, was clapping energetically. "She may have a bomb somewhere concealed among those ribbons and frills," he said to Lloyd when the applause was waxing loudest, and Lloyd laughed.

As for Ellen, when the storm of applause burst at her feet, she stood still for a moment bewildered. Then she bowed again and turned to go, then the compelling uproar brought her back. She stood there quite piteous in her confusion. This was too much triumph, and, moreover, she had not the least idea of the true significance of it all. She was like a chemist who had brought together, quite ignorantly and unwittingly, the two elements of an explosive. She thought that her valedictory must have been well done, that they liked it, and that was all. She had no sooner finished reading than the ushers began in the midst of the storm of applause to approach the stage with her graduating presents. They were laden with great bouquets and baskets of flowers, with cards conspicuously attached to most of them. Cynthia Lennox had sent a basket of roses. Ellen took it on her arm, and wondered when she saw the name attached to the pink satin bow on the handle. She did not look again towards Cynthia since the old impulse of concealment on her account came over her. Ellen had great boxes of candy from her boy admirers, that being a favorite token of young affection upon such occasions. She had a gift-book from her former school-teacher, and a ninety-eight-cent gilded vase from Eva and Amabel, who had been saving money to buy it. She heard a murmur of admiration when she had finally reached her seat, after the storm of applause had at last subsided, and she unrolled the packages with trembling fingers.

"My, ain't that handsome!" said Floretta, pressing her muslin-clad shoulder against Ellen's. "My, didn't they clap you, Ellen! What's that in that package?"

The package contained Ellen's new watch and chain. Floretta had already received hers, and it lay in its case on her lap. Ellen looked at the package, not hearing in the least the Baptist minister who had taken his place on the stage, and was delivering an address. She had felt her aunt Eva's and Amabel's eager eyes on her when she unrolled the gaudy vase; now she felt her father's and mother's. The small, daintily tied package was inscribed "Ellen Brewster, from Father and Mother."

"Why don't you open it?" came in her ear from Floretta. Maria was leaning forward also, over her lapful of carnations which John Sargent had presented to her.

"Why don't she open it?" she whispered to Floretta. They were all quite oblivious of the speaker, who moved nervously back and forth in front of them, so screening them somewhat from the observation of the audience. Still Ellen hesitated, looking at the little package and feeling her father's and mother's eyes on her face.

Finally she untied the cord and took out the jeweler's case from the wrapping-paper. "My, you've got one too, I bet!" whispered Floretta. Ellen opened the box, and gazed at her watch and chain; then she glanced at her father and mother down in the audience, and the three loving souls seemed to meet in an ineffable solitude in the midst of the crowd. All three faces were pale — Ellen's began to quiver. She felt Floretta's shoulder warm through her thin sleeve against hers.

"My! you've got one — I said so," she whispered. "It isn't chased as much as mine, but it's real handsome. My, Ellen Brewster, you ain't going to cry before all these people!"

Ellen smiled against a sob, and she gave her head a defiant toss. Down in the audience Fanny had her handkerchief to her eyes, and Andrew sat looking sternly at the speaker. Ellen said to herself that she would not cry — she would not, but she sat gazing down at her flower-laden lap and the presents. The golden disk under her fixed eyes waxed larger and larger, until it seemed to fill her whole comprehension as with a golden light of a suffering, self-denying love which was her best reward of life and labor on the earth.

Chapter XVIII

*A*fter the exhibition there was a dance. The Brewsters, even Mrs. Zelotes, remained to see the last of Ellen's triumph. Mrs. Zelotes was firmly convinced that Ellen's appearance excelled anyone's in the hall. Not a girl swung past them in the dance but she eyed her white dress scornfully, then her rosy face, and sniffed with high nostrils like an old warhorse. "Jest look at that Vining girl's dress, coarse enough to strain through," she said to Fanny, leaning across Andrew, who was sitting rapt, his very soul dancing with his daughter, his eyes never leaving her one second, following her fair head and white flutter of muslin ruffles and ribbons around the hall.

"Yes, that's so," assented Fanny, but not with her usual sharpness. A wistful softness and sweetness was on her coarsely handsome face. Once she reached her hand over Andrew's and pressed it, and blushed crimson as she did so. Andrew turned and smiled at her. All that annoyed Andrew was that Ellen danced with Granville Joy often, and also with other boys. It disturbed him a little, even while it delighted him, that she should dance at all, that she should have learned to dance. Andrew had been brought up to look upon dancing as an amusement for Louds rather than for Brewsters. It had not been in vogue among the aristocracy of this little New England city when he was young.

Mrs. Zelotes watched Ellen dance with inward delight and outward disapproval. "I don't approve of dancing, never did," she said to Andrew, but she was furious once when Ellen sat through a dance. Towards the end of the evening she saw with sudden alertness Ellen dancing with a new partner, a handsome young man, who carried himself with more assurance than the school-boys. Mrs. Zelotes hit Andrew with her sharp elbow.

"Who's that dancing with her now?" she said.

"That's young Lloyd," answered Andrew. He flushed a little, and looked pleased.

"Norman Lloyd's nephew?" asked his mother, sharply.

"Yes, he's on here from St. Louis. He's goin' into business with his uncle," replied Andrew. "Sargent was telling me about it yesterday. Young Lloyd came into the post office while we were there." Fanny had been listening. Immediately she married Ellen to young Lloyd, and the next moment she went to live in a grand new house built in a twinkling in a vacant lot next to Norman Lloyd's residence, which was the wonder of the city. She reared this castle in Spain with inconceivable swiftness, even while she was turning her head towards Eva on the other side, and prodding her with an admonishing elbow as Mrs. Zelotes had prodded Andrew. "That's Norman Lloyd's nephew dancing with her now," she said. Eva looked at her, smiling. Directly the idea of Ellen's marriage with the young man with whom she was dancing established full connections and ran through the line of Ellen's relatives as though an electric wire.

As for Ellen, dancing with this stranger, who had been introduced to her by the school-master, she certainly had no thought of a possible marriage with him, but she had looked into his face with a curious, ready leap of sympathy and understanding of this other soul which she met for the first time. It seemed to her that she must have known him before, but she knew that she had not. She began to reflect as they were whirling about the hall, she gazed at that secret memory of hers, which she had treasured since her childhood, and discovered that what had seemed familiar to her about the young man was the face of a familiar thought. Ever since Miss Cynthia Lennox had told her about her nephew, the little boy who had owned and loved the doll, Ellen had unconsciously held the thought of him in her mind. "You are Miss Cynthia Lennox's nephew," she said to young Lloyd.

"Yes," he replied. He nodded towards Cynthia, who was sitting on the opposite side from the Brewsters, with the Norman Lloyds and Lyman Risley. "She used to be like a mother to me," he said. "You know I lost my mother when I was a baby."

Ellen nodded at him with a look of pity of that marvelous scope which only a woman in whom the maternal slumbers ready to awake can compass. Ellen, looking at the handsome face of the young man, saw quite distinctly in it the face of the little motherless child, and all the tender pity which she would have felt for that child was in her eyes.

"What a beautiful girl she is," thought the young man. He smiled at her admiringly, loving her look at him, while not in the least understanding it. He had asked to be presented to Ellen from curiosity. He had not been at the exhibition, and had heard the school-master and Risley talking about the valedictory. "I didn't know that you taught anarchy in school, Mr. Harris," Risley had said. He laughed as he said it, but Harris had colored with an uneasy look at Norman Lloyd, whose face wore an expression of amusement. "Perhaps I should have," he began, but Lloyd interrupted him. "My dear fellow," he said, "you don't imagine that any man in his senses could take seriously enough to be annoyed by it that child's effusion on her nice little roll of foolscap tied with her pretty white satin ribbon?"

"She is just as sweet as she can be," said Mrs. Norman, "and I thought her composition was real pretty. Didn't you, Cynthia?"

"Very," replied Cynthia.

"What your are worrying about it for, Edward, I don't see," said Mrs. Norman to the school-master.

"Well, I am glad if it struck you that way," said he, "but when I heard the applause from all those factory people" — he lowered his voice, since a number were sitting near — "I didn't know, but —" He hesitated.

"That the spark that would fire the mine might be in that pretty little beribboned roll of foolscap," said Risley, laughing. "Well, it was a very creditable production, and it was written with the energy of conviction. The Czar and that little schoolgirl would not live long in one country, if she goes on as she has begun."

It was then that young Lloyd, who had just come in, and was standing beside the school-master, turned eagerly to him, and asked who the girl was, and begged him to present him.

"Perhaps he'll fall in love with her," said Mrs. Norman, directly, when the two men had gone across the hall in quest of Ellen. Her husband laughed.

"You have not seen your aunt for a long time," Ellen said to young Lloyd, when they were sitting out a dance after their waltz together.

"Not since — I — I came on — with my father when he died," he replied. Again Ellen looked at him with that wonderful pity in her face, and again the young man thought he had never seen such a girl.

"I think your aunt is beautiful," Ellen said, presently, gazing across at Cynthia.

"Yes, she must have been a beauty when she was young."

"I think she is now," said Ellen, quite fervently, for she was able to disabuse her mind of associations and rely upon pure observation, and it was quite true that leaving out of the question Cynthia's age and the memory of her face in stronger lights at closer view, she was as beautiful from where they sat as some graceful statue. Only clear outlines showed at that distance, and her soft hair, which was quite white, lay in heavy masses around the intense repose of her face.

"Yes — s," admitted Robert, somewhat hesitatingly. "She used to think everything of me when I was a little shaver," he said.

"Doesn't she now?"

"Oh yes, I suppose she does, but it is different now. I am grown up. A man doesn't need so much done for him when he is grown up."

Then again he looked at Ellen with eyes of pleading which would have made of the older woman what he remembered her to have been in his childhood, and hers answered again.

Robert did not say anything to her about the valedictory until just before the close of the evening, when their last dance together was over.

"I am sorry I did not have a chance to hear your valedictory," he said. "I could not come early."

Ellen blushed and smiled, and made the conventional schoolgirl response. "Oh, you didn't miss anything," said she.

"I am sure I did," said the young man, earnestly. Then he looked at her and hesitated a little. "I wonder if you would be willing to lend it to me?" he said, then. "I would be very careful of it, and would return it immediately as soon as I had read it. I should be so interested in reading it."

"Certainly, if you wish," said Ellen, "but I am afraid you won't think it is good."

"Of course I shall. I have been hearing about it, how good it was, and how you broke up the whole house."

Ellen blushed. "Oh, that was only because it was the valedictory. They always clap a good deal for the valedictory."

"It was because it was you, you dear beauty," thought the young man, gazing at her, and the impulse to take her in his arms and kiss that blush seized upon him. "I know they applauded your valedictory because it was worthy of it," said he, and Ellen's eyes fell before his, and the blush crept down over her throat, and up to the soft toss of hair on her temples. The two were standing, and the man gazed at Ellen's pink arms and neck through the lace of her dress, those incomparable curves of youthful bloom shared by a young girl and a rose; he gazed at that noble, fair head bent not so much before him as before the mystery of life, of which a perception had come to her through his eyes, and he said to himself that there never was such a girl, and he also wondered if he saw aright, he being one who seldom entirely lost the grasp of his own leash. Having the fancy and the heart of a young man, he was given like others of his kind to looking at every new girl who attracted him in the light of a problem, the unknown quantity being her possible interest for him, but he always worked it out calmly. He kept himself out of his own shadow, when it came to the question of emotions, in something the same fashion that his uncle Norman did. Now, looking at Ellen Brewster with the whole of his heart setting towards her in obedience to that law which had brought him into being, he yet was saying quite coolly and loudly in his own inner consciousness, "Wait, wait, wait! Wait until tomorrow, see how you feel then. You have felt in much this way before. Wait! Perhaps you don't see it as it is. Wait!"

He realized his own wisdom all the more clearly when Ellen led him to the settee where her relatives sat guarding her graduation presents and her precious valedictory. She presented him gracefully enough. Ellen knew nothing of society etiquette, she had never introduced such a young gentleman as this to anyone in her life, but her inborn dignity of character kept her self-poise perfect. Still, when young Lloyd saw the mother coarsely perspiring and fairly aggressive in her delight over her daughter, when poor Andrew hoped he saw him well, and Mrs. Zelotes eyed him with sharp approbation, and Eva, conscious of her shabbiness, bowed with a stiff toss of her head and sat back sullenly, and little Amabel surveyed him with uncanny wisdom divided between himself and Ellen, he became conscious of a slight disappearance of his glamour. He thanked Ellen most heartily for the privilege which she granted him, when she took the valedictory from the heap of flowers, and took his leave with a bow which made Fanny nudge Andrew, almost before the young man's back was turned.

Then she looked at Ellen, but she said nothing. A sudden impulse of delicacy prevented her. There was something about this beloved daughter of hers which all at once seemed strange to her. She began to associate her with the sacred mystery of life as she had never done. Then, too, there was the more superficial association with one of another class which she held in outward despite but inward awe.

Ellen gathered up her presents into her lap, and sat there a few minutes through the last dance, which she had refused to Granville Joy, who went away with nervous alertness for another girl, and nobody spoke to her.

When young Lloyd and Cynthia Lennox and the others left, as they did directly, Fanny murmured, "They've gone," and they all knew what she meant. She was thinking — and so were they all, except Ellen — that that was the reason, because he had to go, that he had not asked Ellen for the last dance.

As for Ellen, she sat looking at her gold watch and chain, which she had taken out of the case. Her face grew intensely sober, and she did not notice when young Lloyd left. All at once she had reflected how her father had never owned a watch in his whole life, though he was a man, but he had given one to her. She reflected how he had so little work, how shabby his clothes were, how he must have gone without himself to buy this for her, and the girl had such a heart of gold that it rose triumphantly loyal to its first loves and tendernesses, and her father's old, worn face came between her and that of the young man who might become her lover.

Chapter XIX

*T*he day after Ellen's graduation there might have been seen a touching little spectacle passing along the main street of Rowe about ten o'clock in the fore-noon. It was touching because it gave evidence of that human vanity common to all, which strives to perpetuate the few small, good things that come into the hard lives of poor souls, and strives with such utter futility. Ellen held up her fluffy skirts daintily, the wind caught her white ribbons and the loose locks of her yellow hair under her white hat. She carried Cynthia Lennox's basket of roses on her arm, and each of the others was laden with bouquets. Little Amabel clasped both slender arms around a great sheaf of roses; the thorns pricked through her thin sleeves, but she did not mind that, so upborne with the elation of the occasion was she. Her small, pale face gazed over the mass of bloom with challenging of admiration from everyone whom she met. She was jealous lest anyone should not look with full appreciation of Ellen.

Ellen was the one in the little procession who had not unmixed delight in it. She had a certain shamefacedness about going through the streets in such a fashion. She avoided looking at the people whom she met, and kept her head slightly bent and averted, instead of carrying it with the proud directness which was her habit. She felt vaguely that this was the element of purely personal vanity which degrades a triumph, and the weakness of delight and gloating in the faces of her relatives irritated her. It was a sort of unveiling of love, and the girl was sensitive enough to understand it. "Oh, mother, I don't want to have us all go through the street with all these flowers, and me in my white dress," she had said. She had looked at her mother with a shrinking in her eyes which was incomprehensible to the other coarser-natured woman.

"Nonsense," she had said. "Sometimes you have real silly notions, Ellen." Fanny said it adoringly, for even silliness in this girl was in a way worshipful to her. Ellen, with her heart still softened almost to grief by the love shown her on the day before, had yielded, but she was glad when they arrived at the photograph studio. She had particularly dreaded passing Lloyd's, for the thought came to her that possibly young Mr. Lloyd might see her. She supposed that he was likely to be in the office. When they passed the office-windows she looked the other way, but before she was well past, her aunt Eva hit her violently and laughed loudly. Ellen shrank, coloring a deep crimson. Then her mother also laughed, and even Amabel, shrilly, with precocious recognition of the situation. Only Mrs. Zelotes stalked along in silent dignity.

"Don't laugh so loud, he'll hear you," said she, severely.

"It was that young man who was at the hall last night, and he was looking at you awful sharp," said little Amabel to Ellen, squeezing her warm arm, and sending out that shrill peal of laughter again.

"Don't, dear," said Ellen. She felt humiliated, and the more so because she was ashamed of being humiliated by her own mother and aunt. "Why should I be so sensitive to things in which they see no harm?" she asked herself, reprovingly.

As for young Lloyd, he had, ever since he parted with the girl the night before, that sensation of actual contact which survives separation, and had felt the light pressure of her hand in his all night, and along with it that ineffable pain of longing which would draw the substance of a dream to actuality and cannot. He saw her with her coarsely exultant relatives, the inevitable blur of her environments, and felt himself not so much disillusioned as confirmed. He had been constantly saying to himself, when the girl's face haunted his eyes, and her hand in his own, that he was a fool, that he had felt so before, that he must have, that there was no sense in it, that he was Robert Lloyd, and she a good girl, a beautiful girl, but a common sort of girl, born of common people to a common lot. "Now," he said to himself, with a kind of bitter exultation, "there, I told you so." The inconceivable folly of that glance of the mother at him, then at Ellen, and the meaning laughter, repelled him to the point of disgust. He turned his back to the window and resumed his work, but, in spite of himself, the pathos of the picture which he had seen began to force itself upon him, and he thought almost tenderly and forgivingly that she, the girl, had not once looked his way. He even wondered, pityingly, if she had been mortified and annoyed by her mother's behavior. A great anger on Ellen's behalf with her mother seized upon him. How pretty she did look moving along in that little flower-laden procession, he thought, how very pretty. All at once a desire for the photograph which would be taken seized him, for he divined the photograph. However, he said to himself that he would send back the valedictory which he had not yet read by post, with a polite note, and that would be the end.

But it was only the next evening that Robert Lloyd with the valedictory in hand got off the trolley-car in front of the Brewster house. He had proved to himself that it was an act of actual rudeness to return anything so precious and of so much importance to the owner by the post, that he ought to call and deliver it in person. When he regained his equilibrium from the quick sidewise leap from the car, and stood hesitating a little, as one will do before a strange house, for he was not quite sure as to his bearings, he saw a white blur as of feminine apparel in the front doorway. He advanced tentatively up the little path between two rows of flowering bushes, and Ellen rose.

"Good-evening, Mr. Lloyd," she said, in a slightly tremulous voice.

"Oh, good-evening, Miss Brewster," he cried, quickly. "So I am right! I was not sure as to the house."

"People generally tell by the cherry trees in the yard," replied Ellen, taking refuge from her timidity in the security of commonplace observation, as she had done the night before, giving thereby both a sense of disappointment and elusiveness.

"Won't you walk in?" she added, with the prim politeness of a child who accosts a guest according to rule and precept. Ellen had never, in fact, had a young man make a formal call upon her before. She reflected now, both with relief and trepidation, that her mother was away, having gone to her aunt Eva's. She had an instinct which she resented, that her mother and this young man were on two parallels which could never meet. Her father was at home, seated in the south door with John Sargent and Nahum Beals and Joe Atkins, but she never thought of such a thing as her father's receiving a young man caller, though she would not have doubted so much his assimilating with Robert Lloyd. She understood that the young man might look at her mother with dissent, while she resented it, but with her father it was different.

The group of men at the south door were talking in loud, fervent voices which seemed to rise and fall like waves. Nahum Beals's strained, nervous tones were paramount. "Mr. Beals is talking about the labor question, and he gets quite excited," Ellen remarked, somewhat apologetically, as she ushered young Lloyd into the parlor.

Lloyd laughed. "It sounds as if he were leading an army," he said.

"He is very much in earnest," said the girl.

She placed painstakingly for her guest the best chair, which was a spring rocker upholstered with crush-plush. The little parlor was close and stuffy, and the kerosene-lamp, with the light dimmed by a globe decorated with roses, heated the room still further. This lamp was Fanny's pride. It had, in her eyes, the double glory of high art and cheapness. She was fond of pointing at it, and inquiring, "How much do you think that cost?" and explaining with the air of one who expects her truth to be questioned that it only cost forty-nine cents. This lamp was hideous, the shape was aggressive, a discordant blare of brass, and the roses on the globe were blasphemous. Somehow this lamp was the first thing which struck Lloyd on entering the room. He could not take his eyes from it. As for Ellen, long acquaintance had dulled her eyes. She sat in the full glare of this hideous lamp, and Lloyd considered that she was not so pretty as he had thought last night. Still, she was undeniably very pretty. There was something in the curves of her shoulders, in her pink-and-white cotton waist, that made one's fingers tingle, and heart yearn, and there was an appealing look in her face which made him smile indulgently at her as he might have done at a child. After all, it was probably not her fault about the lamp, and lamps were a minor consideration, and he was finical, but suppose she liked it? Lloyd, sitting there, began to speculate if it were possible for one's spiritual nature to be definitely damaged by hideous lamps. Then he caught sight of a plate decorated with postage-stamps, with a perforated edge through which ribbons were run, and he wondered if she possibly made that.

"They are undoubtedly perfectly moral people," he told his aunt Cynthia afterwards, "but I wonder that they keep such an immoral plate." However, that was before he fell in love with Ellen, while he was struggling with himself in his desire to do so, and making all manner of sport of himself by way of hindrance.

Ellen at that age could have had no possible conception of the sentiment with which the young man viewed her environment. She was sensitive to spiritual discords which might arise from meeting with another widely different nature, but when it came to material things, she was at a loss. Then, too, she was pugnaciously loyal to the glories of the best parlor. She was innocently glad that she had such a nice room into which to usher him. She felt that the marble-top table, the plush lambrequin on the mantle-shelf, the gilded vases, the brass clock, the Nottingham lace curtains, the olive-and-crimson furniture, the pictures in cheap gilt frames, the heavily gilded wall-paper, and the throws of thin silk over the picture corners must prove to him the standing of her family. She felt an ignoble satisfaction in it, for a certain measure of commonness clung to the girl like a cobweb. She was as yet too young to bloom free of her environment, her head was not yet over the barrier of her daily lot; her heart never would be, and that was her glory. Young Lloyd handed her the roll of valedictory as soon as he entered.

"I am very much obliged to you for allowing me to read it," he said.

Ellen took it, blushing. Her heart sank a little. She thought to herself that he probably did not like it. She looked at him proudly and timidly, like a child half holding, half withdrawing its hand for a sweet. It suddenly came to her that she would rather this young man would praise her valedictory than anyone else, that if he had been present when she read it in the hall, and she had seen him standing applauding, she could not have contained her triumph and pride. She was not yet in love with him, but she began to feel that in his approbation lay the best coin of her realm.

"It is very well written, Miss Brewster," said Robert, and she flushed with delight.

"Thank you," she said.

But the young man was looking at her as if he had something besides praise in mind, and she gazed at him, shrinking a little as before a blow whose motion she felt in the air. However, he laughed pleasantly when he spoke.

"Do you really believe that?" he asked.

"What?" she inquired, vaguely.

"Oh, all that you say in your essay. Do you really believe that all the property in the world ought to be divided, that kings and peasants ought to share and share alike?"

She looked at him with round eyes. "Why, of course I do!" she said. "Don't you?"

Robert laughed. He had no mind to enter into an argument with this beautiful girl, nor even to express himself forcibly on the opposite side.

"Well, there are a number of things to be considered," he said. "And do you really believe that employer and employés should share alike?"

"Why not?" said she.

Her blue eyes flashed, she tossed her head. Robert smiled at her.

"Why not?" she repeated. "Don't the men earn the money?"

"Well, no, not exactly," said Robert. "There is the capital."

"The profit comes from the labor, not from the capital," said Ellen, quickly. "Doesn't it?" she continued, with fervor, and yet there was a charming timidity, as before some authority.

"Possibly," replied Robert, guardedly; "but the question is how far we should go back before we stop in searching for causes."

"How far back ought we to go?" asked Ellen, earnestly.

"I confess I don't know," said Robert, laughingly. "I have thought very little about it all."

"But you will have to, if you are to be the head of Lloyd's," Ellen said, with a severe accent, with grave, blue eyes full on his face.

"Oh, I am not the head of Lloyd's yet," he answered, easily. "My uncle is far from his dotage. Then, too, you know that I was never intended for a business man, but a lawyer, like my father, if there had not been so little for my father's second wife and the children —" He stopped himself abruptly on the verge of a confidence. "I think I saw you on your way to the photographer today," he said, and Ellen blushed, remembering her aunt Eva's violent nudge, and wondering if he had noticed. She gave him a piteous glance.

"Yes," she said. "All the girls have their pictures taken in their graduating dresses with their flowers."

"You looked to me as if the picture would be a great success," said Robert. He longed to ask for one and yet did not, for a reason unexplained to himself. He knew that this innocent, unsophisticated creature would see no reason on earth why he should not ask, and no reason why she should not grant, and on that account he felt prohibited. That night, after he had gone, Ellen wondered why he had not asked for one of her pictures, and felt anxious lest he should have seen the nudge.

"Well," she said to herself, "if he finds any fault with anything that my mother has done, I don't want him to have one."

Robert stayed a long time. He kept thinking that he ought to go, and also that he was bored, and yet he felt a singular unwillingness to leave, possibly because of his sense that the visit was in a measure forbidden by prudence. The longer he remained, the prettier Ellen looked to him. New beauties of line and color seemed to grow apparent in the soft glow from the hideous lamp. There was a wonderful starry radiance in her eyes now and then, and when she turned her head her eyeballs gleamed crimson and her hair seemed to toss into flame. When she spoke, he was conscious of unknown depths of sweetness in her voice, and it was so with her smile and her every motion. There was about the girl a mystery, not of darkness but of light, which seemed to draw him on and on and on without volition. And yet she said nothing especially remarkable, for Ellen was only a young girl, reared in a little provincial city in common environments. She would have been a great genius had she more than begun to glimpse the breadth and freedom of the outer world through her paling of life. She was too young and too unquestioning of what she had learned from her early loves.

"Have you always lived here in Rowe?" asked Lloyd.

"Yes," said she. "I was born here, and I have lived here ever since."

"And you have never been away?"

"Only once. Once I went to Dragon Beach and stayed a fortnight with mother." She said this with a visible sense of its importance. Dragon Beach was some ten miles from Rowe, a cheap seashore place, built up with flimsy summer cottages of factory hands. Andrew had hired one for a fortnight once when Ellen was ailing, and it had been the event of a lifetime to the family. They hereafter dated from the year "we went to Dragon Beach."

Lloyd looked with a quick impulse of compassionate tenderness at this child who had been away from Rowe once to Dragon Beach. He had his own impressions of Dragon Beach and also of Rowe.

"I suppose you enjoyed that?" said he.

"Very much. The sea is beautiful."

So, after all, it was the sea which she had cared for at Dragon Beach, and not the clam-bakes and merry-go-rounds and women in wrappers in the surf. Robert felt rebuked for thinking of anything but the sea in his memory of Dragon Beach; there was a wonderful water-view there.

All the time they sat there in the parlor, the murmur of conversation at the south door continued, and now and again over it swelled the fervid exhortations of Nahum Beals. Not a word could be distinguished, but the meaning was beyond doubt. That voice was full of denunciation, of frenzied appeal, of warning.

"Who is it?" asked Lloyd, after an unusually loud burst.

"Mr. Beals," replied Ellen, uneasily. She wished that he would not talk so loud.

"He sounds as if he were preaching fire and brimstone," said Robert.

"No, he is talking about the labor question," replied Ellen.

Then she looked confused, for she remembered that this young man's uncle was the head of Lloyd's, that he himself would be the head of Lloyd's some day. All at once, along with another feeling which seemed about to conquer her, came a resentment against this young man with his fine clothes and his gentle manners. Two men passed the windows and one of them looked in, and when the electric-light flashed on his face she saw Granville Joy, and the man with him was in his shirt-sleeves. She saw those white shirt-sleeves swing into the darkness, and felt at once antagonized against herself and against Robert, and yet she knew that she had never seen a man like him.

"I suppose he has settled it," said Robert.

"I don't know," replied Ellen.

"He sounds dangerous."

"Oh, no. He is a good man. He wouldn't hurt anybody. He has always talked that way. He used to come here and talk when I was a child. It used to frighten me at first, but it doesn't now. It is only the way that poor people are treated that frightens me."

Again Robert had a sensation of moving unobtrusively aside from a direct encounter. He looked across the room and started at something which he espied for the first time.

"Pardon me," he said, rising, "but I am interested in dolls. I see you still keep your doll, Miss Brewster."

Ellen sat stupefied. All at once it dawned upon her what might happen. In the corner of the parlor sat her beloved doll, still beloved, though the mother and not the doll had outgrown her first condition of love. The doll, in the identical dress in which she had come from Cynthia's so many years ago, sat staring forth with the fixed radiance of her kind, seated stiffly in a tiny rocking-chair, also one of the treasures of Ellen's childhood. It was a curious feature for the best parlor, but Ellen had insisted upon it. "She isn't going to be put away up garret because I have outgrown her," said she. "She's going to sit in the parlor as long as she lives. Suppose I outgrew you, and put you up in the garret; you wouldn't like it, would you, mother?"

"You are a queer child," Fanny had said, laughing, but she had yielded.

When young Lloyd went close to examine the doll, Ellen's heart stood still. Suppose he should recognize it? She tried to tell herself that it was impossible. Could any young man recognize a doll after all those years? How much did a boy ever care for a doll, anyway? Not enough to think of it twice after he had given it up. It was different with a girl. Her doll meant — God only knew what her doll meant to her; perhaps it had a meaning of all humanity. But the boy, what had he cared for the doll? He had gone away out West and left it.

But Lloyd remembered. He stared down at the doll a moment. Then he took her up gingerly in her fluffy pink robes of an obsolete fashion. He held her at arm's length, and stared and stared. Suddenly he parted the flaxen wig and examined a place on the head. Then he looked at Ellen.

"Why, it is my old doll," he cried, with a great laugh of wonder and incredulity. "Yes, it is my old doll! How in the world did you come by my doll, Miss Brewster? Account for yourself. Are you a child kidnapper?"

Ellen, who had risen and come forward, stood before him, absolutely still, and very pale.

"Yes, it is my doll," said Lloyd, with another laugh. "I will tell you how I know. Of course I can tell her face. Dolls look a good deal alike, I suppose, but I tell you I loved this doll, and I remember her face, and that little cast in her left eye, and that beautiful, serene smile; but there's something besides. Once I burned her head with the red-hot end of the poker to see if she would wake up. I always had a notion when I was a child that it was only a question of violence to make her wake up and demonstrate some existence besides that eternal grin. So I burned her, but it made no difference; but here is the mark now — see."

Ellen saw. She had often kissed it, but she made no reply. She was occupied with considerations of the consequences.

"How did you come by her, if you don't mind telling?" said the young man again. "It is the most curious thing for me to find my old doll sitting here. Of course Aunt Cynthia gave her to you, but I didn't know that she was acquainted with you. I suppose she saw a pretty little girl getting around without a doll after I had gone, and sent her, but —"

Suddenly between the young man's face and the girl's flashed a look of intelligence. Suddenly Robert remembered all that he had heard of Ellen's childish escapade. He *knew*. He looked from her to the doll, and back again. "Good Lord!" he said. Then he set the doll down in her little chair all of a heap, and caught Ellen's hand, and shook it.

"You are a trump, that is what you are," he said; "a trump. So she —" He shook his head, and looked at Ellen, dazedly. She did not say a word, but looked at him with her lips closed tightly.

"It is better for you not to tell me anything," he said; "I don't want to know. I don't understand, and I never want to, how it all happened, but I do understand that you are a trump. How old were you?" Robert's voice took on a tone of tenderness.

"Eight," replied Ellen, faintly.

"Only a baby," said the young man, "and you never told! I would like to know where there is another baby who would do such a thing." He caught her hand and shook it again. "She was like a mother to me," he said, in a husky voice. "I think a good deal of her. I thank you."

Suddenly to the young man looking at the girl a conviction as of some subtle spiritual perfume came; he had seen her beauty before, he had realized her charm, but this was something different. A boundless approbation and approval which was infinitely more precious than admiration seized him. Her character began to reveal itself, to come in contact with his own; he felt the warmth of it through the veil of flesh. He felt a sense of reliance as upon an inexhaustibility of goodness in another soul. He felt something which was more than love, being purely unselfish, with as yet no desire of possession. "Here is a good, true woman," he said to himself. "Here is a good, true woman, who has blossomed from a good, true child." He saw a wonderful faithfulness shining in her blue eyes, he saw truth itself on her lips, and could have gone down at the feet of the little girl in the pink cotton frock. Going home he tried to laugh at himself, but could not succeed. It is easy to shake off the clasp of a hand of flesh, but not the clasp of another soul.

Ellen on her part was at once overwhelmed with delight and confusion. She felt the fervor of admiration in the young man's attitude towards her, but she was painfully conscious of her undeservingness. She had always felt guilty about her silence and disobedience towards her parents, and as for any self-approbation for it, that had been the farthest from her thoughts. She murmured something deprecatingly, but Lloyd cut her short.

"It's no use crying off," said he; "you are one girl in a thousand, and I thank you, I thank you from the bottom of my heart. It might have made awful trouble. My aunt Lizzie told me what a commotion there was over it."

"I ran away," said Ellen, anxiously. Suddenly it occurred to her he might think Cynthia worse than she had been.

"Never mind," said Lloyd — "never mind. I know what you did. You held your blessed little tongue to save somebody else, and let yourself be blamed."

The door which led into the sitting room opened, and Andrew looked in.

He made a shy motion when he saw Lloyd; still, he came forward. His own callers had gone, and he had heard voices in the parlor, and had feared Granville Joy was calling upon Ellen.

As he came forward, Ellen introduced him shyly. "This is Mr. Lloyd, father," she said. "Mr. Lloyd, this is my father." Then she added, "He came to bring back my valedictory." She was very awkward, but it was the charming awkwardness of a beautiful child. She looked exceedingly childish standing beside her father, looking into his worn, embarrassed face.

Lloyd shook hands with Andrew, and said something about the valedictory, which he had enjoyed reading.

"She wrote it all herself without a bit of help from the teacher," said Andrew, with wistful pride.

"It is remarkably well written," said Robert.

"You didn't hear it read at the hall?" said Andrew.

"No, I had not that good fortune."

"You ought to have heard them clap," said Andrew.

"Oh, father," murmured Ellen, but she looked innocently at her father as if she delighted in his pride and pleasure without a personal consideration.

The front door opened. "That's your mother," said Andrew.

Fanny looked into the lighted parlor, and dodged back with a little giggle.

Ellen colored painfully. "It is Mr. Lloyd, mother," she said.

Then Fanny came forward and shook hands with Robert. Her face was flaming — she cast involuntary glances at Andrew for confirmation of her opinion. She was openly and shamelessly triumphant, and yet all at once Robert ceased to be repelled by it. Through his insight into the girl's character, he had seemed to gain suddenly a clearer vision for the depths of human love and pity which are beneath the coarse and the common. When Fanny stood beside her daughter and looked at her, then at Robert, with the reflection of the beautiful young face in her eyes of love, she became at once pathetic and sacred.

"It is all natural," he said to himself as he was going home.

Chapter XX

Robert Lloyd when he came to Rowe was confronted with one of the hardest tasks in the world, that of adjustment to circumstances which had hitherto been out of his imagination. He had not dreamed of a business life in connection with himself. Though he had always had a certain admiration for his successful uncle, Norman Lloyd, yet he had always had along with the admiration a recollection of the old tale of the birthright and the mess of pottage. He had expected to follow the law, like his father, but when he had finished college, about two years after his father's death, he had to face the unexpected. The stocks in which the greater part of the elder Lloyd's money had been invested had depreciated; some of them were for the time being quite worthless as far as income was concerned. There were two little children — girls — by his father's second marriage, and there was not enough to support them and their mother and allow Robert to continue his reading for the law. So he pursued, without the slightest hesitation, but with bitter regret, the only course which he saw open before him. He wrote to his uncle Norman, and was welcomed to a position in his factory with more warmth than he had ever seen displayed by him. In fact, Norman Lloyd, who had no son of his own, saw with a quickening of his pulses the handsome young fellow of his own race who had in a measure thrown himself upon his protection. He had never shared his wife's longing for children as children, and had never cared for Robert when a child; but now, when he was a man grown and bore his name, he appealed to him.

Norman Lloyd was supposed to be heaping up riches, and wild stories of his wealth were told in Rowe. He gave large sums to public benefactions, and never stinted his wife in her giving within certain limits. It would have puzzled anyone when faced with facts to understand why he had the name of a hard man, but he had it, whether justly or not. "He's as hard as nails," people said. His employés hated him — that is, the more turbulent and undisciplined spirits hated him, and the others regarded him as slaves might a stern master. When Robert started his work in his uncle's office he started handicapped by this sentiment towards his uncle. He looked like his uncle, he talked like him, he had his same gentle stiffness, he was never unduly familiar. He was at once placed in the same category by the workmen.

Robert Lloyd did not concern himself in the least as to what the employés in his uncle's factory thought of him. Nothing was more completely out of his mind. He was conscious of standing on a firm base of philanthropic principle, and if ever these men came directly under his control, he was resolved to do his duty by them so far as in him lay.

*E*llen, since her graduation, had been like an animal which circles about in its endeavors to find its best and natural place of settlement.

"What shall I do next?" she had said to her mother. "Shall I go to work, or shall I try to find a school somewhere in the fall, or shall I stay here, and help you with some work I can do at home? I know father cannot afford to support me always at home."

"I guess he can afford to support his only daughter at home a little while after she has just got out of school," Fanny had returned indignantly, with a keen pain at her heart.

Fanny mentioned this conversation to Andrew that night after Ellen had gone to bed.

"What do you think — Ellen was asking me this afternoon what she had better do!" said she.

"What she had better do?" repeated Andrew, vaguely. He looked shrinkingly at Fanny, who seemed to him to have an accusing air, as if in some way he were to blame for something. And, indeed, there were times when Fanny in those days did blame Andrew, but there was some excuse for her. She blamed him when her own back was filling her very soul with the weariness of its ache as she bent over the seams of those grinding wrappers, and when her heart was sore over doubt of Ellen's future. At those times she acknowledged to herself that it seemed to her that Andrew somehow might have gotten on better. She did not know how, but somehow. He had not had an expensive family. "Why had he not succeeded?" she asked herself. So there was in her tone an unconscious recrimination when she answered his question about Ellen.

"Yes — what she had better go to work at," said Fanny, dryly, her black eyes cold on her husband's face.

Andrew turned so white that he frightened her. "Go to work!" said he. Then all at once he gave an exceedingly loud and bitter groan. It betrayed all his pride in and ambition for his daughter and his disgust and disappointment over himself. "Oh! my God, has it come to this," he groaned, "that I cannot support my one child!"

Fanny laid down her work and looked at him. "Now, Andrew," said she, "there's no use in your taking it after such a fashion as this. I told Ellen that it was all nonsense — that she could stay at home and rest this summer."

"I guess, if she can't —" said Andrew. He dropped his grey head into his hands, and began to sob dryly. Fanny, after staring at him a moment, tossed her work onto the floor, went over to him, and drew his head to her shoulder.

"There, old man," said she, "ain't you ashamed of yourself? I told her there was no need for her to worry at present. Don't do so, Andrew; you've done the best you could, and I know it, if I stop to think, though I do seem sort of impatient sometimes. You've always worked hard and done your best. It ain't your fault."

"I don't know whether it is or not," said Andrew, in a high, querulous voice like a woman's. "It seems as if it must be somebody's fault. If it ain't my fault, whose is it? You can't blame the Almighty."

"Maybe it ain't anybody's fault."

"It must be. All that goes wrong is somebody's fault. It can't be that it just happens — that would be worse than the other. It is better to have a God that is cruel than one that don't care, and it is better to be to blame yourself, and have it your fault, than His. Somehow, I have been to blame, Fanny. I must have. It would have been enough sight better for you, Fanny, if you'd married another man."

"I didn't want another man," replied Fanny, half angrily, half tenderly. "You make me all out of patience, Andrew Brewster. What's the need of Ellen going to work right away? Maybe by-and-by she can get an easy school. Then, we've got that money in the bank."

Andrew looked away from her with his face set. Fanny did not know yet about his withdrawal of the money for the purpose of investing in mining-stocks. He never looked at her but the guilty secret seemed to force itself between them like a wedge of ice.

"Then Grandma Brewster has got a little something," said Fanny.

"Only just enough for herself," said Andrew. Then he added, fiercely, "Mother can't be stinted of her little comforts even for Ellen."

"I ain't never wanted to stint your mother of her comforts," Fanny retorted, angrily.

"She ain't got but a precious little, unless she spends her principal," said Andrew. "She ain't got more'n a hundred and fifty or so a year clear after her taxes and insurance are paid."

"I ain't saying anything," said Fanny. "But I do say you're dreadful foolish to take on so when you've got so much to fall back on, and that money in the bank. Here you haven't had to touch the interest for quite a while and it has been accumulating."

It was agreed between the two that Ellen must say nothing to her grandmother Brewster about going to work.

"I believe the old lady would have a fit if she thought Ellen was going to work," said Fanny. "She ain't never thought she ought to lift her finger."

So Ellen was charged on no account to say anything to her grandmother about the possible necessity of her going to work.

"Your grandmother's awful proud," said Fanny, "and she's always thought you were too good to work."

"I don't think anybody is too good to work," replied Ellen, but she uttered the platitude with a sort of mental reservation. In spite of herself, the attitude of worship in which she had always seen all who belonged to her had spoiled her a little. She did look at herself with a sort of compunction when she realized the fact that she might have to go to work in the shop some time. School-teaching was different, but could she earn enough school-teaching? There was a sturdy vein in the girl. All the time she pitied herself she blamed herself.

"You come of working-people, Ellen Brewster. Why are you any better than they? Why are your hands any better than their hands, your brain than theirs? Why are you any better than the other girls who have gone to work in the shops? Do you think you are any better than Abby Atkins?"

And still Ellen used to look at herself with a pitying conviction that she would be out of place at a bench in the shoe-factory, that she would suffer a certain indignity by such a course. The realization of a better birthright was strong upon her, although she chided herself for it. And everybody abetted her in it. When she said once to Abby Atkins, whom she encountered one day going home from the shop, that she wondered if she could get a job in her room in the fall, Abby turned upon her fiercely.

"Good Lord, Ellen Brewster, you ain't going to work in a shoe-shop?" she said.

"I don't see why not as well as you," returned Ellen.

"Why not?" repeated the other girl. "Look at yourself, and look at us!"

As she spoke, Ellen saw projected upon her mental vision herself passing down the street with the throng of factory operatives which her bodily eyes actually witnessed. She had come opposite Lloyd's as the six o'clock whistle was blowing. She saw herself in her clean, light summer frock, slight and dainty, with little hands like white flowers in the blue folds of her skirt, with her fine, sensitive outlook of fair face, and her dainty carriage; and she saw others — those girls and women in dingy skirts and bagging blouses, with coarse hair strained into hard knots of exigency from patient, or sullen faces, according to their methods of bearing their lots; all of them rank with the smell of leather, their coarse hands stained with it, swinging their poor little worn bags which had held their dinners. There were not many foreigners among them, except the Irish, most of whom had been born in this country, and a sprinkling of fair-haired, ruddy Swedes and keen Polanders, who bore themselves better than the Americans, being not so apparently at odds with the situation.

The factory employés in Rowe were a superior lot, men and women. Many of the men had put on their worn coats when they emerged from the factory, and their little bags were supposed to disguise the fact of their being dinner satchels. And yet there was a difference between Ellen Brewster and the people among whom she walked, and she felt it with a sort of pride and indignation with herself that it was so.

"I don't see why I should be any better than the rest," said she, defiantly, to Abby Atkins. "My father works in a shop, and you are my best friend, and you do. Why shouldn't I work in a shop?"

"Look at yourself," repeated the other girl, mercilessly. "You are different. You ain't to blame for it anymore than a flower is to blame for being a rose and not a common burdock. If you've got to do anything, you had better teach school."

"I would rather teach school," said Ellen, "but I couldn't earn so much unless I got more education and got a higher position than a district school, and that is out of the question."

"I thought maybe your grandmother could send you," said Abby.

"Oh no, grandma can't afford to. Sometimes I think I could work my own way through college, if it wasn't for being a burden in the meantime, but I don't know."

Suddenly Abby Atkins planted herself on the sidewalk in front of Ellen, and looked at her sharply, while an angry flush overspread her face.

"I want to know one thing," said she.

"What?"

"It ain't true what I heard the other day, is it?"

"I don't know what you heard."

"Well, I heard you were going to be married."

Ellen turned quite pale, and looked at the other girl with a steady regard of grave, indignant blue eyes.

"No, I am not," said she.

"Well, don't be mad, Ellen. I heard real straight that you were going to marry Granville Joy in the fall."

"Well, I am not," repeated Ellen.

"I didn't suppose you were, but I knew he had always wanted you."

"Always wanted me!" said Ellen. "Why, he's only just out of school!"

"Oh, I know that, and he's only just gone to work, and he can't be earning much, but I heard it."

The stream of factory operatives had thinned; many had taken the trolley-cars, and others had gone to the opposite side of the street, which was shady. The two girls were alone, standing before a vacant lot grown to weeds, rank bristles of burdock, and slender spikes of evanescent succory. Abby burst out in a passionate appeal, clutching Ellen's arm hard.

"Ellen, promise me you never will," she cried.

"Promise you what, Abby?"

"Oh, promise me you never will marry anybody like him. I know it's none of my business — I know that is something that is none of anybody's business, no matter how much they think of anybody; but I think more of you than any man ever will, I don't care who he is. I know I do, Ellen Brewster. And don't you ever marry a man like Granville Joy, just an ordinary man who works in the shop, and will never do anything but work in the shop. I know he's good, real good and steady, and it ain't against him that he ain't rich and has to work for his living, but I tell you, Ellen Brewster, you ain't the right sort to

marry a man like that, and have a lot of children to work in shops. No
man, if he thinks anything of you, ought to ask you to; but all a man
thinks of is himself. Granville Joy, or any other man who wanted you,
would take you and spoil you, and think he'd done a smart thing." Abby
spoke with such intensity that it redeemed her from coarseness. Ellen
continued to look at her, and two red spots had come on her cheeks.

"I don't believe I'll ever get married at all," she said.

"If you've got to get married, you ought to marry somebody like
young Mr. Lloyd," said Abby.

Then Ellen blushed, and pushed past her indignantly.

"Young Mr. Lloyd!" said she. "I don't want him, and he doesn't want
me. I wish you wouldn't talk so, Abby."

"He would want you if your were a rich girl, and your father was boss
instead of a workman," said Abby.

Then she caught hold of Ellen's arm and pressed her own thin one
in its dark-blue cotton sleeve lovingly against it.

"You ain't mad with me, are you, Ellen?" she said, with that indescribable gentleness tempering her fierceness of nature which gave her caresses the fascination of some little, untamed animal. Ellen pressed her
round young arm tenderly against the other.

"I think more of you than any man I know," said she, fervently. "I
think more of you than anybody except father and mother, Abby."

The two girls walked on with locked arms, and each was possessed
with that wholly artless and ignorant passion often seen between two
young girls. Abby felt Ellen's warm round arm against hers with a
throbbing of rapture, and glanced at her fair face with adoration. She
held her in a sort of worship, she loved her so that she was fairly afraid
of her. As for Ellen, Abby's little, leather-stained, leather-scented figure,
strung with passion like a bundle of electric wire, pressing against her,
seemed to inform her farthest thoughts.

"If I live longer than my father and mother, we'll live together, Abby,"
said she.

"And I'll work for you, Ellen," said Abby, rapturously.

"I guess you won't do all the work," said Ellen. She gazed tenderly
into Abby's little, dark, thin face. "You're all worn out with work now,"
said she, "and there you bought that beautiful pin for me with your
hard earnings."

"I wish it had been a great deal better," said Abby, fervently.

She had given Ellen a gold brooch for a graduating-gift, and had paid
a week's wages for it, and gone without her new dress, and stayed away
from the graduation, but that last Ellen never knew; Abby had told her
that she was sick.

*T*hat evening Robert Lloyd and his aunt Cynthia Lennox called on the Brewsters. Ellen was under the trees in the west yard when she heard a carriage stop in front of the house and saw the sitting room lamp travel through the front entry to the front door. She wondered indifferently who it was. Carriages were not given to stopping at their house of an evening; then she reflected that it might be someone to get her mother to do some sewing, and remained still.

It was a bright moonlight night; the whole yard was a lovely dapple of lights and shadows. Ellen had a vivid perception of the beauty of it all, and also that unrest and yearning which comes often to a young girl in moonlight. This beauty and strangeness of familiar scenes under the silver glamour of the moon gave her, as it were, an assurance of other delights and beauties of life besides those which she already knew, and along with the assurance came that wild yearning. Ellen seemed to scent her honey of life, and at the same time the hunger for it leaped to her consciousness. She had begun by thinking of what Abby had said to her that afternoon, and then the train of thought led her on and on. She quite ignored all about the sordid ways and means of existence, about toil and privation and children born to it. All at once the conviction was strong upon her that love, and love alone, was the chief end and purpose of life, at once its source and its result, the completion of its golden ring of glory. Her thought, started in whatever direction, seemed to slide always into that one all-comprehending circle — she could not get her imagination away from it. She began to realize that the mind of mortal man could not get away from the law which produced it. She began to understand dimly, as one begins to understand any great truth, that everything around her obeyed that unwritten fundamental law of love, expressed it, sounded it, down to the leaves of the trees casting their flickering shadows on the silver field of moonlight, and the long-drawn chorus of the insects of the summer night. She thought of Abby and how much she loved her; then that love seemed the step which gave her an impetus to another love. She began to remember Granville Joy, how he had kissed her that night over the fence and twice since, how he had walked home with her from entertainments, how he had looked at her. She saw the boy's face and his look as plain as if he stood before her, and her heart leaped with a shock of pain which was joy.

Then she thought of Robert Lloyd, and his face came before her. Ellen had not thought as much of Robert as he of her. For some two weeks after his call she had watched for him to come again; she had put on a pretty dress and been particular about her hair, and had stayed at home expecting him; then when he had not come, she had put him out of mind resolutely. When her mother and aunt had joked her about him she had been sensitive and half angry. "You know it is nothing, mother," she said; "he only came to bring back my valedictory. You know he wouldn't think of me. He'll marry somebody like Maud Hemingway." Maud Hemingway was the daughter of the leading physician in Rowe, and regarded with a mixture of spite and admiration by daughters of the factory operatives. Maud Hemingway was attending college, and rode a saddle-horse when home on her vacations. She had been to Europe.

But that evening in the moonlight Ellen began thinking again of Robert Lloyd. His face came before her as plainly as Granville Joy's. She had arrived at that stage when life began to be as a picture-gallery of love. Through this and that face the goddess might look, and the look was what she sought; as yet, the man was a minor quantity.

All at once it seemed to Ellen, looking at her mental picture of young Lloyd, that she could see love in his face yet more plainly, more according to her conception of it, than in the other. She began to build an air-castle which had no reference whatever to Robert's position, and to his being the nephew of the richest factory-owner in Rowe, and so far as that went he had not a whit the advantage of Granville Joy in her eyes. But Robert's face wore to her more of the guise of that for which the night and the moonlight, and her youth, had made her long. So she began innocently to imagine a meeting with him at a picnic which would be held some time at Liberty Park. She imagined their walking side by side, through a lovely dapple of moonlight like this, and saying things to each other. Then all at once the man of her dreams touched her hand in a dream, and a faintness swept over her. Then suddenly, gathering shape out of the indetermination of the shadows and the moonlight, came a man into the yard, and Ellen thought with awe and delight that it was he; but instead Granville Joy stood before her, lifting his hat above his soft shock of hair.

"Hullo!" he said.

"Good-evening," responded Ellen, and Granville Joy felt abashed. He lay awake half the night reflecting that he should have greeted her with a "Good-evening" instead of "Hullo," as he had been used to do in their school-days; that she was now a young lady, and that Mr. Lloyd had accosted her differently. Ellen rose with a feeling of disappointment that Granville was himself, which is the hardest greeting possible for a guest, involving the most subtle reproach in the world — the reproach for a man's own individuality.

"Oh, don't get up, Ellen," the young man said, awkwardly. "Here — I'll sit down here on the rock." Then he flung himself down on the ledge of rock which cropped out like a bare rib of the earth between the trees, and Ellen seated herself again in her chair.

"Beautiful night, ain't it?" said Granville.

Ellen noticed that Granville said "ain't" instead of "isn't," according to the fashion of his own family, although he was recently graduated from the high-school. Ellen had separated herself, although with no disparaging reflections, from the language of her family. She also noticed that Granville presently said "wa'n't" instead of "wasn't." "Hot yesterday, wa'n't it?" said he.

"Yes, it was very warm," replied Ellen. That "wa'n't" seemed to insert a tiny wedge between them. She would have flown at anyone who had found fault with her father and mother for saying "wa'n't," but with this young man in her own rank and day it was different. It argued something in him, or a lack of something. An indignation all out of proportion to the offence seized her. It seemed to her that he had in this simple fashion outraged that which was infinitely higher than he himself. He had not lived up to her thought of him, and fallen short by a little slip in English which argued a slip in character. She wanted to reproach him sharply — to ask him if he had ever been to school.

He noticed her manner was cool, and was as far as the antipodes from suspecting the cause. He never knew that he said "ain't" and "wa'n't," and would die not knowing. All that he looked at was the substance of thought behind the speech. And just then he was farther than ever from thinking of it, for he was single-hearted with Ellen.

The boy crept nearer her on the rock with a shy, nestling motion; the moonlight shone full on his handsome young face, giving it a stern quality. "Ellen, look at here," he said.

Then he stopped. Ellen waited, not dreaming what was to follow. She had never had a proposal; then, too, he had just been chased out of her mental perspective by the other man.

"Look at here, Ellen," said Granville. He stopped again; then when he spoke his voice had an indescribably solemn, beseeching quality. "Oh, Ellen," he said, reaching up and catching her hand. He dragged himself nearer, leaned his cheek against her hand, which it seemed to burn; then he began kissing it with soft, pouting lips.

Ellen tried to pull her hand away. "Let my hand go this minute, Granville Joy," she said, angrily.

The boy let her hand go immediately, and stood up, leaning over her.

"Don't be angry; I didn't mean any harm, Ellen," he whispered.

"I shall be angry if you do such a thing again," said Ellen. "We aren't children; you have no right to do such a thing, and you know it."

"But I thought maybe you wouldn't mind, Ellen," said Granville. Then he added, with his voice all husky with emotion and a kind of fear: "Ellen, you know how I feel about you. You know how I have always felt."

Ellen made no reply. It seemed inconceivable that she for the minute should not know his meaning, but she was bewildered.

"You know I've always counted on havin' you for my wife some day when we were both old enough," said the boy, "and I've gone to work now, and I hope to get bigger pay before long, and —"

Ellen rose with sudden realization. "Granville Joy," cried she, with something like panic in her voice, "you must not! Oh, if I had known! I would not have let you finish. I would not, Granville." She caught his arm, and clung to it, and looked up at him pitifully. "You know I wouldn't have let you finish," she said. "Don't be hurt, Granville."

The boy looked at her as if she had struck him.

"Oh, Ellen," he groaned. "Oh, Ellen, I always thought you would!"

"I am not going to marry anybody," said Ellen. Her voice wavered in spite of herself; the young man's look and voice were shaking her through weakness of her own nature which she did not understand, but which might be mightier than her strength. Something crept into her tone which emboldened the young man to seize her hand again. "You do, in spite of all you say —" he began; but just then a long shadow fell athwart the moonlight, and Ellen snatched her hand away imperceptibly, and young Lloyd stood before them.

Chapter XXI

Granville Joy was employed in Lloyd's, and Robert had seen him that very day and spoken to him, but he did not recognize him, not until Ellen spoke. "This is Mr. Joy, Mr. Lloyd," she said; "perhaps you know him. He works in your uncle's shop." She said it quite simply, as if it was a matter of course that Robert was on speaking terms with all the employés in his uncle's factory.

Granville colored. "I saw Mr. Lloyd this afternoon in the cutting-room," he said, "and we had some talk together; but maybe he don't remember, there are so many of us." Granville said "so many of us" with an indescribably bitter emphasis. Suddenly his gentleness seemed changed to gall. It was the terrible protest of one of the herd who goes along with the rest, yet realizes it, and looks ever out from his common mass with fierce eyes of individual dissent at the immutable conditions of things. Immediately, when Granville saw the other young man, this gentleman in his light summer clothes, who bore about him no stain nor odor of toil, he felt that here was Ellen's mate; that he was left behind. He looked at him, not missing a detail of his superiority, and he saw himself young and not ill-looking, but hopelessly common, clad in awkward clothes; he smelled the smell of leather that steamed up in his face from his raiment and his body; and he looked at Ellen, fair and white in her dainty muslin, and saw himself thrust aside, as it were, by his own judgment as to the fitness of things, but with no less bitterness. When he said "there are so many of us," he felt the impulse of revolution in his heart; that he would have liked to lead the "many of us" against this young aristocrat. But Robert smiled, though somewhat stiffly, and bowed. "I beg your pardon, Mr. Joy," he said; "I do remember, but for a minute I did not."

"I don't wonder," said Granville, and again he repeated, "There are so many of us," in that sullen, bitter tone.

"What is the matter with the fellow?" thought Robert; but he said, civilly enough; "Oh, not at all, Mr. Joy. I will admit there are a good many of you, as you say, but that would not prevent my remembering a man to whom I was speaking only a few hours ago. It was only the half-light, and I did not expect to see you here."

"Mr. Joy is a very old friend of mine," Ellen said, quickly, with a painful impulse of loyalty. The moment she saw her old school-boy lover intimidated, and manifestly at a disadvantage before this elegant young gentleman, she felt a fierce instinct of partisanship. She stood a little nearer to him. Granville's face lightened, he looked at her grate-fully, and Robert stared from one to the other doubtfully. He began to wonder if he had interrupted a love-scene, and was at once pained with a curious, new pain, and indignant. Then, too, he scarcely knew what to do. He had been sent to ask Ellen to come into the parlor.

"My aunt is in the house," he said.

"Your aunt?"

"Yes, my aunt, Miss Lennox."

Ellen gave a great start, and stared at him. "Does she want to see me?" she asked, abruptly.

Robert glanced at Granville. He was afraid of being rude towards this possible lover, but the young man was quick to perceive the situation.

"I guess I must be going," he said to Ellen.

"Must you hurry?" she returned, in the common, polite rejoinder of her class in Rowe.

"Yes, I guess I must," said Granville. He held out his hand towards Ellen, then drew it away, but she extended hers resolutely, and so forced his back again. "Good-night," she said, kindly, almost tenderly, and again Robert thought with that sinking at his heart that here was quite possibly the girl's lover, and all his dreams were thrown away.

As for Granville, he glowed with a sudden triumph over the other. Again he became almost sure that Ellen loved him after all, that it was only her maiden shyness which had led her to refuse him. He pressed her hand hard, and held it as long as he dared; then he turned to Robert. "I'll bid you good-evening, sir," he said, with awkward dignity, and was gone.

"I will go in and see your aunt," Ellen said to Robert, regarding him as she spoke with a startled expression. It had flashed through her mind that Miss Lennox had possibly come to confess the secret of so many years ago, and she shrank with terror as before the lowering of some storm of spirit. She knew how little was required to lash her mother's violent nature into fury. "She was not — ?" she began to say to Robert, then she stopped; but he understood. "Don't be afraid, Miss Brewster," he said, kindly. "It is not a matter of bygones, but the future. My aunt has a plan for you which I think you will like."

Ellen looked at him wonderingly, but she went with him across the moonlit yard into the house.

She found Miss Cynthia Lennox, fair and elegant in a filmy black gown, and a broad black hat draped with lace and violets shading her delicate, clear-cut face, and her father and mother. Fanny's eyes were red. She looked as if she had been running — in fact, one could easily hear her breathe across the room. "Ellen, here is Miss Lennox," she said. Ellen approached the lady, who rose, and the two shook hands. "Good-evening, Miss Brewster," said Cynthia, in the same tone which she might have used towards a society acquaintance. Ellen would never have known that she had heard the voice before. As she remembered it, it was full of intensest vibrations of maternal love and tenderness and protection beyond anything which she had ever heard in her own mother's voice. Now it was all gone, and also the old look from her eyes. Cynthia Lennox was, in fact, quite another woman to the young girl from what she had been to the child. In truth, she cared not one whit for Ellen, but she was possessed with a stern desire of atonement, and far stronger than her love was the appreciation of what that mother opposite must have suffered during that day and night when she had forcibly kept her treasure. The agony of that she could present to her consciousness very vividly, but she could not awaken the old love which had been the baby's for this young girl. Cynthia felt much more affection for Fanny than for Ellen. When she had unfolded her plan for sending Ellen to college, and Fanny had almost gone hysterical with delight, she found it almost impossible to keep her tears back. She knew so acutely how this other woman felt that she almost seemed to lose her own individuality. She began to be filled with a vicarious adoration of Ellen, which was, however, dissipated the moment she actually saw her. She realized that this grown-up girl, who could no longer be cuddled and cradled, was nothing to her, but her sympathy with the mother remained.

Ellen remained standing after she had greeted Cynthia. Robert went over to the mantle-piece and stood leaning against it. He was completely puzzled and disturbed by the whole affair. Ellen looked at Cynthia, then at her parents. "Ellen, come here, child," said her father, suddenly, and Ellen went over to him, sitting on the plush sofa beside her mother.

Andrew reached up and took hold of Ellen's hands, and drew her down on his knee as if she had been a child. "Ellen, look here," he said, in an intense, almost solemn voice, "father has got something to tell you."

Fanny began to weep almost aloud. Cynthia looked straight ahead, keeping her features still with an effort. Robert studied the carpet pattern.

"Look here, Ellen," said Andrew; "you know that father has always wanted to do everything for you, but he ain't able to do all he would like to. God hasn't prospered him, and it seems likely that he won't be able to do anymore than he has done, if so much, in the years to come. You know father has always wanted to send you to college, and give you an extra education so you could teach in a school where you would make a good living, and now here Miss Lennox says she heard your composition, and she has heard a good deal about you from Mr. Harris, how well you stood in the high-school, and she says she is willing to send you to Vassar College."

Ellen turned pale. She looked long at her father, whose pathetic, worn, half-triumphant, half-pitiful face was so near her own; then she looked at Cynthia, then back again. "To Vassar College?" she said.

"Yes, Ellen, to Vassar College, and she offers to clothe you while you are there, but we thank her, and tell her that ain't necessary. We can furnish your clothes."

"Yes, we can," said Fanny, in a sobbing voice, but with a flash of pride.

"Well, what do you say to it, Ellen?" asked Andrew, and he asked it with the expression of a martyr. At that moment indescribable pain was the uppermost sensation in his heart, over all his triumph and gladness for Ellen. First came the anticipated agony of parting with her for the greater part of four years, then the pain of letting another do for his daughter what he wished to do himself. No man would ever look in Ellen's eyes with greater love and greater shrinking from the pain which might come of love than Andrew at that moment.

"But —" said Ellen; then she stopped.

"What, Ellen?"

"Can you spare me for so long? Ought I not to be earning money before that, if you don't have much work?"

"I guess we can spare you as far as all that goes," cried Andrew. "I guess we can. I guess we don't want you to support us."

"I rather guess we don't," cried Fanny.

Ellen looked at her father a moment longer with an adorable look, which Robert saw with a sidewise glance of his downcast eyes, then at her mother. Then she slid from her father's knee and crossed the room and stood before Cynthia. "I don't know how to thank you enough," she said, "but I thank you very much, and not only for myself but for them"; she made a slight, graceful, backward motion of her shoulder towards her parents. "I will study hard and try to do you credit," said she. There was something about Ellen's direct, childlike way of looking at her, and her clear speech, which brought back to Cynthia the little girl of so many years ago. A warm flush came over her delicate cheeks; her eyes grew bright with tenderness.

"I have no doubt as to your doing your best, my dear," she said, "and it gives me great pleasure to do this for you."

With that, said with a graceful softness which was charming, she made as if to rise, but Ellen still stood before her. She had something more to say. "If ever I am able," she said — "and I shall be able some day if I have my health — I will repay you." Ellen spoke with the greatest sweetness, yet with an inflexibility of pride evident in her face. Cynthia smiled. "Very well," she said, "if you feel better to leave it in that way. If ever you are able you shall repay me; in the meantime I consider that I am amply paid in the pleasure it gives me to do it." Cynthia held out her slender hand to Ellen, who took it gratefully, yet a little constrainedly.

In the opposite corner the doll sat staring at them with eyes of blank blue and her vacuous smile. A vague sense of injury was over Ellen, in spite of her delight and her gratitude — a sense of injury which she could not fathom, and for which she chided herself. However, Andrew felt it also.

After this surprising benefactress and Robert had gone, after repeated courtesies and assurances of obligation on both sides, Andrew turned to Fanny. "What does she do it for?" he asked.

"Hush; she'll hear you."

"I can't help it. What does she do it for? Ellen isn't anything to her."

Fanny looked at him with a meaning smile and nod which made her tear-stained face fairly grotesque.

"What do you mean lookin' that way?" demanded Andrew.

"Oh, you wait and see," said Fanny, with meaning, and would say no more. She was firm in her conclusion that Cynthia was educating their girl to marry her favorite nephew, but that never occurred to Andrew. He continued to feel, while supremely grateful and overwhelmed with delight at this good fortune for Ellen, the distrust and resentment of a proud soul under obligation for which he sees no adequate reason, and especially when it is directed towards a beloved one to whom he would fain give of his own strength and treasure.

As for Ellen, she was in a tumult of wonder and delight, but when she looked at the doll in her corner there came again that vague sense of injury, and she felt again as if in some way she were being robbed instead of being made the object of benefit.

After Ellen had gone to bed that night she wondered if she ought to go to college, and maybe gain thereby a career which was beyond anything her own loved ones had known, and if it were not better for her to go to work in the shop after all.

Chapter XXII

When Mrs. Zelotes was made acquainted with the plan for sending Ellen to Vassar she astonished Fanny. Fanny ran over the next morning, after Andrew had gone to work, to tell her mother-in-law. She sat a few minutes in the sitting room, where the old lady was knitting, before she unfolded the burden of her errand.

"Cynthia Lennox came to our house last night with Robert Lloyd," she said, finally.

"Did they?" remarked Mrs. Zelotes, who had known perfectly well that they had come, having recognized the Lennox carriage in the moonlight, and having been ever since devoured with curiosity, which she would have died rather than betray.

"Yes, they did," said Fanny. Then she added, after a pause which gave wonderful impressiveness to the news, "Cynthia Lennox wants to send Ellen to college — to Vassar College."

Then she jumped, for the old woman seemed to spring at her like released wire.

"Send her to college!" said she. "What does she want to send her to college for? What right has Cynthia Lennox got to send Ellen Brewster anywhere?"

Fanny stared at her dazedly.

"What right has she got interfering?" demanded Mrs. Zelotes again.

"Why," replied Fanny, stammering, "she thought Ellen was so smart. She heard her valedictory, and the school-teacher had talked about her, what a good scholar she was, and she thought it would be nice for her to go to college, and she should be very much obliged herself, and feel that we were granting her a great pleasure and privilege if we allowed her to send Ellen to Vassar."

All unconsciously Fanny imitated to the life Cynthia's soft elegance of speech and language.

"Pshaw!" said Mrs. Zelotes; but still she said it not so much angrily as doubtfully. "It's the first time I ever heard of Cynthia Lennox doing such a thing as that," said she. "I never knew she was given to sending girls to college. I never heard of her giving anything to anybody."

Fanny looked mysteriously at her mother-in-law with sudden confidence. "Look here," she said.

"What?"

The two women looked at each other, and neither said a word, but the meaning of one flashed to the other like telegraphy.

"Do you s'pose that's it?" said Mrs. Zelotes, her old face relaxing into half-shamed, half-pleased smiles.

"Yes, I do," said Fanny, emphatically.

"You do?"

"Yes, I ain't a doubt of it."

"He did act as if he couldn't take his eyes off her at the exhibition," agreed Mrs. Zelotes, reflectively; "mebbe you're right."

"I know I'm right just as well as if I'd seen it."

"Well, mebbe you are. What does Andrew say?"

"Oh, he wishes he was the one to do it."

"Of course he does — he's a Brewster," said his mother.

"But he's got sense enough to be pleased that Ellen has got the chance."

"He ain't anymore pleased than I be at anything that's a good chance for Ellen," said the grandmother; but all the same, after Fanny had gone, her joy had a sharp sting for her. She was not one who could take a gift to heart without feeling its sharp edge.

Had Ellen's sentiment been analyzed, she felt in something the same way that her grandmother did. However, she had begun to dream definitely about Robert, and the reflection had come, too, that this might make her more his equal, as nearly his equal as Maud Hemingway.

Maud Hemingway went to college, and so would she. Of the minor accessories of wealth she thought not so much. She looked at her hands, which were very small and as delicately white as flowers, and reflected with a sense of comfort, of which she was ashamed, that she would not need ever to stain them with leather now. She looked at the homeward stream of dingy girls from the shops, and thought with a sense of escape that she would never have to join them; but she was conscious of loving Abby better, and Maria, who had also entered Lloyd's. Abby, when she heard the news about Vassar, had looked at her with a sort of fierce exultation.

"Thank the Lord, you're out of it, anyhow!" she cried, fervently, as a soul might in the midst of flames.

Maria had smiled at her with the greatest sweetness and a certain wistfulness. Maria was growing delicate, and seemed to inherit her father's consumptive tendencies.

"I am so glad, Ellen," she said. Then she added, "I suppose we shan't see so much of you."

"Of course we shan't, Maria Atkins," interposed Abby, "and it won't be fitting we should. It won't be best for Ellen to associate with shop-girls when she's going to Vassar College."

But Ellen had cast an impetuous arm around a neck of each.

"If ever I do such a thing as that!" said she. "If ever I turn a cold shoulder to either of you for such a reason as that! What's Vassar College to hearts? That's at the bottom of everything in this world, anyhow. I guess you'll see it won't make any difference unless you keep on thinking such things. If you do — if you think I can do anything like that — I won't love you so much."

Ellen faced them both with gathering indignation. Suddenly this ignoble conception of herself in the minds of her friends stung her to resentment. But Abby seized her in two wiry little arms.

"I never did, I never did!" she cried. "Don't I know what you are made of, Ellen Brewster? Don't you think I know? But after all, it might be better for you if you were worse. That was all I meant."

Ellen, one afternoon, set out in her pretty challis, a white ground with long sprays of blue flowers running over it, and a blue ribbon at her neck and waist, and her leghorn hat with white ribbons, and a knot of forget-me-nots under the brim. She wore her one pair of nice gloves, too, but those she did not put on until she reached the corner of the street where Cynthia lived. Then she rubbed them on carefully, holding up her challis skirts under one arm.

Cynthia was at home, seated on the back veranda, in a rattan chair, with a book which she was not reading. Ellen stood before her, in her cheap attire, which she wore with an air which seemed to make it precious, such faith she had in it. Ellen regarded her coarse blue-flowered challis with an innocent admiration which seemed almost able to glorify it into silk. Cynthia took in at a glance the exceeding commonness of it all; she saw the hat, the like of which could be seen in the milliners' windows at fabulously low prices; the foam of spurious lace and the spray of wretched blue flowers made her shudder. "The poor child, she must have something better than that," she thought, and insensibly she also thought that the girl must lose her evident faith in the splendor of such attire; must change her standard of taste. She rose and greeted Ellen sweetly, though somewhat reservedly. When the two were seated opposite each other, Cynthia tried to talk pleasantly, but all the time with a sub-consciousness as one will have of some deformity which must be ignored. The girl looked so common to her in this array that she began to have a hopeless feeling of disgust about it all. Was it not manifestly unwise to try to elevate a girl who took such evident satisfaction in a gown like that, in a hat like that? Ellen wore her watch and chain ostentatiously. The watch was too large for a chatelaine, but she had looped the heavy chain across her bosom, and pinned it with the brooch which Abby Atkins had given her, so it hung suspended. Cynthia riveted her eyes helplessly upon that as she talked.

"I hope you are having a pleasant vacation," said she, as she looked at the watch, and all at once Ellen knew.

Ellen replied that she was having a very pleasant vacation, then she plunged at once into the subject of her call, though with inward trembling.

"Miss Lennox," said she — and she followed the lines of a little speech which she had been rehearsing to herself all the way there — "I am very grateful to you for what you propose doing for me. It will make a difference to me during my whole life. I cannot begin to tell you how grateful I am."

"I am very grateful to be allowed to do it," replied Cynthia, with her unfailing refrain of gentle politeness, but a kindly glance was in her eyes. Something in the girl's tone touched her. It was exceedingly earnest, with the simple earnestness of childhood. Moreover, Ellen was regarding her with great, steadfast, serious eyes, like a baby's who shrinks and yet will have her will of information.

"I wanted to say," Ellen continued — and her voice became insensibly hushed, and she cast a glance around at the house and the leafy grounds, as if to be sure that no one was within hearing — "that I should never under any circumstances have said anything regarding what happened so long ago. That I never have and never should have, that I never thought of doing such a thing."

Then the elder woman's face flushed a burning red, and she knew at once what the girl had suspected. "You might proclaim it on the house-tops if it would please you," she cried out, vehemently. "If you think — if you think —"

"Oh, I do not!" cried Ellen, in an agony of pleading. "Indeed, I do not. It was only that — I — feared lest you might think I would be mean enough to tell."

"I would have told, myself, long ago if there had been only myself to consider," said Cynthia, still red with anger, and her voice strained. All at once she seemed to Ellen more like the woman of her childhood. "Yes, I would," said she, hotly — "I will now."

"Oh, I beg you not!" cried Ellen.

"I will go with you this minute and tell your mother," Cynthia said, rising.

Ellen sprang up and moved towards her as if to push her back in her chair. "Oh, please don't!" she cried. "Please don't. You don't know mother; and it would do no good. It was only because I wondered if you could have thought I would tell, if I would be so mean."

"And you thought, perhaps, I was bribing you not to tell, with Vassar College," Cynthia said, suddenly. "Well, you have suspected me of something which was undeserved."

"I am very sorry," Ellen said. "I did not suspect, really, but I do not know why you do this for me." She said the last with her steady eyes of interrogation on Cynthia's face.

"You know the reasons I have given."

"I do not think they were the only ones," Ellen replied, stoutly. "I do not think my valedictory was so good as to warrant so much, and I do not think I am so smart as to warrant so much, either."

Cynthia laughed. She sat down again. "Well," she said, "you are not one to swallow praise greedily." Then her tone changed. "I owe it to you to tell you why I wish to do this," she said, "and I will. You are an honest girl, with yourself as well as with other people — too honest, perhaps, and you deserve that I should be honest with you. I am not doing this for you in the least, my dear."

Ellen stared at her.

"No, I am not," repeated Cynthia. "You are a very clever, smart girl, I am sure, and it will be a nice thing for you to have a better education, and be able to take a higher place in the world, but I am not doing it for you. When you were a little child I would have done everything, given my life almost, for you, but I never care so much for children when they grow up. I am not doing this for you, but for your mother."

"My mother?" said Ellen.

"Yes, your mother. I know what agony your mother must have been in, that time when I kept you, and I want to atone in some way. I think this is a good way. I don't think you need to hesitate about letting me do it. You also owe a little atonement to your mother. It was not right for you to run away, in the first place."

"Yes, I was very naughty to run away," Ellen said, starting. She rose, and held out her hand. "I hope you will forgive me," she said. "I am very grateful, and it will make my father and mother happier than anything else could, but indeed I don't think — it is so long ago — that there was any need —"

"I do, for the sake of my own distress over it," Cynthia said, shortly. "Suppose, now, we drop the subject, my dear. There is a taint in the New England blood, and you have it, and you must fight it. It is a suspicion of the motives of a good deed which will often poison all the good effect from it. I don't know where the taint came from. Perhaps the Pilgrim Fathers', being necessarily always on the watch for the savage behind his gifts, have affected their descendants. Anyway, it is there. I suppose I have it."

"I am very sorry," said Ellen.

"I also am sorry," said Cynthia. "I did you a wrong, and your mother a wrong, years ago. I wonder at myself now, but you don't know the temptation. You will never know how you looked to me that night."

Cynthia's voice took on a tone of ineffable tenderness and yearning. Ellen saw again the old expression in her face; suddenly she looked as before, young and beautiful, and full of a boundless attraction. The girl's heart fairly leaped towards her with an impulse of affection. She could in that minute have fallen at her feet, have followed her to the end of the world. A great love and admiration which had gotten its full growth in a second under the magic of a look and a tone shook her from head to foot. She went close to Cynthia, and leaned over her, putting her round, young face down to the elder woman's. "Oh, I love you, I love you," whispered Ellen, with a fervor which was strange to her.

But Cynthia only kissed her lightly on her cheek, and pushed her away softly. "Thank you, my dear," she said. "I am glad you came and spoke to me frankly, and I am glad we have come to an understanding."

Ellen, after she had taken her leave, was more in love than she had ever been in her life, and with another woman. She thought of Cynthia with adoration; she dreamed about her; the feeling of receiving a benefit from her hand became immeasurably sweet.

Chapter XXIII

*E*llen, under the influence of that old fascination which Cynthia had exerted over her temporarily in her childhood, and which had now assumed a new lease of life, would have loved to see her every day, but along with the fascination came a great timidity and fear of presuming. She felt instinctively that the fascination was an involuntary thing on Cynthia's part. She kept repeating to herself what she had said, that she was not sending her to Vassar because she loved her. Strangely enough, this did not make Ellen unhappy in the least, she was quite content to do all the loving and adoring herself. She made a sort of divinity of the older woman, and who expects a divinity to step down from her marble heights, and love and caress? Ellen began to remember all Cynthia's ways and looks, as a scholar remembers with a view to imitation. She became her disciple. She began to move like Cynthia, and to speak like her, though she did not know it. Her imitation was totally unconscious; indeed, it was hardly to be called imitation; it was rather the following out of the leading of that image of Cynthia which was always present before her mind. Ellen saw Cynthia very seldom. Once or twice she arrayed herself in her best and made a formal call of gratitude, and once Fanny went with her. Ellen saw the incongruity of her mother in Cynthia's drawing room with a torture which she never forgot. Going home she clung hard to her mother's arm all the way. She was fairly fierce with love and loyalty. She was so indignant with herself that she had seen the incongruity. "I think our parlor is enough sight prettier than hers," she said, defiantly, when they reached home and the hideous lamp was lighted. Ellen looked around the ornate room, and then at her mother, as with a challenge in behalf of loyalty, and of that which underlies externals.

"I rather guess it is," agreed Fanny, happily, "and I don't s'pose it cost half so much. I dare say that mat on her hearth cost as much as all our plush furniture and the carpet, and it is a dreadful dull, homely thing."

"Yes, it is," said Ellen.

"I wish I'd been able to keep my hands as white as Miss Lennox's, an' I wish I'd had time to speak so soft and slow," said Fanny, wistfully. Then Ellen had her by both shoulders, and was actually shaking her with a passion to which she very seldom gave rein.

"Mother," she cried — "mother, you know better, you know there is nobody in the whole world to me like my own mother, and never will be. It isn't being beautiful, nor speaking in a soft voice, nor dressing well, it's the being you — *you.* You know I love you best, mother, you know, and I love my own home best, and everything that is my own best, and I always will." Ellen was almost weeping.

"You silly child," said Fanny, tenderly. "Mother knows you love her best, but she wishes for your sake, and especially since you are going to have advantages that she never had, that she was a little different."

"I don't, I don't," said Ellen, fiercely. "I want you just as you are, just exactly as you are, mother."

Fanny laughed tearfully, and rubbed her coarse black head against Ellen's lovingly with a curious, catlike motion, then bade her run away or she would not get her dress done. A dressmaker was coming for a whole week to the Brewster house to make Ellen's outfit. Mrs. Zelotes had furnished most of the materials, and Andrew was to pay the dressmaker. "You can take a little more of that money out of the bank," Fanny said. "I want Ellen to go looking so she won't be ashamed before the other girls, and I don't want Cynthia Lennox thinking she ain't well enough dressed, and we ought to have let her do it. As for being beholden to her for Ellen's clothes, I won't."

"I rather guess not," said Andrew, but he was sick at heart. Only that afternoon the man from whom he had borrowed the money to buy Ellen's watch and chain had asked him for it. He had not a cent in advance for his weekly pay; he could not see where the money for Ellen's clothes was coming from. It was long since the "Golden Hope" had been quoted in the stock-list, but the next morning Andrew purchased a morning paper. He had stopped taking one regularly. He put on his spectacles, and spread out the paper in his shaking hands, and scrutinized the stock-list eagerly, but he could not find what he wanted. The "Golden Hope" had long since dropped to a still level below all record of fluctuations. A young man passing to his place at the bench looked over his shoulder. "Counting up your dividends, Brewster?" he asked, with a grin.

Andrew folded up the paper gloomily and made no reply.

"Irish dividends, maybe," said the man, with a chuckle at his own wit, and a backward roll of a facetious eye.

"Oh, shut up, you're too smart to live," said the man who stood next at the bench. He was a young fellow who had been a school-mate of Ellen in the grammar-school. He had left to go to work when she had entered the high-school. His name was Dixon. He was wiry and alert, with a restless sparkle of bright eyes in a grimy face, and he cut the leather with lightninglike rapidity. Dixon had always thought Ellen the most beautiful girl in Rowe. He looked after Andrew with a sharp pain of sympathy when he went away with the roll of newspaper sticking out of his pocket.

"Poor old chap," he said to the facetious man, thrusting his face angrily towards him. "He has had a devil of a time since he begun to grow old. You ought to be ashamed of yourself. Wait till you begin to drop behind. It's what's bound to come to the whole boiling of us."

"Mind your jaw," said the first man, with a scowl.

"You'd better mind yours," said Dixon, slashing furiously at the leather.

That noon Dixon offered Andrew, shamefacedly, taking him aside lest the other men see, a piece of pie of a superior sort which his mother had put into his dinner bag, but Andrew thanked him kindly and refused it. He could eat nothing whatever that noon. He kept thinking about the dressmaker, and how Fanny would ask him again to take some of that money out of the bank to pay her, and how the money was already taken out.

That evening, when he sat down to the tea-table furnished with the best china and frosted cake in honor of the dressmaker, and heard the radiant talk about Ellen's new frills and tucks, he had a cold feeling at his heart. He was ashamed to look at the dressmaker.

"You won't know your daughter when we get her fixed up for Vassar," she told Andrew, with a smirk which covered her face with a network of wrinkles under her blond fluff of hair.

"Do have some more cake, Miss Higgins," said Fanny. She was radiant. The image of her daughter in her new gowns had gone far to recompense her for all her disappointments in life, and they had not been few. "What, after all, did it matter?" she asked herself, "if a woman was growing old, if she had to work hard, if she did not know where the next dollar was coming from, if all the direct personal savor was fast passing out of existence, when one had a daughter who looked like that?" Ellen, in a new blue dress, was ravishing. The mother looked at her when she was trying it on, with the possession of love, and the dressmaker as if she herself had created her.

After supper Ellen had to try on the dress again for her father, and turn about slowly that he might see all its fine points.

"There, what do you think of that, Andrew?" asked Fanny, triumphantly.

"Ain't she a lady?" asked the dressmaker.

"It is very pretty," said Andrew, smiling with gloomy eyes. Then he heaved a great sigh, and went out of the south door to the steps. "Your father is tired tonight," Fanny said to Ellen with a meaning of excuse for the dressmaker.

The dressmaker reflected shrewdly on Andrew's sigh when she was on her way home. "Men don't sigh that way unless there's money to pay," she thought. "I don't believe but he has been speculating." Then she wondered if there was any doubt about her getting her pay, and concluded that she would ask for it from day to day to make sure.

So the next night after tea she asked, with one of her smirks of amiability, if it would be convenient for Mrs. Brewster to pay her that night. "I wouldn't ask for it until the end of the week," said she, "but I have a bill to pay." She said "bill" with a murmur which carried conviction of its deception. Fanny flushed angrily. "Of course," said she, "Mr. Brewster can pay you just as well every night if you need it." Fanny emphasized the "need" maliciously. Then she turned to Andrew. "Andrew," said she, "Miss Higgins needs the money, if you can pay her for yesterday and today."

Andrew turned pale. "Yes, of course," he stammered. "How much?"

"Six dollars," said Fanny, and in her tone was unmistakable meaning of the dearness of the price. The dressmaker was flushed, but her thin mouth was set hard. It was as much as to say, "Well, I don't care so long as I get my money." She was unmarried, and her lonely condition had worked up her spirit into a strong attitude of defiance against all masculine odds. She had once considered men from a matrimonial point of view. She had wondered if this one and that one wanted to marry her. Now she was past that, and considered with equal sharpness if this one or that one wanted to cheat her. She had missed men's love through some failing either of theirs or hers. She did not know which, but she was determined that she would not lose money. So she bore Fanny's insulting emphasis with rigidity, and waited for her pay.

Andrew pulled out his old pocketbook, and counted the bills. Miss Higgins saw that he took every bill in it, unless there were some in another compartment, and of that she could not be quite sure. But Andrew knew. He would not have another penny until the next week when he received his pay. In the meantime there was a bill due at the grocery store, and one at the market, and there was the debt for Ellen's watch. However, he felt as if he would rather owe every man in Rowe than this one small, sharp woman. He felt the scorn lurking within her like a sting. She seemed to him like some venomous insect. He went out to the doorstep again, and wondered if she would want her pay the next night when she went home.

Chapter XXIV

*E*llen had a flower-garden behind the house, and a row of sweet-peas which was her pride. It had occurred to her that she might venture, although Cynthia Lennox had her great garden and conservatories, to carry her a bunch of these sweet-peas. She had asked her mother what she thought about it. "Why, of course, carry her some if you want to," said Fanny. "I don't see why you shouldn't. I dare say she's got sweet-peas, but yours are uncommon handsome, and, anyway, it ought to please her to have some given her. It ain't altogether what's given, it's the giving."

So Ellen had cut a great bouquet of the delicate flowers, selecting the shades carefully, and set forth. She was as guiltily conscious as a lover that she was making an excuse to see Miss Lennox. She hurried along in delight and trepidation, her great bouquet shedding a penetrating fragrance around her, her face gleaming white out of the dusk. She had to pass Granville Joy's house on her way, and saw with some dismay, as she drew near, a figure leaning over the gate.

He pushed open the gate when she drew near, and stood waiting.

"Good-evening, Ellen," he said. He was mindful not to say "Hullo" again. He bowed with a piteous imitation of Robert Lloyd, but Ellen did not notice it.

"Good-evening," she returned, rather stiffly, then she added, in a very gentle voice, to make amends, that it was a beautiful night.

The young man cast an appreciative glance at the crescent moon in the jewellike blue overhead, and at the soft shadows of the trees.

"Yes, beautiful," he replied, with a sort of gratitude, as if the girl had praised him instead of the night.

"May I walk along with you?" he asked, falling into step with her.

"I am going to take these sweet-peas to Miss Lennox," said Ellen, without replying directly.

She was in terror lest Granville should renew his appeal of a few weeks before, and she was in terror of her own pity for him, and also of that mysterious impulse and longing which sometimes seized her to her own wonder and discomfiture. Sometimes, in thinking of Granville Joy, and his avowal of love, and the touch of his hand on hers, and his lips on hers, she felt, although she knew she did not love him, a softening of her heart and a quickening of her pulse which made her wonder as to her next movement, if it might be something which she had not planned. And always, after thinking of Granville, she thought of Robert Lloyd; some mysterious sequence seemed to be established between the two in the girl's mind, though she was not in love with either.

Ellen was just at that period almost helpless before the demands of her own nature. No great stress in her life had occurred to awaken her to a stanchness either of resistance or yielding. She was in the full current of her own emotions, which, added to a goodly flood inherited from the repressed passion of New England ancestors, had a strong pull upon her feet. Sooner or later she would be given that hard shake of life which precipitates and organizes in all strong natures, but just now she was in a ferment. She walked along under the crescent moon, with the young man at her side whose every thought and imagination was dwelling upon her with love. She was conscious of a tendency of her own imagination in his direction, or rather in the direction of the love and passion which he represented, and all the time her heart was filled with the ideal image of another woman. She was prostrated with that hero-worship which belongs to young and virgin souls, and yet she felt the drawing of that other admiration which is more earthly and more fascinating, as it shows the jewel tints in one's own soul as well as in the other.

As for Granville Joy, who had scrubbed his hands and face well with scented soap to take away the odor of the leather, and put on a clean shirt and collar, being always prepared for the possibility of meeting this dainty young girl whom he loved, he walked along by her side, casting, from time to time, glances which were pure admiration at the face over the great bunch of sweet-peas.

"Don't you want me to carry them for you?" he asked.

"No, thank you," replied Ellen. "They are nothing to carry."

"They're real pretty flowers," said Granville, timidly.

"Yes, I think they are."

"Mother planted some, but hers didn't come up. Mother has got some beautiful nasturtiums. Perhaps you would like some," he said, eagerly.

"No, thank you, I have some myself," Ellen said, rather coldly. "I'm just as much obliged to you."

Granville quivered a little and shrank as a dog might under a blow. He saw this dainty girl-shape floating along at his side in a flutter of wonderful draperies, one hand holding up her skirts with maddening revelations of whiteness. If a lily could hold up her petals out of the dust she might do it in the same fashion as Ellen held her skirts, with no coarse clutching nor crumpling, not immodestly, but rather with disclosures of modesty itself. Ellen's wonderful daintiness was one of her chief charms. There was an immaculateness about her attire and her every motion which seemed to extend to her very soul, and hedged her about with the lure of unapproachableness. It was more that than her beauty which roused the imagination and quickened the pulses of a young man regarding her.

Granville Joy did not feel the earth beneath his feet as he walked with Ellen. The scent of the sweet-peas came in his face, he heard the soft rustle of Ellen's skirts and his own heart-beats. She was very silent, since she did not wish him to go with her, though she was all the time reproaching herself for it. Granville kept casting about for something to say which should ingratiate him with her. He was resolved to say nothing of love to her.

"It is a beautiful night," he said.

"Yes, it is," agreed Ellen, and she looked at the moon. She felt the boy's burning, timid, worshipful eyes on her face. She trembled, and yet she was angry and annoyed. She felt in an undefined fashion that she herself was the summer night and the flowers and the crescent moon, and all that was fair and beautiful in the whole world to this other soul, and shame seized her instead of pride. He seemed to force her to a sight of her own pettiness, as is always the case when love is not fully returned. She made an impatient motion with the shoulder next Granville, and walked faster.

"You said you were going to Miss Lennox's," he remarked, anxiously, feeling that in some way he had displeased her.

"Yes, to carry her some sweet-peas."

"She must have been real good-looking when she was young," Granville said, injudiciously.

"When she was young," retorted Ellen, angrily. "She is beautiful now. There is not another woman in Rowe as beautiful as she is."

"Well, she is good-looking enough," agreed Granville, with unreasoning jealousy. He had not heard of Ellen's good fortune. His mother had not told him. She was a tenderly sentimental woman, and had always had her fancies with regard to her son and Ellen Brewster. When she heard the news she reflected that it would perhaps remove the girl from her boy immeasurably, that he would be pained, so she said nothing. Every night when he came home she had watched his face to see if he had heard.

Now Ellen told him. "You know what Miss Cynthia Lennox is going to do for me," she said, abruptly, almost boastfully, she was so eager in her partisanship of Cynthia.

Granville looked at her blankly. They were coming into the crowded, brilliantly lighted main street of the city, and their two faces were quite plain to each other's eyes.

"No, I don't," said he. "What is it, Ellen?"

"She is going to send me to Vassar College."

Granville's face whitened perceptibly. There was a queer sound in his throat.

"To Vassar College!" he repeated.

"Yes, to Vassar College. Then I shall be able to get a good school, and teach, and help father and mother."

Granville continued to look at her, and suddenly an intense pity sprang into life in the girl's heart. She felt as if she were looking at some poor little child, instead of a stalwart young man.

"Don't look so, Granville," she said, softly.

"Of course I am glad at any good fortune which can come to you, Ellen," Granville said then, huskily. His lips quivered a little, but his eyes on her face were brave and faithful. Suddenly Ellen seemed to see in this young man a counterpart of her own father. Granville had a fine, high forehead and contemplative outlook. He had been a good scholar. Many said that it was a pity he had to leave school and go to work. It had been the same with her father. Andrew had always looked immeasurably above his labor. She seemed to see Granville Joy in the future just such a man, a finer animal harnessed to the task of a lower, and harnessed in part by his own loving faithfulness towards others. Ellen had often reflected that, if it hadn't been for her and her mother, her father would not have been obliged to work so hard. Now in Granville she saw another man whom love would hold to the plowshare. A great impulse of loyalty as towards her own came over her.

"It won't make any difference between me and my old friends if I do go to Vassar College," she said, without reflecting on the dangerous encouragement of it.

"You can't get into another track of life without its making a difference," returned Granville, soberly. "But I am glad. God knows I'm glad, Ellen. I dare say it is better for you than if —" He stopped then and seemed all at once to see projected on his mirror of the future this dainty, exquisite girl, with her fine intellect, dragging about a poor house, with wailing children in arm and at heel, and suddenly a great courage of renunciation came over him.

"It *is* better, Ellen," he said, in a loud voice, like a hero's, as if he were cheering his own better impulses on to victory over his own passions. "It is better for a girl like you, than to —"

Ellen knew that he meant to say, "to marry a fellow like me." Ellen looked at him, the sturdy backward fling of his head and shoulders, and the honest regard of his pained yet unflinching eyes, and a great weakness of natural longing for that which she was even now deprecating nearly overswept her. She was nearer loving him that moment than ever before. She realized something in him which could command love — the renunciation of love for love's sake.

"I shall never forget my old friends, whatever happens," she said, in a trembling voice, and it might have all been different had they not then arrived at Cynthia Lennox's.

"Shall I wait and go home with you, Ellen?" Granville asked, timidly.

"No, thank you. I don't know how long I shall stay," Ellen replied. "You are real kind, but I am not a bit afraid."

"It is sort of lonesome going past the shops."

"I can take a car," Ellen said. She extended her hand to Granville, and he grasped it firmly.

"Good-night, Ellen; I am always glad of any good fortune that may come to you," he said.

But Granville Joy, going alone down the brilliant street, past the blaze of the shop windows and the knots of loungers on the corners, reflected that he had seen the fiery tip of a cigar on the Lennox veranda, that it might be possible that young Lloyd was there, since Miss Lennox was his aunt, and that possibly the aunt's sending Ellen to Vassar might bring about something in that quarter which would not otherwise have happened, and he writhed at the fancy of that sort of good fortune for Ellen, but held his mind to it resolutely as to some terrible but necessary grindstone for the refinement of spirit. "It would be a heap better for her," he said to himself, quite loud, and two men whom he was passing looked at him curiously. "Drunk," said one to the other.

When he was on his homeward way he overtook a slender girl struggling along with a kerosene-can in one hand and a package of sugar in the other, and, seeing that it was Abby Atkins, he possessed himself of both. She only laughed and did not start. Abby Atkins was not of the jumping or screaming kind, her nerves were so finely balanced that they recovered their equilibrium, after surprises, before she had time for manifestations. There was a curious healthfulness about the slender, wiry little creature who was overworked and under-fed, a healthfulness which seemed to result from the action of the mind upon a meager body.

"Hullo, Granville Joy!" she said, in her good-comrade fashion, and the two went on together. Presently Abby looked up in his face.

"Know about Ellen?" said she. Granville nodded.

"Well, I'm glad of it, aren't you?" Abby said, in a challenging tone.

"Yes, I am," replied Granville, meeting her look firmly.

Suddenly he felt Abby's little, meager, bony hand close over the back of his, holding the kerosene-can. "You're a good fellow, Granville Joy," said she.

Granville marched on and made no response. He felt his throat fill with sobs, and swallowed convulsively. Along with this womanly compassion came a compassion for himself, so hurt on his little field of battle. He saw his own wounds as one might see a stranger's.

"Think of Ellen dogging around to a shoe-shop like me and the other girls," said Abby, "and think of her draggin' around with half a dozen children and no money. Thank the Lord she's lifted out of it. It ain't you nor me that ought to grudge her fortune to her, nor wish her where she might have been otherwise."

"That's so," said the young man.

Abby's hand tightened over the one on the kerosene-can. "You are a good fellow, Granville Joy," she said again.

Chapter XXV

Robert Lloyd was sitting on the veranda behind the green trail of vines when Ellen came up the walk. He never forgot the girl's face looking over her bunch of sweet-peas. There was in it something indescribably youthful and innocent, almost angelic. The light from the window made her hair toss into gold; her blue eyes sought Cynthia with the singleness of blue stars. It was evident whom she had come to see. She held out her flowers towards her with a gesture at once humble and worshipful, like that of some devotee at a shrine.

She said "Good-evening" with a shy comprehensiveness, then, to Cynthia, like a child, "I thought maybe you would like some of my sweet-peas."

Both gentlemen rose, and Risley looked curiously from the young girl to Cynthia, then placed his chair for her, smiling kindly.

"The sweet-peas are lovely," Cynthia said. "Thank you, my dear. They are much prettier than any I have had in my garden this year. Please sit down," for Ellen was doubtful about availing herself of the proffered chair. She had so hoped that she might find Cynthia alone. She had dreamed, as a lover might have done, of a tête-à-tête with her, what she would say, what Cynthia would say. She had thought, and trembled at the thought, that possibly Cynthia might kiss her when she came or went. She had felt, with a thrill of spirit, the touch of Cynthia's soft lips on hers, she had smelt the violets about her clothes. Now it was all spoiled. She remembered things which she had heard about Mr. Risley's friendship with Cynthia, how he had danced attendance upon her for half a lifetime, and thought that she did not like him. She looked at his smiling, grizzled, blond face with distrust. She felt intuitively that he saw straight through her little subterfuge of the flowers, that he divined her girlish worship at the shrine of Cynthia, and was making fun of her.

"Do you object to a cigar, Miss Brewster?" asked Robert, and Risley looked inquiringly at her.

"Oh, no," replied Ellen, with the eager readiness of a child to fit into new conditions. She thought of the sitting room at home, blue with the rank pipe-smoke of Nahum Beals and his kind. She pictured them to herself sitting about on these warm evenings in their shirt-sleeves, and she saw the two gentlemen in their light summer clothes with their fragrant cigars at their lips, and all of a sudden she realized that between these men and the others there was a great gulf, and that she was trying to cross it. She did not realize, as later, that the gulf was one of externals, and of width rather than depth, but it seemed to her then that from one shore she could only see dimly the opposite. A great fear and jealousy came over her as to her own future accessibility to those of the other kind among whom she had been brought up, like her father and Granville.

Ellen felt all this as she sat beside Cynthia, who was casting about in her mind, in rather an annoyed fashion, for something to say to this young beneficiary of hers which should not have anything to do with the benefit.

Finally she inquired if she were having a pleasant vacation, and Ellen replied that she was. Risley looked at her beautiful face with the double radiance of the electric-light and the lamp-light from the window on it, giving it a curious effect. It suddenly occurred to him to wonder why everybody seemed to have such an opinion as to the talents of this girl. Why did Cynthia consider that her native ability warranted this forcible elevation of her from her own sphere and setting her on a height of education above her kind? She looked and spoke like an ordinary young girl. She had a beautiful face, it is true, and her shyness seemed due to the questioning attitude of a child rather than to self-consciousness, but, after all, why did she give people that impression? Her valedictory had been clever, no doubt, and there was in it a certain fire of conviction, which, though crude, was moving; but, after all, almost any bright girl might have written it. She had been a fine scholar, no doubt, but any girl with a ready intelligence might have done as well. Whence came this inclination of all to rear the child upon a pedestal? Risley wondered, looking at her, narrowing his keen, light eyes under reflective brows, puffing at his cigar; then he admitted to himself that he was one with the crowd of Ellen's admirers. There was somehow about the girl that which gave the impression of an enormous reserve out of all proportion to any external evidence. "The child says nothing remarkable," he told Cynthia, after she had gone that evening, "but somehow she gives me an impression of power to say something extraordinary, and do something extraordinary. There is electricity and steel behind that soft, rosy flesh of hers. But all she does which is evident to the eye of man is to worship you, Cynthia."

"Worship me?" repeated Cynthia, vaguely.

"Yes, she has one of those aberrations common to her youth and her sex. She is repeating a madness of old Greece, and following you as a nymph might a goddess."

"It is only because she is grateful," returned Cynthia, looking rather annoyed.

"Gratitude may be a factor in it, but it is very far from being the whole of the matter. It is one of the spring madnesses of life; but don't be alarmed, it will be temporary in the case of a girl like that. She will easily be led into her natural track of love. Do you know, Cynthia, that she is one of the most normal, typical young girls I ever saw, and that makes me wonder more at this impression of unusual ability which she undoubtedly gives. She has all the weaknesses of her age and sex, she is much younger than some girls of her age, and yet there is the impression which I cannot shake off."

"I have it, too," said Cynthia, rather impatiently.

"Cynthia Lennox, I don't believe you care in the least for this young devotee of yours, for all you are heaping benefits upon her," Risley said, looking at her quizzically.

"I am not sure that I do," replied Cynthia, calmly.

"Then why on earth — ?"

Suddenly Cynthia began speaking rapidly and passionately, straightening herself in her chair. "Oh, Lyman, do you think I could do a thing like that, and not repent it and suffer remorse for it all these years?" she cried.

"A thing like that?"

"Like stealing that child," Cynthia replied, in a whisper.

"Stealing the child? You did not steal the child."

"Yes, I did."

"Why, it was only a few hours that you kept her."

"What difference does it make whether you steal anything for a few hours or a lifetime? I kept her, and she was crying for her mother, and her mother was suffering tortures all that time. Then I kept it secret all these years. You didn't know what I have suffered, Lyman."

Cynthia regarded him with a wan look.

Risley half laughed, then checked himself. "My poor girl, you have the New England conscience in its worst form," he said.

"You yourself told me it was a serious thing I was doing," Cynthia said, half resentfully. "One does not wish one's sin treated lightly when one has hugged its pricks to one's bosom for so long — it detracts from the dignity of suffering."

"So I did, but all those years ago!"

"If you don't leave me my remorse, how can I atone for the deed?"

"Cynthia, you are horribly morbid."

"Maybe you are right, maybe it is worse than morbid. Sometimes I think I am unnatural, out of drawing, but I did not make myself, and how can I help it?" Cynthia spoke with a pathetic little laugh.

She leaned her head back in her chair, and looked at a star through a gap in the vines. The shadows of the leaves played over her long, white figure. Again to Risley, gazing at her, came the conviction as of subtle spiritual deformity in the woman; she was unnatural in something the same fashion that an orchid is unnatural, and it was worse, because presumably the orchid does not know it is an orchid and regret not being another, more evenly developed, flower, and Cynthia had a full realization and a mental mirror clear enough to see the twist in her own character.

Risley had never kissed her in his life, but that night, when they parted, he laid a hand on her soft, grey hair, and smoothed it back with a masculine motion of tenderness, leaving her white forehead, which had a candid, childish fullness about the temples, bare. Then he put his lips to it.

"You are a silly girl, Cynthia," he said.

"I wish I were different, Lyman," she responded, and, he felt, with a double meaning.

"I don't," he said, and stroked her hair with a great tenderness, which seemed for the time to quite fill and satisfy his heart. He was a man of measureless patience, born to a firm conviction of the journey's end.

"There are worse things than loving a good woman your whole life and never having her," he said to himself as he went home, but he said it without its full meaning. Risley's "nerves" were always lighted by the lamp of his own hope, which threw a gleam over unknown seas.

Chapter XXVI

Robert Lloyd accompanied Ellen home, though she had said timidly that she was not in the least afraid, that she would not trouble anyone, that she could take a car. Cynthia herself had insisted that Robert should escort her.

"It's too late for you to be out alone," she said, and the girl seemed to perceive dimly a hedge of conventionality which she had not hitherto known. She had often taken a car when she was alone of an evening, without a thought of anything questionable. Some of the conductors lived near Ellen, and she felt as if she were under personal friendly escort. "I know the conductor on that car, and it would take me right home, and I am not in the least afraid," she said to Robert, as the car came rocking down the street when they emerged from Cynthia's grounds.

"It's a lovely night," Robert said, speaking quickly as they paused on the sidewalk. "I am not going to let you go alone, anyway. We will take the car if you say so, but what do you say to walking? It's a lovely night."

It actually flashed through Ellen's mind — to such small issues of finance had she been accustomed — that the young man might insist upon paying her car-fare if he went with her on the car.

"I would like to walk, but I am sorry to put you to so much trouble," she said, a little awkwardly.

"Oh, I like to walk," returned Robert. "I don't walk half enough," and they went together down the lighted street. Suddenly to Ellen there came a vivid remembrance, so vivid that it seemed almost like actual repetition of the time when she, a little child, maddened by the sudden awakening of the depths of her nature, had come down this same street. She saw that same brilliant market-window where she had stopped and stared, to the momentary forgetfulness of her troubles in the spectacular display of that which was entirely outside them. Curiously enough, Robert drew her to a full stop that night before the same window. It was one of those strange cases of apparent telepathy which one sometimes notices. When Ellen looked at the market-window, with a flash of reminiscence, Robert immediately drew her to a stop before it. "That is quite a study in color," he said. "I fancy there are a good many unrecognized artists among market-men."

"Yes, it is really beautiful," agreed Ellen, looking at it with eyes which had changed very little from their childish outlook. Again she saw more than she saw. The window differed materially from that before which she had stood fascinated so many years ago, for that was in a different season. Instead of frozen game and winter vegetables, were the products of summer gardens, and fruits, and berries. The color scheme was dazzling with great heaps of tomatoes, and long, emerald ears of corn, and baskets of apples, and gold crooks of summer squashes, and speckled pods of beans.

"Suppose," said Robert, as they walked on, "that all the market-men who had artistic tastes had art educations and set up studios and painted pictures, who would keep the markets?"

He spoke gaily. His manner that night was younger and merrier than Ellen had ever seen it. She was naturally rather grave herself. What she had seen of life had rather disposed her to a hush of respect than to hilarity, but somehow his mood began to infect her.

"I don't know," she answered, laughing, "I suppose somebody would keep the markets."

"Yes, but they would not be as good markets. That is, they would not do as artistic markets, and they would not serve the higher purpose of catering to the artistic taste of man, as well as to his bodily needs."

"Perhaps a picture like that is just as well and better than it would be painted and hung on a wall," Ellen admitted, reflectively.

"Just so — why is it not?" Robert said, in a pleased voice.

"Yes, I think it is," said Ellen. "I do think it is better, because everybody can see it there. Ever so many people will see it there who would not go to picture-galleries to see it, and then —"

"And then it may go far to dignify their daily needs," said Robert. "For instance, a poor man about to buy his tomorrow's dinner may feel his soul take a little fly above the prices of turnips and cabbages."

"Maybe," said Ellen, but doubtfully.

"Don't you think so?"

"The prices of turnips and cabbages may crowd other things out," Ellen replied, and her tone was sad, almost tragic. "You see I am right in it, Mr. Lloyd," she said, earnestly.

"You mean right in the midst of the kind of people whom necessity forces to neglect the æsthetic for the purely useful?"

"Yes," said Ellen. Then she added, in an indescribably pathetic voice, "People have to live first before they can see, and they can't think until they are fed, and one needs always to have had enough turnips and cabbages to eat without troubling about the getting them, in order to see in them anything except food."

Lloyd looked at her curiously. "Decidedly this child can think," he reflected. He shrugged his arm, on which Ellen's hand lay, a little closer to his side.

Just then they were passing the great factories — Lloyd's, and Briggs's, and Maguire's. Many of the windows in Briggs's and Maguire's reflected light from the moon and the electric-lamps on the street. Lloyd's was all dark except for one brilliant spark of light, which seemed to be threading the building like a will-o'-the-wisp. "That is the night-watchman," said Robert. "He must have a dull time of it."

"I should think he might be afraid," said Ellen.

"Afraid of what?"

"Of ghosts."

"Ghosts in a shoe-shop?" asked Robert, laughing.

"I don't believe there has been another building in the whole city which has held so many heart-aches, and I always wondered if they didn't make ghosts instead of dead people," Ellen said.

"Do you think they have such a hard time?"

"I know they do," said Ellen. "I think I ate the knowledge along with my first daily bread."

Robert Lloyd looked down at the light, girlish figure on his arm, and again the resolution that he would not talk on such topics with a young girl like this came over him. He felt a reluctance to do so which was quite apart from his masculine scorn of a girl's opinion on such matters. Somehow he did not wish to place Ellen Brewster on the same level of argument on which another man might have stood. He felt a jealousy of doing so. She seemed more within his reach, and infinitely more for his pleasure, where she was. He looked admiringly down at her fair face fixed on his with a serious, intent expression. He was quite ready to admit that he might fall in love with her. He was quite ready to ask now why he should not. She was a beautiful girl, an uncommon girl. She was going to be thoroughly educated. It would probably be quite possible to divorce her entirely from her surroundings. He shuddered when he thought of her mother and aunt, but, after all, a man, if he were firm, need not marry the mother or aunt. And all this was in spite of a resolution which he had formed on due consideration after his last call upon Ellen. He had said to himself that it would not in any case be wise, that he had better not see more of her than he could help. Instead of going to see her, he had gone riding with Maud Hemingway, who lived near his uncle's, in an old Colonial house which had belonged to her great-grandfather. The girl was a good comrade, so good a comrade that she shunted, as it were, love with flings of ready speech and friendly greeting, and tennis-rackets and riding-whips and foils. Robert had been teaching Maud to fence, and she had fenced too well. Still, Robert had said to himself that he might some day fall in love with her and marry her. He charged his memory with the fact that this was a much more rational course than visiting a girl like Ellen Brewster, so he stayed away in spite of involuntary turnings of his thoughts in that direction. However, now when the opportunity had seemed to be fairly forced upon him, what was he to do? He felt that he was stirred as he had never been before. The girl's very soul seemed to meet his when she looked up at him with those serious blue eyes of hers. He knew that there had never been any like her for him, but he felt as if in another minute, if they did not drop topics which he might as well have discussed with another man, this butterfly of femininity which so delighted him would be beyond his hand. He wanted to keep her to her rose.

"But the knowledge must not embitter your life," he said. "It is not for a little, delicate girl to worry herself over the problems which are too much for men."

In spite of himself a tenderness had come into his voice. Ellen looked down and away from him. She trembled.

"It seems to me that the problems of life, like those in the algebra we studied at school, are for everybody who can read them, whether men or women," said she, but her voice was unsteady.

"Some of them are for men to read and struggle with for the sake of the women," said Robert. His voice had a tender inflection. They were passing a garden full of old-fashioned flowers, bordered with box. The scent of the box seemed fairly to clamor over the garden fence, drowning out the smaller fragrances of the flowers, like the clamor of a mob. Even the sweetness of the mignonette was faintly perceived.

"How strong the box is," said Ellen, imperceptibly shrinking a little from Robert.

When they reached the Brewster house Robert said, as kindly as Granville Joy might have done, "Cannot we get better acquainted, Miss Brewster? May I call upon you sometimes?"

"I shall be happy to see you," Ellen said, repeating the formula of welcome like a child, but she knew when she repeated it that it was very true. After she had parted from young Lloyd, she went into the sitting room where were her mother and father, her mother sewing on a wrapper, her father reading the paper. Both of them looked up as the girl entered, and both stared at her in a bewildered way without rightly knowing why. Ellen's cheeks were a wonderful color, her eyes fairly blazed with blue light, her mouth was smiling in that ineffable smile of a simple overflow of happiness.

"Did you ride home on the car?" asked Fanny. "I didn't hear it stop."

"No, mother."

"Did you come home alone?" asked Andrew, abruptly.

"No," said Ellen, blinking before the glare of the lamp. Fanny looked at Andrew. "Who did come home with you?" she asked, in a foolish, fond voice.

"Mr. Robert Lloyd. He was sitting on the piazza when I got there. I told Miss Lennox I had just as soon come on the cars alone, but she wouldn't let me, and then he said it would be pleasant to walk, and —"

"Oh, you needn't make so many excuses," said Fanny, laughing.

Ellen colored until her face was a blaze of roses, she blinked harder, and turned her head away impatiently.

"I am not making excuses," said she, as if her modesty were offended. "I wish you wouldn't talk so, mother. I couldn't help it."

"Of course you couldn't," her mother called out jocularly, as Ellen went into the other room to get her lamp to go to bed.

Fanny was radiant with delight. After Ellen had gone upstairs, she kept looking at Andrew, and longing to confide in him her anticipation with regard to Ellen and young Lloyd, but she refrained, being doubtful as to how he would take it. Andrew looked very sober. The girl's beautiful, metamorphosed face was ever before his eyes, and it was with him as if he were looking after the flight of a beloved bird into a farther blue which was sacred, even from the following of his love.

Chapter XXVII

*E*llen's first impulse, when she really began to love Robert Lloyd, was not yielding, but flight; her first sensation, not happiness, but shame. When he left her that night she realized, to her unspeakable dismay and anger, that he had not left her, that he would never in her whole life, or at least it seemed so, leave her again. Everywhere she looked she saw his face projected by her memory before her with all the reality of life. His face came between her and her mother's and father's, it came between her and her thoughts of other faces. When she was alone in her chamber, there was the face. She blew out the lamp in a panic of resentment and undressed in the dark, but that made no difference. When she lay in bed, although she closed her eyes resolutely, she could still see it.

"I won't have it; I won't have it," she said, quite aloud in her shame and rebellion. "I won't have it. What does this mean?"

In spite of herself the sound of his voice was in her ears, and she resented that; she fought against the feeling of utter rapture which came stealing over her because of it. She felt as if she wanted to spring out of bed and run, run far away into the freedom of the night, if only by so doing she could outspeed herself. Ellen began to realize the tyranny of her own nature, and her whole soul arose in revolt.

But the girl could no more escape than a nymph of old the pursuit of the god, and there was no friendly deity to transform her into a flower to elude him. When she slept at last she was overtaken in the innocent passion of dreams, and when she awoke it was, to her angry sensitiveness, not alone.

When she went downstairs all her rosy radiance of the night before was eclipsed. She looked pale and nervous. She recoiled whenever her mother began to speak. It seemed to her that if she said anything, and especially anything congratulatory about Robert Lloyd, she would fly at her like a wild thing. Fanny kept looking at her with loving facetiousness, and Ellen winced indescribably; still, she did not say anything until after breakfast, when Andrew had gone to work. Andrew was unusually sober and preoccupied that morning. When he went out he passed close to Ellen, as she sat at the table, and tilted up her face and kissed her. "Father's blessin'," he whispered, hoarsely, in her ear. Ellen nestled against him. This natural affection, before which she need not fly nor be ashamed, which she had always known, seemed to come before her like a shield against all untried passion. She felt sheltered and comforted. But Andrew passed Eva Tenny coming to the house on his way out of the yard, and when she entered Fanny began at once:

"Who do you s'pose came home with Ellen last night?" said she. She looked at Eva, then at Ellen, with a glance which seemed to uncover a raw surface of delicacy. Ellen flushed angrily.

"Mother, I do wish —" she began; but Fanny cut her short.

"She's pretendin' she don't like it," she said, almost hilariously, her face glowing with triumph, "but she does. You ought to have seen her when she came in last night."

"I guess I know who it was," said Eva, but she echoed her sister's manner half-heartedly. She was looking very badly that morning, her face was stained, and her eye hard with a look as if tears had frozen in them. She had come in a soiled waist, too, without any collar.

"For Heaven's sake, Eva Tenny, what ails you?" Fanny cried.

Eva flung herself for answer on the floor, and fairly writhed. Words were not enough expression for her violent temperament. She had to resort to physical manifestations or lose her reason. As she writhed, she groaned as one might do who was dying in extremity of pain.

Ellen, when she heard her aunt's groans, stopped, and stood in the entry viewing it all. She thought at first that her aunt was ill, and was just about to call out to know if she should go for the doctor, all her grievances being forgotten in this evidently worse stress, when her mother fairly screamed again, stooping over her sister, and trying to raise her.

"Eva Tenny, you tell me this minute what the matter is."

Then Eva raised herself on one elbow, and disclosed a face distorted with wrath and woe, like a mask of tragedy.

"He's gone! he's gone!" she shrieked out, in an awful, shrill voice, which was like the note of an angry bird. "He's gone!"

"For God's sake, not — Jim?"

"Yes, he's gone! he's gone! Oh, my God! my God! he's gone!"

All at once the little Amabel appeared, slipping past Ellen silently. She stood watching her mother. She was vibrating from head to foot as if strung on wires. She was not crying, but she kept catching her breath audibly; her little hands were twitching in the folds of her frock; she winked rapidly, her lids obscuring and revealing her eyes until they seemed a series of blue sparks. She was no paler than usual — that was scarcely possible — but her skin looked transparent, pulses were evident all over her face and her little neck.

"You don't mean he's gone with — ?" gasped Fanny.

Suddenly Eva raised herself with a convulsive jerk from the floor to her feet. She stood quite still. "Yes, he has gone," she said, and all the passion was gone from her voice, which was much more terrible in its calm.

"You don't mean with — ?"

"Yes; he has gone with Aggie." Eva spoke in a voice like a deaf-mute's, quite free from inflections. There was something dreadful about her rigid attitude. Little Amabel looked at her mother's eyes, then cowered down and began to cry aloud. Ellen came in and took her in her arms, whispering to her to soothe her. She tried to coax her away, but the child resisted violently, though she was usually so docile with Ellen.

Eva did not seem to notice Amabel's crying. She stood in that horrible inflexibility, with eyes like black stones fixed on something unseeable.

Fanny clutched her violently by the arm and shook her.

"Eva Tenny," said she, "you behave yourself. What if he has run away? You ain't the first woman whose husband has run away. I'd have more pride. I wouldn't please him nor her enough. If he's as bad as that, you're better off rid of him."

Eva turned on her sister, and her calm broke up like ice under her fire of passion.

"Don't you say one word against him, not one word!" she shrieked, throwing off Fanny's hand. "I won't hear one word against my husband."

Then little Amabel joined in. "Don't you say one word against my papa!" she cried, in her shrill, childish treble. Then she sobbed convulsively, and pushed Ellen away. "Go away!" she said, viciously, to her. She was half mad with terror and bewilderment.

"Don't you say one word against Jim," said Eva again. "If ever I hear anybody say one word against him I'll —"

"You don't mean you're goin' to stan' up for him, Eva Tenny?"

"As long as I draw the breath of life, and after, if I know anything," declared Eva. Then she straightened herself to her full height, threw back her shoulders, and burst into a furious denunciation like some prophetess of wrath. The veins on her forehead grew turgid, her lips seemed to swell, her hair seemed to move as she talked. The others shrank back and looked at her; even little Amabel hushed her sobs and stared, fascinated. "Curses on the grinding tyranny that's brought it all about, and not on the poor, weak man that fell under it!" she cried. "Jim ain't to blame. He's had bigger burdens put on his shoulders than the Lord gave him strength to bear. He had to drop 'em. Jim has tried faithful ever since we were married. He worked hard, and it wa'n't never his fault that he lost his place, but he kept losin' it. They kept shuttin' down, or dischargin' him for no reason at all, without a minute's warnin'. An' it wa'n't because he drank. Jim never drank when he had a job. He was just taken up and put down by them over him as if he was a piece on a checker-board. He lost his good opinion of himself when he saw others didn't set anymore by him than to shove him off or on the board as it suited their play. He began to think maybe he wa'n't a man, and then he began to act as if he wasn't a man. And he was ashamed of his life because he couldn't support me and Amabel, ashamed of his life because he had to live on my little earnin's. He was ashamed to look me in the face, and ashamed to look his own child in the face. It was only night before last he was talkin' to me, and I didn't know what he meant then, but I know now. I thought then he meant something else, but now I know what he meant. He sat a long time leanin' his head on his hands, whilst I was sewin' on wrappers, after Amabel had gone to bed, and finally he looks up and says, 'Eva, you was right and I was wrong.'

"'What do you mean, Jim?' says I.

"'I mean you was right when you thought we'd better not get married, and I was wrong,' says he; and he spoke terrible bitter and sad. I never heard him speak like it. He sounded like another man. I jest flung down my sewin' and went over to him, and leaned his poor head against my shoulder. 'Jim,' says I, 'I ain't never regretted it.' And God knows I spoke the truth, and I speak the truth when I say it now. I ain't never regretted it, and I don't regret it now." Eva said the last with a look as if she were hurling defiance, then she went on in the same high, monotonous key above the ordinary key of life. "When I says that, he jest gives a great sigh and sort of pushes me away and gets up. 'Well, I have,' says he; 'I have, and sometimes I think the best thing I can do is to take myself out of the way, instead of sittin' here day after day and seein' you wearin' your fingers to the bone to support me, and seein' my child, an' bein' ashamed to look her in the face. Sometimes I think you an' Amabel would be a damned sight better off without me than with me, and I'm done for anyway, and it don't make much difference what I do next.'

"'Jim Tenny, you jest quit talkin' in such a way as this,' says I, for I thought he meant to make away with himself, but that wa'n't what he meant. Aggie Bemis had been windin' her net round him, and he wa'n't nothin' but a man, and all discouraged, and he gave in. Any man would in his place. He ain't to blame. It's the tyrants that's over us all that's to blame." Eva's voice shrilled higher. "Curse them!" she shrieked. "Curse them all! — every rich man in this gold-ridden country!"

"Eva Tenny, you're beside yourself," said Fanny, who was herself white to her lips, yet she viewed her sister indignantly, as one violent nature will view another when it is overborne and carried away by a kindred passion.

"Wonder if you'd be real calm in my place?" said Eva; and as she spoke the dreadful impassibility of desperation returned upon her. It was as if she suffered some chemical change before their eyes. She became silent and seemed as if she would never speak again.

"You hadn't ought to talk so," said Fanny, weakly, she was so terrified. "You ought to think of poor little Amabel," she added.

With that, Eva's dreadful, expressionless eyes turned towards Amabel, and she held out her hand to her, but the child fairly screamed with terror and clung to Ellen. "Oh, Aunt Eva, don't look at her so, you frighten her," Ellen said, trembling, and leaning her cheek against Amabel's little, cold, pale one. "Don't cry, darling," she whispered. "It is just because poor mother feels so badly."

"I am afraid of my mamma, and I want papa!" screamed Amabel, quivering, and stiffening her slender back.

Eva continued to keep her eyes fixed upon her, and to hold out that commanding hand.

Fanny went close to her, seized her by both shoulders, and shook her violently. "Eva Tenny, you behave yourself!" said she. "There ain't no need of your acting this way if your man has run away with another woman, and as for that child goin' with you, she shan't go one step with any woman that looks and acts as you do. Actin' this way over a good-for-nothin' fellow like Jim Tenny!"

Again that scourge of the spirit aroused Eva to her normal state. She became a living, breathing, wrathful, loving woman once more. "Don't you dare say a word against Jim!" she cried out; "not one word, Fanny Brewster; I won't hear it. Don't you dare say a word!"

"Don't you say a word against my papa!" shrilled Amabel. Then she left Ellen and ran to her mother, and clung to her. And Eva caught her up, and hugged the little, fragile thing against her breast, and pounced upon her with kisses, with a fury as of rage instead of love.

"She always looked like Jim," she sobbed out; "she always did. Aggie Bemis shall never get her. I've got her in spite of all the awful wrong of life; it's the good that had to come out of it whether or no, and God couldn't help Himself. I've got this much. She always looked like Jim."

Eva set Amabel down and began leading her out of the room.

"You ain't goin'?" said Fanny, who had herself begun to weep. "Eva, you ain't goin'? Oh, you poor girl!"

"Don't! — you said that like Jim," Eva cried, with a great groan of pain.

"Eva, you ain't goin'? Wait a little while, and let me do somethin' for you."

"You can't do anything. Come, Amabel."

Eva and Amabel went away, the child rolling eyes of terror and interrogation at them, Eva impervious to all her sister's pleading.

When Andrew heard what had happened, and Fanny repeated what Eva had said, his blame for Jim Tenny was unqualified. "I've had a hard time enough, knocked about from pillar to post, and I know what she means when she talks about a checker-board. God knows I feel myself sometimes as if I wasn't anything but a checker-piece instead of a man," he said, "but it's all nonsense blamin' the shoe-manufacturers for his runnin' away with that woman. A man has got to use what little freedom he's got right. It ain't any excuse for Jim Tenny that he's been out of work and got discouraged. He's a good-for-nothing cur, an' I'd like to tell him so."

"It won't do for you to talk to Eva that way," said Fanny. They were all at the supper-table. Ellen was listening silently.

"She does right to stand up for her husband, I suppose," said Andrew, "but anybody's got to use a little sense. It don't make it any better for Jim, tryin' to shove blame off his shoulders that belongs there. The manufacturers didn't make him run off with another woman and leave his child. That was a move he made himself."

"But he wouldn't have made that move if the manufacturers hadn't made theirs," Ellen said, unexpectedly.

"That's so," said Fanny.

Andrew looked uneasily at Ellen, in whose cheeks two red spots were burning, and whose eyes upon his face seemed narrowed to two points of brightness. "There's nothing for you to worry about, child," he said.

All this was before the dressmaker, who listened with no particular interest. Affairs which did not directly concern her did not awaken her to much sharpness of regard. She had been forced by circumstances into a very narrow groove of life, a little foot-path as it were, fenced in from destruction by three dollars a day. She could not, view it as keenly as she might, see that Jim Tenny's elopement had anything whatever to do with her three dollars per day. She, therefore, ate her supper. At first Andrew had looked warningly at Fanny when she began to discuss the subject before the dressmaker, but Fanny had replied, "Oh, land, Andrew, she knows all about it now. It's all over town."

"Yes, I heard it this morning before I came," said the dressmaker. "I think a puff on the sleeves of the silk waist will be very pretty, don't you, Mrs. Brewster?"

Ellen looked at the dressmaker with wonder; it seemed to her that the woman was going on a little especial side track of her own outside the interests of her kind. She looked at her pretty new things and tried them on, and felt guilty that she had them. What business had she having new clothes and going to Vassar College in the face of that misery? What was an education? What was anything compared with the sympathy which love demanded of love in the midst of sorrow? Should she not turn her back upon any purely personal advantage as she would upon a moral plague?

When Ellen's father said that to her at the supper-table she looked at him with unchildlike eyes. "I think it is something for me to worry about, father," she said. "How can I help worrying if I love Aunt Eva and Amabel?"

"It's a dreadful thing for Eva," said Fanny. "I don't see what she is going to do. Andrew, pass the biscuits to Miss Higgins."

"It seems to me that the one that is the farthest behind anything that happens on this earth is the one to blame," said Ellen, reverting to her line of argument.

"I don't know but you've got to go back to God, then," said Andrew, soberly, passing the biscuits. Miss Higgins took one.

"No, you haven't," said Ellen — "you haven't, because men are free. You've got to stop before you get to God. When a man goes wrong, you have got to look and see if he is to blame, if he started himself, or other men have been pushing him into it. It seems to me that other men have been pushing Uncle Jim into it. I don't think factory-owners have any right to discharge a man without a good reason, anymore than he has a right to run the shop."

"I don't think so, either," said Fanny. "I think Ellen is right."

"I don't know. It is all a puzzle," said Andrew. "Something's wrong somewhere. I don't know whether it's because we are pushed or because we pull. There's no use in your worrying about it, Ellen. You've got to study your books." Andrew said this with a look of pride at Ellen and sidelong triumph at the dressmaker to see if she rightly understood the magnitude of it all, of the whole situation of making dresses for this wonderful young creature who was going to Vassar College.

"I don't know but this is more important than books," said Ellen.

"Oh, maybe you'll find out something in your books that will settle the whole matter," said Andrew. Ellen was not eating much supper, and that troubled him. Andrew always knew just how much Ellen ate.

"I don't know what Aunt Eva and poor little Amabel will do," said she. Ellen's lip quivered.

"Pass the cake to Miss Higgins," said Fanny, sharply, to Andrew. She gave him a significant wink as she did so, not to talk more about it.

"Try some of that chocolate cake, Miss Higgins."

"Thank you," said Miss Higgins, unexcitedly.

Andrew had his own cause of worry, and finally reverted to it, eating his food with no more conception of the savor than if it were in another man's mouth. He was sorry enough for his wife's sister, and recognized it as an added weight to his own burden, but just at present all he could think of was the question if Miss Higgins would ask for her pay again that night. He had not a dollar in his pocket. He had been dunned that afternoon by the man who had lent the money to buy Ellen's watch, there were two new dunning letters in his pocket, and now if that keen little dressmaker, who fairly looked to him like a venomous insect, as she sat eating rather voraciously of the chocolate cake, should ask him again for the three dollars due her that night! He would not have cared so much, if it were not for the fact that she would ask him before his wife and Ellen, and the question about the money in the savings-bank, which was a species of nightmare to him, would be sure to come to the front.

Suddenly it struck Andrew that he might run away, that he might slip out after supper, and either go into his mother's house or down the street. He finally decided on the former, since he reasoned, with a pitiful cunning, that if he went down the street he would have to take off his slippers and put on his shoes, and that would at once betray him and lead to the possible arrest of his flight.

So after supper, while Miss Higgins was trying a waist on Ellen, and Fanny was clearing the table, Andrew, bareheaded and in his slippers, prepared to carry his plan into execution. He got out without being seen, and hurried around the rear of the house, out of view from the sitting room windows, resolving on the way that in order to avert the danger of a possible following him to the sanctuary of his mother's house, he had perhaps better slip down into the orchard behind it and see if the porter apples were ripe. But when, stooping as if beneath some invisible shield, and moving with a low glide of secrecy, he had gained the yard between the two houses, the yard where the three cherry trees stood, he heard Fanny's high, insistent voice calling him, and knew that it was all over. Fanny had her head thrust out of her bedroom window. "Andrew! Andrew!" she called.

Andrew stopped. "What is it?" he asked, in a gruff voice. He felt at that moment savage with her and with fate. He felt like some badgered animal beneath the claws and teeth of petty enemies which were yet sufficient to do him to death. He felt that retreat and defense were alike impossible and inglorious. He was aware of a monstrous impatience with it all, which was fairly blasphemy. "What is it?" he said, and Fanny realized that something was wrong.

"Come here, Andrew Brewster," she said, from the bedroom window, and Andrew pressed close to the window through a growth of sweetbrier which rasped his hands and sent up a sweet fragrance in his face. Andrew tore away the clinging vines angrily.

"Well, what is it?" he said again.

"Don't spoil that bush, Ellen sets a lot by it," said Fanny. "What makes you act so, Andrew Brewster?" Then she lowered her voice. "She wants to know if she can have her pay tonight," she whispered.

"I ain't got a cent," replied Andrew, in a dogged, breathless voice.

"You ain't been to the bank today, then?"

"No, I ain't."

Fanny still suspected nothing. She was, in fact, angry with the dressmaker for insisting upon her pay in such a fashion. "I never heard of such a thing as her wantin' to be paid every night," she whispered, angrily, "and I'd tell her so, if I wasn't afraid she'd think we couldn't pay her. I'd never have had her; I'd had Miss Patch, if I'd know she'd do such a mean thing, but, as it is, I don't know what to do. I ain't got but a dollar and seventy-three cents by me. You ain't got enough to make it up?"

"No, I ain't."

"Well, all is, I've got to tell her that it ain't convenient for me to pay her tonight, and she shall have it all together tomorrow night, and tomorrow you'll have to go to the bank and take out the money, Andrew. Don't forget it."

"Well," said Andrew.

Fanny retreated, and he heard her high voice explaining to Miss Higgins. He tore his way through the clinging sweetbrier bushes and ran with an unsteady, desperate gait down to the orchard behind his mother's home, and flung himself at full length in the dewy grass under the trees with all the abandon, under stress of fate, of a child.

Chapter XXVIII

Andrew Brewster, lying in the dewy grass under the apple trees, giving way for almost the first time since his childhood to impulses which had hitherto, from his New England heredity, stiffened instead of relaxed his muscles of expression, felt as if he were being stung to death by ants. He was naturally a man of broad views, who felt the indignity of coping with such petty odds. "For God's sake, if I had to be done to death, why couldn't it have been for something?" he groaned, speaking with his lips close to the earth as if it were a listening ear. "Why need it all have been over so little? It's just the little fight for enough to eat and wear that's getting the better of me that was a man, and able to do a man's work in the world. Now it has come to this! Here I am runnin' away from a woman because she wants me to pay her three dollars, and I am afraid of another woman because — I've been and fooled away a few hundred dollars I had in the savings-bank. I'm afraid — yes, it has come to this. I am afraid, afraid, and I'd run away out of life if I knew where it would fetch me to. I'm afraid of things that ain't worth being afraid of, and it's all over things that's beneath me." There came over Andrew, with his mouth to the moist earth, feeling the breath and the fragrance of it in his nostrils, a realization of the great motherhood of nature, and a contempt for himself which was scorching and scathing before it. He felt that he came from that mighty breast which should produce only sons of might, and was spending his whole life in an ignominy of fruitless climbing up mole-hills. "Why couldn't I have been more?" he asked himself. "Oh, my God, is it my fault?" He said to himself that if he had not yielded to the universal law and longing of his kind for a home and a family, it might have been better. He asked himself that question which will never be answered with a surety of correctness, whether the advancement of the individual to his furthest compass is more to the glory of life than the blind following out of the laws of existence and the bringing others into the everlasting problem of advance. Then he thought of Ellen, and a great warmth of conviction came over the loving heart of the man; all his self-contempt vanished. He had

her, this child who was above pearls and rubies, he had her, and in her
the furthest reach of himself and progression of himself to greater
distances than he could ever have accomplished in any other way, and
it was a double progress, since it was not only for him, but also for the
woman he had married. A great wave of love for Fanny came over him.
He seemed to see that, after all, it was a shining road by which he had
come, and he saw himself upon it like a figure of light. He saw that he
lived and could never die. Then, as with a remorseless hurl of a high
spirit upon needle-pricks of petty cares, he thought again of the dressmaker, of the money for Ellen's watch, of the butcher's bill, and the
grocer's bills, and the money which he had taken from the bank, and
again he cowered beneath and loathed his ignoble burden. He dug his
hot head into the grass. "Oh, my God! oh, my God!" he groaned. He
fairly sobbed. Then he felt a soft wind of feminine skirts caused by the
sudden stoop of someone beside him, and Ellen's voice, shrill with
alarm, rang in his ears. "Father, what is the matter? Father!"

Such was the man's love for the girl that his first thought was for her
alarm, and he pushed all his own troubles into the background with a
lightninglike motion. He raised himself hastily, and smiled at her with
his pitiful, stiff face. "It's nothing at all, Ellen, don't you worry," he
said.

But that was not enough to satisfy her. She caught hold of his arm
and clung to it. "Father," she said, in a tone which had in it, to his
wonder, a firm womanliness — his own daughter seemed to speak to
him as if she were his mother — "you are not telling me the truth.
Something is the matter, or you wouldn't do like this."

"No, there's nothin', nothin' at all, dear child," said Andrew. He tried
to loosen her little, clinging hand from his arm. "Come, let's go back
to the house," he said. "Don't you mind anything about it. Sometimes
father gets discouraged over nothin'."

"It isn't over nothing," said Ellen. "What is it about, father?"

Andrew tried to laugh. "Well, if it isn't over nothin', it's over nothin'
in particular," said he; "it's over jest what's happened right along.
Sometimes father feels as if he hadn't made as much as he'd ought to
out of his life, and he's gettin' older, and he's feelin' kind of discouraged,
that's all."

"Over money matters?" said Ellen, looking at him steadily.

"Over nothin'," said her father. "See here, child, father's ashamed
that he gave way so, and you found him. Now don't you worry one mite
about it — it's nothing at all. Come, let's go back to the house," he said.

Ellen said no more, but she walked up from the field holding tightly
to her father's poor, worn hand, and her heart was in a tumult. To behold

any convulsion of nature is no light experience, and when it is a storm of the spirit in one beloved the beholder is swept along with it in greater or less measure. Ellen trembled as she walked. Her father kept looking at her anxiously and remorsefully. Once he reached around his other hand and chucked her playfully under the chin. "Scared most to death, was she?" he asked, with a shamefaced blush.

"I know something is the matter, and I think it would be better for you to tell me, father," replied Ellen, soberly.

"There's nothing to tell, child," said Andrew. "Don't you worry your little head about it." Between his anxiety lest the girl should be troubled, and his intense humiliation that she should have discovered him in such an abandon of grief which was almost like a disclosure of the nakedness of his spirit, he was completely unnerved. Ellen felt him tremble, and heard his voice quiver when he spoke. She felt towards her father something she had never felt before — an impulse of protection. She felt the older and stronger of the two. Her grasp on his hand tightened, she seemed in a measure to be leading him along.

When they reached the yard between the houses Andrew cast an apprehensive glance at the windows. "Has she gone?" he asked.

"Who, the dressmaker?"

"Yes."

"She hadn't when I came out. I saw you come past the house, and I thought you walked as if you didn't feel well, so I thought I would run out and see."

"I was all right," replied Andrew. "Have you got to try on anything more tonight?"

"No."

"Well, then, let's run into grandma's a minute."

"All right," said Ellen.

Mrs. Zelotes was sitting at her front window in the dusk, looking out on the street, as was her favorite custom. The old woman seldom lit a lamp in the summer evening, but sat there staring out at the lighted street and the people passing and repassing, with her mind as absolutely passive as regarded herself as if she were traveling and observing only that which passed without. At those times she became in a fashion sensible of the motion of the world, and lost her sense of individuality in the midst of it. When her son and granddaughter entered she looked away from the window with the expression of one returning from afar, and seemed dazed for a moment.

"Hullo, mother!" said Andrew.

The room was dusky, and they moved across between the chairs and tables like two shadows.

"Oh, is it you, Andrew?" said his mother. "Who is that with you — Ellen?"

"Yes," said Ellen. "How do you do, grandma?"

Mrs. Zelotes became suddenly fully awake to the situation; she collected her scattered faculties; her keen old eyes gleamed in a shaft of electric-light from the street without, which fell full upon her face.

"Set down," said she. "Has the dressmaker gone?"

"No, she hadn't when I came out," replied Ellen, "but she's most through for tonight."

"How do your things look?"

"Real pretty, I guess."

"Sometimes I think you'd better have had Miss Patch. I hope she ain't got your sleeves too tight at the elbows."

"They seem to fit very nicely, grandma."

"Sleeves are very particular things; a sleeve wrong can spoil a whole dress."

Suddenly the old woman turned on Ellen with a look of extremest facetiousness and intelligence, and the girl winced, for she knew what was coming. "I see you goin' past with a young man last night, didn't I?" said she.

Ellen flushed. "Yes," she said, almost indignantly, for she had a feeling as if the veil of some inner sacredness of her nature were continually being torn aside. "I went over to Miss Lennox, to carry some sweet-peas, and Mr. Robert Lloyd was there, and he came home with me."

"Oh!" replied her grandmother.

Ellen's patience left her at the sound of that "Oh," which seemed to rasp her very soul. "You have none of you any right to talk and act as you do," said she. "You make me ashamed of you, you and mother; father has more sense. Just because a young man makes me a call to return something, and then walks home with me, because he happened to be at the house where I call in the evening! I think it's a shame. You make me feel as if I couldn't look him in the face."

"Never mind, grandma didn't mean any harm," Andrew said, soothingly.

"You needn't try to excuse me, Andrew Brewster," cried his mother, angrily. "I guess it's a pretty to-do, if I can't say a word in joke to my own granddaughter. If it had been a poor, good-for-nothing young feller workin' in a shoe-factory, I s'pose she'd been tickled to death to be joked about him, but now when it begins to look as if somebody that was worth while had come along —"

"Grandma, if you say another word about it, I will never speak to Robert Lloyd again as long as I live," declared Ellen.

"Never mind, child," whispered Andrew.

"I do mind, and I mean what I say," Ellen cried. "I won't have it. Robert Lloyd is nothing to me, and I am nothing to him. He is no better than Granville Joy. There is nothing between us, and you make me too ashamed to think of him."

Then the old woman cried out, in a tone of triumph, "Well, there he is, turnin' in at your gate now."

Chapter XXIX

*E*llen rose without a word, and fled out of the room and out of the house. It seemed to her, after what had happened, after what her mother and grandmother had said and insinuated, after what she herself had thought and felt, that she must. She longed to see Robert Lloyd, to hear him speak, as she had never longed for anything in the world, and yet she ran away as if she were driven to obey some law which was coeval with the first woman and beyond all volition of her individual self.

When she reached the head of the little cross street on which the Atkinses lived, she turned into it with relief. The Atkins house was a tiny cottage, with a little kitchen ell, and a sagging piazza across the front. On this piazza were shadowy figures, and the dull, red gleam of pipes, and one fiery tip of a cigar. Joe Atkins, and Sargent, and two other men were sitting out there in the cool of the evening. Ellen hurried around the curve of the foot-path to the kitchen door. Abby was in there, working with the swift precision of a machine. She washed and wiped dishes as if in a sort of fury, her thin elbows jerking, her mouth compressed.

When Ellen entered, Abby stared, then her whole face lighted up, as if from some internal lamp. "Why, Ellen, is that you?" she said, in a surprisingly sweet voice. Sometimes Abby's sharp American voice rang with the sweetness of a soft bell.

"I thought I'd run over a minute," said Ellen.

The other girl looked sharply at her. "Why, what's the matter?" she said.

"Nothing is the matter. Why?"

"Why, I thought you looked sort of queer. Maybe it's the light. Sit down; I'll have the dishes done in a minute, then we'll go into the sitting room."

"I'd rather stay out here with you," said Ellen.

Abby looked at her again. "There is something the matter, Ellen Brewster," said she; "you can't cheat me. You would never have run over here this way in the world. What has happened?"

"Let's go up to your room after the dishes are done, and then I'll tell you," whispered Ellen. The men's voices on the piazza could be heard quite distinctly, and it seemed possible that their own conversation might be overheard in return.

"All right," said Abby. "Of course I have heard about your aunt," she added, in a low voice.

"Yes," said Ellen, and she felt shamed and remorseful that her own affairs had been uppermost in her mind, and that Abby had supposed that she might be disturbed over this great trouble of her poor aunt's.

"I think it is dreadful," said Abby. "I wish I could get hold of that woman." By "that woman" she meant the woman with whom poor Jim Tenny had eloped.

"I do," said Ellen, bitterly.

"But it's something besides that made you run over here," said Abby.

"I'll tell you when we go up to your room," replied Ellen.

When the dishes were finished, and the two girls in Abby's little chamber, seated side by side on the bed, Ellen still hesitated.

"Now, Ellen Brewster, what is the matter? You said you would tell, and you've got to," said Abby.

Ellen looked away from her, blushing. The electric-light from the street shone full in the room, which was wavering with grotesque shadows.

"Well," said she, "I ran away."

"You ran away! What for?"

"Oh, because."

"Because what?"

"Because I saw somebody coming."

"Saw who coming?"

Ellen was silent.

"Not Granville Joy?"

Ellen shook her head.

"Not — ?"

Ellen looked straight ahead.

"Not young Mr. Lloyd?"

Ellen was silent with the silence of assent.

"Did he go into your house?"

Ellen nodded.

"Where were you?"

"In grandma's."

"And you ran away, over here?"

Ellen nodded.

"Why, Ellen Brewster, didn't you want to see him?"

Ellen turned from Abby with an impatient gesture, buried her face in the bed, and began to weep.

Abby leaned over her caressingly. "Ellen dear," she whispered, "what is the matter; what are you crying for? What made you run away?"

Ellen sobbed harder.

Abby looked at Ellen's prostrate figure sadly. "Ellen," she began; then she stopped, for her own voice quivered. Then she went on, quite steadily. "Ellen," she said, "you like him."

"No, I don't," declared Ellen. "I won't. I never will. Nothing shall make me."

But Abby continued to look at her sadly and jealously. "There's a power over us which is too strong for girls," said she, "and you've come under it, Ellen, and you can't help it." Then she added, with a great, noble burst of utter unselfishness: "And I'm glad, I'm glad, Ellen. That man can lift you out of the grind."

But Ellen sat up straight and faced her, with burning cheeks, and eyes shining through tears. "I will never be lifted out of the grind as long as those I love are in it," said she.

"Do you suppose it would make it any better for your folks to see you in it all your life along with them?" said Abby. "Suppose you married a fellow like Granville Joy?"

Chapter XXX

*E*llen looked at the other girl in a kind of rage of maidenly shame. "Why have I got to get married, anyway?" she demanded. "Isn't there anything in this world besides getting married? Why do you all talk so about me? You don't seem so bent on getting married yourself. If you think so much of marriage, why don't you get married yourself, and let me alone?"

"Nobody wants to marry me that I know of," replied Abby, quite simply. Then she, too, blazed out. "Get married!" she cried. "Do you really think I would get married to the kind of man who would marry me? Do you think I could if I loved him?" A great wave of red surged over the girl's thin face, her voice trembled with tenderness. Ellen knew at once, with a throb of sympathy and shame, that Abby did love someone.

"Do you think I would marry him if I loved him?" demanded Abby, stiffening herself into a soldierlike straightness. "Do you think? I tell you what it is," she said, "I was lookin' only today at David Mendon at the cutting-bench, cutting away with his poor little knife. I'd like to know how many handles he's worn out since he began. There he was, putting the pattern on the leather, and cuttin' around it, standin' at his window, that's a hot place in summer and a cold one in winter, and there's where he's stood for I don't know how many years since before I was born. He's one of the few that Lloyd's has hung on to when he's got older, and I thought to myself, good Lord, how that poor man must have loved his wife, and how he must love his children, to be willin' to turn himself into a machine like that for them. He never takes a holiday unless he's forced into it; there he stands and cuts and cuts. If I were his wife, I would die of shame and pity that I ever led him into it. Do you think I would ever let a man turn himself into a machine for me, if I loved him? I guess I wouldn't! And that's why, when I see a man of another sort that you won't have to break your own heart over, whether you marry him or not, payin' attention to you, I am glad. It's a different thing, marriage with a man like Robert Lloyd, and a man like that would never think of me. I'm right in the ranks, and you ain't."

"I am," said Ellen, stoutly.

"No, you ain't; you don't belong there, and when I see a chance for you to get out where you belong —"

"I don't intend to make marriage a stepping-stone," said Ellen. "Sometimes —" She hesitated.

"What?" asked the other girl.

"Sometimes I think I would rather not go to college, after all."

"Ellen Brewster, are you crazy? Of course, you will go to college unless you marry Robert Lloyd. Perhaps he won't want to wait." Then Abby, dauntless as she was, shrank a little before Ellen's wrathful retort.

"Abby Atkins, you ought to be ashamed of yourself!" she cried. "There he's been to see me just twice, the first time on an errand, and the next with his aunt, and he's walked home with me once because he couldn't help it; his aunt told him to!"

"But here he is again tonight," said Abby, apologetically.

"What of that? I suppose he has come on another errand."

"Then what made you run away?"

"Because you have all made me ashamed of my life to look at him," said Ellen, hotly.

Then down went her head on the bed again, and Abby was leaning over her, caressing her, whispering fond things to her like a lover.

"There, there, Ellen," she whispered. "Don't be mad, don't feel bad. I didn't mean any harm. You are such a beauty — there's nobody like you in the world — that everybody thinks that any man who sees you must want you."

"Robert Lloyd doesn't, and if he did I wouldn't have him," sobbed Ellen.

"You shan't if you don't want him," said Abby, consolingly.

After a while the two girls bathed their eyes with cold water, and went downstairs into the sitting room. Maria was making herself a blue muslin dress, and her mother was hemming the ruffles. There was a cheap blue shade on the lamp, and Maria herself was clad in a blue gingham. All the blue color and the shade on the lamp gave a curious pallor and unreality to the homely room and the two women. Mrs. Atkins's hair was strained back from her hollow temples, which had noble outlines.

"I'm going to walk a little way with Ellen, she's going home," said Abby.

"Very well," said her mother. Maria looked wistfully at them as they went out. She went on sewing on her blue muslin, rather sadly. She coughed a little.

"Why don't you put up your sewing for tonight and go to bed, child?" said her mother.

"I might as well sit here and sew as go to bed and lie there. I shouldn't sleep," replied Maria, with the gentlest sadness conceivable. There was in it no shadow of complaining. Of late years all the fire of resistance had seemed to die out in the girl. She was unfailingly sweet, but nerveless. Often when she raised a hand it seemed as if she could not even let it fall, as if it must remain poised by some curious inertia. Still, she went to the shop every day and did her work faithfully. She pasted linings in shoes, and her slender little fingers used to fly as if they were driven by some more subtle machine than any in the factory. Often Maria felt vaguely as if she were in the grasp of some mighty machine worked by a mighty operator; she felt, as she pasted the linings, as if she herself were also a part of some monstrous scheme of work under greater hands than hers, and there was never any getting back of it. And always with it all there was that ceaseless, helpless, bewildered longing for something, she was afraid to think what, which often saps the strength and life of a young girl. Maria had never had a lover in her life; she had not even good comrades among young men, as her sister had. No man at that time would have ever looked twice at her, unless he had fallen in love with her, and had been disposed to pick her up and carry her along on the hard road upon which they fared together. Maria was half fed in every sense; she had not enough nourishing food for her body, nor love for her heart, nor exercise for her brain. She had no time to read, as she was forced to sew when out of the shop if she would have anything to wear. When at last she went upstairs to bed, before Abby returned, she sat down by her window, and leaned her little, peaked chin on the sill and looked out. The stars were unusually bright for a summer night; the whole sky seemed filled with a constantly augmenting host of them. The scent of tobacco came to her from below. To the lonely girl the stars and the scent of the tobacco served as stimulants; she formed a forcible wish. "I wish," she muttered to herself, "that I was either an angel or a man." Then the next minute she chided herself for her wickedness. A great wave of love for God, and remorse for impatience and melancholy in her earthly lot, swept over her. She knelt down beside her bed and prayed. An exultation half-physical, half-spiritual, filled her. When she rose, her little, thin face was radiant. She seemed to measure the short-ness of the work and woe of the world as between her thumb and finger. The joy of the divine filled all her longing. When Abby came home, who shared her chamber, she felt no jealousy. She only inquired whether she had gone quite home with Ellen. "Yes, I did," replied Abby. "I don't think it is safe for her to go past that lonely place below the Smiths'."

"I'm glad you did," said Maria, with an angelic inflection in her voice.

"Robert Lloyd came to see Ellen, and she ran away over here, and wouldn't see him, because they had all been plaguing her about him," said Abby. "I wish she wouldn't do so. It would be a splendid thing for her to marry him, and I know he likes her, and his aunt is going to send her to college."

"That won't make any difference to Ellen, and everything will be all right anyway, if only she loved God," said Maria, still with that rapt, angelic voice.

"Shucks!" said Abby. Then she leaned over her sister, caught her by her little, thin shoulders and shook her tenderly. "There, I didn't mean to speak so," said she. "You're awful good, Maria. I'm glad you've got religion if it's so much comfort to you. I don't mean to make light of it, but I'm afraid you ain't well. I'm goin' to get you some more of that tonic tomorrow."

Chapter XXXI

*W*hen Ellen reached home that night she found no one there except her father, who was sitting on the doorstep in the north yard. Her mother had gone to see her aunt Eva as soon as the dressmaker had left. "Who was that with you?" Andrew asked, as she drew near.

"Abby," replied Ellen.

"So you went over there?"

Ellen sat down on a lower step in front of her father. "Yes," said she. She half laughed up in his face, like a child who knows she has been naughty, yet knows she will not be blamed since she can count so surely on the indulgent love of the would-be blamer.

"Ellen, your mother didn't like it."

"They had said so many things to me about him that I didn't feel as if I could see him, father," she said.

Andrew put a hand on her head. "I know what you mean," he replied, "but they didn't mean any harm; they're only looking out for your best good, Ellen. You can't always have us; it ain't in the course of nature, you know, Ellen."

There was a tone of inexorable sadness, the sadness of fate itself in Andrew's voice. He had, as he spoke, the full realization of that stage of progress which is simply for the next, which passes to make room for it. He felt his own nothingness. It was the throe of the present before the future; it was the pang of anticipatory annihilation.

"Don't talk that way, father," said Ellen. "Neither you nor mother are old people."

"Oh, well, it's all right, don't you worry," said Andrew.

"How long did he stay?" asked Ellen. She did not look at her father as she spoke.

"Oh, he didn't stay at all, after they found out you had gone."

Ellen sighed. After a second Andrew sighed also. "It's gettin' late," said he, heavily; "mebbe we'd better go in before your mother comes, Ellen. Mebbe you'll get cold out here."

"Oh no, I shall not," said Ellen, "and I want to hear about poor Aunt Eva. I don't see what she is going to do."

"It's a dreadful thing makin' a mistake in marriage," said Andrew.

"Uncle Jim was a good man if he hadn't had such a hard time."

Andrew looked at her, then he spoke impressively. "Look here, Ellen," he said, "you are a good scholar, and you are smarter in a good many ways than father has ever been, but there's one thing you want to remember; you want to be sure before you blame the Lord or other men for a man's goin' wrong, if it ain't his own fault at the bottom of things."

"There's mother," cried Ellen; "there's mother and Amabel. Where's Aunt Eva? Oh, father, what do you suppose has happened? Why do you suppose mother is bringing Amabel home?"

"I don't know," replied Andrew, in a troubled voice.

He and Ellen rose and hastened forward to meet Fanny and Amabel. The child hung at her aunt's hand in a curious, limp, disjointed fashion; her little face, even in the half light, showed ghastly. When she saw Ellen she let go of Fanny's hand and ran to her and threw both her little arms around her in a fierce clutch as of terror, then she began to sob wildly, "Mamma, mamma, mamma!"

Fanny leaned her drawn face forward, and whispered to Andrew and Ellen over Amabel's head, under cover of her sobs, "Hush, don't say anything. She's gone mad, and, and — she tried to — kill Amabel."

Chapter XXXII

*A*mabel was a very nervous child, and she was in such terror from her really terrific experience that she threatened to go into convulsions. Andrew went over for his mother, whom he had always regarded as an incontestable authority about children. She, after one sharp splutter of wrath at the whole situation, went to work with the resolution of an old soldier.

"Heat some water, quick," said she to Andrew, "and get me a wash-tub."

Then she told Fanny to brew a mess of sage tea, and began stripping off Amabel's clothes.

"Let me alone! Mamma, mamma, mamma!" shrieked the child. She fought and clawed like a little, wild animal, but the old woman, in whose arms great strength could still arise for emergencies, and in whose spirit great strength had never died, got the better of her.

When Amabel's clothing was stripped off, and her little, spare body, which was brown rather than rosy, although she was a blonde, was revealed, she was as pitiful to see as a wound. Every nerve and pulse in that tiny frame, about which there was not an ounce of superfluous flesh, seemed visible. The terrible sensitiveness of the child appeared on the surface. She shrank, and wailed in a low, monotonous tone like a spent animal overtaken by pursuers. But Mrs. Zelotes put her in the tub of warm water, and held her down, though Amabel's face, emerging from it, had the expression of a wild thing.

"There, you keep still!" said she, and her voice was tender enough, though the decision of it could have moved an army.

When Amabel had had her hot bath, and had drunk her sage tea by compulsory gulps, and been tucked into Ellen's bed, her childhood reasserted itself. Gradually her body and her bodily needs gained the ascendancy over the unnatural strain of her mind. She fell asleep, and lay like one dead. Then Ellen crept downstairs, though it was almost midnight, where her father and mother and grandmother were still talking over the matter. Fanny seemed almost as bad as her sister. It was evident that there was in the undisciplined Loud family a dangerous strain if too far pressed. She was lying down on the lounge, with Andrew holding her hand.

"Oh, my God! Oh, my God! Poor Eva!" she kept repeating.

Then she threw off Andrew's hand, sprang to her feet, and began to walk the room.

"She'll be as bad as her sister if she keeps on," said Mrs. Zelotes, quite audibly, but Fanny paid no attention to that.

"What is goin' to be done? Oh, my God, what is goin' to be done?" she wailed. "There she is locked up with two men watchin' her lest she do herself a harm, and it's got to cost eighteen dollars a week, unless she's put in with the State poor, and then nobody knows how she'll be treated. Oh, poor Eva, poor Eva! Albert Riggs told me there were awful things done with the State poor in the asylums. He's been an attendant in one. He says we've got to pay eighteen dollars a week if we want to have her cared for decently, and where's the money comin' from?" Fanny raised her voice higher still.

"Where's the money comin' from?" she demanded, with an impious inflection. It was as if she questioned that which is outside of, and the source of, life. Everything with this woman, whose whole existence had been bound and tainted by the need of money, resolved itself into that fundamental question. All her woes hinged upon it; even her misery was deteriorated by mammon.

"Where's the money comin' from?" she demanded again. "There's Jim gone, and all his mother's got is that little, mortgaged place, and she feeble, and there ain't a cent anywhere, unless —" She turned fiercely to Andrew, clutching him hard by the arm.

"You must take every cent of that money out of the savings-bank," she cried, "every cent of it. I'm your wife, and I've been a good wife to you, you can't say I haven't."

"Yes, of course you have, poor girl! Don't, don't!" said Andrew, soothingly. He was very pale, and shook from head to foot as he tried to calm Fanny.

"Yes, I've been a good, faithful wife," Fanny went on, in her high, hysterical voice. "Even your mother can't say that I haven't; and Eva is my own sister, and you ought to help her. Every cent of that money will have to come out of the savings-bank, and the house here will have to be mortgaged; it's only my due. I would do as much for you if it was your sister. Eva ain't goin' to suffer."

"I guess if you mortgage this house that you had from your father, to keep a woman whose husband has gone off and left her," said Mrs.

Zelotes, "I guess if you don't go and get him back, and get the law to tackle him!"

Then Fanny turned on her. "Don't you say a word," said she. "My sister ain't goin' to suffer, I don't care where the money comes from. It's mine as much as Andrew's. I've half supported the family myself sewin' on wrappers, and I've got a right to have my say. My sister ain't goin' to suffer! Oh, my God, what's goin' to become of her? Poor Eva, poor Eva! Eighteen dollars a week; that's as much as Andrew ever earned. Oh, it was awful, it was awful! There, when I got in there, she had a — knife, the — carving knife, and she had Amabel's hair all gathered up in one hand, and her head tipped back, and poor old mother Tenny was holding her arms, and screamin', and it was all I could do to get the knife away," and Fanny stripped up her sleeves, and showed a glancing cut on her arm.

"She did that before I got it away from her," she said. "Think of it, my own sister! My own sister, who always thought so much of me, and would have had her own fingers cut to the bone before she would have let anyone touch me or Ellen! Oh, poor Eva, poor Eva! What is goin' to become of her, what is goin' to become of her?"

Mrs. Zelotes went out of the house with a jerk of angry decision, and presently returned with a bottle half full of whiskey.

"Here," said she to Ellen, "you pour out a quarter of a tumbler of this, and fill it up with hot water. I ain't goin' to have the whole family in an asylum because Jim Tenny has run off with another woman, if I can help it!"

The old woman's steady force of will asserted itself over the hysterical nature of her daughter-in-law. Fanny drank the whiskey and water and went to bed, half stupefied, and Mrs. Zelotes went home.

"You ring the bell in the night if she's taken worse, and I'll come over," said she to her son.

When Ellen and her father were left alone they looked at each other, each with pity for the other. Andrew laid a tender, trembling hand on the girl's shoulder. "Somehow it will all come out right," he whispered. "You go to bed and go to sleep, and if Amabel wakes up and makes any trouble you speak to father."

"Don't worry about me, father," returned Ellen. "It's you who have the most to worry over." Then she added — for the canker of need of money was eating her soul, too — "Father, what is going to be done? You can't pay all that for poor Aunt Eva. How much money have you got in the bank?"

"Not much, not much, Ellen," replied Andrew, with a groan.

"It wouldn't last very long at eighteen dollars a week?"

"No, no."

"It doesn't seem as if you ought to mortgage the house when you and mother are getting older. Father —"

"What, Ellen?"

"Nothing," said Ellen, after a little pause. It had been on her lips to tell him that she must go to work, then she refrained. There was something in her father's face which forbade her doing so.

"Go to bed, Ellen, and get rested," said Andrew. Then he rubbed his head against hers with his curious, doglike method of caress, and kissed her forehead.

"You go to sleep and get rested yourself, father," said Ellen.

"I guess I won't undress tonight, but I'll lay on the lounge," said Andrew.

"Well, you speak to me if mother wakes up and takes on again. Maybe I can do something."

"All right, dear child," said Andrew, lovingly and wearily. He had a look as if some mighty wind had passed over him and he were beaten down under it, except for that one single uprearing of love which no tempest could fairly down.

Ellen went upstairs, and lay down beside poor little Amabel without undressing herself. The child stirred, but not to awake, when she settled down beside her, and reached over her poor little claw of a hand to the girl, who clasped it fervently, and slipped a protecting arm under the tiny shoulders. Then the little thing nestled close to Ellen, with a movement of desperate seeking for protection. "There, there, darling, Ellen will take care of you," whispered Ellen. But Amabel did not hear.

Chapter XXXIII

*T*he next afternoon poor Eva Tenny was carried away, and Andrew accompanied the doctor who had her in charge, as being the only available male relative. As he dressed himself in his Sunday suit, he was aware — to such pitiful passes had financial straits brought him — of a certain self-congratulation, that he would not be at home when the dressmaker asked for money that night, and that no one would expect him to go to the bank under such circumstances. But Andrew, in his petty consideration as to personal benefit from such dire calamity, reckoned without another narrow traveler. Miss Higgins stopped him as he was going out of the door, looking as if bound to a funeral in his shabby Sunday black, with his solemn, sad face under his well-brushed hat.

"I hate to say anything when you're in such trouble, Mr. Brewster," said she, "but I do need the money to pay a bill, and I was wondering if you could leave what was due me yesterday, and what will be due me today."

But Fanny came with a rush to Andrew's relief. She was in that state of nervous tension that she was fairly dangerous if irritated. "Look here, Miss Higgins," said she. "We hesitated a good deal about havin' you come here today, anyway. Ellen wanted to send you word not to. We are in such awful trouble, that she said it didn't seem right for her to be thinkin' about new clothes, but I told her she'd got to have the things if she was going to college, and so we decided to have you come, but we ain't had any time nor any heart to think of money. We've got plenty to pay you in the bank, but my husband ain't had any time to go there this mornin', what with seein' the doctor, and gettin' the certificate for my poor sister, and all I've got to say is: if you're so dreadful afraid as all this comes to, that you have to lose all sense of decency, and dun folks so hard, in such trouble as we be, you can put on your things and go jest as quick as you have a mind to, and I'll get Miss Patch to finish the work. I've been more than half a mind to have her, anyway. I was very strongly advised to. Lots of folks have talked to me against your fittin', but I've always had you, and I thought I'd give you the chance. Now if you don't want it, you jest pack up and go, and the quicker the better. You shall have your pay as soon as Mr. Brewster can get round after he has carried my poor sister to the asylum. You needn't worry." Fanny said the last with a sarcasm which seemed to reach out with a lash of bitterness like a whip. The other woman winced, her eyes were hard, but her voice was appeasing.

"Now, I didn't think you'd take it so, Mrs. Brewster, or I wouldn't have said anything," she almost wheedled. "You know I ain't afraid of not gettin' my pay, I —"

"You'd better not be," said Fanny.

"Of course I ain't. I know Mr. Brewster has steady work, and I know your folks have got money."

"We've got money enough not to be beholden to anybody," said Fanny. "Andrew, you'd better be goin' along or you'll be late."

Andrew went out of the yard with his head bent miserably. He had felt ashamed of his fear, he felt still more ashamed of his relief. He wondered, going down the street, if it might not be a happier lot to lose one's wits like poor Eva, rather than have them to the full responsibility of steering one's self through such straits of misery.

"I hope you won't think I meant any harm," the dressmaker said to Fanny, quite humbly.

There was that about the sister of another woman who was being carried off to an insane asylum which was fairly intimidating.

Miss Higgins sewed meekly during the remainder of the day, having all the time a wary eye upon Fanny. She went home before supper, urging a headache as an excuse. She was in reality afraid of Fanny.

Andrew was inexpressibly relieved when he reached home to find that the dressmaker was gone, and Fanny, having sent Amabel to bed, was chiefly anxious to know how her sister had reached the asylum. It was not until the latter part of the evening that she brought up the subject of the bank. "Do look out tomorrow, Andrew Brewster, and be sure to take that money out of the bank to pay Miss Higgins," she said. "As for being dunned again by that woman, I won't! It's the last time I'll ever have her, anyway. As far as that is concerned, all the money will have to come out of the bank if poor Eva is to be kept where she is. How much money was there that she had?"

"Just fifty-two dollars and seventy cents," replied Andrew. "Jim had left a little that he'd scraped together somehow, with the letter he wrote to her, and he told her if he had work he'd send her more."

"I'd die before I'd touch it," said Fanny, fiercely. Then she looked at Andrew with sudden pity. "Poor old man," she said; "it's mighty hard on you when you're gettin' older, and you never say a word to complain. But I don't see any other way than to take that money, do you?"

"No," said Andrew.

"And you don't think I'm hard to ask it, Andrew?"

"No."

"God knows if it was your sister and my money, I would take every dollar. You know I would, Andrew."

"Yes, I know," replied Andrew, hoarsely.

"Mebbe she'll get better before it's quite gone," said Fanny. "You say the doctor gave some hope?"

"Yes, he did, if she was taken proper care of."

"Well, she shall be. I'll go out and steal before she shan't have proper care. Poor Eva!" Fanny burst into the hysterical wailing which had shaken her from head to foot at intervals during the last twenty-four hours. Andrew shuddered, thinking that he detected in her cries a resemblance to her sister's ravings. "Don't, don't, Fanny," he pleaded. "Don't, poor girl." He put his arm around her, and she wept on his shoulder, but with less abandon. "After all, we've got each other, and we've got Ellen, haven't we, Andrew?" she sobbed.

"Yes, thank God," said Andrew. "Don't, Fanny."

"That — that's more than money, more than all the wages for all the labor in the world, and that we've got, haven't we, Andrew? We've got what comes to us direct from God, haven't we? Don't think I'm silly, Andrew — haven't we?"

"Yes, yes, we have — you are right, Fanny," replied Andrew.

"I guess I am, too," she assented, looking up in Andrew's poor, worn face with eyes of sudden bravery. "We'll get along somehow — don't you worry, old man. I guess we'll come out all right, somehow. We'll use that money in the bank as far as it goes, and then I guess some way will be opened."

Then there came over Andrew's exaltation, to which Fanny's words had spurred his flagging spirit, a damper of utter mortification and guilt. He felt that he could bear this no longer. He opened his mouth to tell her what he had done with the money in the bank, when there came a knock on the door, and Fanny fled into the bedroom. She had unfastened her dress, and her face was stained with tears. She shut the bedroom door tightly as Andrew opened the outer one.

The man who had loaned him the money to buy Ellen's watch stood there. His name was William Evarts, and he worked in the stitching-room of McGuire's factory, in which Andrew was employed. He was reported well-to-do, and to have amassed considerable money from judicious expenditures of his savings, and to be strictly honest, but hard in his dealings. He was regarded with a covert disfavor by his fellow-workmen, as if he were one of themselves who had somehow elevated himself to a superior height by virtue of their backs. If William Evarts had acquired prosperity through gambling in mines, they would have had none of that feeling; they would have recognized the legitimacy of luck in the conduct of affairs. He was in a way a reproach to them. "Why can't you get along and save as well as William Evarts?" many a man's monitor asked of him. "He doesn't earn anymore than you do, and has had as many expenses in his family." The man not being able to answer the question to his own credit, disliked William Evarts who had insti-gated it.

Andrew, who had in his character a vein of sterling justice, yet felt that he almost hated William Evarts as he stood there before him, small and spare, snapping as it were with energy like electric wires, the strong lines in his clean-shaven face evident in the glare of the street-lamp.

"Good-evening," Andrew said, and he spoke like a criminal before a judge, and at that moment he felt like one.

"Good-evening," responded the other man. Then he added, in a hushed voice at first, for he had fineness to appreciate a sort of indecency in dunning, in asking a man for even his rightful due, and he had a regard for possible listening ears of femininity, "I was passing by, and I thought I'd call and see if it was convenient for you to pay me that money."

"I'm sorry," Andrew responded, with utter subjection. He looked and felt ignoble. "I haven't got it, Evarts."

"When are you going to have it?" asked the other, in a slightly raised, ominous voice.

"Just as soon as I can possibly get it," replied Andrew, softly and piteously. Ellen's chamber was directly overhead. He thought of the possibility of her overhearing.

"Look at here, Andrew Brewster," said the other man, and this time with brutal, pitiless force. When it came to the prospect of losing money he became as merciless as a machine. Something diabolical in remorselessness seemed to come to the surface, and reveal wheels of grinding for his fellow-men. "Look at here," he said, "I want to know right out, and no dodging. Have you got the money to pay me — yes or no?"

"No," said Andrew then, with a manliness born of desperation. He had the feeling of one who will die fighting. He wished that Evarts would speak lower on account of Ellen, but he was prepared to face even that. The man's speech came with the gliddering rush of an electric car; it was a concentration of words into one intensity of meaning; he elided everything possible, he ran all his words together. He spoke something in this wise: "GoddamnyouAndrewBrewster, for comin'to borrow money to buy your girl a watch when you had nothin' to pay for't with, whatbusinesshadyourgirlwithawatchanyhow,I'dliket'know?   My girl'ain'tgotno   watch.   I'veputmymoneyinthebank.   It'srobbery. I'llhavethelawonye. I'llsueyou. I'll —"

At that moment something happened. The man, William Evarts, who was talking with a vociferousness which seemed cutting and lacerating to the ear, who was brandishing an arm for emphasis in a circle of frenzy, fairly jumped to one side. The girl, Ellen Brewster, in a light wrapper, which she had thrown over her nightgown, came with such a speed down the stairs which led to the entry directly before the door, that she seemed to be flying. White ruffles eddied around her little feet, her golden hair was floating out like a flag. She came close to William Evarts. "Will you please not speak so loud," said she, in a voice which her father had never heard from her lips before. It was a voice of pure command, and of command which carried with it the consciousness of power to enforce. She stood before William Evarts, and her fine smallness seemed intensified by her spirit to magnificence. The man shrank back a little, he had the impression as of someone overtowering him, and yet the girl came scarcely to his shoulder. "Please do not speak so loud, you will wake Amabel," she said, and Evarts muttered, like a dog under a whip, that he didn't want to wake her up.

"You must not," said Ellen. "Now here is the watch and chain. I suppose that will do as well as your money if you cannot afford to wait for my father to pay you. My father will pay you in time. He has never borrowed anything of any man which he has not meant to pay back, and will not pay back. If you cannot afford to wait, take the watch and chain."

The man looked at her stupefied.

"Here," said Ellen; "take it."

"I don't want your watch an' chain," muttered Evarts.

"You have either got to take them or wait for your money," said Ellen.

"I'll wait," said Evarts. He was looking at the girl's face with mingled sentiments of pity, admiration, and terror.

"Very well, then," said Ellen. "I will promise you, and my father will, that you shall have your money in time, but how long do you want to wait?"

"I'll wait any time. I ain't in any straits for the money, if I get it in the end," said Evarts.

"You will get it in the end," said Ellen. Evarts turned to Andrew.

"Look here, give me your note for six months," said he, "and we'll call it all right."

"All right," said Andrew, again.

"If you are not satisfied with that," said Ellen, with a tone as if she were conferring inestimable benefits, so proud it was, "you can take the watch and chain. It is not hurt in the least. Here." She was fairly insolent. Evarts regarded her with a mixture of admiration and terror. He told somebody the next day that Andrew Brewster had a stepper of a daughter, but he did not give his reasons for the statement. He had a sense of honor, and he had been in love with a girl as young before he married his wife, who had been a widow older than he, worth ten thousand dollars from her first husband. He could no more have taken the girl's watch and chain than he would have killed her.

"I'm quite satisfied," he replied to her, making a repellant motion towards the watch and dangling chain glittering in the electric-light.

"Very well, then," said Ellen, and she threw the chain over her neck.

"You just bring that I O U to the shop to-mor-mor," said Evarts to Andrew; then, with a "Good-evening," he was off. They heard him hail an electric-car passing, and that, although he never took a car, but walked to save the fare. He had been often heard to say that he for one did not support the street railroad.

After he had gone, Ellen turned to her father, and flung a silent white arm slipping from her sleeve loose around his neck, and pulled his head to her shoulder. "Now look here, father," she said, "you've been through lots today, and you'd better go to bed and go to sleep. I don't think mother was waked up — if she had been, she would have been out here."

"Look here, Ellen, I want to tell you," Andrew began, pitifully. He was catching his breath like a child with sobs.

"I don't want to hear anything," replied Ellen, firmly. "Whatever you did was right, father."

"I ought to tell you, Ellen!"

"You ought to tell me nothing," said Ellen. "You are all tired out, father. You can't do anything that isn't right for me. Now go to bed and go to sleep."

Ellen stroked her father's thin grey hair with exactly the same tender touch with which he had so often stroked her golden locks. It was an inheritance of love reverting to its original source. She kissed him on his lined forehead with her flowerlike lips, then she pushed him gently away. "Go softly, and don't wake mother," whispered she; "and, father, there's no need to trouble her with this. Good-night."

Chapter XXXIV

*E*llen's deepest emotion was pity for her father, so intense that it was actual physical pain.

"Poor father! Poor father! He had to borrow the money to buy me my watch and chain," she kept repeating to herself. "Poor father!"

To her New England mind, borrowing seemed almost like robbing. She actually felt as if her father had committed a crime for love of her, but all she looked at was the love, not the guilt. Suddenly a conviction which fairly benumbed her came over her — the money in the savings-bank; that little hoard, which had been to the imagination of herself and her mother a sheet-anchor against poverty, must be gone. "Father must have used if for something unbeknown to mother," she said to herself — "he must, else he would not have told Mr. Evarts that he could not pay him." It was a hot night, but the girl shivered as she realized for the first time the meaning of the wolf at the door. "All we've got left is this house — this house and — and — our hands," thought Ellen. She saw before her her father's poor, worn hands, her mother's thin, tired hands, jerking the thread in and out of those shameful wrappers; then she looked at her own, as yet untouched by toil, as white and small and fair as flowers. She thought of the four years before her at college, four years before she could earn anything — and in the meantime? She looked at the pile of her school-books on the table. She had been studying hard all summer. The thirst for knowledge was as intense in her as the thirst for stimulants in a drunkard.

"I ought to give up going to college, and go to work in the shop," Ellen said to herself, and she said it as one might drive a probing-knife into a sore. "I ought to," she repeated. And yet she was far from resolving to give up college. She began to argue with herself the expediancy, supposing that the money in the bank was gone, of putting a mortgage on the house. If her father continued to have work, they might get along and pay for her aunt, who might, as the doctor had said, not be obliged to remain long in the asylum if properly cared for. Would it not, after all, be better, since by a course at college she would be fitted to command a larger salary than she could in any other way. "I can support them all," reflected Ellen. At that time the thought of Robert Lloyd, and that awakening of heart which he had brought to pass, were in abeyance. Old powers had asserted themselves. This love for her own blood and their need came between her and this new love, half of the senses, half of the spirit.

Amabel waked up in the early sultry dawn of the summer day with the bewilderment of one in a new world. She stared at the walls of the room, at the shaft of sunlight streaming in the window, then at Ellen.

"Where am I?" she inquired, in a loud, querulous plaint. Then she remembered, but she did not cry; instead, her little face took on a painfully old look.

"You are here with cousin Ellen, darling, don't you know?" Ellen replied, leaning over her, and kissing her.

Amabel wriggled impatiently away, and faced to the wall. "Yes, I know," said she.

That morning Amabel would not eat any breakfast, and Fanny suggested that Ellen take her for a ride on the street-cars. "We can get along without you for an hour," she whispered, "and I am afraid that child will be sick."

So Ellen and Amabel set out, leaving Fanny and the dressmaker at work, and when they were returning past the factories the noon whistles were blowing and the operatives were streaming forth.

Ellen was surprised to see her father among them as the car swept past. He walked down the street towards home, his dinner-bag dangling at his side, his back more bent than ever.

She wondered uneasily if her father was ill, for he never went home to dinner. She looked back at him as the car swept past, but he did not seem to see her. He walked with an air of seeing nothing, covering the ground like an old dog with some patient, dumb end in view, heeding nothing by the way. It puzzled her also that her father had come out of Lloyd's instead of McGuire's, where he had been employed all summer. Ellen, after she reached home, watched anxiously for her father to come into the yard, but she did not see him. She assisted about the dinner, which was a little extra on account of the dressmaker, and all the time she glanced with covert anxiety at the window, but her father did not pass it. Finally, when she went out to the pump for a pitcher of water, she set the pitcher down, and sped to the orchard like a wild thing. A suspicion had seized her that her father was there.

Sure enough, there he was, but instead of lying face down on the grass, as he had done before, he was sitting back against a tree. He had the air of having settled into such a long lease of despair that he had sought the most comfortable position for it. His face was ghastly. He looked at Ellen as she drew near, and opened his mouth as if to speak, but instead he only caught his breath. He stared hard at her, then he closed his eyes as if not to see her, and motioned her away with one hand with an inarticulate noise in his throat.

But Ellen sat down beside him. She caught his two hands and looked at him. "Father, look at me," said she, and Andrew opened his eyes. The expression in them was dreadful, compounded of shame and despair and dread, but the girl's met them with a sort of glad triumph and strength of love. "Now look here, father," she said, "you tell me all about it. I didn't want to know last night. Now I want to know. What is the matter?"

Andrew continued to look at her, then all at once he spoke with a kind of hoarse shout. "I'm discharged! I'm discharged," he said, "from

McGuire's; they've got a boy who can move faster in my place — a boy for less pay, who can move faster. I hurried over to Lloyd's to see if they would take me on again; I've always thought I should get back into Lloyd's, and I saw the foreman, and he told me to my face that I was too old, that they wanted younger men. And I went into the office to see Lloyd, pushed past the foreman, with him damning me, and I saw Lloyd."

"Was young Mr. Lloyd there?" asked Ellen, with white lips.

"No; I guess he had gone to dinner. And Lloyd looked at me, and I believe he counted every grey hair in my head, and he saw my back, and he saw my hands, and he said — he said I was too old."

Andrew snatched his hands from Ellen's grasp, pressed them to his face, and broke into weeping. "Oh, my God, I'm too old, I'm too old!" he sobbed; "I'm out of it! I'm too old!"

Ellen regarded him, and her face had developed lines of strength hitherto unrevealed. There was no pity in it, hardly love; she looked angry and powerful. "Father, stop doing so, and look at me," she said. She dragged her father's hands from his face, and he stared at her with his inflamed eyes, half terrified, half sustained. At that moment he realized a strength of support as from his own lost youth, a strength as of eternal progress which was more to be relied upon than other human strength. For the first time he leaned on his child, and realized with wonder the surety of the stay.

"Now, father, you stop doing so," said Ellen. "You can get work somewhere; you are not old. Call yourself old! It is nonsense. Are you going to give in and be old because two men tell you that you are? What if your hair is grey! Ever so many young men have grey hair. You are not old, and you can get work somewhere. McGuire's and Lloyd's are not the only factories in the country."

"That ain't all," said Andrew, with eyes like a beseeching dog's on her face.

"I know that isn't all," said Ellen. "You needn't be afraid to tell me, father. You have taken the money out of the savings-bank for something."

Again Andrew would have snatched his hands from the girl's and hidden his face, but she held them fast. "Yes, I have," he admitted, in a croaking voice.

"Well, what if you have?" asked Ellen. "You had a right to take it out, didn't you? You put it in. I don't know of anybody who had a better right to take it out than you, if you wanted to."

Andrew stared at her, as if he did not hear rightly. "You don't know what I did with it, Ellen," he stammered.

"It is nobody's business," replied Ellen. She had an unexplained sensation as if she were holding fast to her father's slipping self-respect which was dragging hard at her restraining love.

"I put it in a worthless gold-mine out in Colorado — the same one your uncle Jim lost his money in," groaned Andrew.

"Well, it was your money, and you had a perfect right to," said Ellen. "Of course you thought the mine was all right or you wouldn't have put the money into it."

"God knows I did."

"Well, the best business men in the world make mistakes. It is nobody's business whether you took the money out or not, or what you used it for, father."

"I don't see how the bills are going to be paid, and there's your poor aunt," said Andrew. He was leaning more and more heavily upon this new tower of strength, this tender little girl whom he had hitherto shielded and supported. The beautiful law of reverse of nature had come into force.

Ellen set her mouth firmly. "Don't you worry, father," said she. "We will think of some way out of it. There's a little money to pay for Aunt Eva, and maybe she won't be sick long. Does mother know, father?"

"She don't know about anything, Ellen," replied Andrew, wretchedly.

"I know she doesn't know about your getting thrown out of work — but about the bank?"

"No, Ellen."

Ellen rose. "You stay here, where it is cool, till I ring the dinner-bell, father," she said.

"I don't want any dinner, child."

"Yes, you do, father. If you don't eat your dinner you will be sick. You come when the bell rings."

Andrew knew that he should obey, as he saw the girl's light dress disappear among the trees.

Ellen went back to the pump, and carried her pitcher of water into the house. Her mother met her at the door. "Where have you been all this time, Ellen Brewster?" she asked, in a high voice. "Everything is getting as cold as a stone."

Ellen caught her mother's arm and drew her into the kitchen, and closed the door. Fanny turned pale as death and looked at her. "Well, what has happened now?" she said. "Is your father killed?"

"No," said Ellen, "but he is out of work, and he can't get a job at Lloyd's, and he took all that money out of the savings-bank a long time ago, and put it into that gold-mine that Uncle Jim lost in."

Fanny clutched the girl's arm in a grasp so hard that it left a blue mark on the tender flesh. She looked at her, but did not speak one word.

"Now, mother," said Ellen, "you must not say one word to father to scold him. He's got enough to bear as it is."

Fanny pushed her away with sudden fierceness. "I guess I don't need to have my own daughter teach me my duty to my husband," said she. "Where is he?"

"Down in the orchard."

"Well, ring the bell for dinner loud, so he can hear it."

When Andrew came shuffling wearily up from the orchard, Fanny met him at the corner of the house, out of sight from the windows. She was flushed and perspiring, clad in a coarse cotton wrapper, revealing all her unkempt curves. She went close to him, and thrust one large arm through his. "Look here, Andrew," said she, in the tenderest voice he had ever heard from her, a voice so tender that it was furious, "you needn't say one word. What's done's done. We shall get along somehow. I ain't afraid. Come in and eat your dinner!"

The dressmaking work went on as usual after dinner. Andrew had disappeared, going down the road towards the shop. He tried for a job at Briggs's, with no success, then drifted to the corner grocery.

Ellen sat until nearly three o'clock sewing. Then she went upstairs and got her hat, and went secretly out of the back door, through the west yard, that her mother should not see her. However, her grandmother called after her, and wanted to know where she was going.

"Down street, on an errand," answered Ellen.

"Well, keep on the shady side," called her grandmother, thinking the girl was bound to the stores for some dressmaking supplies.

That night Miss Higgins did not ask for her pay; she had made up her mind to wait until her week was finished. She went away after supper, and Ellen followed her to the door. "We won't want you tomorrow, Miss Higgins," said she, "and here is your pay." With that she handed a roll of bills to the woman, who stared at her in amazement and growing resentment.

"If my work ain't satisfactory," said she —

"Your work is satisfactory," said Ellen, "but I don't want anymore work done. I am not going to college."

There was something conclusive and intimidating about Ellen's look and tone. The dressmaker, who had been accustomed to regard her as a child, stared at her with awe, as before a sudden revelation of force. Then she took her money, and went down the walk.

When Ellen reentered the sitting room her father and mother, who had overheard every word, confronted her.

"Ellen Brewster, what does this mean?"

Andrew looked as if he would presently fall to the floor.

"It means," said Ellen — and she looked at her parents with the brave enthusiasm of a soldier on her beautiful face — she even laughed — "it means that I am going to work — I have got a job in Lloyd's."

When Ellen made that announcement, her mother did a strange thing. She ran swiftly to a corner of the room, and stood there, staring at the girl, with back hugged close to the intersection of the walls, as if she would withdraw as far as possible from some threatening ill. At that moment she looked alarmingly like her sister; there was something about Fanny in her corner, calculated, when all circumstances were taken into consideration, to make one's blood chill, but Andrew did not look at her. He was intent upon Ellen, and the facing of the worst agony of his life, and Ellen was intent upon him. She loved her mother, but the fear as to her father's suffering moved her more than her mother's. She was more like her father, and could better estimate his pain under stress. Andrew rose to his feet and stood looking at Ellen, and she at him. She tried to meet the drawn misery and incredulousness of his face with a laugh of reassurance.

"Yes, I've got a job in Lloyd's," said she. "What's the matter, father?"

Then Andrew made an almost inarticulate response; it sounded like a croak in an unknown tongue.

Ellen continued to look at him, and to laugh.

"Now look here, father," said she. "There is no need for you and mother to feel bad over this. I have thought it all over, and I have made up my mind. I have got a good high-school education now, and the four years I should have to spend at Vassar I could do nothing at all. There is awful need of money here, and not only for us, but for Aunt Eva and Amabel."

"You shan't do it!" Andrew burst out then, in a great shout of rage. "I'll mortgage the house — that'll last awhile. You shan't, I say! You are my child, and you've got to listen. You shan't, I say!"

"Now, father," responded Ellen's voice, which seemed to have in it a wonderful tone of firmness against which his agonized vociferousness broke as against a rock, "this is nonsense. You must not mortgage the house. The house is all you have got for your and mother's old age. Do you think I could go to college, and let you give up the house in order to keep me there? And as for grandma Brewster, you know what's hers is hers as long as she lives — we don't want to think of that. I have got this job now, which is only three dollars a week, but in a year the foreman said I might earn fifteen or eighteen, if I was quick and smart, and I will be quick and smart. It is the best thing for us all, father."

"You shan't!" shouted Andrew. "I say you shan't!"

Suddenly Andrew sank into a chair, his head lopped, he kept moving a hand before his eyes, as if he were brushing away cobwebs. Then Fanny came out of her corner.

"Get the camphor, quick!" she said to Ellen. "I dun'no' but you've killed your father."

Fanny held her husband's head against her shoulder, and rubbed his hands frantically. The awful strained look had gone from her face. Ellen came with the camphor, and then went for water. Fanny rubbed Andrew's forehead with the camphor, and held the bottle to his nose. "Smell it, Andrew," she said, in a voice of ineffable tenderness and pity. Ellen returned with a glass of water, and Andrew swallowed a little obediently. Finally he made out to stagger into the bedroom with Fanny's and Ellen's assistance. He sat down weakly on the bed, and Fanny lifted his legs up. Then he sank and closed his eyes as if he were spent. In fact, he was. At that moment of Ellen's announcement some vital energy in him suddenly relaxed like overstrained rubber. His face, sunken in the pillow, was both ghastly and meek. It was the face of a man who could fight no more. Ellen knelt down beside him, sobbing.

"Oh, father!" she sobbed, "I think it is for the best. Dear father, you won't feel bad."

"No," said Andrew, faintly. There was a slight twitching in his hand, as if he wished to put it on her head, then it lay thin and inert on the coverlid. He tried to smile, but his face settled into that look of utter acquiescence of fate.

"I s'pose it's the best you can do," he muttered.

"Have you told Miss Lennox?" gasped Fanny.

"Yes."

"What did she say?"

"She was sorry, but she made no objection," replied Ellen, evasively.

Fanny came forward abruptly, caught up the camphor-bottle, and began bathing Andrew's forehead again.

"We won't say anymore about it," said she, in a harsh voice. "You'd better go over to your grandma Brewster's and see if she has got any whiskey. I think your father needs to take something."

"I don't want anything," said Andrew, feebly.

"Yes, you do, too, you are as white as a sheet. Go over and ask her, Ellen."

Ellen ran across the yard to her grandmother's, and the old woman met her at the door. She seemed to have an instinctive knowledge of trouble.

"What's the matter?" she asked.

"Father's a little faint, and mother wants me to borrow the whiskey," said Ellen. She had not at that time the courage to tell her grandmother what she had done.

Mrs. Zelotes ran into the house, and came out with the bottle.

"I'm comin' over," she announced. "I'm kind of worried about your father; he ain't looked well for some time. I wonder what made him faint. Maybe he ate something which hurt him."

Ellen said nothing. She fled upstairs to her chamber, as her grandmother entered the bedroom. She felt cowardly, but she thought that she would let her mother tell the news.

She sat down and waited. She knew that presently she would hear the old woman's voice at the foot of the stairs. She was resolved upon her course, and knew that she could not be shaken in it, yet she dreaded unspeakably the outburst of grief and anger which she knew would come from her grandmother. She felt as if she had faced two fires, and now before the third she quailed a little.

It was not long before the expected summons came.

"Ellen — Ellen Brewster, come down here!"

Ellen went down. Her grandmother met her at the foot of the stairs. She was trembling from head to foot; her mouth twisted and wavered as if she had the palsy.

"Look here, Ellen Brewster, this ain't true?" she stammered.

"Yes, grandma," answered Ellen. "I have thought it all over, and it is the only thing for me to do."

Her grandmother clutched her arm, and the girl felt as if she were in the grasp of another will, which was more conclusive than steel.

"You shan't!" she said, whispering, lest Andrew should hear, but with intense force.

"I've got to, grandma. We've got to have the money."

"The money," said the old woman, with an inflection of voice and a twist of her features indicative of the most superb scorn — "the money! I guess you ain't goin' to lose such a chance as that for money. I guess I've got two hundred and ten dollars a year income, and I'll give up a half of that, and Andrew can put a mortgage on the house, if that Tenny woman has got to be supported because her husband has run off and left her and her young one. You shan't go to work in a shop."

"I've got to, grandma," said Ellen.

The old woman looked at her. It was like a duel between two strong wills of an old race. "You shan't," she said.

"Yes, I shall, grandma."

Then the old woman turned upon her in a fury of rage.

"You're a Loud all over, Ellen Brewster," said she. "You ain't got a mite of Brewster about you. You ain't got any pride! You'd just as soon settle down and work in a shop as do anything else."

Fanny pushed before her. "Look here, Mother Brewster," said she, "you can just stop! Ellen is my daughter, and you ain't any right to talk to her this way. I won't have it. If anybody is goin' to blame her, it's me."

"Who be you?" said Mrs. Zelotes, sniffing.

Then she looked at them both, at Ellen and at her mother.

"If you go an' do what you've planned," said she to Ellen, "an' if you uphold her in it," to Fanny, "I've done with you."

"Good riddance," said Fanny, coarsely.

"I ain't goin' to forget that you said that," cried Mrs. Zelotes. She held up her dress high in front and went out of the door. "I ain't comin' over here again, an' I'll thank you to stay at home," said she. Then she went away.

Soon after Fanny heard Ellen in the dining room setting the table for supper, and went out.

"Where did you get that money you paid the dressmaker with?" she asked, abruptly.

"I borrowed it of Abby," replied Ellen.

"Then she knows?"

"Yes."

Fanny continued to look at Ellen with the look of one who is settling down with resignation under some knife of agony.

"Well," said she, "there's no need to talk anymore about it before your father. Now I guess you had better toast him some bread for his supper."

"Yes, I will," replied Ellen. She looked at her mother pitifully, and yet with that firmness which had seemed to suddenly develop in her. "You know it is the best thing for me to do, mother?" she said, and although she put it in the form of a question, the statement was commanding in its assertiveness.

"When are you — goin' to work?" asked Fanny.

"Next Monday," replied Ellen.

Chapter XXXV

*W*hen Ellen had gone to the factory to apply for work neither of the Lloyds were in the office, only a girl at the desk, whom she knew slightly. Ellen had hesitated a little as she approached the girl, who looked around with a friendly smile.

"I want to see —" Ellen began, then she stopped, for she did not exactly know for whom she should ask. The girl, who was blond and trim, clad coquettishly in a blue shirt-waist and a duck skirt, with a large, cheap rhinestone pin confining the loop of her yellow braids, looked at her in some bewilderment. She had heard of Ellen's good-fortune, and knew she was to be sent to Vassar by Cynthia Lennox. She did not dream that she had come to ask for employment.

"You want to see Mr. Lloyd?" she asked.

"Oh no!" replied Ellen.

"Mr. Robert Lloyd?" The girl, whose name was Nellie Stone, laughed a little meaningly as she said that.

Ellen blushed. "No," she said. "I think I want to see the foreman."

"Which foreman?"

"I don't know," replied Ellen. "I want to get work if I can. I don't know which foreman I ought to see."

"To get work?" repeated the girl, with a subtle change in her manner.

"Yes," said Ellen. She could hear her heart beat, but she looked at the other girl's pretty, common face with the most perfect calmness.

"Mr. Flynn is the one you want to see, then," said the girl. "You know Ed Flynn, don't you?"

"A little," replied Ellen. He had been a big boy when she entered the high-school, and had left the next spring.

"Well, he's the one you want," said Nellie Stone. Then she raised her voice to a shrill peal as a boy passed the office door.

"Here, you, Jack," said she, "ask Mr. Flynn to come here a minute, will you?"

"He don't want to see you," replied the boy, who was small and spare, laden heavily with a great roll of wrapping paper borne bayonet fashion over his shoulder. His round, impish face grinned back at the girl at the desk.

"Quit your impudence," she returned, half laughing herself. "I don't want to see him; it is this young lady here; hurry up."

The boy gave a comprehensive glance at Ellen. "Guess he'll come," he called back.

Flynn appeared soon. He was handsome, well shaven and shorn, and he held himself smartly. He also dressed well in a business suit which would not have disgraced the Lloyds. His face lit up with astonishment and pleasure when he saw Ellen. He bowed and greeted her in a rich voice. He was of Irish descent but American born. Both his motions and his speech were adorned with flourishes of grace which betrayed his race. He placed a chair for Ellen with a sweep which would have been a credit to the stage. All his actions had a slight exaggeration as of fresco painting, which seemed to fit them for a stage rather than a room, and for an audience rather than chance spectators.

"No, thank you," replied Ellen. Then she went straight to the matter in hand. "I have called to see if I could get a job here?" she said. She had been formulating her speech all the way thither. Her first impulse was to ask for employment, but she was sure as to the manner in which a girl would ordinarily couch such a request. So she asked for a job.

Flynn stared at her. "A job?" he repeated.

"Yes, I want very much to get one," replied Ellen. "I thought there might be a vacancy."

"Why, I thought —" said the young man. He was very much astonished, but his natural polish could rise above astonishment. Instead of blurting out what was in his mind as to her change of prospects, he reasoned with incredible swiftness that the change must be a hard thing to this girl, and that she was to be handled the more tenderly and delicately because she was such a pretty girl. He became twice as polite as before. He moved the chair nearer to her.

"Please sit down," he said. He handed to her the wooden armchair as if it had been a throne. Nellie Stone bent frowning over her day-book.

"Now let me see," said the young man, seriously, with perfect deference of manner, only belied by the rollicking admiration in his eyes. "You have never held a position in a factory before, I think?"

"No," replied Ellen.

"There is at present only one vacancy that I can think of," said Flynn, "and that does not pay very much, but there is always a chance to rise for a smart hand. I am sure you will be that," he added, smiling at her.

Ellen did not return the smile. "I shall be contented to begin for a little, if there is a chance to rise," she said.

"There's a chance to rise to eighteen dollars a week," said Flynn. He smiled again, but it was like smiling at seriousness itself. Ellen's downright, searching eyes upon his face seemed almost to forbid the fact of her own girlish identity.

"What is the job you have for me?" said she.

"Tying strings in shoes," answered Flynn. "Easy enough, only child's play, but you won't earn more than three dollars a week to begin with."

"I shall be quite satisfied with that," said Ellen. "When shall I come?"

"Why, tomorrow morning; no, tomorrow is Friday. Better come next Monday and begin the week. That will give you one day more off, and the hot wave a chance to get past." Flynn spoke facetiously. It was a very hot day, and the air in the office like a furnace. He wiped his forehead, to which the dark rings of hair clung. The girl at the desk glanced around adoringly at him.

"I would rather not stop for that if you want me to begin at once," said Ellen.

Flynn looked abashed. "Oh, we'd rather have you begin on the even week — it makes less bother over the account," he said. "Monday morning at seven sharp, then."

"Yes," said Ellen.

Flynn walked off with an abrupt duck of his head. He somehow felt that he had been rebuffed, and Ellen rose.

"I told you you'd get one," said the girl at the desk. "Catch Ed Flynn not giving a pretty girl a job." She said it with an accent of pain as well as malice. Ellen looked at her with large, indignant eyes. She had not the least idea what she meant, at least she realized only the surface meaning, and that angered her.

"I suppose he gave me the job because there was a vacancy," she returned, with dignity.

The other girl laughed. "Mebbe," said she.

Ellen continued to look at her, and there was something in her look not only indignant, but appealing. Nellie Stone's expression changed again. She laughed uneasily. "Land, I didn't mean anything," said she. "I'm glad for you that you got the job. Of course you wouldn't have got it if there hadn't been a chance. One of the girls got married last week, Maud Millet. I guess it's her place you've got. I'm real glad you've got it."

"Thank you," said Ellen.

"Good-bye," said the girl.

"Good-bye," replied Ellen.

On Monday morning the heat had broken, and an east wind with the breath of the sea in it was blowing. Ellen started for her work at half-past six. She held her father's little, worn leather-bag, in which he had carried his dinner for so many years. The walk was so long that it would scarcely give her time to come home at noon, and as for taking a car, that was not to be thought of for a moment on account of the fare.

Ellen walked along briskly, the east wind blew in her face, she smelled the salt sea, and somehow it at once soothed and stimulated her. Without seeing the mighty waste of waters, she seemed to realize its presence; she gazed at the sky hanging low with a scud of grey clouds, which did not look unlike the ocean, and the sense of irresponsibility in the midst of infinity comforted her.

"I am not Ellen Brewster after all," she thought. "I am not anything separate enough to be worried about what comes to me. I am only a part of greatness which cannot fail of reaching its end." She thought this all vaguely. She had no language for it, for she was very young; it was formless as music, but as true to her.

When she reached the cross-street where the Atkinses lived Abby and Maria came running out.

"My land, Ellen Brewster," said Abby, half angrily, "if you don't look real happy! I believe you are glad to go to work in a shoe-shop!"

Ellen laughed. Maria said nothing, but she pressed close to her as she walked along. She was coughing a little in the east wind. There had been a drop of twenty degrees in the night, and these drops of temperature in New England mean steps to the tomb.

"You make me mad," said Abby. Her voice broke a little. She dashed her hand across her eyes angrily. "Here's Granville Joy," said she; "you'll be in the same room with him, Ellen." She said it maliciously. Distress over her friend made her fairly malicious.

Ellen colored. "You are hard to talk to," said she, in a low voice, for Granville was coming nearer, gaining on them from behind.

"She don't mean it," whispered Maria.

When Granville caught up with them, Ellen pressed so close to Maria that he was forced to walk with Abby or pass on. She returned his "Good-morning," then did not look at him again. Presently Willy Jones appeared, coming so imperceptibly that he seemed almost impossible.

"Where did he come from?" whispered Ellen to Maria.

"Hush," replied Maria; "it's this way 'most every morning. All at once he comes, and he generally walks with me, because he's afraid Abby won't want him, but it's Abby."

This morning, Willy Jones, aroused, perhaps, to self-assertion by the presence of another man, walked three abreast with Abby and Granville, but on the other side of Granville. Now and then he peered around the other man at the girl, with soft, wistful blue eyes, but Abby never seemed to see him. She talked fast, in a harsh, rather loud voice. She uttered bitter witticisms which made her companions laugh.

"Abby is so bright," whispered Maria to Ellen, "but I wish she wouldn't talk so. Abby doesn't feel the way I wish she did. She rebels. She would be happier if she gave up rebelling and believed." Maria coughed as she spoke.

"You had better keep your mouth shut in this east wind, Maria," her sister called out sharply to her.

"I'm not talking much, Abby," replied Maria.

Presently Maria looked at Ellen lovingly. "Do you feel very badly about going to work?" she asked, in a low voice.

"No, not now. I have made up my mind," replied Ellen. The east wind was bringing a splendid color to her cheeks. She held up her head as she marched along, like one leading a charge of battle. Her eyes gleamed as with blue fire, her yellow hair sprung and curled around her temples.

They were now in the midst of a great, hurrying procession bound for the factories. Some of the men walked silently, with a dogged stoop of shoulders and shambling hitch of hips; some of the women moved droopingly, with an indescribable effect of hanging back from the leading of some imperious hand of fate. Many of them, both men and women, walked alertly and chattered like a flock of sparrows. Ellen moved with this rank and file of the army of labor, and all at once a sense of comradeship seized her. She began to feel humanity as she had never felt it before. The sense of her own littleness aroused her to a power of comprehension of the grandeur of the mass of which she was a part. She began to lose herself and sense humanity.

When the people reached the factories, two on one side of the road, one, Lloyd's, on the other, they began streaming up the outside stairs and disappearing like swarms of bees in hives. Two flights of stairs, one on each side, led to a platform in front of the entrance of Lloyd's.

When Ellen set her foot on one of these stairs the seven-o'clock steam-whistle blew, and a mighty thrill shot through the vast building. Ellen caught her breath. Abby came close to her.

"Don't get scared," said she, with ungracious tenderness; "there's nothing to be scared at."

Ellen laughed. "I'm not scared," said she. Then they entered the factory, humming with machinery, and a sensation which she had not anticipated was over her. Scared she was not; she was fairly exultant. All at once she entered a vast room in which eager men were already at the machines with frantic zeal, as if they were driving labor herself. When she felt the vibration of the floor under her feet, when she saw people spring to their stations of toil, as if springing to guns in a battle, she realized the might and grandeur of it all. Suddenly it seemed to her that the greatest thing in the whole world was work and that this was one of the greatest forms of work — to cover the feet of progress of the travelers of the earth from the cradle to the grave. She saw that these great factories, and the strength of this army of the sons and daughters of toil, made possible the advance of civilization itself, which cannot go barefoot. She realized all at once and forever the dignity of labor, this girl of the people, with a brain which enabled her to overlook the heads of the rank and file of which she herself formed a part. She never again, whatever her regret might have been for another life for which she was better fitted, which her taste preferred, had any sense of ignominy in this. She never again felt that she was too good for her labor, for labor had revealed itself to her like a goddess behind a sordid veil. Abby and Maria looked at her wonderingly. No other girl had ever entered Lloyd's with such a look on her face.

"Are you sick?" whispered Abby, catching her arm.

"No," said Ellen. "No, don't worry me, Abby. I think I shall like it."

"I declare you make me mad," said Abby, but she looked at her adoringly. "Here's Ed Flynn," she added. "He'll look out for you. Good-bye, I'll see you at noon." Abby went away to her machine. She was stitching vamps by the piece, and earning a considerable amount. The Atkinses were not so distressed as they had been, and Abby was paying off a mortgage.

When the foreman came towards Ellen she experienced a shock. His gay, admiring eyes on her face seemed to dispel all her exaltation. She felt as if her feet touched earth, and yet the young man was entirely respectful, and even thoughtful. He bade her "Good-morning," and conducted her to the scene of her labor. One other girl was already there at work. She gave a sidewise glance at Ellen, and went on, making her fingers fly. Mr. Flynn showed Ellen what to do. She had to tie the shoes together with bits of twine, laced through eyelet holes. Ellen took a piece of twine and tied it in as Flynn watched her. He laughed pleasantly.

"You'll do," he said, approvingly. "I've been in here five years, and you are the first girl I ever saw who tied a square knot at the first trial. Here's Mamie Brady here, she worked a solid month before she got the hang of the square knot."

"You go along," admonished the girl spoken of as "Mamie Brady." Her words were flippant, even impudent, but her tone was both dejected and childish. She continued to work without a glance at either of them. Her fingers flew, tying the knots with swift jerks.

"Well, you help Miss Brewster, if she needs any help," said Flynn, as he went away.

"We don't have any misses in this shop," said the girl to Ellen, with sarcastic emphasis.

"I don't care anything about being called miss," replied Ellen, picking up another piece of string.

"What's your first name?"

"Ellen."

"Oh, land! I know who you be. You read that essay at the high-school graduation. I was there. Well, I shouldn't think you would want to be called miss if you feel the way you said you did in that."

"I don't want to," said Ellen.

The girl gave a swift, comprehensive glance at her as her fingers manipulated the knots.

"You won't earn twenty cents a week at the rate you're workin'," she said; "look at me."

"I don't believe you worked any faster than I do when you hadn't been here any longer," retorted Ellen.

"I did, too; you can't depend on a thing Ed Flynn says. You're awful slow. He praises you because you are good-lookin'."

Ellen turned and faced her. "Look here," said she.

The other girl looked at her with unspeakable impudence, and yet under it was that shadow of dejection and that irresponsible childishness.

"Well, I am lookin'," said she, "what is it?"

"You need not speak to me again in that way," said Ellen, "and I want you to understand it. I will not have it."

"My, ain't you awful smart," said the other girl, sneeringly, but she went on with her work without another word. Presently she said to Ellen, kindly enough: "If you lay the shoes the way I do, so, you can get them faster. You'll find it pays. Every little saving of time counts when you are workin' by the piece."

"Thank you," said Ellen, and did as she was instructed. She began to work with exceeding swiftness for a beginner. Her fingers were supple, her nervous energy great. Flynn came and stood beside her, watching her.

"If you work at that rate, you'll make it pretty profitable," he said.

"Thank you," said Ellen.

"And a square knot every time," he added, with almost a caressing inflection. Mamie Brady tied in the twine with compressed lips. Granville Joy passed them, pushing a rack full of shoes to another department, and he glanced at them jealously. Still he was not seriously alarmed as to Flynn, who, although he was good-looking, was a Catholic. Mrs. Zelotes seemed an effectual barrier to that.

"Ed Flynn talks that way to everybody," Mamie Brady said to Ellen, after the foreman had passed on. She said it this time quite inoffensively. Ellen laughed.

"If I *do* tie the knots square, that is the main thing," she said.

"Then you don't like him?"

"I never spoke two words to him before the day I applied for work," Ellen replied, haughtily. She was beginning to feel that perhaps the worst feature of her going to work in a factory would be this girl.

"I've known girls who would be willing to go down on their knees and tie his shoes when they hadn't seen more of him than that," said the girl. "Ed Flynn is an awful masher."

Ellen went on with her work. The girl, after a side glance at her, went on with hers.

Gradually Ellen's work began to seem mechanical. At first she had felt as if she were tying all her problems of life in square knots. She had to use all her brain upon it; after a while her brain had so informed her fingers that they had learned their lesson well enough to leave her free to think, if only the girl at her side would let her alone. The girl had a certain harsh beauty, coarsely curling red hair, a great mass of it, gathered in an untidy knot, and a brilliant complexion. Her hands were large and red. Ellen's contrasted with them looked like a baby's.

"You ain't got hands for workin' in a shoe-shop," said Mamie Brady, presently, and it was impossible to tell from her tone whether she envied or admired Ellen's hands, or was proud of the superior strength of her own.

"Well, they've got to work in a shoe-shop," said Ellen, with a short laugh.

"You won't find it so easy to work with such little mites of hands when it comes to some things," said the girl.

It began to be clear that she exulted in her large, coarse hands as being fitted for her work.

"Maybe mine will grow larger," said Ellen.

"No, they won't. They'll grow all bony and knotty, but they won't grow any bigger."

"Well, I shall have to get along with them the best way I can," replied Ellen, rather impatiently. This girl was irritating to a degree, and yet there was all the time that vague dejection about her, and withal a certain childishness, which seemed to insist upon patience. The girl was really older than Ellen, but she was curiously unformed. Some of the other girls said openly that she was "lacking."

"You act stuck up. Are you stuck up?" asked Mamie Brady, suddenly, after another pause.

Ellen laughed in spite of herself. "No," said she, "I am not. I know of no reason that I have for being stuck up."

"Well, I don't know of any either," said the other girl, "but I didn't know. You sort of acted as if you felt stuck up."

"Well, I don't."

"You talk stuck up. Why don't you talk the way the rest of us do? Why do you say 'am not,' and 'ar'n't'; why don't you say 'ain't'?"

The girl mimicked Ellen's voice impishly.

Ellen colored. "I am going to talk the way I think best, the way I have been taught is right, and if that makes you think I am stuck up, I can't help it."

"My, don't get mad. I didn't mean anything," said the other girl.

All the time while Ellen was working, and even while the exultation and enthusiasm of her first charge in the battle of labor was upon her, she had had, since her feminine instincts were, after all, strong with her, a sense that Robert Lloyd was under the same great factory roof, in the same human hive, that he might at any moment pass through the room. That, however, she did not think very likely. She fancied the Lloyds seldom went through the departments, which were in charge of foremen. Mr. Norman Lloyd was at the mountains with his wife, she knew. They left Robert in charge, and he would have enough to do in the office. She looked at the grimy men working around her, and she thought of the elegant young fellow, and the utter incongruity of her being among them seemed so great as to preclude the possibility of it. She had said to herself when she thought of obtaining work in Lloyd's that she need not hesitate about it on account of Robert. She had heard her father say that the elder Lloyd almost never came in contact with the men, that everything was done through the foremen. She reasoned that it would be the same with the younger Lloyd. But all at once the girl at her side gave her a violent nudge, which did not interrupt for a second her own flying fingers.

"Say," she said, "ain't he handsome?"

Ellen glanced over her shoulder and saw Robert Lloyd coming down between the lines of workmen. Then she turned to her work, and her fingers slipped and bungled, her ears rang. He passed without speaking.

Mamie Brady openly stared after him. "He's awful handsome, and an awful swell, but he's awful stuck up, just like the old boss," said she. "He never notices any of us, and acts as if he was afraid we'd poison him. My, what's the matter with you?"

"Nothing," said Ellen.

"You look white as a sheet; ain't you well?"

Ellen turned upon her with sudden fury. She had something of the blood of the violent Louds and of her hot-tempered grandmother. She had stood everything from this petty, insistent tormentor.

"Yes, I am well," she replied, "and I will thank you to let me alone, and let me do my work, and do your own."

The other girl stared at her a minute with curiously expressive, uplifted eyebrows.

"Whew!" she said, in a half whistle then, and went on with her work, and did not speak again.

Ellen was thankful that Robert Lloyd had not spoken to her in the factory, and yet she was cut to the quick by it. It fulfilled her anticipations to the letter. "I was right," she said to herself; "he can never think of me again. He is showing it." Somehow, after he had passed, her enthusiasm, born of a strong imagination, and her breadth of nature failed her somewhat. The individual began to press too closely upon the aggregate. Suddenly Ellen Brewster and her own heartache and longing came to the front. She had put herself out of his life as completely as if she had gone to another planet. Still, feeling this, she realized no degradation of herself as a cause of it. She realized that from his point of view she had gone into a valley, but from hers she was rather on an opposite height. She on the height of labor, of skilled handiwork, which is the manifestation in action of brain-work, he on the height of pure brain-work unpressed by physical action.

At noon, when she was eating her dinner with Abby and Maria, Abby turned to her and inquired if young Mr. Lloyd had spoken to her when he came through the room.

"No, he didn't," replied Ellen.

Abby said nothing, but she compressed her lips and gave her head a hard jerk. A girl who ran a machine next to Abby's came up, munching a large piece of pie, taking clean semicircular bites with her large, white teeth.

"Say," she said, "did you see the young boss's new suit? Got up fine, wasn't he?"

"I'd like to see him working where I be for an hour," said a young fellow, strolling up, dipping into his dinner-bag. He was black and greasy as to face and hands and clothing. "Guess his light pants and vest would look rather different," said he, and everybody laughed except the Atkins girls and Ellen.

"I guess he washed his hands, anyway, before he ate his dinner," said Abby, sharply, looking at the young man's hands with meaning.

The young fellow colored, though he laughed. "There ain't a knife in this shop so sharp as some women's tongues," said he. "I pity the man that gets you."

"There won't be any man get me," retorted Abby. "I've seen all I want to see of men, working with 'em every day."

"Mebbe they have of you," called back the young fellow, going away.

"The saucy thing!" said the girl who stitched next to Abby.

"There isn't any excuse for a man's eating his dinner with hands like that," said Abby. "It's worse to poison yourself with your own dirt than with other folks'. It hurts your own self more."

"He ain't worth minding," said the girl.

"Do you suppose I do mind him?" returned Abby. Maria looked at her meaningly. The young man, whose name was Edison Bartlett, had once tried to court Abby, but neither she nor Maria had ever told of it.

"His clothes were a pearl grey," said the girl at the stitching-machine, reverting to the original subject.

"Good gracious, who cares what color they were?" cried Abby, impatiently.

"He looked awful handsome in 'em," said the girl. "He's awful handsome."

"You'd better look at handsome fellows in your own set, Sadie Peel," said Abby, roughly.

The girl, who was extremely pretty, carried herself well, and dressed with cheap fastidiousness, colored.

"I don't see what we have to think about sets for," said she. "I guess way back the Peels were as good as the Lloyds. We're in a free country, where one is as good as another, ain't we?"

"No one is as good as another, except in the sight of the Lord, in any country on the face of this earth," said Abby.

"If you are as good in your own sight, I don't see that it makes much difference about the sight of other human beings," said Ellen. "I guess that's what makes a republic, anyway."

Sadie Peel gave a long, bewildered look at her, then she turned to Abby.

"Do you know where I can get somebody to do accordion-plaiting for me?" she asked.

"No," said Abby. "I never expect to get to the height of accordion-plaiting."

"I know where you can," said another girl, coming up. She had light hair, falling in a harsh, uncurled bristle over her forehead; her black gown was smeared with paste, and even her face and hands were sticky with it.

"There's a great splash of paste on your nose, Hattie Wright," said Abby.

The girl took out a crumpled handkerchief and began rubbing her nose absently while she went on talking about the accordion-plaiting.

"There's a woman on Joy Street does it," said she. "She lives just opposite the school-house, and she does it awful cheap, only three cents a yard." She thrust the handkerchief into her pocket.

"You haven't got it half off," said Abby.

"Let it stay there, then," said the girl, indifferently. "If you work pasting linings in a shoe-shop you've got to get pasted yourself."

Ellen looked at the girl with a curious reflection that she spoke the truth, that she really was pasted herself, that the soil and the grind of her labor were wearing on her soul. She had seen this girl out of the shop — in fact, only the day before — and no one would have known her for the same person. When her light hair was curled, and she was prettily dressed, she was quite a beauty. In the shop she was a slattern, and seemed to go down under the wheels of her toil.

"On Joy Street, you said?" said Sadie Peel.

"Yes. Right opposite the school-house. Her name is Brackett."

Then the one-o'clock whistle blew, and everybody, Ellen with the rest, went back to their stations. Robert Lloyd did not come into the room again that afternoon. Ellen worked on steadily, and gained swiftness. Every now and then the foreman came and spoke encouragingly to her.

"Look out, Mamie," he said to the girl at her side, "or she'll get ahead of you."

"I don't want to get ahead of her," said Ellen, unexpectedly.

Flynn laughed. "If you don't, you ain't much like the other girls in this shop," said he, passing on with his urbane, slightly important swing of shoulders.

"Did you mean that?" asked Mamie Brady.

"Yes, I did. It seems to me you work fast enough for any girl. A girl isn't a machine."

"You're a queer thing," said Mamie Brady. "If I were you, I would just as soon get ahead as not, especially if Ed Flynn was goin' to come and praise me for it."

Ellen shrugged her shoulders and tied another knot.

"You're a queer thing," said Mamie Brady, while her fingers flew like live wires.

Chapter XXXVI

*T*hat night, when Ellen went down the street towards home with the stream of factory operatives, she computed that she must have earned about fifty cents, perhaps not quite that. She was horribly tired. Although the work in itself was not laborious, she had been all day under a severe nervous tension.

"You look tired to death, Ellen Brewster," Abby said, in a half-resentful, half-compassionate tone. "You can never stand this in the world."

"I am no more tired than anyone would be the first day," Ellen returned, stoutly, "and I'm going to stand it."

"You act to me as if you liked it," said Abby, with an angry switch like a cat.

"I do," Ellen returned, almost as angrily. Then she turned to Abby. "Look here, Abby Atkins, why can't you treat me halfway decent?" said she. "You know I've got to do it, and I'm making the best of it. If anybody else treated me the way you are doing, I don't know what you would do."

"I would kill them," said Abby, fiercely; "but it's different with me. I'm mad to have you go to work in the shop, and act as if you liked it, because I think so much of you." Abby and Ellen were walking side by side, and Maria followed with Sadie Peel.

"Well, I can't help it if you are mad at me," said Ellen. "I've had everything to contend against, my father and mother, and my grandmother won't even speak to me, and now if you —" Ellen's voice broke.

Abby caught her arm in a hard grip.

"I ain't," said she; "you can depend on me. You know you can, in spite of everything. You know why I talk so. If you've set your heart on doing it, I won't say another word. I'll do all I can to help you, and I'd like to hear anybody say a word against you for going to work in the shop, that's all."

Ellen and Abby almost never kissed each other; Abby was not given to endearments of that kind. Maria was more profuse with her caresses.

That night when they reached the corner of the cross street where the Atkinses lived, Maria went close to Ellen and put up her face.

"Good-night," said she. Then she withdrew her lips suddenly, before Ellen could touch them.

"I forgot," said she. "You mustn't kiss me. I forgot my cough. They say it's catching."

Ellen caught hold of her little, thin shoulders, held her firmly, and kissed her full on her lips.

"Good-night," said she.

"Good-night, Ellen," called Abby, and her sharp voice rang as sweet as a bird's.

When Ellen came in sight of her grandmother's house, she saw a window-shade go down with a jerk, and knew that Mrs. Zelotes had been watching for her, and was determined not to let her know it. Mrs. Pointdexter came out of her grand house as Ellen passed, and took up her station on the corner to wait for a car. She bowed to Ellen with an evasive, little, sidewise bow. Her natural amiability prompted her to shake hands with her, call her "my dear," and inquire how she had got on during her first day in the factory, but she was afraid of her friend, whose eye she felt upon her around the edge of the drawn curtain.

It was unusually dark that night for early fall, and the rain came down in a steady drizzle, as it had come all day, and the wind blew from the ocean on the east. The lamp was lighted in the kitchen when Ellen turned into her own door-yard, and home had never looked so pleasant and desirable to her. For the first time in her life she knew what it was to come home for rest and shelter after a day of toil, and she seemed to sense the full meaning of home as a refuge for weary labor.

When she opened the door, she smelled at once a particular kind of stew of which she was very fond, and knew that her mother had been making it for her supper. There was a rush of warm air from the kitchen which felt grateful after the damp chill outside.

Ellen went into the kitchen, and her mother stood there over the stove, stirring the stew. She looked up at the girl with an expression of intense motherliness which was beyond a smile.

"Well, so you've got home?" she said.

"Yes."

"How did you get along?"

"All right. It isn't hard work. Not a bit hard, mother."

"Ain't you tired?"

"Oh, a little. But no more than anybody would be at first. I don't look very tired, do I?" Ellen laughed.

"No, you don't," said Fanny, looking at her cheeks, reddened with the damp wind. The mother's look was admiring and piteous and brave. No one knew how the woman had suffered that day, but she had kept her head and heart above it. The stew for Ellen's supper was a proof of that.

"Where's father?" asked Ellen, taking off her hat and cape, and going to the sink to wash her face and hands. Fanny saw her do that with a qualm. Ellen had always used a dainty little set in her own room. Now she was doing exactly as her father had always done on his return from the shop — washing off the stains of leather at the kitchen sink. She felt instinctively that Ellen did it purposely, that she was striving to bring herself into accord with her new life in all the details.

Little Amabel came running out of the dining room, and threw her arms around Ellen's knees as she was bending over the sink. "I've set the table!" she cried.

"Look out or you'll get all splashed," laughed Ellen.

"And I dusted," said Amabel.

"She's been as good as a kitten all day, and a sight of help," said Fanny.

"She's a good girl," said Ellen. "Cousin Ellen will kiss her as soon as she gets her face washed."

She caught hold of a fold of the roller towel, and turned her beautiful, dripping face to her mother as she did so.

"That stew does smell so good," said she. "Where did you say father was?"

"I thought we'd just have some bread and milk for dinner, and somethin' hearty tonight, when you came home," said Fanny. "I thought maybe a stew would taste good."

"I guess it will," said Ellen, stooping down to kiss Amabel. "Where did you say father was?"

"Uncle Andrew has been lyin' down all day most," whispered Amabel.

"Isn't he well?" Ellen asked her mother, in quick alarm.

"Oh yes, he's well enough." Fanny moved close to the girl with a motion of secrecy. "If I were you I wouldn't say one word about the shop, nor what you did, before father tonight; let him kind of get used to it. Amabel mustn't talk about it, either."

"I won't," said Amabel, with a wise air.

"You know father had set his heart on somethin' pretty different for you," said Fanny.

Fanny hushed her voice as Andrew came out of the dining room, staggering a little as if the light blinded him. His nervous strength of the morning had passed and left him exhausted. He moved and stood with a downward lope of every muscle, expressing unutterable patience, which had passed beyond rebellion and questioning.

He stood before Ellen like some old, spent horse. He was expecting to hear something about the shop — expecting, as it were, a touch on a sore, and he waited for it meekly.

Ellen turned her lovely, glowing face towards him.

"Father," she said, as if nothing out of the common had happened, "are you going down-town tonight?"

Andrew brightened a little. "I can if you want anything, Ellen," he said.

"Well, I don't want you to go on purpose, but I do want a book from the library."

"I'd just as soon go as not, Ellen," said Andrew.

"It'll do him good," whispered Fanny, as she passed Ellen, carrying the dish of stew to the dining room.

"Well, then, I'll give you my card after supper," said Ellen. "Supper is ready now, isn't it, mother? I'm as hungry as a bear."

Andrew, when he was seated at the table and was ladling out the stew, had still that air of hopeless and defenseless apology towards life, but he held his head higher, and his frown of patient gloom had relaxed.

Then Ellen said something else. "Maybe I can write a book some time," said she.

A sudden flash illumined Andrew's face. It was like the visible awakening of hope and ambition.

"I don't see why you can't," he said, eagerly.

"Maybe she can," said Fanny. "Give her some more of the potatoes, Andrew."

"I'll have plenty of time after — evenings," said Ellen.

"I guess lots of folks write books that sell, and sell well, that don't have anymore talent than you," said Andrew. "Only think how they praised your valedictory."

"Well, it can't do any harm to try," said Ellen, "and you could copy it for me, couldn't you, father? Your writing is so fine, it would be as good as a typewriter."

"Of course I can," said Andrew.

When Andrew went down to the library, passing along the drenched streets, seeing the lamps through shifting veils of heavy mist, he was as full of enthusiasm over Ellen's book as he had been over the gold-mine. The heart of a man is always ready to admit a ray of sunshine, and it takes only a small one to dispel the shadows when love dwells therein.

Chapter XXXVII

*E*llen actually went to work, with sheets of foolscap and a new bottle of ink, on a novel, which was not worth the writing; but no one could estimate the comfort and encouragement it was to Andrew. Ellen worked an hour or two every evening on the novel, and next day Andrew copied it in a hand like copperplate — large, with ornate flourishes. Andrew's handwriting had always been greatly admired, and, strangely enough, it was not in the least indicative of his character, being wholly acquired. He had probably some ability for drawing, but this had been his only outlet.

At the head of every chapter of Ellen's novel were birds and flowers done in colored inks, and every chapter had a tail-piece of elegant quirls and flourishes. Fanny admired it intensely. She was not quite so sure of Ellen's work as she was of her husband's. She felt herself a judge of one, but not of the other.

"If Ellen could only write as well as you copy, it will do," she often said to Andrew.

"What she is writing is beautiful," said Andrew, fervently. He was quite sure in his own mind that such a book had never been written, and his pride in his decorations was a minor one.

Ellen, although she was not versed in the ways of books, yet had enough of a sense of the fitness of things, and of the ridiculous, to know that the manuscript, with its impossible pen-and-ink birds and flowers heading and finishing every chapter, was grotesque in the extreme. She felt divided between a desire to laugh and a desire to cry whenever she looked at it. About her own work she felt more than doubtful; still, she was somewhat hopeful, since her taste and judgment, as well as her style, were alike crude. She told Abby and Maria what she was doing, under promise of strict secrecy, and after a while read them a few chapters.

"It's beautiful," said Maria — "perfectly beautiful. I had a Sunday-school book this week which I know wasn't half as good."

Ellen looked at Abby, who was silent. The three girls were up in Ellen's room. It was midwinter, some months after she had gone to work in the shop, and she had a fire in her little, air-tight stove.

"Well, what do you think of it, Abby?" asked Ellen. Ellen's cheeks were flushed as if with fever. She looked eagerly at the other girl.

"Do you want me to tell you the truth?" asked Abby, bluntly.

"Yes, of course I do."

"Well, then, I don't know a thing about books, and I'd knock anybody else down that said it, but it seems to me it's trash."

"Oh, Abby," murmured Maria.

"Never mind," said Ellen, though she quivered a little, "I want to know just how it looks to her."

"It looks to me just like that," said Abby — "like trash. It sounds as if, when you began to write it, you had mounted upon stilts, and didn't see things and people the way they really were. It ain't natural."

"Do you think I had better give it up, then?" asked Ellen.

"No, I don't, on account of your father."

"I believe it would about break father's heart," said Ellen.

"I don't know but it's worth as much to write a book for your father, to please him, and keep his spirits up, as it is to write one for the whole world," said Abby.

"Only, of course, she can't get any money for it," said Maria. "But I don't believe Abby is right, and don't you get discouraged, Ellen. It sounds beautiful to me."

"Well, I suppose it is worth keeping on with for father's sake," said Ellen; but she had a discouraged air. She never again wrote with any hope or heart; she had faith in Abby's opinion, for she knew that she was always predisposed to admiration in her case.

Ellen at that time was earning more, for she had advanced, and had long ago left her station beside Mamie Brady; and now in a month or two she would have a machine. The girls, many of them, said openly that her rapid promotion was due to favoritism, and that Ed Flynn wouldn't do as much for anybody but Ellen Brewster. Flynn hung about her in the shop a good deal, but he had made no efforts to pay her decided attention. His religion was the prime factor for his hesitation. He could not see his way clear towards open addresses with a view to marriage. Still, he had a sharp eye for other admirers, and Ellen had not been in the factory two months before Granville Joy was sent into another room. Robert Lloyd, to whom the foreman appealed for confirmation of the plan, coincided with readiness.

"That fellow ain't strong enough to run that machine he's doing now," said Flynn.

"Then put him on another," Robert said, coloring. It was not quite like setting his rival in the front of the battle; still, he felt ashamed of himself. Quicker than lightning it had flashed through his mind that young Joy could thus be sent into a separate room from Ellen Brewster.

"I think he had better take one of the heel-shaving machines below," said Flynn, "and let that big Swede, that's as strong as an ox, and never jumped at anything in his life, take his place here."

"All right," said Lloyd, assuming a nonchalant air. "Make the change if you think it advisable, Flynn."

While such benevolence towards a possible rival had its suspicious points, yet there was, after all, some reason for it. Granville Joy, who was delicately organized as to his nerves, was running a machine for cutting linings, and this came down with sharp thuds which shook the factory, and it was fairly torture to him. Every time the knife fell he cringed as if at a cannon report. He had never grown accustomed to it. His face had acquired a fixed expression of being screwed to meet a shock of sound. He was manifestly unfit for his job, but he received the order to leave with dismay.

"Hasn't my work been satisfactory?" he asked Flynn.

"Satisfactory enough," replied the foreman, genially, "but it's too hard for you, man."

"I ain't complained," said Joy, with a flash of his eyes. He thought he knew why this solicitude was shown him.

"I know you ain't," said Flynn, "but you ain't got the muscle and nerve for it. That's plain enough to see."

"I ain't complained, and I'd rather stay where I be," said Joy, angrily.

"You'll go where you are sent in this factory, or be damned," cried Flynn, walking off.

Joy looked after him with an expression which transformed his face. But the next morning the stolid Swede, who would not have started at a bomb, was at his place, and he was below, where he could not see Ellen.

Robert never spoke to Ellen in the factory, and had never called upon her since she entered. Now and then he met her on the street and raised his hat, that was all. Still, he began to wonder more and more if his aunt had not been mistaken in her view of the girl's motive for giving up college and going to work. Then, later on, he learned from Lyman Risley that a small mortgage had been put on the Brewster house some time before. In fact, Andrew, not knowing to whom to go, and remembering his kindness when Ellen was a child, had applied to him for advice concerning it. "He had to do it to keep his wife's sister in the asylum," he told Robert; "and that poor girl went to work because she was forced into it, not because she preferred it, you may be sure of that."

The two men were walking down the street one windswept day in December, when the pavement showed ridges of dust as from a mighty broom, and travelers walked bending before it with backward-flying garments.

"You may be right," said Robert; "still, as Aunt Cynthia says, so many girls have that idea of earning money instead of going to school."

"I know the pitiful need of money has tainted many poor girls with a monstrous and morbid overvalue of it," said Risley, "and for that I cannot see they are to blame; but in this case I am sure it was not so. That poor child gave up Vassar College and went to work because she was fairly forced into it by circumstances. The aunt's husband ran away with another woman, and left her destitute, so that the support of her and her child came upon the Brewsters; and Brewster has been out of work a long time now, I know. He told me so. That mortgage had to be raised, and the girl had to go to work; there was no other way out of it."

"Why didn't she tell Aunt Cynthia so?" asked Robert.

"Because she is Ellen Brewster, the outgrowth of the child who would not —" Risley checked himself abruptly.

"I know," said Robert, shortly.

The other man started. "How long have you known — she did not tell?"

Robert laughed a little. "Oh no," he replied. "Nobody told. I went there to call, and saw my own old doll sitting in a little chair in a corner of the parlor. She did not tell, but she knew that I knew. That child was a trump."

"Well, what can you expect of a girl who was a child like that?" said Risley. "Mind you, in a way I don't like it. This power for secretiveness and this rigidity of pride in a girl of that age strike me rather unpleasantly. Of course she was too proud to tell Cynthia the true reason, and very likely thought they would blame her father, or Cynthia might feel that she was in a measure hinting to her to do more."

"It would have looked like that," said Robert, reflecting.

"Without any doubt that was what she thought; still, I don't like this strength in so young a girl. She will make a more harmonious woman than girl, for she has not yet grown up to her own character. But depend upon it, that girl never went to work of her own free choice."

"You say the father is out of work?" Robert said.

"Yes, he has not had work for six months. He said, with the most dejected dignity and appeal that I ever saw in my life, that they begin to think him too old, that the younger men are preferred."

"I wonder," Robert began, then he stopped confusedly. It had been on his tongue to say that he wondered if he could not get some employment for him at Lloyd's; then he remembered his uncle, and stopped. Robert had begun to understand the older man's methods, and also to understand that they were not to be caviled at or disputed, even by a nephew for whom he had undoubtedly considerable affection.

"It is nonsense, of course," said Risley. "The man is not by any means old or past his usefulness, although I must admit he has that look. He cannot be any older than your uncle. Speaking of your uncle, how is Mrs. Lloyd?"

"I fear Aunt Lizzie is very far from well," replied Robert, "but she tries to keep it from Uncle Norman."

"I don't see how she can. She looked ghastly when I met her the other day."

"That was when Uncle Norman was in New York," said Robert. "It is different when he is at home." As he spoke, an expression of intensest pity came over the young man's face. "I wonder what a woman who loves her husband will not do to shield him from any annoyance or suffering," he said.

"I believe some women are born fixed to a sort of spiritual rack for the sake of love, and remain there through life," said Risley. "But I have always liked Mrs. Lloyd. She ought to have good advice. What is it, has she told you?"

"Yes," said Robert.

"It will be quite safe with me."

Robert whispered one word in his ear.

"My God!" said Risley, "that? And do you mean to say that she has had no advice except Dr. Story?"

"Yes, I took her to New York to a specialist some time ago. Uncle Norman never knew it."

"And nothing can be done?"

"She could have an operation, but the success would be very doubtful."

"And that she will not consent to?"

"She has not yet."

"How long?"

"Oh, she may live for years, but she suffers horribly, and she will suffer more."

"And you say he does not know?"

"No."

"Why, look here, Robert, dare you assume the responsibility? What will he say when he finds out that you have kept it from him?"

"I don't care," said Robert. "I will not break an oath exacted by a woman in such straits as that, and I don't see what good it could do to tell him."

"He might persuade her to have the operation."

"His mere existence is persuasion enough, if she is to be persuaded. And I hope she may consent before long. She has seemed a little more comfortable lately, too."

"I suppose sometimes those hideous things go away as mysteriously as they come," said Risley.

"Yes," replied Robert. "Going back to our first subject —"

Risley laughed. "Here she is coming," he said.

In fact, at that moment they came abreast the street that led to the factories, and the six-o'clock whistle was just dying away in a long reverberation, and the workmen pouring out of the doors and down the stairs. Ellen had moved quickly, for she had an errand at the grocery-store before she went home. She was going to get some oysters for a hot stew for supper, of which her father was very fond. She had a little oyster-can in her hand when she met the two gentlemen. She had grown undeniably thinner since summer, but she was charming. Her short black skirt and her coarse grey jacket fitted her as well as if they had been tailor-made. There was nothing tawdry or slatternly about her. She looked every inch a lady, even with the drawback of an oyster-can, and mittens instead of gloves.

Both Risley and Robert raised their hats, and Ellen bowed. She did not smile, but her face contracted curiously, and her color obviously paled. Risley looked at Robert after they had passed.

"I have called on her twice," said Robert, as if answering a question. His relations with the older man had become very close, almost like those of father and son, though Risley was hardly old enough for that relation.

"And you haven't been since she went to work?"

"No."

"But you would have, had she gone to college instead of going to work in a shoe-factory?" Risley's voice had a tone of the gentlest conceivable sarcasm.

Robert colored. "Yes, I suppose so," he said. Then he turned to Risley with a burst of utter frankness. "Hang it! old fellow," he said, "you know how I have been brought up; you know how she — you know all about it. What is a fellow to do?"

"Do what he pleases. If it would please me to call on that splendid young thing, I should call if I were the Czar of all the Russias."

"Well, I will call," said Robert.

Chapter XXXVIII

*T*he very next evening Robert Lloyd went to call on Ellen. As he started out he was conscious of a strange sensation of shock, as if his feet had suddenly touched firm ground. All these months since Ellen had been working in the factory he had been vacillating. He was undoubtedly in love with her; he did not for a moment cheat himself as to that. When he caught a glimpse of her fair head among the other girls, he realized how unspeakably dear she was to him. Ellen never entered nor left the factory that he did not know it. Without actually seeing her, he was conscious of her presence always. He acknowledged to himself that there was no one like her for him, and never would be. He tried to interest himself in other young women, but always there was Ellen, like the constant refrain of a song. All other women meant to him not themselves, but Ellen. Womanhood itself was Ellen for his manhood. He knew it, and yet that strain of utterly impassionate judgment and worldly wisdom which was born in him kept him from making any advances to her. Now, however, the radicalism of Risley had acted like a spur to his own inclination. His judgment was in abeyance. He said to himself that he would give it up; he would go to see the girl — that he would win her if he could. He said to himself that she had been wronged, that Risley was right about her, that she was good and noble.

As the car drew near the Brewsters, his tenderness seemed to outspeed the electricity. The girl's fair face was plain before his eyes, as if she were actually there, and it was idealized and haloed as with the light of gold and precious stones. All at once, since he had given himself loose rein, he overtook, as it were, the true meaning of her. "The dear child," he thought, with a rush of tenderness like pain — "the dear child. There she gave up everything and went to work, and let us blame her, rather than have her father blamed. The dear, proud child. She did that rather than seem to beg for more help."

When Robert got off the car he was ready to fall at her feet, to push between her and the roughness of life, between her and the whole world.

He went up the little walk between the dry shrubs and rang the bell. There was no light in the front windows nor in the hall. Presently he heard footsteps, and saw a glimmer of light advancing towards him through the length of the hall. There were muslin-curtained sidelights to the door. Then the door opened, and little Amabel Tenny stood there holding a small kerosene lamp carefully in both hands. She held it in such a manner that the light streamed up in Robert's face and nearly blinded him. He was dimly conscious of a little face full of a certain chary innocence and pathos regarding him.

"Is Miss Ellen Brewster at home?" asked Robert, smiling down at the little thing.

"Yes, sir," replied Amabel.

Then she remained perfectly still, holding the lamp, as if she had been some little sculptured light-bearer. She did not return his smile, and she did not ask him in. She simply regarded him with her sharp, innocent, illuminated face. Robert felt ridiculously nonplussed.

"Did you say she was in, my dear?" he asked.

"Yes, sir," replied Amabel, then relapsed into silence.

"Can I see her?" asked Robert, desperately.

"I don't know," replied Amabel. Then she stood still, as before, holding the lamp.

Robert began to wonder what he was to do, when he heard a woman's voice calling from the sitting room at the end of the hall, the door of which had been left ajar:

"Amabel Tenny, what are you doin'? You are coldin' the house all off! Who is it?"

"It's a man, Aunt Fanny," called Amabel.

"Who is the man?" asked the voice. Then, much to Robert's relief, Fanny herself appeared.

She colored a flaming red when she saw him. She looked at Amabel as if she had an impulse to shake her.

"Why, Mr. Lloyd, is it you?" she cried.

"Good-evening, Mrs. Brewster; is — is your daughter at home?" asked Robert. He felt inclined to roar with laughter, and yet a curious dismay was beginning to take possession of him.

"Yes, Ellen is at home," replied Fanny, with alacrity. "Walk in, Mr. Lloyd." She was blushing and smiling as if she had been her own daughter. It was foolish, yet pathetic. Although Fanny asked the young man to walk in, and snatched the lamp peremptorily from Amabel's hand, she still hesitated. Robert began to wonder if he should ever be admitted. He did not dream of the true reason for the hesitation. There was no fire in the parlor, and in the sitting room were Andrew, John

Sargent, and Mrs. Wetherhed. It seemed to her highly important that Ellen should see her caller by herself, but how to take him into that cold parlor?

Finally, however, she made up her mind to do so. She opened the parlor door.

"Please walk in this way, Mr. Lloyd," said she, and Robert followed her in.

It was a bitter night outside, and the temperature in the unused room was freezing. The windows behind the cheap curtains were thickly furred with frost.

"Please be seated," said Fanny.

She indicated the large easy chair, and Robert seated himself without removing his outer coat, yet the icy cold of the cushions struck through him.

Fanny ignited a match to light the best lamp with its painted globe. Her fingers trembled. She had to use three matches before she was successful.

"Can't I assist you?" asked Robert.

"No, thank you," replied Fanny; "I guess the matches are damp. I've got it now." Her voice shook. She turned to Robert when the lamp was lighted, still holding the small one, which she had set for the moment on the table. The strong double light revealed her face of abashed delight, although the young man did not understand it. It was the solicitude of the mother for the child which dignified all coarseness and folly.

"I guess you had better keep on your overcoat a little while till I get the fire built," said she. "This room ain't very warm."

Robert tried to say something polite about not feeling cold, but the lie was too obvious. Instead, he remarked that his coat was very warm, as it was, indeed, being lined with fur.

"I'll have the fire kindled in a minute," Fanny said.

"Now don't trouble yourself, Mrs. Brewster," said Robert. "I am quite warm in this coat, unless," he added, lamely, "I could go out where you were sitting."

"There's company out there," said Fanny, with embarrassed significance. She blushed as she spoke, and Robert blushed also, without knowing why.

"It's no trouble at all to start a fire," said Fanny; "this chimney draws fine. I'll speak to Ellen."

Robert, left alone in the freezing room, felt his dismay deepen. Barriers of tragedy are nothing to those of comedy. He began to wonder if he were not, after all, doing a foolish thing. The hall door had been left ajar, and he presently became aware of Amabel's little face and luminous eyes set therein.

Robert smiled, and to his intense astonishment the child made a little run to him and snuggled close to his side. He lifted her up on his knee, and wrapped his fur coat around her. Amabel thrust out one tiny hand and began to stroke the sable collar.

"It's fur," said she, with a bright, wise look into Robert's face.

"Yes, it's fur," said he. "Do you know what kind?"

She shook her head, with bright eyes still on his.

"It is sable," said Robert, "and it is the coat of a little animal that lives very far north, where it is as cold and colder than this all the time, and the ice and snow never melts."

Suddenly Amabel slipped off his knee, pushing aside his caressing arm with a violent motion. Then she stood aloof, eying him with unmistakable reproof and hostility. Robert laughed.

"What is the matter?" he said.

"What does he do without his coat if it is as cold as that where he lives?" asked Amabel, severely. There was almost an accent of horror in her childish voice.

"Why, my dear child," said Robert, "the little animal is dead. He isn't running around without his coat. He was shot for his fur."

"To make you a coat?" Amabel's voice was full of judicial severity.

"Well, in one way," replied Robert, laughing. "It was shot to get the fur to make somebody a coat, and I bought it. Come back here and have it wrapped round you; you'll freeze if you don't."

Amabel came back and sat on his knee, and let him wrap the fur-lined garment around her. A strange sensation of tenderness and protection came over the young man as he felt the little, slender body of the child nestle against his own. He had begun to surmise who she was. However, Amabel herself told him in a moment.

"My mamma's sick, and they took her to an asylum. And my papa has gone away," she said.

"You poor little soul," said Robert, tenderly. Amabel continued to look at him with eyes of keenest intelligence, while one little cheek was flattened against his breast.

"I live with Uncle Andrew and Aunt Fanny now," said she, "and I sleep with Ellen."

"But you like living here, don't you, you dear?" asked Robert.

"Yes," said Amabel, "and I like to stay with Ellen, but — but — I want to see my mamma and papa," she wailed, suddenly, in the lowest and most pitiful wail imaginable.

"Poor little darling," said Robert, stroking her flaxen hair. Amabel looked up at him with her little face all distorted with grief.

"If you had been my papa, would you have gone away and left Amabel?" she asked, quiveringly. Robert gathered her to him in a strong clasp of protection.

"No, you little darling, I never should," he cried, fervently.

At that moment he wished devoutly that he had the handling of the man who had deserted this child.

"I like you most as well as my own papa," said Amabel. "You ain't so big as my papa." She said that in a tone of evident disparagement.

Then the sitting room door opened, and Fanny and Ellen and Andrew appeared, the last with a great basket of wood and kindlings.

Robert set down Amabel, and sprang to his feet to greet Andrew and Ellen. Andrew, after depositing his basket beside the stove, shook hands with a sort of sad awkwardness. Robert saw that the man had aged immeasurably since he had last seen him.

"It is a cold night, Mr. Brewster," he said, and knew the moment he said it that it was not a happy remark.

"It is pretty cold," agreed Andrew, "and it's cold here in this room."

"Oh, it'll be warm in a minute; this stove heats up quick," cried Fanny, with agitated briskness. She began pulling the kindlings out of the basket.

"Here, you let me do that," said Andrew, and was down on his knees beside her. The two were cramming the fuel into the little, air-tight stove, while Robert was greeting Ellen. The awkwardness of the situation was evidently overcoming her. She was quite pale, and her voice trembled as she returned his good-evening. Amabel left the young man, and clung tightly to Ellen's hand, drawing her skirt around her until only her little face was visible above the folds.

The fumes from a match filled the room, and the fire began to roar.

"It'll be warm in a minute," said Fanny, rising. "You leave the register open till it's real good and hot, Ellen, and there's plenty more wood in the basket. Here, Amabel, you come out in the other room with Aunt Fanny."

But Amabel, instead of obeying, made a dart towards Robert, who caught her up, laughing, and smuggled her into the depths of his fur-lined coat.

"Come right along, Amabel," said Fanny.

But Amabel clung fast to Robert, with a mischievous roll of an eye at her aunt.

"Amabel," said Fanny, authoritatively.

"Come, Amabel," said Andrew.

"Oh, let her stay," Robert said, laughing. "I'll keep her in my coat until it is warm."

"I'm afraid she'll bother you," said Fanny.

"Not a bit," replied Robert.

"You are a naughty girl, Amabel," said Fanny; but she went out of the room, with Andrew at her heels. She did not know what else to do, since the young man had expressed a desire to keep the child. She had thought he would have preferred a *tête-à-tête* with Ellen. Ellen sat down on the sofa covered with olive-green plush, beyond the table, and the light of the hideous lamp fell full upon her face. She was thin, and much of her lovely bloom was missing between her agitation and the cold; but Robert, looking at her, realized how dear she was to him. There was something about that small figure, and that fair head held with such firmness of pride, and that soul outlooking from steady blue eyes, which filled all his need of life. His love for the pearl quite ignored its setting of the common and the ridiculous. He looked at her and smiled. Ellen smiled back tremulously, then she cast down her eyes. The fire was roaring, but the room was freezing. The sitting room door was opened a crack, and remained so for a second, then it was widened, and Andrew peeped in. Then he entered, tiptoeing gingerly, as if he were afraid of disturbing a meeting. He brought a blue knitted shawl, which he put over Ellen's shoulders.

"Mother thinks you had better keep this on till the room gets warm," he whispered. Then he withdrew, shutting the door softly.

Robert, left alone with Ellen in this solemnly important fashion, felt utterly at a loss. He had never considered himself especially shy, but an embarrassment which was almost ridiculous was over him. Ellen sat with her eyes cast down. He felt that the child on his knee was regarding them both curiously.

"If you have come to see Ellen, why don't you speak to her?" demanded Amabel, suddenly. Then both Robert and Ellen laughed.

"This is your aunt's little girl, isn't she?" asked Robert.

Amabel answered before Ellen was able. "My mamma is sick, and they carried her away to the asylum," she told Robert. "She — she tried to hurt Amabel; she tried to" — Amabel made that hideous gesture with her tiny forefinger across her throat. "Mamma was sick or she wouldn't," she added, challengingly, to Robert.

"Of course she wouldn't, you poor little soul," said Robert.

Suddenly Amabel burst into tears, and began to wriggle herself free from his arms. "Let me go," she demanded; "let me go. I want Ellen."

When Robert loosened his grasp she fled to Ellen, and was in her lap with a bound.

"I want my mamma — I want my mamma," she moaned.

Ellen leaned her cheek against the poor little flaxen head. "There, there, darling," she whispered, "don't. Mamma will come home as soon as she gets better."

"How long will that be, Ellen?"

"Pretty soon, I hope, darling. Don't."

Poor Eva Tenny had been in the asylum some four months, and the reports as to her condition were no more favorable. Ellen's voice, in spite of herself, had a hopeless tone, which the child was quick to detect.

"I want my mamma," she repeated. "I want her, Ellen. It has been tomorrow, and tomorrow, and tomorrow after that, and the tomorrows are yesterdays, and she hasn't come."

"She will come some time, darling."

Robert sat eying the two with intensest pity. "Do you like chocolates, Amabel?" he asked.

The child repeated that she wanted her mother still, as with a sort of mechanical regularity of grief, but she fastened her eyes on him.

"Because I am going to send you a big box of them tomorrow," said Robert.

Amabel turned to Ellen. "Does he mean it?" she asked.

"I guess so," replied Ellen, laughing.

Amabel, looking from one to the other, also began to laugh unwillingly.

Then the sitting room door opened, and Fanny called sharply and imperatively, "Amabel, Amabel; come!"

Amabel clung more tightly to Ellen, who began to gently loosen her arms.

"Amabel Tenny, come this minute. It is your bedtime," said Fanny.

"I guess you had better go, darling," whispered Ellen.

"I don't want to go to bed till you do, Ellen," whispered the child.

Ellen gently but firmly unclasped the clinging arms. "Run along, dear," she whispered.

"I will send those chocolates tomorrow," suggested Robert.

Amabel seemed to do everything by sudden and violent impulses. All at once she ceased resisting. She slid down from Ellen's lap as quickly as she had gotten into it. She clutched her neck with two little wiry arms, kissed her hard on the mouth, darted across the room to Robert, threw her arms around his neck and kissed him, then flew out of the room.

"She is an interesting child," said Robert, who felt, like most people, the delicate flattery of a child's unsolicited caresses.

"I am very fond of her," replied Ellen.

Then the two were silent. Robert suddenly realized that there was little to say unless he ventured on debatable ground. It would be too absurd of him to commence making love at once, and as for asking Ellen about her work, that seemed a subject better let alone.

Ellen herself opened the conversation by inquiring for his aunt.

"Aunt Cynthia is very well," replied Robert. "I was in there last evening. You have not been to see her lately, Miss Brewster."

Robert realized as soon as he had said that that he had made a mistake.

"No," replied Ellen. She obviously paled a little, and looked at him wistfully. The young man could not stand it any longer, so straight into the heart of the matter he lunged.

"Look here, Miss Brewster," he said, "why on earth didn't you tell Aunt Cynthia?"

"Tell her?" repeated Ellen, vaguely.

"Yes; make a clean breast of it to her. Tell her just why you went to work, and gave up college?"

Ellen colored, and looked at him half defiantly, half piteously. "I told her all I ought to," she said.

"But you did not; pardon me," said Robert, "you did not tell her half enough. You let her think that you actually of your own free choice went to work in the factory rather than go to college."

"So I did," replied Ellen, looking at him proudly.

"Of course you did, in one sense, but in another you did not. You deliberately chose to make a sacrifice; but it was a sacrifice. You cannot deny that it was a sacrifice."

Ellen was silent.

"But you gave Aunt Cynthia the impression that it was not a sacrifice," said Robert, almost severely.

Ellen's face quivered a little. "I saw no other way to do," she said, faintly. The authoritative tone which this young man was taking with her stirred her as nothing had ever stirred her in her life before. She felt like a child before him.

"You have no right to give such a false impression of your own character," said Robert.

"It was either that or a false impression of another," returned Ellen, tremulously.

"You mean that she might have blamed your parents, and thought that they were forcing you into this?"

Ellen nodded.

"And I suppose you thought, too, that maybe Aunt Cynthia would suspect, if you told her all the difficulties, that you were hinting for more assistance."

Ellen nodded, and her lip was quivering. Suddenly all her force of character seemed to have deserted her, and she looked more like a child than Amabel. She actually put both her little fists to her eyes. After all, the girl was very young, a child forced by the stress of circumstances to premature development, but she could relapse before the insistence of another nature.

Robert looked at her, his own face working, then he could bear it no longer. He was over on the sofa beside Ellen and had her in his arms. "You poor little thing," he whispered. "Don't. I have loved you ever since the first time I saw you. I ought to have told you so before. Don't you love me a little, Ellen?"

But Ellen released herself with a motion of firm elusiveness and looked at him. The tears still stood in her eyes, but her face was steady. "I have been putting you out of my mind," said she.

"But could you?" whispered Robert, leaning over her.

Ellen did not reply, but looked down and trembled.

"Could you?" repeated Robert, and there was in his voice that masculine insistence which is a true note of nature, and means the subjugation of the feminine into harmony.

Ellen did not speak, but every line in her body betrayed helpless yielding.

"You know you could not," said Robert with triumph, and took her in his arms again.

But he reckoned without the girl, who was, after all, stronger than her natural instincts, and able to rise above and subjugate them. She freed herself from him resolutely, rose, and stood before him, looking at him quite unfalteringly and accusingly.

"Why do you come now?" she asked. "You say you have loved me from the first. You came to see me, you walked home with me, and said things to me that made me think —" She stopped.

"Made you think what, dear?" asked Robert. He was pale and indescribably anxious and appealing. It was suddenly revealed to him that this plum was so firmly attached to its bough of individuality that possibly love itself could not loosen it.

"You made me think that perhaps you did care a little," said Ellen, in a low but unfaltering voice.

"You thought quite right, only not a little, but a great deal," said Robert, firmly.

"Then," said Ellen, "the moment I gave up going to college and went to work you never came to see me again; you never even spoke to me in the shop; you went right past me without a look."

"Good God! child," Robert interposed, "don't you know why I did that?"

Ellen looked at him bewildered, then a burning red overspread her face. "Yes," she replied. "I didn't. But I do now. They would have talked."

"I thought you would understand that," said Robert. "I had only the best motives for that. I cannot speak to you in the factory anymore than I have done. I cannot expose you to remark; but as for my not calling, I believed what you said to my aunt and to me. I thought that you had deliberately preferred a lower life to a higher one — that you preferred earning money to something better. I thought —"

Robert fairly started as Ellen began talking with a fire which seemed to make her scintillate before his eyes.

"You talk about a lower and a higher life," said she. "Is it true? Is Vassar College any higher than a shoe-factory? Is any labor which is honest, and done with the best strength of man, for the best motives, to support the lives of those he loves, or to supply the needs of his race, any higher than another? Where would even books be without this very labor which you despise — the books which I should have learned at college? Instead of being benefited by the results of labor, I have become part of labor. Why is that lower?"

Robert stared at her.

"I have come to feel all this since I went to work," said Ellen, speaking in a high, rapid voice. "When I went to work, it was, as you thought, for my folks, to help them, for my father was out of work, and there was no other way. But since I have been at work I have realized what work really is. There is a glory over it, as there is over anything which is done faithfully on this earth for good motives, and I have seen the glory, and I am not ashamed of it; and while it was a sacrifice at first, now, while I should like the other better, I do not think it is. I am proud of my work."

The girl spoke with a sort of rapt enthusiasm. The young man stared, bewildered.

Robert caught Ellen's little hands, which hung, tightly clinched, in the folds of her dress, and drew her down to his side again. "See here, dear," he said, "maybe you are right. I never looked at it in this way before, but you do not understand. I love you; I want to marry you. I want to make you my wife, and lift you out of this forever."

Then again Ellen freed herself, and straightened her head and faced him. "There is nothing for me to be lifted out of," said she. "You speak as if I were in a pit. I am on a height."

"My God! child, how many others feel as you, do you think, out of the whole lot?" cried Robert.

"I don't know," replied Ellen, "but it is true. What I feel is true."

Robert caught up her little hand and kissed it. Then he looked at its delicate outlines. "Well, it may be true," he said, "but look at yourself. Can't you see that you are not fashioned for manual labor? Look at this little hand."

"That little hand can do the work," Ellen replied, proudly.

"But, dear," said Robert, "admitting all this, admitting that you are not in a position to be lifted — admitting everything — let us come back to our original starting-point. Dear, I love you, and I want you for my wife. Will you marry me?"

"No, I never can," replied Ellen, with a long, sobbing breath of renunciation.

"Why not? Don't you love me?"

"Yes. I think it must be true that I do. I said I wouldn't; I have tried not to, but I think it must be true that I do."

"Then why not marry me?"

"Because it will be impossible for my father and mother to get along and support Amabel and Aunt Eva without my help," said Ellen, directly.

"But I —" began Robert.

"Do you think I will burden you with the support of a whole family?" said Ellen.

"Ellen, you don't know what I would be willing to do if I could have you," cried the young man, fervently. And he was quite in earnest. At that moment it seemed to him that he could even come and live there in that house, with the hideous lamp, and the crushed-plush furniture, and the eager mother; that he could go without anything and everything to support them if only he could have this girl who was fairly storming his heart.

"I wouldn't be willing to have you," said Ellen, firmly. "As things are now I cannot marry you, Mr. Lloyd. Then, too," she added, "you asked me just now how many people looked at all this labor as I do, and I dare say not very many. I know not many of your kind of people. I know how your uncle looks at it. It would hurt you socially to marry a girl from a shoe-shop. Whether it is just or not, it would hurt you. It cannot be, as matters are now, Mr. Lloyd."

"But you love me?"

Ellen suddenly, as if pushed by some mighty force outside herself, leaned towards him, and he caught her in his arms. He tipped back her face and kissed her, and looked down at her masterfully.

"We will wait a little," he said. "I will never give you up as long as I live if you love me, Ellen."

Chapter XXXIX

When Ellen went out into the sitting room that evening, after Robert Lloyd had taken leave, her father and mother were still there, although the callers had gone. Both of them looked furtively at her as she went through the room to the kitchen to get a lamp, then they looked at each other. Fanny was glowing with half shamefaced triumph; Andrew was pale. Ellen did not reenter the room, but simply paused at the door, before going upstairs, and they had a vision of a face in a tumult of emotions, with eyes and hair illuminated to excess of brilliancy by the lamp which she held.

"Good-night," she called, and her voice did not sound like her own.

"Something has happened," Fanny whispered to Andrew, when Ellen's chamber door had closed.

"Do you suppose she's goin' to?" whispered Andrew, in a sort of breathless fashion. His eyes on his wife's face were sad and wistful.

"Hush! How do I know?" asked Fanny. "I always told you he liked her."

However, Fanny looked disturbed. Presently she went out in the kitchen to mix up some bread, and she wept a little, standing in a corner, with her face hidden in the folds of an old shawl which hung there on a peg. Dictatorial towards circumstances as she was when her beloved daughter came in question, and proud as she was at the prospect of an advantageous marriage for her, she remembered her sister in the asylum, she remembered how Andrew was out of work, and she could not understand how it was to be managed. And all this was aside from the grief which she would have felt in any case at losing Ellen.

As for Andrew, the next morning he put on his best clothes and went by trolley-cars to the next manufacturing town, not a city like Rowe, but a busy little place with two large factories, and tried in vain to get a job there. As he came home on the crowded car, his face was so despairing that the people looked curiously at him. Andrew had always been mild and peaceable, but at that moment anarchistic principles began to ferment in him. When a portly man, swelling ostentatiously with broadcloth and fine linen, wearing a silk hat, and carrying a gold-headed cane like a wand of office, got into the car, Andrew looked at him with a sidelong glance which was almost murderous. The spiritual bomb, which is in all our souls for our fellow-men, began to swell towards explosion. This man was the proprietor of one of the great factories in Leavitt, the town where Andrew had vainly sought a job. He had been in the office when Andrew entered, and the latter had heard his low voice of instruction to the foreman that the man was too old. The manufacturer, who weighed heavily, and described a vast curve of opulence from silk hat to his patent-leathers, sat opposite, his gold-headed cane planted in the aisle, his countenance a blank of complacent power. Andrew felt that he hated him.

The man's face was not intellectual, not as intellectual as Andrew's. He gave the impression of the force of matter oncoming and irresistible, some inertia which had started Heaven knew how. This man had inherited great wealth, as Andrew knew. He had capital with which to begin, and he had strength to roll the accumulating ball. Andrew felt more and more how he hated this man. He had told his foreman that Andrew was too old, and Andrew knew that he was no older, if as old, as the man himself.

"If I had been born under the Czar, and done with it, I should have felt differently," he told himself. "But who is this man? What right has he to say that his fellow-men shall or shall not? Does even his own property give him the right of dictation over others? What is property? Is it anything but a temporary lease while he draws the breath of life? What of it in the tomb, to which he shall surely come? Shall a temporary possession give a man the right to wield eternal power? For the power of giving or withholding the means of life may produce eternal results."

When the man rose and moved down the car, oscillating heavily, steadying himself with his gold-headed cane, and got out in front of a portentous mansion, Andrew would scarcely have recognized the look in his own eyes had he seen himself in a mirror.

"That chap is pretty well fixed," said a man next him, to one on the other side.

"A cool half-million," replied the other.

"More than that," said the first speaker. "His father left him half a million to start with, besides the business, and he's been piling up ever since."

"Do you work there?"

"Did, but I had what was mighty nigh a sunstroke last summer; had to quit. It was damned hot up there under the roof. It's the same old factory his father had."

"Goin' to work again?"

"Next week, if I'm able, but I dun'no' whether I can stay there longer than till spring. It's damned hot up there under the roof."

The man who spoke had a leaden hue of face, something ghastly, as if the deadly heat had begun a work of decomposition. Andrew looked at him, and his hatred against the rich man who had built himself a stately mansion, and kept his fellow-creatures at work for him in an unhealthy factory in tropical heat, and had condemned him for being too old, was redoubled.

"Andrew Brewster, where have you been?" Fanny asked, when he got home.

"I've been to Leavitt," answered Andrew, shortly.

"To see if you could get a job there?"

"Yes."

Fanny did not ask if he had been successful. She sighed, and took another stitch in the wrapper which she was making. That sigh almost drove Andrew mad.

"I don't see what has got you into such a habit of sighing," he said, brutally.

Fanny looked at him with reproachful anger. "Andrew Brewster, you ain't like yourself," said she.

"I can't help it."

"There's no need for you to pitch into me because you can't get work; I ain't to blame. I'm doing all I can. I won't stand it, and you might as well know it first as last."

Fanny glared angrily at her husband, then the tears sprang to her eyes.

Andrew hesitated a moment, then he leaned over her and put his thin cheek against her rough black hair. "The Lord knows I don't mean to be harsh to you, you poor girl," said he, "but I wish I was dead."

Fanny seemed to spring into resistance like a wire. "Then you are a coward, Andrew Brewster," said she, hotly. "Talk about wishin' you was dead. I ain't got time to die. You'd 'nough sight better go out into the yard and split up some of that wood."

"I didn't mean to speak so, Fanny," said Andrew, "but sometimes I get desperate, and I've been thinking of Ellen."

"Don't you suppose I have?" asked Fanny, angrily.

"Well, there's one thing about it; we won't stand in her way," said Andrew.

"No, we won't," replied Fanny. "I'll go out washing first."

"She hasn't said anything?"

"No."

As time went on Ellen still said nothing. She had made a curious compact for a young girl with her lover. She had stipulated that no engagement was to exist, that she should be perfectly free — when she said that she thought of Maud Hemingway, but she said it without a tremor — and if years hence both were free and of the same mind they might talk of it again.

Robert had rebelled strenuously. "You know this will shut me off from seeing much of you," he said. "You know I told you how it will be about my even talking much to you in the factory."

"Yes, I understand that now," replied Ellen, blushing; "and I understand, too, that you cannot come to see me very often under such circumstances without making talk."

"How often?" Robert asked, impetuously.

Ellen hesitated, her lip quivered a little, but her voice was firm. "Not oftener than two or three times a year, I am afraid," said she.

"Great Scott!" cried Robert. Then he caught her in his arms again. "Do you suppose I can stand that?" he whispered. "Ellen, I cannot consent to this!"

"It is the only way," said she. She freed herself from him enough to look into his eyes with a brave, fearless gaze of comradeship, which somehow seemed to make her dearer than anything else.

"But to see you to speak to only two or three times a year!" groaned Robert. "You are cruel, Ellen. You don't know how I love you."

"There isn't any other way," said Ellen. Then she looked up into his face with a brave innocence of confession like a child. "It hurts me, too," said she.

Robert had her in his arms, and was covering her face with kisses. "You darling," he whispered. "It shall not be long. Something will happen. We cannot live so. We will let it go so a little while, but something will turn up. I shall have a more responsible place and a larger salary, then —"

"Do you think I will let you?" asked Ellen, with a great blush.

"I will, whether you will let me or not," cried Robert; and at that moment he felt inclined to marry the entire Brewster family rather than give up this girl.

However, as he went home, walking that he might think the better, he had to confess to himself that the girl was right; that, as matters were, anything definite was out of the question. He had to admit that it might be a matter of years.

Chapter XL

When Ellen had been at work in the factory a year, she was running a machine and working by the piece, and earning on an average eighteen dollars a week. Of course that was an unusual advance for a girl, but Ellen was herself unusual. She came to work in those days with such swiftness and unswerving accuracy that she seemed fairly a part of the great system of labor itself. While she was at her machine, her very individuality seemed lost; she became an integral part of a system.

"She's one of the best hands we ever had," Flynn told Norman Lloyd one day.

"I am glad to hear that," Lloyd responded, smiling with that peculiar smile of his which was like a cold flash of steel.

"Curse him, he thinks no more of anybody in this shop than he does of the machine they work," Flynn thought as he watched the proprietor walking with his stately descent down the stairs. The noon whistle was blowing, and the younger Lloyd went leaping down the stairs and joined his uncle, then the two walked down the street, away from the factory. The factory at that time of year began to present, in spite of its crude architecture, quite a charming appearance, from the luxuriant vines which covered it and were beginning to get autumnal tints of red and russet. All the front of Lloyd's was covered with vines, which had grown with amazing swiftness. Mrs. Lloyd often used to look at them and reflect upon them with complacency.

"I should think it would make it pleasanter for the men to work in the factory, when it looks so pretty and green," she told her husband one of the hottest days of the preceding summer. As she spoke she compressed her lips in a way which was becoming habitual to her. It meant the endurance of a sharp stab of vital pain. There was a terrible pathos in the poor woman's appearance at that time. She still kept about. Her malady did not seem to be on the increase, but it endured. Her form had changed indescribably. She had not lost flesh, but she had a curious, distorted look, and one on seeing her had a bewildered feeling, and looked again to be sure that he had seen aright. Her ghastly pallor she concealed in a manner which she thought distinctly sinful. She painted and powdered. She did not dare purchase openly the concoctions which were used for improving her complexion, but she went to a manicure and invested in a colored salve for her fingernails. This, with rather surprising skill for such a conscience-pricked tyro, she applied to the pale curves of her cheeks and her blue lips. She took more pains than ever before with her dress, and it was all to deceive her husband, that he should not be annoyed. She felt a desperate shame because of her illness; she felt it to be a direct personal injury to this masculine power which had been set over her gentle femininity. It was not so much because she was afraid of losing his affection that she concealed her affliction from him, as because she felt that the affliction itself was somehow an act of disloyalty. Her terrible malady had in a way affected her reasoning powers, so that they had become distorted by a monstrous growth of suffering, like her body. She would not give up going about as usual, and was never absent from church. She drove about with her husband in his smart trap. Twice she had gone with Robert to consult the New York specialist, taking times when Norman was away on business. She still would not consent to an operation, and lately the specialist had been lukewarm in advising it. He had indeed been doubtful from the first.

Mrs. Lloyd treated Robert with a soft affection which was almost like that of a mother. One night, when he returned late from a call on Ellen, she sat up waiting for him. He had not called on Ellen before for several months, and it was nearly midnight when he returned.

"Why, Aunt Lizzie, are you up?" he cried, as he entered the library door and saw his aunt's figure, clad in shining black satin, gleaming with jet, in the depths of an easy chair.

Mrs. Lloyd looked up at him with an expression of patient suffering. "I couldn't go to sleep if I went to bed, Robert," she replied, in a hushed voice. She found it a comfort sometimes to confess her pain to him.

Robert went over to her, and drew her large, crinkled, blond head to his shoulder as if she had been a child.

"Poor thing," he whispered, stroking her face pitifully. "Is it very terrible?" he asked, with his lips close to her ear.

"Terrible," she whispered back. "Oh, Robert, you do not know; pray God you may never know."

"I wish to God I could bear it for you, Aunt Lizzie," Robert said, fervently.

"Oh, hush! If you or Norman had to bear anything like this, I should curse God and die," she answered, and she shut her mouth hard, and her whole face was indicative of a repressed shriek.

"Aunt Lizzie, don't you think you ought to go to New York, that you ought —" Robert began, but she stopped him with an almost fierce peremptoriness. "Robert Lloyd, I have trusted you," she said. "For God's sake, don't forsake me. Don't say a word to me about that; when I can I will. It means my death, anyhow. Dr. Evarts thought so; you can't deny it."

"I think he thought there was a chance, Aunt Lizzie," Robert returned, but he said it faintly.

"You can't cheat me," replied Mrs. Lloyd. "I know." She had a lapse from pain, and her features began to assume their natural expression. She looked at him almost smiling, and as if she turned her back upon her own misery. "Where have you been, Robert?" she asked.

Robert colored a little, but he answered directly enough. "I have been to make a call on Miss Brewster," he said.

"You don't go there very often," said Mrs. Lloyd.

"No, not very often."

"She's a beautiful girl, as beautiful a girl as I ever laid eyes on, if she does work in the shop," said Mrs. Lloyd, "and she's a good girl, too; I know she is. She was the sweetest little thing when she was a child, and she ain't altered a mite!" Then Mrs. Lloyd looked with a sort of wistful curiosity at Robert.

"I think it is all true, what you say, Aunt Lizzie," replied Robert.

Mrs. Lloyd continued to look at him with that wistful scrutiny.

"Robert," she began, then she hesitated.

"What, Aunt Lizzie?"

"If — ever you wanted to marry that girl, I don't see any reason why you shouldn't, for my part."

Robert pulled a chair close to his aunt, and sat down beside her, still holding her hand.

"I've a good mind to tell you the whole story, Aunt Lizzie," he said.

"I wish you would, Robert. You know I think as much of you as if you were my own son, and I won't tell anybody, not even your uncle, if you don't want me to."

"Well, then, it is all in a nutshell," said Robert. "I like her, you know, and I think I have ever since I saw her in her little white gown at the high-school exhibition."

"Wasn't she sweet?" said his aunt.

"And she likes me, too, I think."

"Of course she does."

"But you know what my salary is, and her whole family is in a measure dependent upon her."

"Hasn't her father got work?"

"No."

"I'll speak to Norman," cried Mrs. Lloyd, quickly. "I know he would do it for me."

"But even then, Aunt Lizzie, there is the aunt in the asylum, and the child, and —"

"Your uncle will pay you more."

"It isn't altogether that; in fact, it isn't that at all which is at the bottom of the difficulty. The difficulty is with Ellen herself. She will never consent to my marrying her, and having to support her family, while matters are as now. You don't know how proud she is, Aunt Lizzie."

"She is a splendid girl."

"As far as I am concerned I would marry the whole lot on a little more than I have now, but she would not let me do it. There's nothing to do but to wait."

"Perhaps the aunt will get well and her husband will come back; and I will see, anyway, if Norman won't give her father work," said Mrs. Lloyd.

"I think you had better not, Aunt Lizzie."

"Why not, Robert?"

"There are reasons why I think you had better not." Robert would not tell her that Ellen had begged him not to use any influence of his to get her father work.

"After the way father has been turned off, I can't stand it," she had said, with a sort of angry dignity which was unusual to her. In fact, her father himself had begged her not to make use of Robert in any way for his own advancement.

"If they don't want me for my work, I don't want to crawl in because the nephew of the boss likes my daughter," he had said. This speech was fairly rough for him, but Ellen had understood.

"I know what you mean, father," she said.

"I'd rather work in the road," said Andrew. That autumn he was getting jobs of clearing up yards of fallen leaves, and gathering feed-corn and pumpkins, and earning a pittance. Fanny continued to work on her wrappers. "It's a mercy wrappers don't go out of fashion," she often said.

"I suppose things that folks can get for nothing ain't so apt to go out of fashion," Andrew retorted, bitterly. He hated the wrappers with a deadly hatred. He hated the sight of the limp row of them on his bedroom wall. Nobody knew how the family pinched and screwed in those days.

They were using the small fund which they secured from the house mortgage, Ellen's earnings, and Fanny's and Andrew's, and every cent had to be counted, but there was something splendid in their loyalty to poor Eva in the asylum. The thought of deserting her in her extremity never occurred to them.

Mrs. Lloyd spoke of her that night, when she and Robert were talking together in the library.

"They are good folks, to keep on doing for that poor woman in the asylum," she said.

"They would never desert a dog that belonged to them," Robert answered, fervently. "I tell you that trait is worth a good many others, Aunt Lizzie."

"I guess it is," said his aunt. Then another paroxysm of pain seized her. She looked at Robert with a convulsed, speechless face. He held her hands more tightly, his own face contracting in sympathy, and watched his aunt with a sort of angry helplessness. But he felt as if he wanted to fight something for the sake of this poor, oppressed, innocent creature; indeed, he felt fairly blasphemous. But this time the pain passed quickly, and Mrs. Lloyd looked at her nephew with an expression of relief and gentleness which was almost angelic. When the pain was over she thought again of the Brewsters, and how they would not have forsaken her in her misery, had she belonged to them, anymore than they had forsaken the insane aunt.

"They are good folks," said she, "and that is the main thing. That is the main thing to consider when you are marrying into a family, Robert. It is more than riches and position. The power they've got of loving and standing by each other is worth more than anything else."

"You are right, Aunt Lizzie, I guess there's no doubt of that," said Robert.

"And that girl's beautiful," said Mrs. Lloyd. She gazed at the young man with a delicate understanding and sympathy which was almost beyond that of a sweetheart. Robert felt as if a soft hand of tenderness and blessing were laid on his inmost heart. He looked at her like a grateful child.

"There isn't anybody like her, is there, Aunt Lizzie?" he asked.

"No, I don't think there is, dear boy," said Mrs. Lloyd. "I do think she is the sweetest little thing I ever saw in my life."

Robert brought his aunt's hand to his lips and kissed it. It seemed to him for a minute as if the love and sympathy of this martyr were almost more precious than the love of Ellen herself.

He realized when he was in his own room, and the house was quiet, how much he loved his aunt, and how hard her pain and probably inevitable doom were for him to bear. Then something came to him which he had never felt before — a great, burning anxiety and tenderness and terror over Ellen, because she was of the weaker half of creation, which is born to the larger share of pain in the world. He felt that he would almost have given her up, yielded up forever all his delight in her, to spare her; for the pain of knighthood, which is in every true lover, awoke in his heart.

Chapter XLI

Nahum Beals was a laster in Lloyd's. Late in the autumn, when Ellen had been in the factory a little over a year, there began to be a subtle condition of discontent and insubordination. Men gathered in muttering groups, of which Nahum Beals seemed always to be the nucleus. His high, rampant voice, restrained by no fear of consequences, always served as the keynote to the chorus of rebellion. Ellen paid little attention to it. She was earning good wages, and personally she had nothing of which to complain. She had come to regard Beals as something of a chronic fanatic, but as she knew that the lasters were fairly paid, she had not supposed it meant anything. However, one night, going home from the factory, her eyes were opened. Abby and Maria Atkins and Mamie Brady were with her, and shortly after they had left the shop Abby stopped Granville Joy, Frank Dixon, and Willy Jones, who with another young man were swinging past without noticing the girls, strange to say. Abby caught Joy by the arm.

"Hold on a minute, Granville Joy," said she. "I want to know what's up with the lasters."

Granville laughed, with an uneasy, sidelong, deprecating glance at Ellen. "Oh, nothing much," said he.

Willy Jones stood still, coloring, gazing at Abby with a half-terrified expression. Dixon walked on, and the other young man, Amos Lee, who was dark and slight and sinewy, stared from one to the other with quick flashes of black eyes. He looked almost as if he had gypsy blood in him, and he came of a family which was further on the outskirts of society than the Louds had been.

When Granville replied "nothing much" to Abby's question, Amos Lee frowned with a swift contraction of dissent, but did not speak until Abby had retorted. "You needn't talk that way to me, Granville Joy," said she. "You can't cheat me. I know something's up."

"It ain't nothin', Abby," said Granville, but it was quite evident that he was lying.

Then Lee spoke up, in a sudden fury of enthusiasm. "There is somethin' up," said he, "and I don't care if you do know it. There's —" he stopped as Granville clutched his arm violently and whispered something.

"Well, maybe you're right," said Lee to Joy. "Look here," he continued to Abby, "you and Ellen come along here a little ways, and I'll tell you."

After Maria and Mamie had passed on, Joy and Jones and Lee, standing close to the two girls, began to talk, Lee leading.

"Well, look here," he said, in a hushed voice. "We've found out — no matter how, but we've found out — that the boss is goin' to dock the lasters' pay."

"How much?" asked Abby.

"Fifteen percent."

"Good Lord!" said Abby.

"We ain't going to stand it," said Lee.

"I don't see how we can stand it," said Willy Jones, with a slightly interrogative tone directed towards Abby. Granville looked at Ellen.

"Are you sure?" she asked.

"Perfectly sure," replied Granville. "What do you think about it, Ellen?"

"What are you going to do?" asked Ellen, thoughtfully.

"Strike for fifteen percent more before he has a chance to dock us," cried Lee, with a hushed vehemence, looking about warily to make sure that no one overheard.

"The worst of it is, I know it all comes from Nahum Beals, and he's half cracked," said Abby, bluntly.

"He's got the right of it, anyhow," said Lee.

The two girls walked on, while the men lingered behind to talk.

"Do you suppose it is true, Abby?" asked Ellen.

"I don't know. I should, if it wasn't for that Lee fellow. I can't bear him. And that Nahum Beals, I believe he's half mad."

"I feel the same way about him," said Ellen; "but think what it would mean, fifteen percent less on their wages."

"It doesn't mean so much for those young fellows, except Willy Jones; he's got enough on his shoulders."

"No, but ever so many of the lasters have large families."

"I hope they don't drag Willy Jones into it," said Abby. She looked back as she spoke. Willy, in the little knot of men, was looking after her, and their eyes met. Abby colored.

"It's a shame to dock his wages," she said.

"Whose — Willy Jones's?"

"Yes. I hope he won't get into any trouble. I can't bear that Lee."

"Still, to dock their wages fifteen percent," said Ellen, thoughtfully. "What right has Mr. Lloyd?"

"I suppose he'd say he has the right because he has the capital."

"I don't see why that gives him the right."

"You'd better go and talk to him," said Abby. "As for me, I made up my mind when I went to work in the shop that I'd got to be a bond-slave, all but my soul. That can kick free, thank the Lord."

"I didn't make up my mind to it," said Ellen. "I am not going to be a slave in any way, and I am not going to approve of others being slaves."

"You think they ought to strike?"

"Yes, if it is true that Mr. Lloyd is going to dock their wages, but I don't feel sure that it is true. Mr. Beals is a queer man. Sometimes I have thought he was dangerous."

Chapter XLII

*T*uesday evening was one of those marvelously clear atmospheres of autumn which seem to be clearer from the contrast to the mists of the recent summer. The stars swarmed out in unnumbered hosts.

"Seems to me I never saw so many stars," one would say to another. The air had the sharp cleave of the frost in it. Everything was glittering with a white rime — the house roofs, and the levels of fields on the outskirts of the little city.

Ellen had an errand down-town that evening, and she wrapped herself up warmly, putting on a fur collar which she had not worn since the winter before. She felt strangely nervous and disturbed as she set out.

"Don't you want your father to go with you?" asked Fanny, for in some occult fashion the girl's perturbation seemed to be communicated to her. She followed her to the door.

"Seems kind of lonesome for you to go alone," she said, anxiously.

"As if I minded! Why, it is as bright as day with the electric-lights, and there are houses almost all the way," laughed Ellen.

"Your father could go with you, or he could go for you."

"No, he couldn't go for me. I want to get one of the new catalogues at the library and pick out a book, and there is no sense in dragging father out. He has a cold, too. Why, there is nothing in the world to be afraid of, mother."

"Well, don't be any longer than you can help," said Fanny.

Ellen, as she passed her grandmother's house, saw a curtain drawn with a quick motion. That happened nearly every time she passed. She knew that the old woman was always on the lookout for her, and always bent on concealing it. Mrs. Zelotes never went into her son's house, and never spoke to Ellen in those days. She had aged rapidly during the past year, and even her erect carriage had failed her. She stooped rigidly when she walked. She was fairly racked with love and hatred of Ellen. She adored her, she could have kissed the ground she walked on, and yet she was so full of wrath against her for thwarting her hopes for her own advancement that she was conscious of cruel impulses in her direction.

Ellen walked along rapidly under the vast canopy of stars, about which she presently began to have a singular impression. She felt as if they were being augmented, swelled as if by constantly oncoming legions of light from the space beyond space, and as if her little space of individuality, her tiny foothold of creation, was being constantly narrowed by them.

"I never saw so many stars," she said to herself. She looked with wonder at the Milky Way, which was like a zone of diamond dust. Suddenly a mighty conviction of God, which was like the blazing forth of a new star, was in her soul. Ellen was not in a sense religious, and had never united with the Congregational Church, which she had always attended with her parents; she had never been responsive to efforts made towards her so-called conversion, but all at once, under the stars that night, she told herself with an absolute certainty of the truth of it. "There is something beyond everything, beyond the stars, and beyond all poor men, and beyond me, which is enough for all needs. We shall have our portion in the end."

She had been feeling discouraged lately, although she would not own it even to herself. She saw Robert but seldom, and her aunt was no better. She often wondered if there could be anything before her but that one track of drudgery for daily bread upon which she had set out. She wondered if she ought not to say positively to Robert that there must be no thought of anything between them in the future. She wondered if she were not wronging him. Once or twice she had seen him riding with Miss Hemingway, and thought that, after all, that was a girl better suited to him, and perhaps if he had no hope whatever of her he might turn to the other to his own advantage. But tonight, with the clear stimulus of the frost in her lungs, and her eyes and soul dazzled with the multiplicity of stars, she began to have a great impetus of courage, like a soldier on the morning of battle. She felt as if she could fight for her joy and the joy of others, and victory would in the end be certain; that the chances of victory ran to infinity, and could not be measured.

However, all the while, in spite of her stimulation of spirits, there was that vague sense of excitement, as over some impending crisis. That she could not throw off. Suddenly she found herself searching the road ahead of her, and often turning at the fancied sound of a footstep. She began to wish that her father had come with her; then she told herself how foolish she was, for he had a cold, and this keen air would have been sure to give him more. The electric-car passed her, and she had a grateful sense of companionship. She looked after its diminishing light in the distance, and almost wished that she had stopped it, but car-fares had to be counted carefully.

She began to dread unspeakably passing the factories. She told herself that there was no sense in it, that it was not late, that the electric-light made it like high noon, that there was a watchman in each building, that there was nothing whatever to fear; but it was in vain. It was only by a great effort of her will that she did not turn and go back home when she reached Lloyd's.

Lloyd's came first; then, a few rods farther, on the other side of the street, McGuire's, and then Briggs's.

Ellen had a library book under her arm, and she clutched her dress-skirt firmly. A terror as to the supernatural was stealing over her. She felt as she had when waking in the night from some dreadful dream, though all the time she was dinning in her ears how foolish she was. She saw the lantern of the night-watchman in Lloyd's moving down a stair which crossed a window.

She came opposite Lloyd's, and, just as she did so, saw a dark figure descending the right-hand flight of stairs from the entrance platform. She thought, from something in the carriage, that it was Mr. Lloyd, and hung back a little, reflecting that she would keep behind him all the way to town.

The man reached the ground at the foot of the stairs, then there was a flash of fire from the shadow underneath, and a shot rang out. Ellen did what she could never have counted upon herself for doing. She ran straight towards the man, who had fallen prostrate like a log, and was down on the ground beside him, with his head on her lap, shouting for the night-watchman, whose name was McLaughlin.

"McLaughlin!" she shouted. But there was no need of it, for he had heard the shot. The cry had not left Ellen's lips before she was surrounded by men, one of whom was Granville Joy, one was Dixon, and one was John Sargent.

Joy and Sargent had met down-town, and were walking home together, when the shot rang out, and they had rushed forward. Then there was McLaughlin, the watchman of Lloyd's, and the two watchmen from Briggs's and McGuire's came pelting down their stairs, swinging their lanterns.

They all stood around the wounded man and Ellen, and stared for a second. They were half stupefied.

"My God! this is a bad job," said Dixon.

"Go for a doctor," cried Ellen, hoarsely.

"We're a pack of fools," ejaculated Sargent, suddenly. Then he gave Granville Joy a push on the back. "Run for your life for the first doctor," he cried, and was down on his knees beside the wounded man. Lloyd seemed to be quite insensible. There was a dark spot which was constantly widening in a hideous circle of death on his shirt-front when Sargent opened his coat and vest tenderly.

"Is he —" whispered Ellen. She held one of Lloyd's hands in a firm clutch as if she would in such wise hold him to life.

"No, not yet," whispered Sargent. Dixon knelt down on the other side, and took Lloyd's other hand and felt his pulse. McLaughlin was rushing aimlessly up and down, talking as he went.

"I never heard a thing till that shot came," he kept repeating. "He'd jest been in to get his pocketbook he'd left in the office. I never heard a thing till I heard that shot."

Sargent was opening Lloyd's shirt. "McLaughlin, for God's sake stop talking and run for another doctor, in case Joy does not get one at once," he cried; "then go to his house, and tell young Lloyd, but don't say anything to his wife."

"Poor Mrs. Lloyd," whispered Ellen.

The sick man sighed audibly. It seemed as if he had heard. The other watchmen stood looking on helplessly.

"Why in thunder don't you two scatter, and see if you can't catch him," cried Dixon to them. "He can't be far off."

But the words had no sooner left his mouth than up came a great Swede who was one of the workmen in Lloyd's, and he had Nahum Beals in a grasp as imperturbable as fate. The assassin, even with the strength of his fury of fanaticism, was as a reed in the grasp of this Northern giant. The Swede held him easily, walking him before him in a forced march. He had a hand of Nahum's in each of his, and he compelled Nahum's right hand to retain the hold of the discharged pistol. There was something terrible about the Swede as he drew near, a captor as unyielding and pitiless as justice itself. He was even smiling with a smile which showed his gums from ear to ear, but there was no joy in his smile, and no triumph. His blue eyes surveyed them all with the placid content of achievement.

"I have him," he said. "I heard him shoot, and I heard him run, and I stood still until he ran into my arms. I have him."

Nahum, in the grasp of this fate, was quivering from head to foot, but not from fear.

"Is he dead?" he shouted, eagerly.

"Hush up, you murderer," cried Dixon. "We didn't want any such work as this, damn you. Keep fast hold of him, Olfsen."

"I will keep him fast," replied the Swede, smiling.

Then there was a swift clatter of wheels, and two doctors drove up, and men came running. The space in front of Lloyd's was black with men. Robert Lloyd was among them. Granville Joy had met him on the street.

"You'd better go down to the factory, quick," he had said, hoarsely. "There's trouble there; your uncle —"

Robert pushed through the crowd, which made way respectfully for him. He knelt down beside the wounded man. "Is he —" he whispered to Sargent.

"Not yet," whispered Sargent, "but I'm afraid it's pretty bad."

"You here?" Robert said to Ellen.

"Yes," she answered, "I was passing when I heard the shot."

"See here," said Robert, "I don't know but I am asking a good deal, but will you get into Dr. James's buggy, and let his man drive you to my aunt's, and you break it to her? She likes you. I must stay with him. I don't want her to know it first when he is brought home."

"Yes, that will be the best way," said the other physician, who was the one regularly employed by the Lloyds. "Someone must tell her first, and if she knows this young lady —"

"I will go," said Ellen.

Dr. Story whispered something to Ellen as she was getting into the buggy. Then Dr. James's man drove her away down the street.

There was a little black mare harnessed to the buggy, and she went with nervous leaps of speed. When Ellen reached the Lloyd house she saw that it was blazing with light. Norman Lloyd was fond of brilliant light, and would have every room in his house illuminated from garret to cellar.

As Ellen went up the stone steps she saw a woman's figure in the room at the right, which moved to an attitude of attention when she rang the bell.

Before Ellen could inquire for Mrs. Lloyd of the maid who answered her ring there was a shrill cry from the room on the right.

"Who is it? Who is it?" demanded the voice.

Then, before Ellen could speak, Mrs. Lloyd came running out.

"What is it?" she said. "Tell me quick. I know something has happened. Tell me quick. You came in Dr. James's buggy, and the man was driving fast. Tell me."

"Oh, Mrs. Lloyd," said Ellen. Then she could say no more, but the other woman knew.

"Is he dead?" she asked, hoarsely.

"Oh, no, no, not dead."

"Hurt?"

Ellen nodded, trembling.

"How?"

"He was shot."

"Who shot him?"

"One of the workmen. They have him. Carl Olfsen found him."

"One of the workmen, when he has always been so good!"

Suddenly Mrs. Lloyd seemed to gather herself together into the strength of action.

"Are they bringing him home?" she asked Ellen, in a sharp, decisive voice.

"I think they must be by this time."

"Then I've got to get ready for him. Come, quick."

There was by that time a man and two women servants standing near them, aghast. Mrs. Lloyd turned to the man.

"Go down to the drug-store and get some brandy, there isn't any in the house," said she; "then come back as quick as you can. Maggie, you see that there is plenty of hot water. Martha, you and Ellen come upstairs with me, quick."

Ellen followed Mrs. Lloyd and the maid upstairs, and, before she knew what she was doing, was assisting to put the room in perfect readiness for the wounded man. The maid was weeping all the time she worked, although she had never liked Mr. Lloyd. There was something about her mistress which was fairly abnormal. She kept looking at her. This gentle, soft-natured woman had risen above her own pain and grief to a sublime strength of misery.

"Get the camphor, quick, Martha," she said to the maid, who flew out, with the tears streaming. Ellen stood on one side of the bed, and Mrs. Lloyd on the other. Mrs. Lloyd had stripped off the blankets, and was pinning the sheet tightly over the mattress. She seemed to know instinctively what to do.

"I wish you would bring that basin over here, and put it on the stand," said Mrs. Lloyd. "Martha, you fetch more towels, and, Maggie, you run up garret and bring down some of those old sheets from the trunk under the window, quick."

This maid, who was as large and as ample as her mistress, fled out of the room with heavy, noiseless pads of flat feet.

All the time Mrs. Lloyd worked she was evidently listening. She paid no attention to Ellen except to direct her. All at once she gave a great leap and stood still.

"They're coming," said she, though Ellen had heard nothing. Ellen went close to her, and took her two fat, cold hands. She could say nothing. Then she heard the roll of carriage-wheels in the street below.

Mrs. Lloyd pulled her hands away from Ellen's and went to the head of the stairs.

"Bring him right up here," she ordered, in a loud voice.

Ellen stood back, and the struggling procession with the prostrate man in the midst labored up the broad stairs.

"Bring him in here," said Mrs. Lloyd, "and lay him on the bed."

When Lloyd was stretched on the bed, the crowd drew back a little, and she bent over him.

Then she turned with a sort of fierceness to the doctors.

"Why don't you do something?" she demanded. She raised a hand with a repellant gesture towards the other men.

"You had better go now," said she. "I thank you very much. If there is anything you can do, I will let you know."

When Mrs. Lloyd was left with the two doctors and a young assistant, Robert, and Ellen, she said, cutting her words short as if she released every one from a mental grip:

"I have got everything ready. Shall I go out now?"

"I think you had better, Mrs. Lloyd," said the family physician, pityingly. He went close to Ellen.

"Can't you stay with her a little while?" he whispered.

Ellen nodded.

Then the physician spoke quite loudly and cheerfully to Mrs. Lloyd.

"We are going to probe for the ball," he said. "We must all hope for the best, Mrs. Lloyd."

Mrs. Lloyd made no reply. She bent again over her husband with a rigid face, and kissed him on his white lips, then she went out, with Ellen following.

Norman Lloyd lived only two hours after he was shot. The efforts to remove the ball had to be abandoned. He was conscious only a few minutes. He suddenly began to look about him with comprehension.

"Robert," he said, in a faraway voice.

Robert stooped closely over his uncle. The dying man looked up at him with an expression which he had never worn in life.

"That man was insane," whispered he, faintly. Then he added, "Look out for her, if she has to go through the operation. Take care of her. Make it as easy for her as you can."

"Then you know, Uncle Norman," gasped Robert.

"All the time, but it — pleased her to think I — did not. Don't let her know I knew. Take care —"

Then Norman Lloyd relapsed into unconsciousness, and the whole room and the whole house became clamorous with his stertorous breathing. Mrs. Lloyd and Ellen came and stood in the doorway. The doctor whispered to them. Then the breathing ceased, although at first it was inconceivable that the silence did not continue to ring with it, and Mrs. Lloyd came into the room.

Chapter XLIII

*W*hen Mrs. Lloyd entered the room, the attention of everyone was taken from the dead man on the bed and concentrated upon the woman. Dr. Story, a nervous, intense, elderly man with a settled frown of perplexity over keen eyes, which he had gotten from a struggle of forty years with unanswerable problems of life and death, stepped towards her hastily. Robert pressed close to her side. Ellen came behind her, holding in a curious, instinctive fashion to a fold of the older woman's gown, as if she had been a mother holding back a child from a sudden topple to its hurt. Everybody expected her to make some heart-breaking manifestation. She did nothing. At that moment the sublime unselfishness of the woman, which was her one strength of character, seemed actually to spread itself, as with wings, before them all. She moved steadily, close to her husband on the bed. She gazed at that profile of rigid calmness and enforced peace, which, although the head lay low, seemed to have an effect of upward motion, as if it were cleaving the mystery of space. Mrs. Lloyd laid her hand upon her husband's forehead; she felt a slight incredulousness of death, because it was still warm. She took his hands, drew them softly together, and folded them upon his breast. Then she turned and faced them all with an angelic expression.

"He did not realize it to suffer much?" she said.

"No, Mrs. Lloyd," replied Dr. Story, quickly. "No, I assure you that he suffered very little."

"He seemed very happy when he died, Aunt Lizzie," said Robert, huskily.

Mrs. Lloyd looked away from them all around the room. It was a magnificent apartment. Norman Lloyd had had an artistic taste as well as wealth. The furnishings had always been rather beyond Mrs. Lloyd's appreciation, but she admired them kindly. She took in every detail; the foam of rich curtains at the great windows, the cut-glass and silver on the dressing-table, the pale softness of a polar-bear skin beside the bed, the lifelike insistence of the costly pictures on the walls.

"He's gone where it is a great deal more beautiful," she said to them, like a child. "He's gone where there's better treasures than these which he had here."

They all looked at her in amazement. It actually seemed as if, for the moment, the woman's sole grief was over the loss to her husband of those things which he had on earth — the treasures of his mortal state.

Robert took hold of his aunt's arm and led her, quite unresisting, from the room, and as she went she felt for Ellen's hand. "It is time she was home," she said to Robert. "Her folks will be worried about her. She's been a real comfort to me."

It was the first time that Ellen had ever seen death, that she had ever seen the living confronted with it. She felt as if a wave were breaking over her own head as she clung fast to Mrs. Lloyd's hand.

"Shan't I stay?" she whispered, pitifully, to her. "If I can send word to my mother —"

"No, you dear child," replied Mrs. Lloyd, "you've done enough, and you will have to be up early in the morning." Then she checked herself. "I forgot," said she to Robert; "the factory will be closed till after the funeral, won't it?"

"Of course it will, Aunt Lizzie."

"And the workmen will be paid just the same, of course," said Mrs. Lloyd. "Now, can't you take her home, Robert?"

"Oh, don't mind about me," cried Ellen.

"You can have a horse put into the buggy," said Mrs. Lloyd.

"Oh, you mustn't leave her now," Ellen whispered to Robert. "Let somebody else take me — Dr. James —"

"I would rather you took her," said Mrs. Lloyd. "And you needn't worry about his leaving me, dear child; the doctor will stay until he comes back."

As Robert was finally going out his aunt caught his arm and looked at him with a radiant expression. "He will never know about *me* now," said she, "and it won't be long before I — Oh, I feel as if I had gotten rid of my own death."

She was filled with inexpressible thankfulness that she had herself to bear what she had dreaded for her husband. "Only think how hard it would have been for Norman," she said to Cynthia, the next day.

Cynthia looked at her wonderingly. She could have understood this feeling over a dearly beloved child. "You are a good woman, Lizzie," she said, in a tone of pitiful respect.

"Not half as good a woman as he was a man," returned Mrs. Lloyd, jealously. "Norman wasn't a professor, I know, but he was a believer. You don't think it is necessary to be a professor in order to be saved, do you, Cynthia?"

"I certainly do not," Cynthia replied. "I wish you would go and lie down, Lizzie."

"Oh, I can't. I wouldn't let anybody do these things but me, for the whole world." Mrs. Lloyd was arranging flowers, tuberoses and white carnations, in vases, and the whole house was scented with them. She looked ghastly, yet still unconquerably happy. She had now no reason to conceal the ravages of disease, and her color was something frightful. Still, she did not suffer as much, for her mind had overborne her body to such an extent that she had the mastery for the time, to a certain extent, of those excruciating stabs of pain. People looked at her incredulously. They could not believe that she felt as she talked, that she was as happy and resigned as she looked, but it was all true. It was either an abnormal state into which her husband's death had thrown her, or one too normal to be credited. She looked at it all with a supreme childishness and simplicity. She simply believed that her husband was in heaven, where she should join him; that he was beyond all suffering which might have come to him through her, and all that troubled her was the one consideration of his having been forced to leave his treasures of earth. She looked at various things which had been prized by the dead man, and found her chief comfort in saying to the minister or Cynthia or Robert that Norman had loved these, but he would have that which was infinitely more precious. She even gazed out of the window, that Tuesday night, and saw her nephew driving away with Ellen, and reflected, with pain, that her husband had been fond and proud of that bay. She was a little at a loss to conceive what could make up to her husband for that in another world, but she succeeded, and evolved from her own loving fancy, and her recollection of the Old Testament, a conception of some wonderful creature, shod with thunder and maned with a whirlwind. Her disease, and a drug she had been taking of late, stimulated her imagination to results of grotesque pathos, but she was comforted.

That night when they were alone, Robert turned to the girl at his side with a sudden motion. It was no time for love-making, for that was in the mind of neither of them, but the bereavement of this other woman, and the tragedy of her state, filled him with a sort of protective pain towards the girl who might some time have to suffer through him the same loss.

"Are you all tired out, dear?" he said, and passed his free arm around her waist.

"No," replied Ellen. Then, since she was only a girl, and overwrought, having been through a severe strain, she broke down, and began to cry.

Robert drew her closer, and she hid her face on his shoulder. "Poor little girl, it has been very hard for you," he whispered.

"Oh, don't think of me," sobbed Ellen. "But I can't bear it, the way she acts and looks. It is sadder than grief."

"She is not going to live long herself, dear," said Robert, in a stifled voice.

"And he — did not know?"

"Hush! yes; but you must never tell anyone. She tried to keep it from him. That is her comfort."

"Oh," said Ellen. She looked up at the white face of the young man bending over her, and suddenly the realization of a love that was mightier than all the creatures who came of it and all who followed it was over her.

Chapter XLIV

*W*hen Ellen did not return, there was some alarm in the Brewster household. Mrs. Zelotes came over, finally, in a quiver of anxiety.

"Maybe I had better start out and see if I can find her," said Andrew.

"I think you had better," returned his mother. "She went before eight o'clock, and it's most midnight, and I've set at my window watchin' ever since. I don't see what you've been thinkin' about, waitin' all this time. I guess if I was a man I shouldn't have waited."

"I think she may have gone in to see Abby Atkins — it's on the way — and not realized how late it was," said Fanny, obstinately, but with a very white face. She drew her thread through with a jerk. It knotted, and she broke it off viciously.

"Fiddlesticks!" said her mother-in-law.

"There's no use imaginin' things," said Fanny, angrily; "but I think myself you'd better go now, Andrew, and see if you can see anything of her."

"I'm goin' with him," announced Mrs. Zelotes.

"Now, mother, you'd better stay where you be," said Andrew, putting on his hat. Then the door flew open, and Amos Lee, who had seen the light in the windows, and was burning to impart the news of the tragedy, rushed in.

"Heard what's happened?" he cried out.

They all thought of Ellen. "What?" demanded Andrew, in a terrible voice. Fanny dropped her work and stared at him, with her chin falling as if she were dying. Mrs. Zelotes made a queer gurgling noise in her throat. Lee stared at them a second, bewildered by the effect of his own words, although they had for him such a tragic import. Andrew caught hold of him in a grasp like the clamp of a machine. "What?" he demanded again.

"The boss has been shot," cried Lee, getting his breath.

Andrew dropped his arm, and they all stared at him. Lee went on fluently, as if he were a fakir at a fair.

"Nahum Beals did it. The boss went back to the office to get his pocketbook; McLaughlin saw him; then he went down the stairs; Nahum, he — he fired; he had been hidin' underneath the stairs. Carl Olfsen caught him, and he's in jail. Your daughter she was there when the shot came, and run up and held his head. The young boss he sent her in Dr. James's buggy to Mrs. Lloyd to break the news. She ain't got home?"

"No," gasped Andrew.

"The boss has been shot; he's dead by this time," repeated Lee. "Beals did it; they've got him." There was the most singular evenness and impartiality in his tone, although he was evidently strained to a high pitch of excitement. It was impossible to tell whether he exulted in or was aghast at the tragedy.

"Oh, that poor woman!" cried Fanny.

"I'd like to know what they'll do next," cried Mrs. Zelotes. "I should call it pretty work."

"Nahum Beals has acted to me as if he was half crazy for some time," said Fanny.

"No doubt about it," said Lee; "but I shouldn't wonder if he had to swing."

"It's dreadful," said Fanny. "I wonder when she's comin' home."

"Seems as if they might have got somebody besides that girl to have gone there," said Mrs. Zelotes.

"She happened to be right on the spot," said Lee, importantly.

Andrew seemed speechless; he leaned against the mantel-shelf, gazing from one to the other, breathing hard. He had had bitter feelings against the murdered man, and a curious sense of guilt was over him. He felt almost as if he were the murderer.

"Andrew, I dun'no' but you'd better go up there and see if she's comin' home," said Fanny; and he answered heavily that maybe he had better, when they heard wheels, which stopped before the house.

"They're bringin' her home," said Lee.

Andrew ran and threw open the front door. He had a glimpse of Robert's pale face, nodding to him from the buggy as he drove away, and Ellen came hastening up the walk.

"Well, Ellen, this is pretty dreadful news," said her father, tremulously. "So you have heard?"

"Amos Lee has just come in. It's a terrible thing, Ellen."

"Yes, it's terrible," returned Ellen, in a quick, strained voice. She entered the sitting room, and when she met her mother's anxious, tender eyes, she stood back against the wall, with her hands to her face, sobbing. Fanny ran to her, but her grandmother was quicker. She had her arms around the girl before the mother had a chance.

"If they couldn't get somebody besides you," she said, in a voice of intensest love and anger, "I should call it pretty work. Now you go straight to bed, Ellen Brewster, and I'm goin' to make a bowl of sage tea, and bring it up, and see if it won't quiet your nerves. I call it pretty work."

"Yes, you'd better go to bed, Ellen," said Andrew, gulping as if he were swallowing a sob.

Mrs. Zelotes fairly forced Ellen towards the door, Fanny following.

"Don't talk and wake Amabel," whispered Ellen, forcing back her sobs.

"Was he dead when you got there, Ellen?" called out Lee.

Mrs. Zelotes turned back and looked at him. "It's after midnight, and time for you to be goin' home," she said. Then the three disappeared. Lee grinned sheepishly at Andrew.

"Your mother is a stepper of an old woman," said he.

"It's awful news," said Andrew, soberly. "Whatever anybody may have felt, nobody expected —"

"Of course they didn't," retorted Lee, quickly. "Nahum went a step too far." He started for the door as he spoke.

"Well, he was crazy, without any doubt!" said Andrew.

"He'll have to swing for it all the same," said Lee, going out.

"It don't seem right, if he wasn't himself when he did it."

"Lord, we're all crazy when it comes to things like that," returned Lee. Before closing the door he flashed his black eyes and white teeth at Andrew, who felt repelled.

He sat down beside the table and leaned his head upon it. To his fancy all creation seemed to circle about that one dead man. Mr. Lloyd had been for years the arbiter of his destiny, almost of his life. Andrew had regarded him with almost feudal loyalty and admiration, and lately with bitter revolt and hatred, and now he was dead. He felt no sorrow, but rather a terrible remorse because he felt no sorrow. All the bitter thoughts which he had ever had against Lloyd seemed to marshal themselves before him like an accusing legion of ghosts. And with it all there was a sense of desolation, as if some force which had been necessary to his full living had gone out of creation.

"It's over thirty years since I went to work under him," Andrew thought, and he gave a dry sob. At that moment a wonderful pity and sorrow for the dead man seemed to spring up in his soul like a light. He felt as if he loved him.

*N*orman Lloyd's funeral was held in the First Baptist Church of Rowe. It was crowded. Mr. Lloyd had been the most prominent manufacturer and the wealthiest man in the city. His employés filled up a great space in the body of the church.

Andrew went with his mother and wife. They arrived quite early. When Andrew saw the employés of Lloyd's marching in, he drew a great sigh. He looked at the solemn black thing raised on trestles before the pulpit with an emotion which he could not himself understand. "That man ain't treated me well enough for me to care anything about him," he kept urging upon himself. "He never paid anymore attention to me than a gravel-stone under his feet; there ain't any reason why I should have cared about him, and I don't; it can't be that I do." Yet arguing with himself in this way, he continued to eye the casket which held his dead employer with an unyielding grief.

Mrs. Zelotes sat like a black, draped statue at the head of the pew, but her eyes behind her black veil were sharply observant. She missed not one detail. She saw everything; she counted the wreaths and bouquets on the casket, and stored in her mind, as vividly as she might have done some old mourning-piece, the picture of the near relatives advancing up the aisle.

Mrs. Lloyd came leaning on her nephew's arm, and there were Cynthia Lennox and a distant cousin, an elderly widow who had been summoned to the house of death.

Ellen sat in the body of the church, with the employés of Lloyd's, between Abby Atkins and Maria. She glanced up when the little company of mourners entered, then cast her eyes down again and compressed her lips. Maria began to weep softly, pressing her handkerchief to her eyes. Ellen's mother had begged her not to sit with the employés, but with her and her father and grandmother in their own pew, but the girl had refused.

"I must sit where I belong," said she.

"Maybe she thinks it would look as if she was putting on airs on account of —" Fanny said to Andrew when Ellen had gone out.

"I guess she's right," returned Andrew.

The employés had contributed money for a great floral piece composed of laurel and white roses, in the shape of a pillow. Mamie Brady, who sat behind Ellen, leaned over, and in a whisper whistled into her ear.

"Ain't it handsome?" said she. "Can you see them flowers from the hands?"

Ellen nodded impatiently. The great green and white decoration was in plain view from her seat, and as she looked at it she wondered if it were a sarcasm or poetic truth beyond the scope of the givers, the pillow of laurel and roses, emblematic of eternal peace, presented by the hard hands of labor to dead capital.

Of course the tragic circumstances of Norman Lloyd's death increased the curiosity of the public. Gradually the church became crowded by a slow and solemn pressure. The aisles were filled. The air was heavy with the funeral flowers. The minister spoke at length, descanting upon the character of the deceased, his uprightness and strict integrity in business, avoiding pitfalls of admissions of weaknesses with the expertness of a juggler. He was always regarded as very apt at funerals, never saying too much and never too little. The church was very still, the whole audience wrapped in a solemn hush, until the minister began to pray; then there was a general bending of heads and devout screening of faces with hands. Then all at once a sob from a woman sounded from the rear of the church. It was hysterical, and had burst from the restraint of the weeper. People turned about furtively.

"Who was that?" whispered Mamie Brady, after a prolonged stare over her shoulders from under her red frizzle of hair. "It ain't any of the mourners."

Ellen shook her head.

"Do keep still, Mamie Brady," whispered Abby Atkins.

The sob came again, and this time it was echoed from the pew where sat the members of the dead man's family. Mrs. Lloyd began weeping convulsively. Her state of mind had raised her above natural emotion, and yet her nerves weakly yielded to it when given such an impetus. She wept like a child, and now and then a low murmur of heart-broken complaint came from her lips, and was heard distinctly over the church. Other women began to weep. The minister prayed, and his words of comfort seemed like the air in a discordant medley of sorrow.

Andrew Brewster's face twitched; he held his hands clutched tightly. Fanny was weeping, but the old woman at the head of the pew sat immovable.

When the services were over, and the great concourse of people had passed around the casket and viewed the face of the dead, with keen, sidewise observation of the funeral flowers, Mrs. Zelotes pressed out as fast as she was able without seeming to crowd, and caught up with Mrs. Pointdexter, who had sat in the rear of the church.

She came alongside as they left the church, and the two old women moved slowly down the sidewalk, with lingering glances at the funeral procession drawn up in front of the church.

"Who was that cryin' so in back; did you see?" asked Mrs. Zelotes of Mrs. Pointdexter, whose eyes were red, and whose face bore an expression of meek endurance of a renewal of her own experience of sorrow.

"It was Joe Martin's wife," said she. "I sat just behind her."

"What made her?"

Then both started, for the woman who had sobbed came up behind them, her brother, an elderly man, trying to hold her back.

"You stop, John," she cried. "I heard what she said, and I'm goin' to tell her. I'm goin' to tell everybody. Nobody shall stop me. There the minister spoke and spoke and spoke, and he never said a word as to any good he'd done. I'm goin' to tell. I wanted to stan' right up in the church an' tell everybody. He told me not to say a word about it, an' I never did whilst he was livin', but now I'm goin' to stan' up for the dead." The woman pulled herself loose from her brother, who stood behind her, frightened, and continually thrusting out a black-gloved hand of remonstrance. People began to gather. The woman, who was quite old, had a face graven with hard lines of habitual restraint, which was now, from its utter abandon, at once pathetic and terrible. She made a motion as if she were thrusting her own self into the background.

"I'm goin' to speak," she said, in a high voice. "I held my tongue for the livin', but I'm goin' to speak for the dead. My poor husband died twenty years ago, got his hand cut in a machine in Lloyd's, and had lockjaw, and I was left with my daughter that had spinal disease, and my little boy that died, and my own health none too good, and — and he — he — came to my house, one night after the funeral, and — and told me he was goin' to look out for me, and he has, he has. That blessed man gave me five dollars every week of my life, and he buried poor Annie when she died, and my little boy, and he made me promise never to say a word about it. Five dollars every week of my life — five dollars."

The woman's voice ended in a long-drawn, hysterical wail. The other women who had been listening began to weep. Mrs. Pointdexter, when she and Mrs. Zelotes moved on, was sobbing softly, but Mrs. Zelotes's face, though moved, wore an expression of stern conjecture.

"I'd like to know how many things like that Norman Lloyd did," said she. "I never supposed he was that kind of a man."

She had a bewildered feeling, as if she had to reconstruct her own idea of the dead man as a monument to his memory, and reconstruction was never an easy task for the old woman.

Chapter XLV

A Short time after Norman Lloyd's death, Ellen, when she had reached the factory one morning, met a stream of returning workmen. They swung along, and on their faces were expressions of mingled solemnity and exultation, as of children let out to play because of sorrow in the house, which will not brook the jarring inconsequence of youth.

Mamie Brady, walking beside a young man as red-haired as herself, called out, with ill-repressed glee, "Turn round, Ellen Brewster; there ain't no shop today."

The young man at her side, nervously meager, looked at Ellen with a humorous contortion of this thin face, then he caught Mamie Brady by the arm, and swung her into a hopity-skip down the sidewalk. Just behind them came Granville Joy, with another man. Ellen stopped. "What is it?" she said to him. "Why is the shop closed?"

Granville stopped, and let the stream of workmen pass him and Ellen. They stood in the midst of it, separating it, as rock will separate a current. "Mrs. Lloyd is dead," Granville replied, soberly.

"I heard she was very low last night," Ellen returned, in a hushed voice.

Then she passed Granville, who stood a second gazing wistfully after her, before he resumed his homeward way. He told himself quite accurately that she had purposely refrained from turning, in order to avoid walking with himself. A certain resentment seized him. It seemed to him that something besides his love had been slighted. "She needn't have thought I was going to make love to her going home in broad daylight with all these folks," he reflected, and he threw up his head impatiently.

The man with whom he had been walking when Ellen appeared lingered for him to rejoin him. "Wonder how many shops they'd shut up for you and me," said the man, with a sort of humorous bitterness. He had a broad face, seemingly fixed in an eternal mask of laughter, and yet there were hard lines in it, and a forehead of relentless judgment overhung his wide bow of mouth and his squat and wrinkled nose.

"Guess not many," replied Granville, echoing the man in a way unusual to him.

"And yet if it wa'n't for us they couldn't keep the shop running at all," said the man, whose name was Tom Peel.

"That's so," said Granville, with a slight glance over his shoulder.

Ellen had met the Atkins girls, and had turned, and was coming back with them. It was as he had thought.

"If the new boss cuts down fifteen percent, as the talk is, what be you goin' to do?" asked Tom Peel.

"I ain't goin' to stand it," replied Granville, fiercely.

"Ain't goin' to be swept clean by the new broom, hey?" said the man, with a widened grin.

"No!" thundered Granville — "not by him, nor anyone like him. Damn him!"

Tom Peel's grin widened still further into an intense but silent laugh. Meantime Ellen was walking with Abby and Maria.

"I wonder how we're going to get along with young Lloyd," said Abby. Ellen looked at her keenly. "Why?" she said.

"Oh, I heard the men talking the other night after I'd gone to bed. Maybe it isn't true that he's thinking of cutting down the wages."

"It can't be," said Ellen.

"I say so, too," said Maria.

"Well, I hope not," said Abby. "You can't tell. Some chimneys always have the wind whistling in them, and I suppose it's about so with a boot and shoe shop. It don't follow that there's going to be a hurricane."

They had come to the entrance of the street where the Atkins sisters lived, and Ellen parted from them.

She kept on her way quite alone. They had walked slowly, and the other operatives had either boarded cars or had gone out of sight.

Ellen, when she turned, faced the northwest, out of which a stiff wind was blowing. She thrust a hand up each jacket-sleeve, folding her arms, but she let the fierce wind smite her full in the face without blenching. She had a sort of delight in facing a wind like that, and her quick young blood kept her from being chilled. The sidewalk was frozen. There was no snow, and the day before there had been a thaw. One could see on this walk, hardened into temporary stability, the footprints of hundreds of the sons and daughters of labor. Read rightly, that sidewalk in the little manufacturing city was a hieroglyphic of toil, and perhaps of toil as tending to the advance of the whole world. Ellen did not think of that, for she was occupied with more personal considerations, thinking of the dead woman in the great Lloyd house. She pictured her lying dead on that same bed whereon she had seen her husband lie dead. All the ghastly concomitants of death came to her mind. "They will turn off all that summer heat, and leave her alone in this freezing cold," she thought. She remembered the sound of that other woman's kind voice in her ears, and she saw her face when she told her the dreadful news of her husband's death. She felt a sob rising in her throat, but forced it back. What Abby had told concerning Mrs. Lloyd's happiness in the face of death seemed to her heart-breaking, though she knew not why. That enormous, almost transcendent trust in that which was absolutely unknown seemed to engulf her.

When she reached home, her mother looked at her in astonishment. She was sewing on the interminable wrappers. Andrew was paring apples for pies. "What be you home for — be you sick?" asked Fanny. Andrew gazed at her in alarm.

"No, I am not sick," replied Ellen, shortly. "Mrs. Lloyd is dead, and the factory's closed."

"I heard she was very low — Mrs. Jones told me so yesterday," said Fanny, in a hushed voice. Andrew began paring another apple. He was quite pale.

"When is the funeral to be, did you hear?" asked Fanny. Ellen was hanging up her hat and coat in the entry.

"Day after tomorrow."

"Have you heard anything about the hands sending flowers?"

"No."

"I suppose they will," said Fanny, "as long as they sent one to him. Well, she was a good woman, and it's a mark of respect, and I ain't anything to say against it, but I can't help feeling as if it was a tax."

Chapter XLVI

*I*t was some time after Mrs. Lloyd's death. Ellen had not seen Robert except as she had caught from time to time a passing glimpse of him in the factory. One night she overheard her father and mother talking about him after she had gone to bed, the sitting room door having been left ajar.

"I thought he'd come and call after his aunt died," she heard Fanny say. "I've always thought he liked Ellen, an' here he is now, with all that big factory, an' plenty of money."

"Mebbe he will," replied Andrew, with a voice in which were conflicting emotions, pride and sadness, and a struggle for self-renunciation.

"It would be a splendid thing for her," said Fanny.

"It would be a splendid thing for *him,*" returned Andrew, with a flash.

"Land, of course it would! You needn't be so smart, Andrew Brewster. I guess I know what Ellen is, as well as you. Any man might be proud to get her — I don't care who — whether he's Robert Lloyd, or who, but that don't alter what I say. It would be a splendid chance for Ellen. Only think of that great Lloyd house, and it must be full of beautiful things — table linen, and silver, and what-not. I say it would be a splendid thing for her, and she'd be above want all her life — that's something to be considered when we ain't got anymore than we have to leave her, and she workin' the way she is."

"Yes, that's so," assented Andrew, with a heavy sigh, as of one who looks upon life from under the mortification of an incubus of fate.

"We'd ought to think of her best good," said Fanny, judiciously. "I've been thinkin' every evening lately that he'd be comin'. I've had the fire in the parlor stove all ready to touch off, an' I've kept dusted in there. I know he liked her, but mebbe he's like all the rest of the big-bugs."

"What do you mean?" asked Andrew, with an inward qualm of repulsion. He always hated unspeakably to hear his wife say "big-bugs" in that tone. Although he was far from being without humility, he was republican to the core in his estimate of his own status in his own free country. In his heart, as long as he kept the law of God and man, he recognized no "big-bugs." It was one of the taints of his wife's ancestry which grated upon him from time to time.

"Oh, well, mebbe he don't want to be seen callin' on a shop-girl."

"Then he'd better keep away, that's all!" cried Andrew, furiously.

"Oh, well, mebbe it ain't so," said Fanny. "He's always seemed to me like a sensible feller, and I know he's liked Ellen, an' lots of girls that work in shops marry rich. Look at Annie Graves, married that factory boss over to Pemberton, an' has everythin'. She'd worked in his factory years. Mebbe it ain't that."

"Ellen don't act as if she minded anything about his not comin'," said Andrew, anxiously.

"Land, no; she ain't that kind. She's too much like her grandmother, but there ain't been a night lately that she ain't done her hair over when she got home from the shop and changed her dress."

"She always changes her dress, don't she?" said Andrew.

"Oh yes, she always has done that. I guess she likes to get rid of the leather smell for a while; but she has put on that pretty, new, red silk waist, and I've seen her watchin', though she's never said anything."

"You don't suppose she —" began Andrew, in a voice of intensest anxiety and indignant tenderness.

"Land, no; Ellen Brewster ain't a girl to fret herself much over any man unless she's sure he wants her; trust her. Don't you worry about that. All I mean is, I know she's had a kind of an idea that he might come."

Ellen, upstairs, lay listening against her will, and felt herself burning with mortified pride and shame. She said to herself that she would never put on that red silk waist again of an evening; she would not even do her hair over. It was quite true that she had thought that Robert might come, that he might renew his offer, now that he was so differently situated, and the obstacles, on his side, at least, removed. She told herself all the time that the obstacles on her own were still far from removed. She asked herself how could she, even if this man loved her and wished to marry her, allow him to support all her family, although he might be able to do so. She often told herself that she ought perhaps to have pride enough to refuse, and yet she watched for him to come. She had reflected at first that it was, of course, impossible for him to seem to take advantage of the deaths which had left him with this independence, that he must stay away for a while from motives of delicacy; but now the months were going, and she began to wonder if he never would come. Every night, when she took off the pretty, red silk waist, donned in vain, and let down her fair lengths of hair, it was with a sinking of her heart, and a sense of incredulous unhappiness. Ellen had always had a sort of sanguinity of happiness and of the petting of Providence as well as of her friends. However, the girl had, in spite of her childlike trust in the beauty of her life, plenty of strength to meet its refutal, and a pride equal to her grandmother's. In case Robert Lloyd should never approach her again, she would try to keep one face of her soul always veiled to her inmost consciousness.

The next evening she was careful not to put on her red silk waist, but changed her shop dress for her old blue woolen, and only smoothed her hair. She even went to bed early in order to prove to her mother that she expected nobody.

"You ain't goin' to bed as early as this, Ellen?" her mother said, as she lighted her lamp.

"Yes, I'm going to bed and read."

"Seems as if somebody might be in," said Fanny, awkwardly.

"I don't know who," Ellen returned, with a gentle haughtiness.

Andrew colored. He was at his usual task of paring apples. Andrew, in lieu of regular work outside, assisted in these household tasks, that his wife might have more time to sew. He looked unusually worn and old that night.

"If anybody does come, Ellen will have to get up, that's all," said Fanny, when the girl had gone upstairs. Then she pricked up her ears, for the electric-car had stopped before the house. Then it went on, with a sharp clang of the bell and a gathering rush of motion.

"That car stopped," Fanny said, breathlessly, her work falling from her fingers. Andrew and she both listened intently, then footsteps were heard plainly coming around the path at the side of the house.

Fanny's face fell. "It's only some of the men," said she, in a low voice. Then there came a knock on the side door, and Andrew ushered in John Sargent, Joe Atkins, and Amos Lee. Nahum Beals did not come in those days, for he was in prison awaiting trial for the murder of Norman Lloyd. However, Amos Lee's note was as impressive as his. He called often with Sargent and Atkins. They could not shake him off. He lay in wait for them at street corners, and joined them. He never saw Ellen alone, and did not openly proclaim his calls as meant for her. She prevented him from doing that in a manner which he could not withstand, full of hot and reckless daring as he was. When he entered that night he looked around with keen furtiveness, and was evidently listening and watching for her, though presently his voice rose high in discussion with the others. After a while the man who lived next door dropped in, and his wife with him. She and Fanny withdrew to the dining room with their sewing — for the woman also worked on wrappers — and left the sitting room to the men.

"It beats all how they like to talk," said the woman, with a large-minded leniency, "and they never get anywhere," she added. "They work themselves all up, and never get anywhere; but men are all like that."

"Yes, they be," assented Fanny.

"Jest hear that Lee feller," said the woman.

Amos Lee's voice was audible over the little house, and could have been heard in the yard, for it had an enormous carrying quality. It was the voice of a public ranter. Ellen, up in her chamber, lying in her bed, with a lamp at her side, reading, closely covered from the cold — for the room was unheated — heard him with a shiver of disgust and repulsion, and yet with a fierce sympathy and loyalty. She could not distinguish every word he said, but she knew well what he was talking about.

Mrs. Lloyd's death had made a certain hush in the ferment of revolt at Lloyd's, but now it was again on the move. There was a strong feeling of dislike to young Lloyd among the workmen. His uncle had heaped up ill-feeling as well as wealth as a heritage for him. The older Lloyd had never been popular, and Robert had succeeded to all his unpopularity, and was fast gathering his own. He was undoubtedly disposed to follow largely his uncle's business methods. He had admired them, they had proved successful, and he had honestly seen nothing culpable in them as business methods go; so it was not strange that he tried to copy them when he came into charge of Lloyd's. He was inclined to meet opposition with the same cool inflexibility of persistency in his own views, and was disposed to consult his own interests and carry out his own plans with no more brooking of interference than the skipper of a man-o'-war. Therefore, when it happened, shortly after his aunt's death, that he conceived a dissatisfaction with some prominent spirits among union men, he discharged them without the slightest reference to the fact that they were old and skillful workmen, and employed non-union men from another town in their places. He had, indeed, the object of making in time his factory entirely non-union. He said to himself that he would be dictated to by no labor organization under the sun, and that went a step beyond his uncle, inasmuch as the elder Lloyd had always made his own opinion subservient to good business policy; but Robert was younger and his blood hotter. It happened, also, a month later, when he began to see that business had fallen off considerably (indeed, it was the beginning of a period of extreme business depression), and that he could no longer continue on the same scale with the same profits, that instead of assembling the men in different departments, communicating the situation to them, and submitting them a reduced price-list for consideration, as was the custom with the more pacific of the manufacturers in the vicinity, he posted it up in the different rooms with no ado whatever. That had been his uncle's method, but never in the face of such brewing discontent as was prevalent in Lloyd's at that time. It was an occasion when the older man would have shut down, but Robert had, along with his arbitrary impetuosity, a real dislike to shut down on account of the men, for which they would have been the last to give him credit. "Poor devils," he told himself, standing in the office window one night, and seeing them pour out and disappear into the early darkness beyond the radius of the electric-lights, "I can't turn them adrift without a dollar in midwinter. I'll try to run the factory a while longer on a reduced scale, if I only meet expenses."

He saw Ellen going out, descending the steps with the Atkins girls, and as she passed the light, her fair head shone out for a second like an aureole. A great wave of tenderness came over him. He reflected that it would make no difference to her, that it was only a question of time before he lifted her forever out of the ranks of toil. The impulse was strong upon him to go to see her that night, but he had set himself to wait three months after his aunt's death, and the time was not yet up. He had a feeling that he might seem to be, and possibly would be, taking advantage of his bereavement if he went sooner, and that Ellen herself might think so.

It was that very night that Ellen had gone to bed early, to prove not only to her mother but to herself that she did not expect him, and the men came to see Andrew. Once she heard Amos Lee's voice raised to a higher pitch than ever, and distinguished every word.

"I tell you he's goin' to cut the wages tomorrow," said he.

There was a low rumble of response, which Ellen could not understand, but Lee's answer made it evident.

"How do I know?" he thundered. "It is in the air. He don't tell anymore than his uncle did; but you wait and see, that's all."

"I don't believe it," the girl upstairs said to herself, indignantly and loyally. "He can't cut the wages of all those poor men, he with all his uncle's money."

But the next morning the reduced price-list was posted on the walls of the different rooms in Lloyd's.

Chapter XLVII

*T*here was a driving snowstorm the next day. When Ellen started for the factory the white twilight of early morning still lingered. Everywhere were the sons and daughters of toil plodding laboriously and noiselessly through the snow, each keeping in the track of the one who went before. There was no wind blowing, and the snow was in a blue-white level; the trees bent stiffly and quietly beneath a heavy shag of white, and now and then came a clamor of birds, which served to accentuate the silence and peace. Ellen could always be forced by an extreme phase of nature to forgetfulness of her own stresses. For the time being she forgot everything; her vain watching for Robert, the talk of trouble in the factory, the disappointment in her home — all were forgotten in the contemplation, or rather in the absorbing, of this new-old wonder of snow.

There was a survival of the old Greek spirit in the girl, and had she come to earth without her background of orthodox traditions, she might have easily found her own deities in nature. The peace of the snow enveloped her soul as well as the earth, and she became a beneficiary of the white storm; the graceful droop of the pine boughs extended to her thoughts, and the clamor of the birds aroused in her a winged freedom, so that she felt at once peace and a sort of ecstasy. She walked in the track of a stolidly plodding man before her, as different a person as if she were an inhabitant of another planet. He was digesting the soggy, sweet griddle-cakes which he had eaten for breakfast, and revolving in his mind two errands for his wife — one, a pail of lard; the other, three yards of black dress braid; he was considering the surface scum of existence, that which pertained solely to his own petty share of it; the girl, the clear residue of life which was, and had been, and would be. Each was on the way to humble labor for daily bread, but with a difference of eternity between them.

But when Ellen reached the end of the cross street where the Atkins girls lived, she heard a sound which dispelled her rapt state. Her far vision became a near one; she saw, as it were, the clouded window-glass between her mortal eyes and the beyond, and the sound of a cough brought it about. Abby and Maria were coming towards her through the snow. Maria was coughing violently, and Abby was scolding her.

"I don't care anything about it, Maria Atkins," Abby was saying, "you ought to be ashamed of yourself coming out such a morning as this. There isn't any sense in it. You know you'll catch cold, and then there'll be two of you to take care of. You don't help a mite doing so, you needn't think you do."

When Abby caught sight of Ellen she hastened forward, while Maria, still coughing, trailed behind, lifting her little, heavy, snow-bound feet wearily.

"Ellen, I wish you'd tell Maria to turn around and go home," she said. "Just hear her cough, and out in all this snow, and getting her skirts draggled. She hasn't got common-sense, you tell her so."

Ellen stopped, nodding assentingly. "I think she's right, Maria," she said. "You ought not to be out such a morning as this. You had better go home."

Maria came up smiling, though her lips were quite white, and she controlled her cough to convulsive motions of her chest.

"I am no worse than usual," said she. "I feel better than I generally do in the morning. I haven't coughed anymore, if I have as much, and I am holding my dress up high, and you know how warm the factory is. It will be enough sight warmer than it is at home. It is cold at home."

"Lloyd don't have to save coal," said Abby, bitterly, "but that don't alter the fact of your getting your skirts draggled."

Maria pulled up her skirts so high that she exposed her slender ankles, then seeing that she had done so, she let them fall with a quick glance at two men behind them.

"The snow will shake right off; it's light, Abby," she said.

"It ain't light. I should think you might listen to Ellen, if you won't to me."

Ellen pressed close to Maria, and pulled her thin arm through her own. "Look here," she said, "don't you think —"

Then Maria burst out with a pitiful emphasis. "I've got to go," she said. "Father had a bad spell last night; he can't get out. He'll lose his place this time, we are afraid, and there's a note coming due that father says he's paid, but the man didn't give it up, and he's got to pay it over again; the lawyer says there is no other way, and we can't let John Sargent do everything. He's got a sister out West he's about supporting since her husband died last fall. I've got to go to work; we've got to have the money, Ellen, and as for my cough, I have always coughed. It hasn't killed me yet, and I guess it won't yet for a while." Maria said the last with a reckless gayety which was unusual to her.

Abby trudged on ahead with indignant emphasis. "I'd like to know what good it is going to do to work and earn and pay up money if everybody is going to be killed by it?" she said, without turning her head.

Ellen pulled up Maria's coat-collar around her neck and put an extra fold of her dress-skirt into her hand.

"There, you can hold it up as high as that, it looks all right," said she.

"I wish Robert Lloyd had to get up at six o'clock and trudge a mile in this snow to his work," said Abby, with sudden viciousness. "He'll be driven down in his Russian sleigh by a man looking like a drum-major, and cut our poor little wages, and that's all he cares. Who's earning the money, he or us, I'd like to know? I hate the rich!"

"If it's true, what you say," said Maria, "it seems to me it's like hating those you have given things to, and that's worse than hating your enemies."

"Don't say given, say been forced to hand over," retorted Abby, fiercely; "and don't preach, Maria Atkins, I hate preaching; and do have sense enough not to talk when you are out in this awful storm. You can keep your mouth shut, if you can't do anything else!"

Ellen had turned quite white at Abby's words.

"You don't think that he means to cut the wages?" she said, eagerly.

"I know he does. I had it straight. Wait till you get to the shop."

"I don't believe it."

"You wait. Norman Lloyd was as hard as nails, and the young one is just like him." Abby looked relentlessly at Ellen.

"Maybe it isn't so," whispered Maria to Ellen.

"I don't believe it is," responded Ellen, but Abby heard them, and turned with a vicious jerk.

"Well, you wait!" said she.

The moment Ellen reached the factory she realized that something unwonted had happened. There were groups of men, talking, oblivious even of the blinding storm, which was coming in the last few minutes with renewed fury, falling in heavy sheets like dank shrouds.

Ellen saw one man in a muttering group throw out an arm, whitened like a branch of a tree, and shake a rasped, red fist at the splendid Russian sleigh of the Lloyd's, which was just gliding out of sight with a flurry of bells and a swing of fur tails, the whole surmounted by the great fur hat of the coachman. Abby turned and looked fiercely at Ellen.

"What did I tell you?" she cried.

Even then Ellen would not believe. She caught a glimpse of Robert's fair head at the office window, and a great impulse of love and loyalty came over her.

"I don't believe it," she said aloud to Maria. Maria held her arm tightly.

"Maybe it isn't so," she said.

But when they entered the room where they worked, there was a sullen group before a placard tacked on the wall. Ellen pressed closely, and saw what it was — a reduced wage-list. Then she went to her machine.

Chapter XLVIII

*E*llen had a judicial turn of mind, as her school-master had once said of her. She was able to look at matters from more than one stand-point, but she reasoned with a New Testament clearness of impartiality. She was capable of uncompromising severity, since she brought such a clear light of youth and childhood to bear upon even those things which needed shadows for their true revelation. Everything was for her either black or white. She had not lived long enough, perhaps she never would, for a comprehension of half-tones. The situation to her mind was perfectly simple, and she viewed it with a candor which was at once terrible and cruel, for it involved cruelty not only to Robert but to herself. She said to herself, here was this rich man, this man with accumulation of wealth, not one dollar of which he had earned himself, either by his hands or his brains, but which had been heaped up for his uncle by the heart and back breaking toil of all these poor men and women; and now he was going to abuse his power of capital, his power to take the bread out of their mouths entirely, by taking it out in part. He was going to reduce their wages, he was deliberately going to cause privation, and even suffering where there were large families. She felt the most unqualified dissent and indignation, and all the love which she had for the man only intensified it. Love, with a girl like this, tended to clearness of vision instead of blindness. She judged him as she would have judged herself. As she stood working at her machine, stitching linings to vamps, she kept a sharply listening ear for what went on about her, but there was very little to hear after work had fairly commenced and the great place was in full hum. The demand of labor was so imperative that the laborers themselves were merged in it; they ceased to be for the time, and, instead of living, they became parts of the struggle for life. A man hustling as if the world were at stake to get his part of a shoe finished as soon as another man, so as not to clog and balk the whole system, had no time for rebellion. He was in the whirlpool which was mightier than himself and his revolt. After all, a man is a small and helpless factor before his own needs. For a time those whirring machines, which had been evolved in the first place from the brains of men, and partook in a manner of both the spirit and the grosser elements of existence, its higher qualities and its sordid mechanism, like man himself, had the best of it. The swart arms of the workmen flew at their appointed tasks, they fed those unsatisfied maws, the factory vibrated with the heavy thud of the cutting-machines like a pulse, the racks with shoes in different stages of completion trundled from one department to another, propelled by men with tense arms and doggedly bent heads.

Ellen worked with the rest, but she was one of the few whose brain could travel faster than her hands. She thought as she worked, for her muscles did not retard her mind. She was composed of two motions, one within the other, and the central motion was so swift that it seemed still.

Ed Flynn came down the room and bent over her.

"Good-morning," he said. He was too gaily confident to be entirely respectful, but he had always a timidity of bearing which sat oddly upon him before Ellen. He looked half boldly, half wistfully at her fair face, and challenged her with gay eyes, which had in their depths a covert seriousness.

Ellen stood between Abby Atkins and Sadie Peel at her work. Sadie Peel turned on the foreman coquettishly and said, "You'd better go an' talk to Mamie Brady, she's got on a new blue bow on her red hair. Why don't you give her some better work than tying those old shoes? Here she's been workin' in this shop two years. You needn't come shinin' round Ellen an' me! We don't want you."

Flynn colored angrily and shot a vicious glance at the girl.

"It's a pretty hard storm," he said to Ellen, as if the other girl had not spoken.

"You needn't pretend you don't hear me, Ed Flynn," called out the girl. Her cheap finery was in full force that morning, not a lock of her brown hair was unstudied in its arrangement, and she was as conscious of her pose before her machine as if she had been on the stage. She knew just how her slender waist and the graceful slope of her shoulders appeared to the foreman, and her voice, in spite of its gay rallying and audacity, was wheedling.

Flynn caught hold of her shoulders, round and graceful under her flannel blouse, and shook her, half in anger, half in weakness.

"You shut up, you witch," said he. Then he turned to Ellen again, and his whole manner and expression changed.

"I'm sorry about that new list," he said, very low, in her ear. Ellen never looked at him, and did not make a motion as if she heard.

"It's a hard storm," the foreman said again, almost appealingly.

"Yes, it is very hard," replied Ellen, slipping another shoe under the needles.

"What on earth ails you this morning, Ellen Brewster?" Sadie Peel said to her, when the foreman had gone. "You look queer and act queer."

"Ellen ain't in the habit of joking with Ed Flynn," said Abby Atkins, on the other side, with sarcastic emphasis.

"My, don't you feel big!" sneered Sadie Peel. There was always a jarring inconsequence about this girl, she was so delicately pretty and refined in appearance, her ribbons were so profuse and cheap, and her manners were so recklessly coarse.

Ellen said nothing, but worked steadily.

"Mame Brady's just gone on Ed Flynn, and he goes with her just enough to keep her hangin', and I don't believe he means to marry her, and I think it's mean," said Sadie Peel.

"She ought to have more sense than to take any stock in him," said Abby.

"She ain't the only one," said Sadie. "Nellie Stone in the office has been daft over him since she's been there, and he don't look at her. I don't see what there is about Ed Flynn, for my part."

"I don't," said Abby, dryly.

"Well, I don't know. He's pretty good-looking," said Sadie Peel, "and he's got a sort of a way with him." All the time the girl was talking her heart was aching. The foreman had paid her some little attention, which she had taken seriously, but nobody except her father had known it, or known when he had fallen off. Sometimes Flynn, meeting the father's gaze as he passed him at his work at the cutting-bench, used to waver involuntarily, though he asked himself with perfect good faith what was it all about, for he had done the girl no harm. He felt more guilty concerning Mamie Brady.

Ellen worked on, with her fingers flying and her forehead tense with thought. The chatter of the girls ceased. They were too busy to keep it up. The hum of work continued. Once Ellen knew, although she did not see him, by some subtle disturbance of the atmosphere, a little commotion which was perfectly silent, that Robert Lloyd had entered the room. She knew when he passed her, and she worked more swiftly than ever. After he had gone out there was a curiously inarticulate sound like a low growl of purely animal dissent over the room; a word of blasphemy sounded above the din of the machines. Then all went on as before until the noon whistle blew.

Even then there was not so much discussion as might have been expected. Robert, since the storm was so heavy, remained in the office, and sent a boy out for a light luncheon, and the foremen were much in evidence. There was always an uncertainty about their sentiments, occupying as they did a position halfway between employer and employés; and then, too, they were not affected by the cut in wages. The sentiments of the unaffected are always a matter of suspicion to those who suffer themselves. There were grumblings carried on in a low key behind Flynn's back, but the atmosphere for the most part was one of depression. Ellen ate her luncheon with Maria and Abby. Willy Jones came up timidly when they were nearly finished, feeling his way with a remark about the storm, which was increasing.

"All the cars are tied up," he said, "and the noon train isn't in."

He leaned, with a curious effort at concealment from them all and himself, upon the corner of the bench near Abby. Then a young man passed them, with such an air of tragedy and such a dead-white face that they all stared after him.

"What in the world ails you, Ben Simmons?" called out Sadie Peel. But he did not act as if he heard. He crossed vehemently to the other side of the room, and stood at a window, looking out at the fierce white slant of the storm.

"What in creation ails him?" cried Sadie Peel.

"I guess I know," Willy Jones volunteered, timidly.

"What?"

"He was going to get married, and this cut in his wages is going to put a stop to it. I heard him say so this morning."

"Married! Who to?" asked Sadie Peel.

"Floretta Vining."

"My land!" cried Sadie Peel. "So she did take up with him after the school-teacher went away. I always said she would. I always knew Edward Harris wouldn't marry her, and I always said Ben Simmons would get her if he hung on long enough. Floretta was bound to marry somebody;

she wasn't going to wind up an old maid; and if she couldn't get one, she'd take another. I suppose Ben has got that sick sister of his to do for since her father died, and thinks he can't get married with any less pay. Floretta won't make a very cheap wife. She's bound to have things whether or no, and Ben ain't never earned so much as some. He's awful steady, but he's slow as cold molasses, and he won't let his sister suffer for no Floretta."

"That's so; I don't believe he would," said Abby. "What any man in his senses wants a doll like that for enough to look as if he was dead when he's got to put off marrying her!"

"That's because you ain't a man, Abby Atkins," said Sadie Peel. "All the men think of is looks, and little fine airs and graces."

"It seems as if they might get along," ventured Willy Jones, "as if they might do with less for a while."

Then Ellen turned to him unexpectedly. "There's no use in talking about doing with less when every single cent has to count," said she, sternly. "Ben Simmons has his taxes and insurance, and a steady doctor's bill for his sister, and medicines to buy. He can't have laid up a cent, for he's slow, though he's a good workman. You can't do with less when you haven't anymore than enough."

"That's so," said Abby. Then she turned a tender, conciliating, indulgent gaze on the young man at her side. "If I were Floretta Vining," said she, "and if Ellen were, we would go without things, and never know it. We'd go to work; but Floretta, she's different. We went to school with Floretta Vining."

"Floretta Vining is dreadful fond of men, but she wouldn't go without a yard of ribbon for one if he was dying," said Sadie Peel, conclusively. "It's awful hard on Ben Simmons, and no mistake."

"What?" said Amos Lee, coming up.

"Oh, what's hard on all of us? What's the use of asking?" said the girl, with a bitter coquetry. "I shouldn't think any man with horse-sense would ask what's hard on us when he's seen the ornaments tacked up all over the shop this morning."

"That's so," said Lee, with a glance over his shoulder. Flynn was at the other end of the room. Granville Joy, Dixon, and one or two other men were sauntering up. For a second the little group looked at one another.

"What are you going to do?" asked Ellen, in a low voice, which had an intonation that caused the others to start.

"I know what I'll do, if I can get enough to back me," cried Lee, in a loud voice.

"Hush up!" said Sadie Peel. Then her father came along smiling his imperturbable smile on his wide face, which had a Slavonic cast, although he was New England born and bred. He looked from one to the other without saying a word.

"We're deciding whether to strike or not, father," said Sadie, in a flippant manner. She raised a hand and adjusted a stray lock of hair as she spoke, then she straightened her ribbon stock. Her father said nothing, but his face assumed a stolidity of expression.

"I know what I'll do," proclaimed Amos Lee again.

"Hush up!" cried Sadie Peel again, with a giggle. "Here's Ed Flynn." And the foreman came sauntering up as the one-o'clock whistle blew, and the workers sprang to their posts of work.

Chapter XLIX

*T*he snow increased all day. When the six-o'clock whistle blew, and the workmen streamed out of the factories, it was a wild waste of winter and storm. The wind had come up, and the light snow arose in the distance like white dancers of death, spinning furiously over the level, then settling into long, gravelike ridges. Ellen glanced into the office as she passed the door, and saw Robert Lloyd talking busily with Flynn and another foreman by the name of Dennison. As she passed, Robert turned with a look as if he had been watching for her, and came forward hastily.

"Miss Brewster!" he called.

Mamie Brady, following close behind, gave Ellen an admonishing nudge. "Boss wants to see you," she whispered, loudly. Ellen stopped, and Robert came up.

"Please step in here a moment, Miss Brewster," he said, and colored a little.

Granville Joy, who was following Ellen, looked keenly at him, someone sniggered aloud, and a girl said quite audibly, "My land!"

Ellen followed Robert into the office, and he bent over her, speaking rapidly, in a low voice.

"You must not walk home in this snow," he said, "and the cars are not running. You must let me take you. My sleigh is at the door."

Ellen turned white. Somehow this protecting care for herself, in the face of all which she had been considering that day, gave her a tremendous shock. She felt at once touched and more indignant than she had ever been in her whole life. She had been half believing that Robert was neglecting her, that he had forgotten her; all day she had been judging his action of cutting the wages of the workmen from her unswerving, childlike, unshadowed point of view, and now this little evidence of humanity towards her, in the face of what she considered wholesale inhumanity towards others, made her at once severe to him and to herself, and she forced back sternly the leap of pleasure and happiness which this thought of her awakened. "No, thank you," she said, shortly; "I am much obliged, but I would rather walk."

"But you cannot, in this storm," pleaded Robert, in a low voice.

"Yes, I can; it is no worse for me than for others. There is Maria Atkins, she has been coughing all day."

"I will take her too. Ellen, you cannot walk. You must let me take you."

"I am much obliged, but I would rather not," replied Ellen, in an icy tone. She looked quite hard in his face.

Robert looked at her perplexed. "But it is drifting," he said.

"It is no worse for me than for the others." Ellen turned to go. Her attitude of rebuff was unmistakable.

Robert colored. "Very well; I will not urge you," he said, coldly. Then he returned to his desk, and Ellen went out. She caught up with Maria Atkins, who was struggling painfully through the drifts, leaning on Abby's arm, and slipped a hand under her thin shoulder.

"I expect nothing but she'll get her death out in this storm," grumbled Abby. "What did he want, Ellen?"

"Nothing in particular," replied Ellen. Uppermost in her mind at that moment was the charge of cruelty against Robert for not taking her hint as to Maria. "He can ask me to ride because he has amused himself with me, but as for taking this poor girl, whom he does not love, when it may mean life or death to her, he did not think seriously of doing that for a moment," she thought.

Maria was coughing, although she strove hard to smother the coughs. Granville Joy, who was plodding ahead, turned and waited until they came up.

"You had better let me carry you, Maria," he said, jocularly, but his honest eyes were full of concern.

"He is enough sight kinder than Robert Lloyd," thought Ellen; "he has a better heart." And then the splendid Lloyd sleigh came up behind them and stopped, tilting to a drift. Robert, in his fur-lined coat, sprang out and went up to Maria.

"Please let me take you home," he said, kindly. "You have a cold, and this storm is too severe for you to be out. Please let me take you home."

Maria looked at him, fairly gasping with astonishment. She tried to speak, but a cough choked her.

"You had better go if Mr. Lloyd will take you," Abby said, decisively. "Thank you, Mr. Lloyd; she isn't fit to be out." She urged her sister towards the sleigh, and Robert assisted her into the fur-lined nest.

"I can sit with the driver," said Robert to Abby, "if you will come with your sister."

"No, thank you," replied Abby. "I am able to walk, but I will be much obliged if you will take Maria home."

Robert sprang in beside Maria, and the sleigh slid out of sight.

"I never!" said Abby. Ellen said nothing, but plodded on, her eyes fixed on the snowy track.

"I am glad she had a chance to ride," said Granville Joy, in a tentative voice. He looked uneasily at Ellen.

"It beats the Dutch," said Abby. She also regarded Ellen with sympathy and perplexity. When they reached the street where she lived, up which the sleigh had disappeared, she let Granville go on ahead, and she spoke to Ellen in a low tone. "Why didn't he ask you?" she said.

"He did," replied Ellen.

"In the office?"

"Yes."

"And you wouldn't?"

"No."

"Why not?"

"I don't care to accept favors from a man who oppresses all my friends!"

"He was good to take in Maria," said Abby, in a perplexed voice. "His uncle would never have thought of it."

Ellen made no reply. She stood still in the drifting snow, with her mouth shut hard.

"You feel as if this cutting wages was a pretty hard thing?" said Abby.

"Yes, I do."

"Well, so do I. I wonder what they will do about it. I don't know how the men feel. Somehow, folks can't seem to think or plan much in a storm like this. There's the sleigh coming back."

"Good-night," Ellen said, hurriedly, and trudged on as fast as she was able in order not to have the Lloyd sleigh pass her; it had to turn after reaching the end of the street. Ellen caught up with Granville Joy. Robert, glancing over the waving fringe of fur tails, saw disappearing in the pale gleam of the electric-light the two dim figures veiled by the drifting snow. He thought to himself, with a sharp pain, that perhaps, after all, Granville Joy was the reason for her rebuff. It never occurred to him that his action in cutting the wages could have anything to do with it.

Ellen went along with Granville, who was anxious to offer her his arm, but did not quite dare. He kept thrusting out an elbow in her direction, and an inarticulate invitation died in his throat. Finally, when they reached an unusually high drift of snow, he plucked up sufficient courage.

"Take my arm, won't you?" he said, with a pitiful attempt at ease, then stared as if he had been shot, at Ellen's reply.

"No, thank you," she said. "I think it is easier to walk alone in snow like this."

"Maybe it is," assented Granville, dejectedly. He walked on, scuffling as hard as he could to make a path for Ellen with the patient faithfulness of a dog.

"What are you going to do about the cut in wages?" Ellen asked, presently.

Granville started. The sudden transition from personalities to generalities confused him.

"What?" he said.

Ellen repeated her question.

"I don't know," said Granville. "I don't think the boys have made up their minds. I don't know what they will do. They have been weeding out union men. I suppose the union would have something to say about it otherwise. I don't know what we will do."

"I shouldn't think there would be very much doubt as to what to do," said Ellen.

Granville stared at her over his shoulder in a perplexed, admiring fashion. "You mean — ?" he asked.

"I shouldn't think there would be any doubt."

"Well, I don't know. It is a pretty serious thing to get out of work in midwinter for a good many of us, and as long as the union isn't in control, other men can come in. I don't know."

"I know," said Ellen.

"You mean — ?"

"I mean that I do not think it right, that it is unjust, and I believe in resisting injustice."

"Men have resisted injustice ever since the Creation," said Granville, in a bitter voice.

"Well, resistance can continue as long as life lasts," returned Ellen. Just then came a fiercer blast than ever, laden with a stinging volley of snow, and seemed to sweep the words from the girl's mouth. She bent before it involuntarily, and the conviction forced itself upon her that, after all, resistance to injustice might be as futile as resistance to storm, that injustice might be one of the primal forces of the world, and one of the conditions of its endurance, and yet with the conviction came the renewed resolution to resist.

"What can poor men do against capital unless they are backed up by some labor organization?" asked Granville. "And I don't believe there are a dozen in the factory who belong to the union. There has been an understanding, without his ever saying so that I know of, that the old boss didn't approve of it. So lots of us kept out of it, we wanted work so bad. What can we do against such odds?"

"When right is on your side, you have all the odds," said Ellen, looking back over her snow-powdered shoulder.

"Then you would strike?"

"I wouldn't submit."

"Well, I don't know how the boys feel," said Granville. "I suppose we'll have to talk it over."

"I shouldn't need to talk it over," said Ellen. "You've gone past your house, Granville."

"I ain't going to let you go home alone in such a storm as this," said Granville, in a tender voice, which he tried to make facetious. "I wouldn't let any girl go home alone in such a storm."

Ellen stopped short. "I don't want you to go home with me, thank you, Granville," she said. "Your mother will have supper ready, and I can go just as well alone."

"Ellen, I won't let you go alone," said the young man, as a wilder gust came. "Suppose you should fall down?"

"Fall down!" repeated Ellen, with a laugh, but her regard of the young man, in spite of her rebuff, was tender. He touched her with his unfailing devotion; the heavy trudging by her side of this poor man meant, she told herself, much more than the invitation of the rich one to ride behind his bays in his luxurious sleigh. This meant the very bone and sinew of love. She held out her little, mittened hand to him.

"Good-night, Granville," she said.

Granville caught it eagerly. "Oh, Ellen," he murmured.

But she withdrew her hand quickly. "We have always been good friends, and we always will be," said she, and her tone was unmistakable. The young man shrank back.

"Yes, we always will, Ellen," he said, in a faithful voice, with a note of pain in it.

"Good-night," said Ellen again.

"Good-night," responded Granville, and turned his plodding back on the girl and retraced his laborious steps towards his own home, which he had just passed. There come times for all souls when the broad light of the path of humanity seems to pale to insignificance before the intensity of the one little search-light of personality. Granville Joy felt as if the eternal problem of the rich and poor, of labor and capital, of justice and equality, was as nothing before the desire of his heart for that one girl who was disappearing from his sight behind the veil of virgin snow.

Chapter L

*W*hen Ellen came in sight of her house that night she saw her father's bent figure moving down the path with sidewise motions of a broom. He had been out at short intervals all the afternoon, that she should not have to wade through drifts to the door. The electric-light shone full on this narrow, cleared track and the toiling figure.

"Hullo, father!" Ellen called out. Andrew turned, and his face lit with love and welcome and solicitude.

"Be you dreadful snowy?" he asked.

"Oh no, father, not very."

"It's an awful storm."

"Pretty bad, but I got along all right. The snow-plow has been out."

"Wait a minute till I get this swept," said Andrew, sweeping violently before her.

"You needn't have bothered, father," said Ellen.

"I ain't anything else to do," replied Andrew, in a sad voice.

"There's mother watching," said Ellen.

"Yes, she's been diggin' at them wrappers all day."

"I suppose she has," Ellen returned, in a bitter tone. Her father stared at her. Ellen never spoke like that. For the first time she echoed him and her mother. Something like terror came over him at the sound of that familiar note of his own life from this younger one. He seemed to realize dimly that a taint of his nature had descended upon his child.

When Ellen entered the house, the warm air was full of savory odors of toast and tea and cooking meat and vegetables.

"You'd better go right upstairs and put on a dry dress, Ellen," said Fanny. "I put your blue one out on your bed, and your shoes are warming by the sitting room stove. I've been worrying as to how you were going to get home all day." Then she stopped short as she caught sight of Ellen's face. "What on earth is the matter, Ellen Brewster?" she said.

"Nothing," said Ellen. "Why?"

"You look queer. Has anything happened?"

"Yes, something has happened."

"What?"

Andrew turned pale. He stood in the entry with his snowy broom in hand, staring from one to the other.

"Nothing that you need worry about," said Ellen. "I'll tell you when I get my dress changed."

Ellen pulled off her rubbers, and went upstairs to her chamber. Fanny and Andrew stood looking at each other.

"You don't suppose —" whispered Andrew.

"Suppose what?" responded Fanny, sharply.

They continued to look at each other. Fanny answered Andrew as if he had spoken, with that jealous pride for her girl's self-respect which possessed her even before the girl's father.

"Land, it ain't that," said she. "You wouldn't catch Ellen lookin' as if anything had come across her for such a thing as that."

"No, I suppose she wouldn't," said Andrew; and he actually blushed before his wife's eyes.

That afternoon Mrs. Wetherhed had been in, and told Fanny that she had heard that Robert Lloyd was to be married to Maud Hemingway; and both Andrew and Fanny had thought of that as the cause of Ellen's changed face.

"You'd better take that broom out into the shed, and get the snow off yourself, and come in and shut the door," Fanny said, shortly. "You're colding the house all off, and Amabel has got a cold, and she's sitting right in the draft."

"All right," replied Andrew, meekly, though Fanny had herself been holding the sitting room door open. In those days Andrew felt below his moral stature as head of the house. Actually, looking at Fanny, who was earning her small share towards the daily bread, she seemed to him much taller than he, though she was a head shorter. He thought so little of himself, he seemed to see himself as through the wrong end of a telescope. Fanny went into the sitting room and shut the door with a bang. Amabel did not look up from her book. She was reading a library book much beyond her years, and sniffing pathetically with her cold. Amabel had begun to discover an omnivorous taste for books, which stuck at nothing. She understood not more than half of what she read, but seemed to relish it like indigestible food.

When Ellen came downstairs, and sat beside the coal stove to change her shoes, she looked at the book which Amabel was reading. "You ought not to read that book, dear," she said. "Let Ellen get you a better one for a little girl tomorrow."

But Amabel, without paying the slightest heed to Ellen's words, looked up at her with amazement, as Andrew and Fanny had done. "What's the matter, Ellen?" she asked, in her little, hoarse voice.

Fanny and Andrew, who had just entered, stood waiting. Ellen bent over her shoe, drawing in the strings firmly and evenly.

"Mr. Lloyd has reduced the wage-list," she said.

"How much?" asked Andrew, in a hoarse voice.

"Ten percent."

There was a dead silence. Andrew and Fanny looked at Ellen like people who are uncertain of their next move; Amabel stared from one to the other with her weak, watery eyes. Ellen continued to lace her shoes.

"What do you think about it, Ellen?" asked Andrew, almost timidly.

"I know of only one thing to think," replied Ellen, in a dogged voice.

As she spoke she pulled the tag off a shoestring because it would not go through the eyelet.

"What is that?" asked Fanny, in a hard voice.

"I think it is cruelty and tyranny," said Ellen, pulling the rough end of the string through the eyelet.

"I suppose the times are pretty hard," ventured Andrew; but Ellen cut him short.

"Robert Lloyd has half a million, which has been accumulated by the labor of poor men in prosperous times," said she, with her childlike severity and pitilessness. "There is no question about the matter."

Then Fanny flung all self-interest to the wind and was at her daughter's side like a whirlwind. The fact that the two were of one blood was never so strongly evident. Red spots glowed in the elder woman's cheeks and her black eyes blazed.

"Ellen's right," said she; "she's right. For a man worth half a million to cut down the wages of poor, hard-working folks in midwinter is cruelty. I don't care who does it."

"Yes, it is," said Ellen.

Fanny opened her mouth to tell Ellen of the rumor concerning Robert's engagement to Maud Hemingway, then she refrained, for some reason which she could not analyze. In her heart she did not believe the report to be true, and considered the telling of it a slight to Ellen, but it influenced her in her indignation against Robert for the wage-cutting.

"What are they going to do?" asked Andrew.

"I don't know," replied Ellen.

"Did he — young Lloyd — talk to the men?"

"No; notices were tacked up all over the shop."

"That was the way his uncle would have done," said Andrew, in a curious voice of bitterness and respect.

"So you don't know what they are going to do?" said Fanny.

"No."

"Well, I know what I would do," said Fanny. "I never would give in, if I starved — never!"

Chapter LI

When Ellen started for the factory the next morning the storm had not ceased; the roads were very heavy, although the snow-plow had been out at intervals all night, and there was a struggling line of shoveling men along the car-track, but the cars were still unable to penetrate the drifts. When Ellen passed her grandmother's house the old woman tapped sharply on the window and motioned her back frantically with one bony hand. The window was frozen to the sill with the snow, and she could not raise it. Ellen shook her head, smiling. Her grandmother continued to wave her back, the lines of forbidding anxiety in her old face as strongly marked as an etching in the window frame. This love, which had at once coerced and fondled the girl since her birth, was very precious to her. This protection, which she was forced to repel, smote her like a pain.

"Poor old grandmother!" she thought; "there she will worry about me all day because I have gone out in the storm." She turned back and waved her hand and nodded laughingly; but the old woman continued that anxiously imperative backward motion until Ellen was out of sight.

Ellen walked in the car-track, as did everybody else, that being better cleared than the rest of the road. She was astonished that she heard nothing of the cut in wages from the men. There seemed to be no excitement at all. They merely trudged heavily along, their whitening bodies bent before the storm. There was an unusual doggedness about this march to the factory this morning, but that was all. Ellen returned the muttered greeting of several, and walked along in silence with the rest. Even when Abby Atkins joined her there was little said. Ellen asked for Maria, and Abby replied that she had taken more cold yesterday, and could not speak aloud; then relapsed into silence, making her way through the snow with a sort of taciturn endurance. Ellen looked at the struggling procession of which she was a part, all slanting with the slant of the storm, and a fancy seized her that rebellion and resistance were hopeless, that those parallel lines of yielding to the onslaughts of fate were as inevitable as life itself, one of its conditions. Men could not help walking that way when the bitter storm-wind was blowing; they could not help living that way when fate was in array against their progress. Then, thinking so, a mightier spirit of revolt than she had ever known awoke within her. She, as she walked, straightened herself. She leaned not one whit before the drive of the storm. She advanced with no yielding in her, her brave face looking ahead through the white blur of snow with a confidence which was almost exultation.

"What do you think the men will do?" she said to Abby when they came in sight of Lloyd's, shaggy with fringes and wreaths and overhanging shelvings of snow, roaring with machinery, with the steady stream of labor pouring in the door.

"Do?" repeated Abby, almost listlessly. "Do about what?"

"About the cut in wages?"

Abby turned on her with sudden fire. "Oh, my God, what can they do, Ellen Brewster?" she demanded. "Haven't they got to live? Hasn't Lloyd got it all his own way? How are men to live in weather like this without work? Bread without butter is better than none at all, and life at any cost is better than death for them you love. What can they do?"

"It seems to me there is only one thing to do," replied Ellen.

Abby stared at her wonderingly. "You don't mean —" she said, as they climbed up the stairs.

"I mean I would do anything, at whatever cost to myself, to defeat injustice," said Ellen, in a loud, clear voice.

Several men turned and looked back at her and laughed bitterly.

"It's easy talking," said one to another.

"That's so," returned the other.

The people all settled to their work as usual. One of the foremen (Dennison), who was anxious to curry favor with his employer, reported to him in an undertone in the office that everything was quiet. Robert nodded easily. He had not anticipated anything else. In the course of the morning he looked into the room where Ellen was employed, and saw with relief and concern her fair head before her machine. It seemed to him that he could not bear it one instant longer to have her working in this fashion, that he must lift her out of it. He still tingled with his rebuff of the night before, but he had never loved her so well, for the idea that the cut in wages affected her relation to him never occurred to him. As he walked through the room none of the workers seemed to notice him, but worked with renewed energy. He might have been invisible for all the attention he seemed to excite. He looked with covert tenderness at the back of Ellen's head, and passed on. He reflected that he had adopted the measure of wage-cutting with no difficulty whatever.

"All it needs is a little firmness," he thought, with a boyish complacency in his own methods. "Now I can keep on with the factory, and no turning the poor people adrift in midwinter."

At noon Robert put on his fur-lined coat and left the factory, springing into the sleigh, which had drawn up before the door with a flurry of bells. He had an errand in the next town that afternoon, and was not going to return. When the sleigh had slid swiftly out of sight through the storm, which was lightening a little, the people in the office turned to one another with a curious expression of liberty, but even then little was said. Nellie Stone was at the desk eating her luncheon; Ed Flynn and Dennison and one of the lasters, who had looked in and then stepped in when he saw Lloyd was gone, were there. The laster, who was young and coarsely handsome, had an admiration for the pretty girl at the desk. Presently she addressed him, with her mouth full of apple-pie.

"Say, George, what are you fellows going to do?" she asked.

Dennison glanced keenly from one to the other; Flynn shrugged his shoulders and looked out of the window.

"Looks as if it was clearing up," he remarked.

"What are you going to do?" asked Nellie Stone again, with a coquettish flirt of her blond fluff of hair.

"Grin and bear it, I s'pose," replied the young laster, with an adoring look at her.

"My land! grin and bear a cut of ten percent? Well, I don't think you've got much spunk, I must say. Why don't you strike?"

"Who's going to feed us?" replied the laster, in a tender voice.

"Feed you? Oh, you don't want much to eat. Join the union. It's ridiculous so few of the men in Lloyd's belong to it, anyway; and then the union will feed you, won't it?"

"The union did not do what it promised in the Scarboro strike," interposed Dennison, curtly.

"Oh, we all know where you are, Frank Dennison," said the girl, with a soft roll of her blue eyes. "Besides, it's easy to talk when you aren't hit. Your wages aren't cut. But here is George May here, he's in a different box."

"He's got nobody dependent on him, anyway," said Flynn.

"If I wasn't going to get married I'd strike," cried the young man, with a fervent glance at the girl. She colored, half pleased, half angry, and the other men chuckled. She took another bite of pie to conceal her confusion. She preferred Flynn to the laster, and while she was not averse to proving to the former the triumph of her charms over another man, did not like too much concessions.

"You'd better go and eat your dinner, George May," she said, in her sweet, shrill voice. "First thing you know the whistle will blow. Here's yours, Ed." With that she pulled out a leather bag from under the desk, where she had volunteered to place it for warmth and safety against the coil of steam-pipes.

"I don't believe your coffee is very cold, Ed," said she.

The laster glared from one to the other jealously. Dennison went towards a shelf where he had stored away his luncheon, when he stopped suddenly and listened, as did the others. There came a great uproar of applause from the next room beyond. Then it subsided, and a girl's clear, loud voice was heard.

"What is going on?" cried Nellie Stone. She jumped up and ran to the door, still eating her pie, and the men followed her.

At the end of one of the work-rooms, backed against a snowy window, clung about with shreds of the driving storm, stood Ellen Brewster, with some other girls around her, and a few men on the outskirts, and a steady, curious movement of all the other workmen towards her, as of iron filings towards a magnet, and she was talking.

Her voice was quite audible all over the great room. It was low-pitched, but had a wonderful carrying quality, and there was something marvelous in its absolute confidence.

"If you men will do nothing, and say nothing, it is time for a girl to say and act," she proclaimed. "I did not dream for a minute that you would yield to this cut in wages. Why should you have your wages cut?"

"The times are pretty hard," said a doubtful voice among her auditors.

"What if the times are hard? What is that to you? Have you made them hard? It is the great capitalists who have made them hard by shifting the wealth too much to one side. They are the ones who should suffer, not you. What have you done, except come here morning after morning in cold or heat, rain or shine, and work with all your strength? They who have precipitated the hard times are the ones who should bear the brunt of them. Your work is the same now as it was then, the strain on your flesh and blood and muscles is the same, your pay should be the same."

"That's so," said Abby Atkins, in a reluctant, surly fashion.

"That's so," said another girl, and another. Then there was a fusillade of hand-claps started by the girls, and somewhat feebly echoed by the men.

One or two men looked rather uneasily back towards Dennison and Flynn and two more foremen who had come forward.

"It ain't as though we had something to fall back on," said a man's grumbling voice. "It's easy to talk when you ain't got a wife and five children dependent on you."

"That's so," said another man, doggedly.

"That has nothing to do with it," said Ellen, firmly. "We can all club together, and keep the wolf from the door for those who are hardest pressed for a while; and as for me, if I were a man —"

She paused a minute. When she spoke again her voice was full of childlike enthusiasm; it seemed to ring like a song.

"If I were a man," said she, "I would go out in the street and dig — I would beg, I would steal — before I would yield — I, a free man in a free country — to tyranny like this!"

There was a great round of applause at that. Dennison scowled and said something in a low voice to another foreman at his side. Flynn laughed, with a perplexed, admiring look at Ellen.

"The question is," said Tom Peel, slouching on the outskirts of the throng, and speaking in an imperturbable, compelling, drawling voice, "whether the free men in the free country are going to kick themselves free, or into tighter places, by kicking."

"If you have got to stop to count the cost of bravery and standing up for your rights, there would be no bravery in the world," returned Ellen, with disdain.

"Oh, I am ready to kick," said Peel, with his masklike smile.

"So am I," said Granville Joy, in a loud voice. Amos Lee came rushing through the crowd to Ellen's side. He had been eating his dinner in another room, and had just heard what was going on. He opened his mouth with a motion as of letting loose a flood of ranting, but somebody interposed. John Sargent, bulky and irresistible in his steady resolution, put him aside and stood before him.

"Look here," he said to them all. "There may be truth in what Miss Brewster says, but we must not act hastily; there is too much at stake. Let us appoint a committee and go to see Mr. Lloyd this evening, and remonstrate on the cutting of the wages." He turned to Ellen in a kindly, half-paternal fashion. "Don't you see it would be better?" he said.

She looked at him doubtfully, her cheeks glowing, her eyes like stars. She was freedom and youth incarnate, and rebellious against all which she conceived as wrong and tyrannical. She could hardly admit, in her fire of enthusiasm, of pure indignation, of any compromise or arbitration. All the griefs of her short life, she had told herself, were directly traceable to the wrongs of the system of labor and capital, and were awakening within her as freshly as if they had just happened.

She remembered her father, exiled in his prime from his place in the working world by this system of arbitrary employment; she remembered her aunt in the asylum; poor little Amabel; her own mother toiling beyond her strength on underpaid work; Maria coughing her life away. She remembered her own life twisted into another track from the one which she should have followed, and there was for the time very little reason or justice in her. That injustice which will arise to meet its kind in equal combat had arisen in her heart. Still, she yielded. "Perhaps you are right," she said to Sargent. She had always liked John Sargent, and she respected him.

"I am sure it is the best course," he said to her, still in that low, confidential voice.

It ended in a committee of four — John Sargent, Amos Lee, Tom Peel, and one of the older lasters, a very respectable man, a deacon in the Baptist Church — being appointed to wait on Robert Lloyd that evening.

When the one-o'clock whistle blew, Ellen went back to her machine. She was very pale, but she was conscious of a curious steadiness of all her nerves. Abby leaned towards her, and spoke low in the roar of wheels.

"I'll back you up, if I die for it," she said.

But Sadie Peel, on the other side, spoke quite openly, with a laugh and shrug of her shoulders. "Land," she said, "father'll be with you. He's bound to strike. He struck when he was in McGuire's. Catch father givin' up anything. But as for me, I wish you'd all slow up an' stick to work, if you do get a little less. If we quit work I can't have a nearseal cape, and I've set my heart on a nearseal cape this winter."

Chapter LII

*E*llen resolved that she would say as little as possible about the trouble at home that night. She did not wish her parents to worry over it until it was settled in one way or another.

When her mother asked what they had done about the wage-cutting, she replied that a committee had been appointed to wait on Mr. Lloyd that evening, and talk it over with him; then she said nothing more.

"He won't give in if he's like his uncle," said Fanny.

Ellen went on eating her supper in silence. Her father glanced at her with sharp solicitude.

"Maybe he will," said he.

"No, he won't," returned Fanny.

Ellen was very pale and her eyes were bright. After supper she went to the window and pressed her face against the glass, shielding her eyes from the indoor light, and saw that the storm had quite ceased. The stars were shining and the white boughs of the trees lashing about in the northwest wind. She went into the entry, where she had hung her hat and coat, and began putting them on.

"Where are you going, Ellen?" asked her mother.

"Just down to Abby's a minute."

"You don't mean to say your are goin' out again in this snow, Ellen Brewster? I should think you were crazy." When Fanny said crazy, she suddenly started and shuddered as if she had struck herself. She thought of Eva. Always the possibility of a like doom was in her own mind.

"It has stopped snowing, mother," Ellen said.

"Stopped snowing! What if it has? The roads ain't cleared. You can't get down to Abby Atkins's without gettin' wet up to your knees. I should think if you got into the house after such a storm you'd have sense enough to stay in. I've worried just about enough."

Ellen took off her coat and hat and hung them up again. "Well, I won't go if you feel so, mother," she said, patiently.

"It seems as if you might get along without seein' Abby Atkins till tomorrow mornin', when you'd seen her only an hour ago," Fanny went on, in the high, nagging tone which she often adopted with those whom she loved the dearest.

"Yes, I can," said Ellen. It seemed to her that she must see somebody with whom she could talk about the trouble in the factory, but she yielded. There was always with the girl a perfect surface docility, as that she seemed to have no resistance, but a little way down was a rock-bed of firmness. She lighted her lamp, and took her library book and went upstairs to bed to read. But she could not read, and she could not sleep when she had put aside her book and extinguished her lamp. She could think of nothing except Robert, and what he would say to the committee. She lay awake all night thinking of it. Ellen was a girl who was capable of the most devoted love, and the most intense dissent and indignation towards the same person. She could love in spite of faults, and she could see faults in spite of love. She thought of Robert Lloyd as of the one human soul whom she loved best out of the whole world, whom she put before everybody else, even her own self, and she also thought of him with a wrath which was pitiless and uncompromising, and which seemed to tear her own heart to pieces, for one cannot be wroth with love without a set-back of torture. "If he does not give in and raise the wages, I shall hate him," thought Ellen; and her heart stung her as if at the touch of a hot iron, and then she could have struck herself for the supposition that he would not give in. "He must," she told herself, with a great fervor of love. "He must."

But when she went down to breakfast the next morning her mother stared at her sharply.

"Ellen Brewster, what is the matter with you?" she cried.

"Nothing. Why?"

"Nothing! You look like a ghost."

"I feel perfectly well," said Ellen. She made an effort to eat as much breakfast as usual in order that her mother should not suspect that she was troubled. When at last she set out for the factory, in the early morning dusk, she was chilled and trembling with excitement.

The storm had quite ceased, and there was a pale rose-and-violet dawn-light in the east, and presently came effects like golden-feathered shafts shooting over the sky. The road was alive with shoveling men, construction-cars of the railroad company were laboring back and forth to clear the tracks, householders were making their way from their doors to their gates, clearing their paths, lifting up the snow in great, glittering, blue-white blocks on their clumsy shovels. Everywhere were the factory employés hastening to their labor; the snow was dropping from the overladen tree branches in great blobs; there was an incessant, shrill chatter of people, and occasional shouts. It was the rally of mankind after a defeat by a primitive force of nature. It was the eternal reassertion of human life and a higher organization over the elemental. Men who had walked doggedly the morning before now moved with a spring of alacrity, although the road was very heavy. There was a new light in their eyes; their cheeks glowed. Ellen had no doubt whatever that if Robert Lloyd had not yielded the attitude of the employés of Lloyd's would be one of resistance. She herself seemed to breathe in resistance to tyranny, and strength for the right in every breath of the clear, crisp morning air. She felt as if she could trample on herself and her own weakness, for the sake of justice and the inalienable good of her kind, with as little hesitation as she trampled on the creaking snow. Yet she trembled with that deadly chill before a sense of impending fate. When she returned the salutations of her friends on the road she felt that her lips were stiff.

"You look dreadful queer, Ellen," Abby Atkins said, anxiously, when she joined her. Maria also was out that morning.

"Have you heard what they are going to do?" Ellen asked, in a sort of breathless fashion.

"You mean about the wage-cutting? Don't look so, Ellen."

Maria pressed close to Ellen, and slid her thin arm through hers.

"Yes," said Ellen. "What did John Sargent say when he got home last night?"

Abby hesitated a second, looking doubtfully at Ellen. "I don't see that there is any need for you to take all this so much to heart," she said.

"What did he say?"

"Well," Abby replied, reluctantly, "I believe Mr. Lloyd wouldn't give in. Ellen Brewster, for Heaven's sake, don't look so!"

Ellen walked on, her head high, her face as white as death. Maria clung closely to her, her own lips quivering.

"What are the men going to do, do you think?" asked Ellen, presently, in a low voice.

"I don't know," replied Abby. "John Sargent seems to think they'll give in. He says he doesn't know what else they can do. The times are hard. I believe Amos Lee and Tom Peel are for striking, but he says he doesn't believe the men will support them. The amount of it all is, a man with money has got it all his own way. It's like fighting with bare hands to oppose him, and getting yourself cut, and not hurting him at all. He's got all the weapons. We simply can't go without work all winter. It is better to do with less than with nothing at all. What can a man like Willy Jones do if he hasn't any work? He and his mother would actually suffer. What could we do?"

"I don't think we ought to think so much about that," said Ellen.

"What do you think we ought to think about, for goodness' sake?"

"Whether we are doing right or not, whether we are furthering the cause of justice and humanity, or hindering it. Whether it is for good in the long run or not. There have always been martyrs; I don't see why it is any harder for us to be martyrs than for those we read about."

Sadie Peel came pressing up behind eagerly, her cheeks glowing, holding up her dress, and displaying a cheap red petticoat. "Ellen Brewster," she exclaimed, "if you dare say anything more today I'm goin' to talk. Father is tearing, though he goes around looking as if he wouldn't jump at a cannon-ball. Do, for Heaven's sake, keep still; and if you can't get what you want, take what you can get. I ain't goin' to be cheated out of my nearseal cape, nohow."

"Sadie Peel, you make me tired," cried Abby Atkins. "I don't say that I'm striking, but I'd strike for all a nearseal cape. I'm ashamed of you."

"I don't care if you be," said the girl, tossing her head. "A nearseal cape means as much to me as some other things to you. I want Ellen Brewster to hold her tongue."

"Ellen Brewster will hold her tongue or not, just as she has a mind to," responded Abby, with a snap. She did not like Sadie Peel.

"Oh, stick up for her if you want to, and get us all into trouble."

"I shall stick up for her, you can be mighty sure of that," declared Abby.

Ellen walked on as if she heard nothing of it at all, with little Maria clinging closely to her. Robert Lloyd got out of his sleigh and went upstairs just before they reached the factory, and she heard a very low, subdued mutter of execration.

"They don't mean to strike," she told herself. "They mean to submit."

All went to their tasks as usual. In a minute after the whistle blew the great pile was in the full hum of labor. Ellen stood for a few moments at her machine, then she left it deliberately, and made her way down the long room to where John Sargent stood at his bench cutting shoes, with a swift faithfulness born of long practice. She pressed close to him, while the men around stared.

"What is going to be done?" she asked, in a low voice.

Sargent turned and looked at her in a troubled fashion, and spoke in a pacific, soothing tone, as her father might have done. He was much older than Ellen.

"Now look here, child," he said, "I don't dare take the responsibility of urging all these men into starvation this kind of weather. The times are hard. Lloyd has some reason —"

Ellen walked away from him swiftly and went to the row of lasting-machines where Amos Lee and Tom Peel stood. She walked up to them and spoke in a loud, clear voice.

"You are not going to give in?" said she. "You don't mean to give in?"

Lee turned and gave her one stare, and left his machine.

"Not another stitch of work will I do under this new wage-list, so help me, God!" he proclaimed.

Tom Peel stood for a second like an automaton, staring at them both. Then he turned back to his post.

"I'm with ye," he said.

The lasters, for some occult reason, were always the most turbulent element in Lloyd's. In less than three minutes the enthusiasm of revolt had spread, and every laster had left his machine. In a half-hour more there was an exodus of workmen from Lloyd's. There were very few left in the factory. Among them were John Sargent, the laster who was a deacon and had formed one of the consulting committee, Sadie Peel, who wanted her nearseal cape, and Mamie Brady, who would do nothing which she thought would displease the foreman, Flynn.

"If father's mind to be such a fool, it's no reason why I should," said Sadie Peel, stitching determinedly away. Mamie Brady looked at Flynn, when he came up to her, with a gentle, wheedling smile. There was no one near, and she fancied that he might steal a kiss. But instead he looked at her, frowning.

"No use you tying away any longer, Mamie," he said. "The strike's on."

Chapter LIII

*T*hat was one of the strangest days which Ellen had ever passed. The enforced idleness gave her an indefinite sense of guilt. She tried to assist her mother about the household tasks, then she tried to sew on the wrappers, but she was awkward about it, from long disuse.

"Do take your book and sit down and read and rest a little, now you've got a chance," said Fanny, with sharp solicitude.

She said never one word concerning it to Ellen, but all the time she thought how Ellen had probably lost her lover. It was really doubtful which suffered the more that day, the mother or the daughter. Fanny, entirely faithful to her own husband, had yet that strange vicarious affection for her daughter's lover, and a realization of her state of mind, of which a mother alone is capable. It is like a cord of birth which is never severed. Not one shadow of sad reflection passed over the bright enthusiastic face of the girl but was passed on, as if driven by some wind of spirit, over the face of the older woman. She reflected Ellen entirely.

As for Andrew, his anxiety was as tender, and less subtle. He did not understand so clearly, but he suffered more. He was clumsy with this mystery of womanhood, but he was unremitting in his efforts to do something for the girl. Once he tiptoed up to Fanny and whispered, when Ellen was in the next room, that he hoped she hadn't made any mistake, that it seemed to him she looked pretty pale.

"Mistake?" cried Fanny, tossing her head, and staring at him proudly. "Haven't you got any spirit, and you a man, Andrew Brewster?"

"I ain't thinking about myself," said Andrew.

And he was quite right. Andrew, left to himself and his purely selfish interests, could have struck with the foremost. He would never have considered himself when it came to a question of a conscientious struggle against injustice, though he was so prone to look upon both sides of an argument that his decision would have been necessarily slow; but here was Ellen to consider, and she was more than himself. While he had been, in the depths of his heart, fiercely jealous of Robert Lloyd, yet the suspicion that his girl might suffer because of her renunciation of him hurt him to the quick. Ellen had told him all she had done in the interests of the strike, and he had no doubt that her action would effectually put an end to all possible relations between the two. He tried to imagine how a girl would feel, and being a man, and measuring all passion by the strength of his own, he exaggerated her suffering. He could eat nothing, and looked haggard. He remained out-of-doors the greater part of the day. After he had cleared his own paths, he secured a job clearing some for a more prosperous neighbor. Andrew in those days grasped eagerly at any little job which could bring him in a few pennies. He worked until dark, and when he went home he saw with a great throb of excitement the Lloyd sleigh waiting before his door.

Robert had heard from Dennison of Ellen's attitude about the strike. He had been incredulous at first, as indeed he had been incredulous about the strike. He had looked out of the office window with the gaze of one who does not believe what he sees when he had heard that retreating tramp of the workmen on the stairs.

"What does all this mean?" he said to Dennison, who entered, pale to his lips.

"It means a strike," replied Dennison. Nellie Stone rolled her pretty eyes around at the two men from under her fluff of blond hair. Flynn came in and stood in a curious, non-committal attitude.

"A strike!" repeated Robert, vaguely. "What for?"

It seemed incredible that he should ask, but he did. The calm masterfulness of his uncle, which could not even imagine opposition, had apparently descended upon him.

Both foremen stared at him. Nellie Stone smiled a little covertly.

"Why, you know you had a committee wait upon you last night, Mr. Lloyd," replied Dennison.

Flynn looked out of the window at the retreating throngs of workmen, and gave a whistle under his breath.

"Have they struck because of the wage-cutting?" asked Robert, in a curious, boyish, incredulous, aggrieved tone. Then all at once he colored violently. "Let them strike, then!" he cried. He threw himself into a chair and took up the morning paper, with its glaring headlines about the unprecedented storm, as if nothing had happened. Nellie Stone, after a sly wink at Flynn, which he did not return, began writing again. Flynn went out, and Dennison remained standing in a rather helpless attitude. A strike in Lloyd's was unprecedented, but this manner of receiving the news was more unprecedented still. The proprietor was apparently reading the morning paper with much interest, when two more foremen, heads of other departments, came hurrying in.

"I have heard already," said Robert, in response to their gasped information. Then he turned another page of the paper.

"What's to be done, sir?" said one of the newcomers, after a prolonged stare at his companion and Dennison. He was a spare man, with a fierce glimmer of blue eyes under bent brows.

"Let them strike if they want to," replied Robert.

It was in his mind to explain at length to these men his reasons for cutting the wages — for his own attitude as he knew it himself was entirely reasonable — but the pride of a proud family was up in him.

"The strike would never have been on, for the men went to work quietly enough, if it hadn't been for that Brewster girl," Dennison said, presently, but rather doubtfully. He was not quite sure how the information would be received.

Robert dropped his paper, and stared at him with angry incredulity.

"What are you talking about?" he said. "What had Miss Brewster to do with it?"

He said "Miss Brewster" with a meaning emphasis of respect, and Dennison was quick to adopt the hint.

"Oh, nothing," he replied, uneasily, "only she talked with them."

"You mean that Miss Brewster talked to the men?"

"Yes; she said a good deal yesterday, and today the men would not have struck if it had not been for her. It only needs a spark to set them off sometimes."

Robert was very pale. "Well," he said, coolly, "there is no need for you to remain longer, since the factory is shut down. You may as well go."

"The engineer is seeing to the fires, Mr. Lloyd," said Dennison.

"Very well." Robert turned to the girl at the desk. "The factory is closed, Miss Stone," he said; "there is no need for you to remain longer today. Come tomorrow at ten o'clock, and I will have something for you to do with regard to settling up accounts. There is nothing in shape now."

That afternoon Robert went to see Ellen. He could not wait until evening.

Fanny greeted him at the door, and there was the inevitable flurry about lighting the parlor stove, and presently Ellen entered.

She had changed the gown which she had worn at her factory-work for her last winter's best one. Her young face was pale, almost severe, and she met him in a way which made her seem a stranger.

Robert realized suddenly that she had, as it were, closed the door upon all their old relations. She seemed years older, and at the same time indefinably younger, since she was letting the childish impulses, which are at the heart of all of us untouched by time and experience, rise rampant and unchecked. She was following the lead of her own convictions with the terrible unswerving of a child, even in the face of her own hurt. She was, metaphorically, bumping her own head against the floor in her vain struggles for mastery over the mighty conditions of her life.

She bowed to Robert, and did not seem to see his proffered hand.

"Won't you shake hands with me?" he asked, almost humbly, although his own wrath was beginning to rise.

"No, I would rather not," she replied, with a straight look at him. Her blue eyes did not falter in the least.

"May I sit down?" he said. "I have something I would like to say to you."

"Certainly, if you wish," she replied. Then she seated herself on the sofa, with Robert opposite in the crushed-plush easy chair.

The room was still very cold, and the breath could be seen at the lips of each in white clouds. Robert had on his coat, but Ellen had nothing over her blue gown. It was on Robert's tongue to ask if she were not cold, then he refrained. The issues at stake seemed to make the question frivolous to offensiveness. He felt that any approach to tenderness when Ellen was in her present mood would invoke an indignation for which he could scarcely blame her, that he must try to meet her on equal fighting-ground.

Ellen sat before him, her little, cold hands tightly folded in her lap, her mouth set hard, her steady fire of blue eyes on his face, waiting for him to speak.

Robert felt a decided awkwardness about beginning to talk. Suddenly it occurred to him to wonder what there was to say. It amounted to this: they were in their two different positions, their two points of view — would either leave for any argument of the other? Then he wondered if he could, in the face of a girl who wore an expression like that, stoop to make an argument, for the utter blindness and deafness of her very soul to any explanation of his position was too evident in her face.

"I called to tell you, if you will permit me, how much I regret the unfortunate state of affairs at the factory," Robert said, and the girl's eyes met his as with a flash of flame.

"Why did you not prevent it, then?" asked she. Ellen had all the fire of her family, but a steadiness of manner which never deserted her. She was never violent.

"I could not prevent it," replied Robert, in a low voice.

Ellen said nothing.

"You mistake my position," said Robert. It was in his mind then to lay the matter fully before her, as he had disdained to do before the committee, but her next words deterred him.

"I understand your position very fully," said she.

Robert bowed.

"There is only one way of looking at it," said Ellen, in her inexpressibly sweet, almost fanatical voice. She tossed her head, and the fluff of fair hair over her temples caught a beam of afternoon sunlight.

"She is only a child," thought Robert, looking at her. He rose and crossed over to the sofa, and sat down beside her with a masterful impatience. "Look here, Ellen," he said, leaving all general issues for their own personal ones, "you are not going to let this come between us?"

Ellen sat stiff and straight, and made no reply.

"All this can make very little difference to you," Robert urged. "You know how I feel. That is, it can make very little difference to you if you still feel as you did. You must know that I have only been waiting — that I am eager and impatient to lift you out of it all."

Ellen faced him. "Do you think I would be lifted out of it now?" she said.

"Why, but, Ellen, you cannot —"

"Yes, I can. You do not know me."

"Ellen, you are under a total misapprehension of my position."

"No, I am not. I apprehend it perfectly."

"Ellen, you cannot let this separate us."

Ellen looked straight ahead in silence.

"You at least owe it to me to tell me if, irrespective of this, your feelings have changed," Robert said, in a low voice.

Ellen said nothing.

"You may have come to prefer someone else," said Robert.

"I prefer no one before my own, before all these poor people who are a part of my life," Ellen cried out, suddenly, her face flaming.

"Then why do you refuse to let me act for their final good? You must know what it means to have them thrown out of work in midwinter. You know the factory will remain closed for the present on account of the strike."

"I did not doubt it," said Ellen, in a hard voice. All the bitter thoughts to which she would not give utterance were in her voice.

"I cannot continue to run the factory at the present rate and meet expenses," said Robert; "in fact, I have been steadily losing for the last month." He had, after all, descended to explanation. "It amounts to my either reducing the wage-list or closing the factory altogether," he continued. "For my own good I ought to close the factory altogether, but I thought I would give the men a chance."

Robert thought by saying that he must have finally settled matters. It did not enter his head that she would really think it advisable for him to continue losing money. The pure childishness of her attitude was something really beyond the comprehension of a man of business who had come into hard business theories along with his uncle's dollars.

"What if you do lose money?" said Ellen.

Robert stared at her. "I beg your pardon?" said he.

"What if you do lose money?"

"A man cannot conduct business on such principles," replied Robert. "There would soon be no business to conduct. You don't understand."

"Yes, I do understand fully," replied Ellen.

Robert looked at her, at the clear, rosy curve of her young cheek, the toss of yellow hair above a forehead as candid as a baby's, at her little, delicate figure, and all at once such a rage of masculine insistence over all this obstinacy of reasoning was upon him that it was all he could do to keep himself from seizing her in his arms and forcing her to a view of his own horizon. He felt himself drawn up in opposition to an opponent at once too delicate, too unreasoning, and too beloved to encounter. It seemed as if the absurdity of it would drive him mad, and yet he was held to it. He tried to give a desperate wrench aside from the main point of the situation. He leaned over Ellen, so closely that his lips touched her hair.

"Ellen, let us leave all this," he pleaded; "let me talk to you. I had to wait a little while. I knew you would understand that, but let me talk to you now."

Ellen sat as rigid as marble. "I wish to talk of nothing besides the matter at hand, Mr. Lloyd," said she. "That is too close to my heart for any personal consideration to come between."

Chapter LIV

When Robert went home in the winter twilight he was more miserable than he had ever been in his life. He felt as if he had been assaulting a beautiful alabaster wall of unreason. He felt as if that which he could shatter at a blow had yet held him in defiance. The idea of this girl, of whom he had thought as his future wife, deliberately setting herself against him, galled him inexpressibly, and in spite of himself he could not quite free his mind of jealousy. On his way home he stopped at Lyman Risley's office, and found, to his great satisfaction, that he was alone, writing at his desk. Even his stenographer had gone home. He turned around when Robert entered, and looked at him with his quizzical, yet kindly, smile.

"Well, how are you, boy?" he said.

Robert dropped into the first chair, and sat therein, haunched up as in a lapse of despair and weariness.

"What is the matter?" asked Risley.

"You have heard about the trouble in the factory?"

For answer Risley held up a night's paper with glaring head-lines.

"Yes, of course it is in the papers," assented Robert, wearily.

Risley stared at him in a lazily puzzled fashion. "Well," he said, "what is it all about? Why are you so broken up about it?" Risley laid considerable emphasis on the *you*.

"Yes," cried Robert, in a sudden stress of indignation. "You look at it like all the rest. Why are all the laborers to be petted and coddled, and the capitalists held up to execration? Good Lord, isn't there any pity for the rich man without his drop of water, in the Bible or out? Are all creation born with blinders on, and can they only see before their noses?"

"What are you talking about, Robert?" said Risley, laughing a little.

"I say why should all the sympathy go to the workmen who are acting like the pig-headed idiots they are, and none for the head of the factory, who has the sharp-edged, red-hot brunt of it all to bear?"

"You wouldn't look at it that way if you were one of the poor men just out on strike such weather as this," said Risley, dryly. He glanced as he spoke at the window, which was beginning to be thickly furred with frost in spite of the heat of the office. Robert followed his gaze, and noted the spreading fairy jungle of crystalline trees and flowers on the broad field of glass.

"Do you think that is the worst thing in the world to bear?" he demanded, angrily.

"What? Cold and hunger not only for yourself, but for those you love?"

"Yes."

"Well, I think it is pretty bad," replied Risley.

"Well, suppose you had to bear that, at least for those you loved, and — and —" said the young man, lamely.

Risley remained silent, waiting.

"If I had been my uncle instead of myself I should simply have shut down with no ado," said Robert, presently, in an angry, argumentative voice.

"I suppose you would; and as it was?"

"As it was, I thought I would give them a chance. Good God, Risley, I have been running the factory at a loss for a month as it is. With this new wage-list I should no more than make expenses, if I did that. What was it to me? I did it to keep them in some sort of work. As for myself, I would much rather have shut down and done with it, but I tried to keep it running on their account, poor devils, and now I am execrated for it, and they have deliberately refused what little I could offer."

"Did you explain all this to the committee?" asked Risley.

"Explain? No! I told them my course was founded upon strict business principles, and was as much for their good as for mine. They understood. They know how hard the times are. Why, it was only last week that Weeks & McLaughlin failed, and that meant a heavy loss. I didn't explain." Then Robert hesitated and colored. "I have just explained to her," he said, with a curious hang of his head, like a boy, "and if my explanation was met in the same fashion by the others in the factory I might as well have addressed the north wind. They are all alike; they are a different race. We cannot help them, and they cannot help themselves, because they are themselves."

"You mean by her, Ellen Brewster?" Risley said.

Robert nodded gloomily.

"That is all in the paper," said Risley — "what she said to the men."

Robert made an impatient move.

"If ever there was a purely normal outgrowth, a perfect flower of her birth and environments and training, that girl is one," said Risley, with an accent of admiration.

"She is infected with the ranting idiocy of those with whom she has been brought in daily contact," said Robert; but even as he spoke he seemed to see the girl's dear young face, and his voice faltered.

"Even as you may be infected with the conservatism of those with whom you are brought in contact," said Risley, dryly.

"What a democrat you are, Risley!" said Robert, impatiently. "I believe you would make a good walking delegate."

Risley laughed. "I think I would myself," he said. "Wouldn't she listen to you, Robert?"

"She listened with such utter dissent that she might as well have been dumb. It is all over between us, Risley."

"How precipitate you are, you young folks!" said the other, good-humoredly.

"How precipitate? Do you mean to say — ?"

"I mean that you are forever thinking you are on the brink of nothingness, when the true horizon-line is too far for you ever to reach in your mortal life."

"Not in this case," said Robert.

"You know nothing about it. But if you will excuse me, it seems to me that the matter of all these people being reduced to starvation in a howling winter is of more importance than the coming together of two people in the bonds of wedlock. It is the aggregate against the individual."

"I don't deny that," said Robert, doggedly, "but I am not responsible for the starvation, and the aggregate have brought it on themselves."

"You have shut down finally?"

"Yes, I have. I would rather shut down than not, as far as I am concerned. It is distinctly for my interest. The only one objection is losing experienced workmen, but in a community like this, and in times like this, that objection is reduced to a minimum. I can hire all I want in the spring if I wish to open again. I should run a risk of losing on every order I should have to fill in the next three months, even with the reduced list. I would rather shut down than not; I only reduced the wages for them."

Robert rose as he spoke. He felt in his heart that he had gotten scant sympathy and comfort. The older man looked with pity at the young fellow's handsome, gloomy face.

"There's one thing to remember," he said.

"What?"

"All the troubles of this world are born with wings." Risley laughed, as he spoke, in his half-cynical fashion.

As Robert walked home — for there was no car due — he felt completely desolate. It seemed to him that everybody was in league against him. When he reached his uncle's splendid house and entered, he felt such an isolation from his kind in the midst of his wealth that something like an actual terror of solitude came over him.

The impecunious cousin of his aunt's who had come to her during her last illness acted as his housekeeper. There was something inexpressibly irritating about this woman, who had suffered so much, and was now nestling, with a sense of triumph over the passing of her griefs, in a luxurious home.

She asked Robert if it were true that the factory was closed, and he felt that she noted his gloomy face, and realized a greater extent of comfort from her own exemption from such questions.

"Business must be a great care," said she, and a look of utter peaceful reflection upon her own lot overspread her face.

After supper Robert went down to his aunt Cynthia's. He had not been there for a long time. The minute he entered she started up with an eagerness which had been completely foreign to her of late years.

"What is the matter, Robert?" she asked, softly. She took both his hands as she spoke, and her look in his face was full of delicate caressing.

Robert succumbed at once to this feminine solicitude, of which he had had lately so little. He felt as if he had relapsed into childhood. A sense of injury which was exquisite, as it brought along with it a sense of his demand upon love and sympathy, seized him.

"I am worried beyond endurance, Aunt Cynthia," said he.

"About the strike? I have read the night papers."

"Yes; I tried to do what was right, even at a sacrifice to myself, and —"

Cynthia had read about Ellen, but she was a woman, and she said nothing as to that.

"I tried to do what was right," Robert said, fairly broken down again.

Cynthia had seated herself, and Robert had taken a low foot-stool at her side. It came over him as he did so that it had been a favorite seat of his when a child. As for Cynthia, influenced by the appealing to the vulnerable place of her nature, she put her slim hands on her nephew's head, and actually seemed to feel his baby curls.

"Poor boy," she whispered.

Robert put both his arms around her and hid his face on her shoulder, for love is a comforter, in whatever guise.

Chapter LV

On the day after the strike Ellen went to McGuire's and to Briggs's, the two other factories in Rowe, to see if she could obtain a position; but she was not successful. McGuire had discharged some of his employés, reducing his force to its smallest possible limits, since he had fewer orders, and was trying in that way to avert the necessity of a cut in wages, and a strike or shut-down. McGuire's was essentially a union factory, as was Briggs's. Ellen would have found in either case difficulty about obtaining employment, because she did not belong to the union, if for no other reason. At Briggs's she encountered the proprietor himself in the office, and he dismissed her with a bluff, almost brutal, peremptoriness which hurt her cruelly, although she held up her head high as she left. Briggs turned to a foreman who was standing by before she was well out of hearing.

"I like that!" he said. "Mrs. Briggs read about that girl in the paper last night, and the strike wouldn't have been on at Lloyd's if it hadn't been for her. I would as soon take a lighted match into a powder-magazine."

The foreman grinned. "She's a pretty, mild-looking thing," he said; "doesn't look as if she could say boo to a goose."

"That's all you can tell," returned Briggs. "Deliver me from a light-complexioned woman. They're all the very devil. Mrs. Briggs says it's the same girl that read that composition that made such a stir at the high-school exhibition. She'd make more trouble in a factory than a dozen ordinary girls, and just now, when everything is darned ticklish-looking."

"That's so," assented the foreman, "and all the more because she's good-looking."

"I don't know what you call good-looking," returned Briggs.

He had two daughters, built upon the same heavy lines as himself and wife, and he adored them. Insensibly he regarded all more delicate feminine beauty as a disparagement of theirs. As Briggs spoke, the foreman seemed to see in the air before his eyes the faces of the two

Briggs girls, large and massive, and dull of hue, the feminine counterpart of their father's.

"Well, maybe you're right," said he, evasively. "I suppose some might call her good-looking."

As he spoke he glanced out of the window at Ellen's retreating figure, moving away over the snow-path with an almost dancing motion of youth and courage, though she was sorely hurt. The girl had scarcely ever had a hard word said to her in her whole life, for she had been in her humble place a petted darling. She had plenty of courage to bear the hard words now, but they cut deeply into her unseasoned heart.

Ellen went on past the factories to the main street of Rowe. She had no idea of giving up her efforts to obtain employment. She said to herself that she must have work. She thought of the stores, that possibly she might obtain a chance to serve as a sales-girl in one of them. She actually began at the end of the long street, and worked her way through it, with her useless inquiries, facing proprietors and superintendents, but with no success. There was not a vacancy in more than one or two, and there they wished only experienced hands. She found out that her factory record told against her. The moment she admitted that she had worked in a factory the cold shoulder was turned. The position of a shop-girl was so far below that of a sales-lady that the effect upon the superintendent was almost as if he had met an unworthy aspirant to a throne. He would smile insultingly and incredulously, even as he regarded her.

"You would find that our goods are too fine to handle after leather. Have you tried all the shops?"

At last Ellen gave that up, and started homeward. She paused once as she came opposite an intelligence office. There was one course yet open to her, but from that she shrank, not on her own account, but she dared not — knowing what would be the sufferings of her relatives should she do so — apply for a position as a servant.

As for herself, strained as she was to her height of youthful enthusiasm for a great cause, as she judged it to be, clamping her feet to the topmost round of her ladder of difficulty, she would have essayed any honest labor with no hesitation whatever. But she thought of her father and mother and grandmother, and went on past the intelligence office.

When she came to her old school-teacher's — Miss Mitchell's — house, she paused and hesitated a moment, then she went up the little path between the snow-banks to the front door, and rang the bell. The door was opened before the echoes had died away. Miss Mitchell had seen her coming, and hastened to open it. Miss Mitchell had not been teaching school for some years, having retired on a small competency of her savings. Her mortgage was paid, and there was enough for herself and her mother to live upon, with infinite care as to details of expenditure. Every postage-stamp and car-fare had its important part in the school-teacher's system of economy; but she was quite happy, and her large face wore an expression of perfect peace and placidity.

She was a woman who was not tortured by any strong, ungratified desires. Her allotment of the gifts of the gods quite satisfied her.

When Ellen entered the rather stuffy sitting room — for Miss Mitchell and her mother were jealous of any breath of cold air after the scanty fire was kindled — it was like entering into a stratum of peace. It seemed quite removed from the turmoil of her own life. The school-teacher's old mother sat in her rocker close to the stove, stouter than ever, filling up her chair with those wandering curves and vague outlines which only the overfleshy human form can assume. She looked as indefinite as a quivering jelly until one reached her face. That wore a fixedness of amiability which accentuated the whole like a high light. She had not seen Ellen for a long time, and she greeted her with delight.

"Bless your heart!" said she, in her sweet, throaty, husky voice. "Go and get her some of them cookies, Fanny, do." The old woman's faculties were not in the least impaired, although she was very old, neither had her hands lost their cunning, for she still retained her skill in cookery, and prepared the simple meals for herself and daughter, seated in a high chair at the kitchen table to roll out pastry or the famous little cookies which Ellen remembered along with her childhood.

There was something about these cookies which Miss Mitchell presently brought to her in a pretty china plate, with a little, fine-fringed napkin, which was like a morsel of solace to the girl. With the first sweet crumble of the cake on her plate, she wished to cry. Sometimes the rush of old, kindly, tender associations will overcome one who is quite equal to the strain of present emergency. But she did not cry; she ate her cookies, and confided to Miss Mitchell and her mother her desire to obtain a position elsewhere, since her factory-work had failed her. It had occurred to her that possibly Miss Mitchell, who was on the school-board, might know of a vacancy in a primary school for the coming spring term, and that she might obtain it.

"I think I know enough to teach a primary school," Ellen said.

"Of course you do, bless your heart," said old Mrs. Mitchell. "She knows enough to teach any kind of a school, don't she, Fanny? You get her a school, dear, right away."

But Miss Mitchell knew of no probable vacancy, since one young woman who had expected to be married had postponed her marriage on account of the strike in Lloyd's, and the consequent throwing out of employment of her sweetheart. Then, also, Miss Mitchell owned with hesitation, in response to Ellen's insistent question, that she supposed that the fact that she had worked in a shop might in any case interfere with her obtaining a position in a school.

"There is no sense in it, dear child, I know," she said, "but it might be so."

"Yes, I supposed so," replied Ellen, bitterly. "They would all say that a shop-girl had no right to try to teach school. Well, I'm much obliged to you, Miss Mitchell."

"What are you going to do?" Miss Mitchell asked, anxiously, following her to the door.

"I'm going to Mrs. Doty, to get some of the wrappers that mother works on, until something else turns up," replied Ellen.

"It seems a pity."

Ellen smiled bravely. "Beggars mustn't be choosers," she said. "If we can only keep along, somehow, I don't care."

There came a vehement pound of a stick on the floor, for that was the way the old woman in the sitting room commanded attention. Miss Mitchell opened the door on a crack, that she might not let in the cold air.

"What is it, mother?" she said.

"You get Ellen a school right away, Fanny."

"All right, mother; I'll do my best."

"Get her the grammar-school you used to have."

"All right, mother."

There was something about the imperative solicitude of the old woman which comforted Ellen in spite of its futility as she went on her way. The good-will of another human soul, even when it cannot be resolved into active benefits, has undoubtedly a mighty force of its own. Ellen, with the sweet of the cookies still lingering on her tongue, and the sweet of the old woman's kindness in her soul, felt refreshed as if by some subtle spiritual cake and wine. She even went to the door of Mrs. Doty's house. Mrs. Doty was the woman who let out wrappers to her impecunious neighbors with an undaunted heart. She had no difficulty there. The demand for cheap wrappers was not on the wane, even in the hard times. When Ellen reached her grandmother's house, with a great parcel under her arm, Mrs. Zelotes opened her side door.

"What have you got there, Ellen Brewster?" she called out sharply.

"Some wrappers," replied Ellen, cheerfully.

"Are you going to work on wrappers?"

"Yes, grandma."

The door was shut with a loud report.

When Ellen entered the house and the sitting room, her mother looked up from a pink wrapper which she was finishing.

"What have you got there?" she demanded.

"Some wrappers."

"Why, I haven't finished the last lot."

"These are for me to make, mother."

Andrew got up and went out of the room. Fanny shut her mouth hard, and drew her thread through with a jerk.

"Well," she said, in a second, "take off your things, and let me show you how to start on them. There's a little knack about it."

Chapter LVI

*T*hat was a hard winter for Rowe. Aside from the financial stress, the elements seemed to conspire against the people who were so ill-prepared to meet their fury. It was the coldest winter which had been known for years; coal was higher, and the poor people had less coal to burn. Storm succeeded storm; then, when there came a warm spell, there was an epidemic of the grippe, and doctors' bills to pay and quinine to buy — and quinine was very dear.

The Brewsters managed to keep up the interest on the house mortgage, but their living expenses were reduced to the smallest possible amount. In those days there was no wood laid ready for kindling in the parlor stove, since there was neither any wood to spare nor expectation of Robert's calling. Ellen and her mother sat in the dining room, for even the sitting room fire had been abolished, and they heated the dining room whenever the weather admitted it from the kitchen stove, and worked on the wrappers for their miserable pittance.

The repeated storms were in a way a boon to Andrew, since he got many jobs clearing paths, and thus secured a trifle towards the daily expenses.

In those days Mrs. Zelotes watched the butcher-cart anxiously when it stopped before her son's house, and she knew just what a tiny bit of meat was purchased, and how seldom. On the days when the cart moved on without any consultation at the tail thereof, the old woman would buy an extra portion, cook it, and carry some over to her son's.

Times grew harder and harder. Few of the operatives who had struck in Lloyd's succeeded in obtaining employment elsewhere, and most of them joined the union to enable them to do so. There was actual privation. One evening, when the strike was some six weeks old, Abby Atkins came over in a pouring rain to see Ellen. There were a number of men in the dining room that night. Amos Lee and Frank Dixon were among them. It was a singular thing that Andrew, taking, as he had done, no active part in any rebellion against authority, should have come to see his house the headquarters for the rallies of dissension. Men seemed to come to Andrew Brewster's for the sake of bolstering themselves up in their hard position of defiance against tremendous odds, though he sat by and seldom said a word. As for Ellen, she and her mother on these occasions sat out in the kitchen, sewing on the endless seams of the endless wrappers. Sometimes it seemed to the girl as if wrappers enough were being made to clothe not only the present, but future generations of poor women. She seemed to see whole armies of hopeless, overburdened women, all arrayed in these slouching garments, crowding the foreground of the world.

That evening little Amabel, who had developed a painful desire to make herself useful, having divined the altered state of the family finances, was pulling out basting-threads, with a puckered little face bent over her work. She was a very thin child, but there was an incisive vitality in her, and somehow Fanny and Ellen contrived to keep her prettily and comfortably clothed.

"I've got to do my duty by poor Eva's child, if I starve," Fanny often said.

When the side door opened, Ellen and her mother thought it was another man come to swell the company in the dining room.

"It beats all how men like to come and sit round and talk over matters; for my part, I ain't got any time to talk; I've got to work," remarked Fanny.

"That's so," rejoined Ellen. She looked curiously like her mother that night, and spoke like her. In her heart she echoed the sarcasm to the full. She despised those men for sitting hour after hour in a store, or in the house of some congenial spirit, or standing on a street corner, and talking — talking, she was sure, to no purpose. As for herself, she had done what she thought right; she had, as it were, cut short the thread of her happiness of life for the sake of something undefined and rather vague, and yet as mighty in its demands for her allegiance as God. And it was done, and there was no use in talking about it. She had her wrappers to make. However, she told herself, extenuatingly, "Men can't sew, so they can't work evenings. They are better off talking here than they would be in the billiard-saloon." Ellen, at that time of her life, had a slight, unacknowledged feeling of superiority over men of her own class. She regarded them very much as she regarded children, with a sort of tolerant good-will and contempt. Now, suddenly, she raised her head and listened. "That isn't another man, it's a woman — it's Abby," she said to her mother.

"She wouldn't come out in all this rain," replied Fanny. As she spoke, a great, wind-driven wash of it came over the windows.

"Yes, it is," said Ellen, and she jumped up and opened the dining room door.

Abby had entered, as was her custom, without knocking. She had left her dripping umbrella in the entry, and her old hat was flattened on to her head with wet, and several damp locks of her hair straggled from under it and clung to her thin cheeks. She still held up her wet skirts around her, as she had held them out-of-doors, but she was gesticulating violently with her other hand. She was repeating what she had said before. Ellen had heard her indistinctly through the door.

"Yes, I mean just what I say," she cried. "Get up and go to work, if you are men! Stop hanging around stores and corners, and talking about the tyranny of the rich, and go to work, and make them pay you something for it, anyhow. This has been kept up long enough. Get up and go to work, if you don't want those belonging to you to starve."

Abby caught sight of Ellen, pale and breathless, in the door, with her mother looking over her shoulder, and she addressed her with renewed violence. "Come here, Ellen," she said, "and put yourself on my side. We've got to give in."

"You go away," cried little Amabel, in a shrill voice, looking around Ellen's arm; but nobody paid any attention to her.

"I never will," returned Ellen, with a great flash, but her voice trembled.

"You've got to," said Abby. "I tell you there's no other way."

"I'll die before I give up," cried Lee, in a loud, threatening voice.

"I'm with ye," said Tom Peel.

Dixon and the young laster who sat beside him looked at each other, but said nothing. Dixon wrinkled his forehead over his pipe.

"Then you'd better go to work quick, before some that I know of, who are enough sight better worth saving than you are, starve," replied

Abby, unshrinkingly. "If I could I would go to Lloyd's and open it on my own account tomorrow. I believe in bravery, but nothing except fools and swine jump over precipices."

Abby passed through the room, sprinkling rain-drops from her drenched skirts, and went into the kitchen with Ellen. Fanny cast an angry glance at her, then a solicitous one at her dripping garments.

"Abby Atkins, you haven't got any rubbers on," said she.

"Rubbers!" repeated Abby.

"You just slip off those wet skirts, and Amabel will fetch you down Ellen's old black petticoat and brown dress. Amabel —"

But Abby seated herself peremptorily before the kitchen stove and extended one soaked little foot in its shabby boot. "I'm past thinking or caring about wet skirts," said she. "Good Lord, what do wet skirts matter? We can't make wrappers any longer. We had to sell the sewing-machine yesterday to pay the rent or be turned out, and we haven't got a thing to eat in the house except potatoes and a little flour. We haven't had any meat for a week. Nice fare for a man like poor father and a girl like Maria! We have come down to the kitchen fire like you, but we can't keep it burning as late as this. The rest went to bed an hour ago to keep warm. Maria has got more cold. She did seem better one spell, but now she's worse again. Our chamber is freezing cold, and we haven't had a fire in it since the strike. John Sargent has ransacked every town within twenty miles for work, but he can't get any, and his sick sister keeps sending to him for money. He looks as if he was just about done, too. He went off somewhere after supper. A great supper! He don't smoke a pipe nowadays. Father don't get the medicine he ought to have, and that cold spell he just about perished for a little whiskey. The bedroom was like ice with no fire in the sitting room, and he didn't sleep warm. It's one awful thing after another happening. Did you know Mamie Brady took laudanum last night?"

"Good land!" said Fanny.

"Yes, she did. Ed Flynn has been playing fast and loose with her for a long time, and she's none too well balanced, and when it came to her not having enough to eat, and to keep her warm, and her mother nagging at her all the time — you know what an awful hard woman her mother is — she got desperate. She gulped it down when the last car went past and Ed Flynn hadn't come; she had been watchin' out for him; then she told her mother, and her mother shook her, then run for Dr. Fox, and he called in Dr. Lord, and they worked with a stomach-pump till morning, and she isn't out of danger yet. Then that isn't all. Willy Jones's mother is failing. He was over to our house last evening, telling us about it, and he fairly cried, poor boy. He said he actually could not get her what she needed to make her comfortable this awful winter. It was all he could do with odd jobs to keep the roof over their heads, that she hadn't actually enough to eat and keep her warm. It seemed as if he would die when he told about it. And that isn't all. Those little Blake children next door are fairly starving. They are going around to the neighbors' swill-buckets — it's a fact — just like little hungry dogs, and it's precious little they find in them. Mrs. Wetherhed has let her sewing-machine go, and Edward Morse is going to be sold out for taxes. And that isn't all." Abby lowered her voice a little. She cast an apprehensive glance at the door of the other room, and at Amabel. "Mamie Bemis has gone to the bad. I had it straight. She's in Boston. She didn't have enough to pay for her board, and got desperate. I know her sister did wrong, but that was no reason why she should have, and I don't believe she would if it hadn't been for the strike. It's all on account of the strike. There's no use talking: before the sparrow flies in the eyes of the tiger, he'd better count the cost."

Fanny, quite white, stood staring from Abby to Ellen, and back again.

Amabel was holding fast to a fold of Ellen's skirt. Ellen looked rigid.

"I knew it all before," she said, in a low voice.

Suddenly Abby jumped up and caught the other girl in a fierce embrace. "Ellen," she sobbed — "Ellen, isn't there any way out of it? I can't see —"

Ellen freed herself from Abby with a curious imperative yet gentle motion, then she opened the door into the other room again. The loud clash of voices hushed, and every man faced towards her standing on the threshold, with her mother and Abby and little Amabel in the background. "I want to say to you all," said Ellen, in a clear voice, "that I think I did wrong. I have been wondering if I had not for some time, and growing more and more certain. I did not count the cost. All I thought of was the principle, but the cost is a part of the principle in this world, and it has to be counted in with it. I see now. I don't think the strike ought ever to have been. It has brought about too much suffering upon those who were not responsible for it, who did not choose it of their own free will. There are children starving, and people dying and breaking their hearts. We have brought too much upon ourselves and others. I am sorry I said what I did in the shop that day, if I influenced anyone. Now I am not going to strike any longer. Let us all accept Mr. Lloyd's terms, and go back to work."

But Ellen's voice was drowned out in a great shout of wrath and dissent from Lee. He directly leaped to the conclusion that the girl took this attitude on account of Lloyd, and his jealousy, which was always smoldering, flamed.

"Well, I guess not!" he shouted. "I rather guess not! I've struck, and I'm going to stay struck! I ain't goin' to back out because a girl likes the boss, damn him!"

Andrew and the young laster rose and moved quietly before Ellen. Tom Peel said nothing, but he grinned imperturbably.

"I ain't had a bit of tobacco, and the less said about what I've had to eat the better," Lee went on, in a loud, threatening voice, "but I ain't going to give up. No, miss; you've het up the fightin' blood in me, and it ain't so easy coolin' of it down."

The door opened, and Granville Joy entered. He had knocked several times, but nobody had heard him. He looked inquiringly from one to another, then moved beside Andrew and the laster.

Dixon got up. "It looks to me as if it was too soon to be giving up now," he said.

"It's easy for a man who's got nobody dependent upon him to talk," cried Abby.

"I won't give up!" cried Dixon, looking straight at Ellen, and ignoring Abby.

"That's so," said Lee. "We don't give up our rights for bosses, or bosses' misses."

As he said that there was a concerted movement of Andrew, the laster, and Granville. Granville was much slighter than Lee, but suddenly his right arm shot out, and the other man went down like a log. Andrew followed him up with a kick.

"Get out of my house," he shouted, "and never set foot in it again! Out with ye!"

Lee was easily cowed. He did not attempt to make any resistance, but gathered himself up, muttering, and moved before the three into the entry, where he had left his coat and hat. Dixon and Peel followed him. When the door was shut, Ellen turned to the others, with a quieting hand on Amabel's head, who was clinging to her, trembling.

"I think it will be best to talk to John Sargent," said she. "I think a committee had better be appointed to wait upon Mr. Lloyd again, and ask him to open the factory. I'm not going to strike any longer."

"I'm sure I'm not," said Abby.

"Abby and I are not going to strike any longer," said Ellen, in an indescribably childlike way, which yet carried enormous weight with it.

Chapter LVII

*E*llen had not arrived at her decision with regard to the strike as suddenly as it may have seemed. All winter, ever since the strike, Ellen had been wondering, not whether the principle of the matter was correct or not, that she never doubted; she never swerved in her belief concerning the cruel tyranny of the rich and the helpless suffering of the poor, and their good reason for making a stand, but she doubted more and more the wisdom of it. She used to sit for hours up in her chamber after her father and mother had gone to bed, wrapped up in an old shawl against the cold, resting her elbows on the windowsill and her chin on her two hands, staring out into the night, and reflecting. Her youthful enthusiasm carried her like a leaping-pole to conclusions beyond her years. "I wonder," she said to herself, "if, after all, this inequality of possessions is not a part of the system of creation, if the righting of them is not beyond the flaming sword of the Garden of Eden? I wonder if the one who tries to right them forcibly is not meddling, and usurping the part of the Creator, and bringing down wrath and confusion not only upon his own head, but upon the heads of others? I wonder if it is wise, in order to establish a principle, to make those who have no voice in the matter suffer for it — the helpless women and children?" She even thought with a sort of scornful sympathy of Sadie Peel, who could not have her nearseal cape, and had not wished to strike. She reflected, as she had done so many times before, that the world was very old — thousands of years old — and inequality was as old as the world. Might it not even be a condition of its existence, the shifting of weights which kept it to its path in the scheme of the universe? And yet always she went back to her firm belief that the strikers were right, and always, although she loved Robert Lloyd, she denounced him. Even when it came to her abandoning her position with regard to the strike, she had not the slightest thought of effecting thereby a reconciliation with Robert.

For the first time, that night when she had gone to bed, after announcing her determination to go back to work, she questioned her affection for Robert. Before she had always admitted it to herself with a sort of shamed and angry dignity. "Other women feel so about men, and why should I not?" she had said; "and I shall never fail to keep the feeling behind more important things." She had accepted the fact of it with childlike straightforwardness as she accepted all other facts of life, and now she wondered if she really did care for him so much. She thought over and over everything Abby had said, and saw plainly before her mental vision those poor women parting with their cherished possessions, the little starving children snatching at the refuse-buckets at the neighbors' back doors. She saw with incredulous shame, and something between pity and scorn, Mamie Bemis, who had gone wrong, and Mamie Brady, who had taken her foolish, ill-balanced life in her own hands. She remembered every word which she had said to the men on the morning of the strike, and how they had started up and left their machines. "I did it all," she told herself. "I am responsible for it all — all this suffering, for those hungry little children, for that possible death, for the ruin of another girl." Then she told herself, with a stern sense of justice, that back of her responsibility came Robert Lloyd's. If he had not cut the wages it would never have been. It seemed to her that she almost hated him, and that she could not wait to strive to undo the harm which she had done. She could not wait for morning to come.

She lay awake all night in a fever of impatience. When she went downstairs her eyes were brilliant, there were red spots on her cheeks, her lips were tense, her whole face looked as if she were strained for some leap of action. She took hold of everything she touched with a hard grip. Her father and mother kept watching her anxiously. Directly after breakfast Ellen put on her hat and coat.

"What are you going to do?" asked Fanny.

"I am going over to see John Sargent, and ask him to get some other men and go to see Mr. Lloyd, and tell him we are willing to go to work again," replied Ellen.

Ellen discovered, when she reached the Atkins house, that John Sargent had already resolved upon his course of action.

"The first thing he said when he came in last night was that he couldn't stand it any longer, and he was going to see the others, and go to Lloyd, and ask him to open the shop on his own terms," said Abby. "I told him how we felt about it."

"Yes, I am ready to go back whenever the factory is opened," said Ellen. "I am glad he has gone."

Ellen did not remain long. She was anxious to return and finish some wrappers she had on hand. Abby promised to go over and let her know the result of the interview with Lloyd.

It was not until evening that Abby came over, and John Sargent with her. Lloyd had not been at home in the morning, and they had been forced to wait until late afternoon. The two entered the dining room, where Ellen and her mother sat at work.

Abby spoke at once, and to the point. "Well," said she, "the shop's going to be opened tomorrow."

"On what terms?" asked Ellen.

"On the boss's, of course," replied Abby, in a hard voice.

"It's the only thing to do," said Sargent, with a sort of stolid assertion. "If we are willing to be crushed under the Juggernaut of principle, we haven't any right to force others under, and that's what we are doing."

"Bread without butter is better than no bread at all," said Abby. "We've got to live in the sphere in which Providence has placed us." The girl said "Providence" with a sarcastic emphasis.

Andrew was looking at Sargent. "Do you think there will be any trouble?" he asked.

Sargent hesitated, with a glance at Fanny. "I don't know; I hope not," said he. "Lee and Dixon are opposed to giving in, and they are talking hard tonight in the store. Then some of the men have joined the union since the strike, and of course they swear by it, because it has been helping them, and they won't approve of giving up. But I doubt if there will be much trouble. I guess the majority want to go to work, even the union men. The amount of it is, it has been such a tough winter it has taken the spirit out of the poor souls." Sargent, evidently, in yielding was resisting himself.

"You don't think there will be any danger?" Fanny said, anxiously, looking at Ellen.

"Oh no, there's no danger for the girls, anyhow. I guess there's enough men to look out for them. There's no need for you to worry, Mrs. Brewster."

"Mr. Lloyd did not offer to do anything better about the wages?" asked Ellen.

Sargent shook his head.

"Catch him!" said Abby, bitterly.

Ellen had a feeling as if she were smiting in the face that image of Robert which always dwelt in her heart.

"Well," said Abby, with a mirthless laugh, "there's one thing: according to the Scriptures, it is as hard for the rich man to get into heaven as it is for the poor men to get into their factories."

"You don't suppose there will be any danger?" Fanny said again, anxiously.

"Danger — no; who's afraid of Amos Lee and a few like him?" cried Abby, contemptuously; "and Nahum Beals is safe. He's going to be tried next month, they say, but they'll make it imprisonment for life, because they think he wasn't in his right mind. If he was here we might be afraid, but there's nobody now that will do anything but talk. I ain't afraid. I'm going to march up to the shop tomorrow morning and go to work, and I'd like to see anybody stop me."

However, before they left, John Sargent spoke aside with Andrew, and told him of a plan for the returning workmen to meet at the corner of a certain street, and go in a body to the factory, and suggested that there might be pickets posted by the union men, and Andrew resolved to go with Ellen.

The next morning the rain had quite ceased, and there was a faint something, rather a reminiscence than a suggestion, of early spring in the air. People caught themselves looking hard at the elm branches to see if they were acquiring the virile fringe of spring or if their eyes deceived them, and wondered, with respect to the tips of maple and horse-chestnut branches, whether or not they were swollen red and glossy. Sometimes they sniffed incredulously when a soft gust of south wind seemed laden with fresh blossom fragrance.

"I declare, if I didn't know better, I should think I smelled apple blossoms," said Maria.

"Stuff!" returned Abby. She was marching along with an alert, springy motion of her lean little body. She was keenly alive to the situation, and scented something besides apple blossoms. She had tried to induce Maria to remain at home. "I don't know but there'll be trouble, and if there is, you'll be just in the way," she told her before they left the house, but not in their parents' hearing.

"Oh, I don't believe there'll be any. Folks will be too glad to get back to work," replied Maria. She had a vein of obstinacy, gentle as she was; then, too, she had a reason which no one suspected for wishing to be present. She would not yield when John Sargent begged her privately not to go. It was just because she was afraid there might be trouble, and he was going to be in it, that she could not bear to stay at home herself.

Andrew had insisted upon accompanying Ellen in spite of her remonstrances. "I've got an errand down to the store," he said, evasively; but Ellen understood.

"I don't think there is any danger, and there wouldn't be any danger for me — not for the girls, sure," she said; but he persisted.

"Don't you say a word to your mother to scare her," he whispered. But they had not been gone long before Fanny followed them, Mrs. Zelotes watching her furtively from a window as she went by.

All the returning employés met, as agreed upon, at the corner of a certain street, and marched in a solid body towards Lloyd's. The men insisted upon placing the girls in the center of this body, although some of them rebelled, notably Sadie Peel. She was on hand, laughing and defiant.

"I guess I ain't afraid," she proclaimed. "Father's keepin' on strikin', but I guess he won't see his own daughter hurt; and now I'm goin' to have my nearseal cape, if it is late in the season. They're cheaper now, that's one good thing. On some accounts the strike has been a lucky thing for me." She marched along, swinging her arms jauntily. Ellen and Maria and Abby were close together. Andrew was on the right of Ellen, Granville Joy behind; the young laster, who had called so frequently evenings, was with him. John Sargent and Willy Jones were on the left. They all walked in the middle of the street like an army. It was covertly understood that there might be trouble. Some of the younger men from time to time put hands on their pockets, and a number carried stout sticks.

The first intimation of disturbance came when they met an electric-car, and all moved to one side to let it pass. The car was quite full of people going to another town, some thirty miles distant, to work in a large factory there. Nearly every man and woman on the car belonged to the union.

As this car slid past a great yell went up from the occupants; men on the platforms swung their arms in execration and derision. "Sc-ab, sc-ab!" they called. A young fellow leaped from the rear platform, caught up a stone and flung it at the returning Lloyd men, but it went wide of its mark. Then he was back on the platform with a running jump, and one of the Lloyd men threw a stone, which missed him. The yell of "Scab, scab!" went up with renewed vigor, until it died out of hearing along with the rumble of the car.

"Sometimes I wish I had joined the union and stuck it out," said one of the Lloyd men, gloomily.

"For the Lord's sake, don't show the white feather now!" cried a young fellow beside him, who was striding on with an eager, even joyous outlook. He had fighting blood, and it was up, and he took a keen delight in the situation.

"It's easy to talk," grumbled the other man. "I don't know but all our help lies in the union, and we've been a pack of fools not to go in with them, because we hoped Lloyd would weaken and take us back. He hasn't weakened; we've had to. Good God, them that's rich have it their own way!"

"I'd have joined the union in a minute, and got a job, and got my nearseal cape, if it hadn't been for father," said Sadie Peel, with a loud laugh. "But, my land! if father'd caught me joinin' the union I dun'no' as there would have been anything left of me to wear the cape."

They all marched along with no disturbance until they reached the corner of the street into which they had to turn in order to approach Lloyd's. There they were confronted by a line of pickets, stationed there by the union, and the real trouble began. Yells of "Scab, scab!" filled the air.

"Good land, I ain't no more of a scab than you be!" shrieked Sadie Peel, in a loud, angry voice. "Scab yourself! Touch me if you dasse!"

Many young men among the returning force had stout sticks in their hands. Granville Joy was one of them. Andrew, who was quite unarmed, pressed in before Ellen. Granville caught him by the arm and tried to draw him back.

"Look here, Mr. Brewster," he said, "you keep in the background a little. I am young and strong, and here are Sargent and Mendon. You'd better keep back."

But Ellen, with a spring which was effectual because so utterly uncalculated, was before Granville and her father, and them all. She reasoned it out in a second that she was responsible for the strike, and that she would be in the front of whatever danger there was in consequence. Her slight little figure passed them all before they knew what she was doing. She was in the very front of the little returning army. She saw the threatening faces of the pickets; she half turned, and waved an arm of encouragement, like a general in a battle. "Strike if you want to," she cried out, in her sweet young voice. "If you want to kill a girl for going back to work to save herself and her friends from starvation, do it. I am not afraid! But kill me, if you must kill anybody, because I am the one that started the strike. Strike if you want to."

The opposing force moved aside with an almost imperceptible motion. Ellen looked like a beautiful child, her light hair tossed around her rosy face, her eyes full of the daring of perfect confidence. She in reality did not feel one throb of fear. She passed the picket-line, and turned instinctively and marched backward with her blue eyes upon them all. Abby Atkins sprang forward to Ellen's side, with Sargent and Joy and Willy Jones and Andrew. Andrew kept calling to Ellen to come back, but she did not heed him.

The little army was several rods from the pickets before a shot rang out, but that was fired into the air. However, it was followed by a fierce clamor of "Scab" and a shower of stones, which did little harm. The

Lloyds marched on without a word, except from Sadie Peel. She turned round with a derisive shout.

"Scab yourselves!" she shrieked. "You dassen't fire at me. You're scabs yourselves, you be!"

"Scabs, scabs!" shouted the men, moving forward.

"Scab yourself!" shouted Sadie Peel.

Abby Atkins caught hold of her arm and shook her violently. "Shut up, can't you, Sadie Peel," she said.

"I'll shut up when I get ready, Abby Atkins! I ain't afraid of them if you be. They dassen't hit me. Scab, scab!" the girl yelled back, with a hysteric laugh.

"Don't that girl know anything?" growled a man behind her.

"Shut up, Sadie Peel," said Abby Atkins.

"I ain't afraid if you be, and I won't shut up till I get ready, for you or anybody else. I'm goin' to have my nearseal cape! Hi!"

"I ain't afraid," said Abby, contemptuously, "but I've got sense."

Maria pressed close to Sadie Peel. "Please do keep still, Sadie," she pleaded. "Let us get into the factory as quietly as we can. Think, if anybody was hurt."

"I ain't afraid," shrieked the girl, with a toss of her red fringe, and she laughed like a parrot. Abby Atkins gripped her arm so fiercely that she made her cry out with pain. "If you don't keep still!" she said, threateningly.

Willy Jones was walking as near as he could, and he carried his right arm half extended, as if to guard her. Now and then Abby turned and gave him a push backward.

"They won't trouble us girls, and you might as well let us and the men that have sticks go first," she said in a whisper.

"If you think —" began the young fellow, coloring.

"Oh, I know you ain't afraid," said Abby, "but you've got your mother to think of, and there's no use in running into danger."

The pickets were gradually left behind; they were, in truth, half-hearted. Many of them had worked in Lloyd's, and had small mind to injure their old comrades. They were not averse to a great show of indignation and bluster, but when it came to more they hesitated.

Presently the company came into the open space before Lloyd's. Robert and Lyman Risley and several foremen were standing at the foot of the stairs. The windows of the factory were filled with faces, and derisive cries came from them. Lloyd's tall shaft of chimney was plumed with smoke. The employés advanced towards the stairs, when suddenly Amos Lee, Dixon, and a dozen others appeared, coming with a rush from around a corner of the building, and again the air was filled with the cry of "Scab!" Ellen and Abby linked arms and sprang forward before the men with an impetuous rush, with Joy and Willy Jones and Andrew following. Ellen, as she rushed on towards the factory stairs, was conscious of no fear at all, but rather of a sort of exaltation of courage. It did not really occur to her that she could be hurt, that it could be in the heart of Lee or Dixon, or any of them, actually to harm her. She was throbbing and intense with indignation and resolution. Into that factory to her work she was bound to go. All that intimidated her in the least was the fear for her father. She rushed as fast as she could that her father might not get before her and be hurt in some way.

"Scab! scab!" shouted Lee and the others.

"Scab yourself!" shrieked Sadie Peel. Her father was one of the opposing party, and that gave her perfect audacity. "Look out you don't hit me, dad," she cried to him. "I'm goin' to get my nearseal cape. Don't you hit your daughter, Tom Peel!" She raced on with a sort of hoppity-skip. She caught a young man near her by the arm and forced him into the same dancing motion.

They were at the foot of the stairs, when Robert, watching, saw Lee with a pistol in his hand aim straight at Ellen. He sprang before her, but Risley was nearer, and the shot struck him. When Risley fell, a great cry, it would have been difficult to tell whether of triumph or horror, went up from the open windows of the other factories, and men came swarming out. Lee and his companions vanished.

A great crowd gathered around Risley until the doctors came and ordered them away, and carried him in the ambulance to the hospital. He was not dead, but evidently very seriously injured.

When the ambulance had rolled out of sight, the Lloyd employés entered the factory, and the hum of machinery began.

Fanny and Andrew stood together before the factory after Ellen had entered. Andrew had started when he had seen his wife.

"You here?" he said.

"I rather guess I'm here," returned Fanny. "Do you s'pose I was goin' to stay at home, and not know whether you and her were shot dead or not?"

"I guess it's all safe now," said Andrew. He was very pale. He looked at the blood-stained place where Lyman Risley had lain. "It's awful work," he said.

"Who did it?" asked Fanny, sharply. "I heard the shot just before I got here."

"I don't know for sure, and guess it's better I don't," replied Andrew, sternly.

Then all at once as they stood there a woman came up with a swift, gliding motion and a long trail of black skirts straight to Fanny, who was the only woman there. There were still a great many men and boys standing about. The woman, Cynthia Lennox, caught Fanny's arm with a nervous grip. Her finely cut face was very white under the nodding plumes of her black bonnet.

"Is he in there?" she asked, in a strained voice, pointing to the shop.

Fanny stared at her. She was half dazed. She did not know whether she was referring to the wounded man or Robert.

Andrew was quicker in his perceptions.

"They carried him off to the hospital in the ambulance," he told her. Then he added, as gently as if he had been addressing Ellen: "I guess he wasn't hurt so very bad. He came to before they took him away."

"You don't know anything about it," Fanny said, sharply. "I heard them say something about his eyes."

"His eyes!" gasped Cynthia. She held tightly to Fanny, who looked at her with a sudden passion of sympathy breaking through her curiosity.

"Oh, I guess he wasn't hurt so very bad; he *did* come to. I heard him speak," she said, soothingly. She laid her hard hand over Cynthia's slim one.

"They took him to the hospital?"

"Yes, in the ambulance."

"Is — my nephew in there?"

"No; he went with him."

Cynthia looked at the other woman with an expression of utter anguish and pleading.

"Look here," said Fanny; "the hospital ain't very far from here. Suppose we go up there and ask how he is? We could call out your nephew."

"Will you go with me?" asked Cynthia, with a heart-breaking gasp.

If Ellen could have seen her at that moment, she would have recognized her as the woman whom she had known in her childhood. She was an utter surprise to Fanny, but her sympathy leaped to meet her need like the steel to the magnet.

"Of course I will," she said, heartily.

"I would," said Andrew — "I would go with her, Fanny."

"Of course I will," said Fanny; "and you had better go home, I guess, Andrew, and see how I left the kitchen fire. I don't know but the dampers are all wide open."

Fanny and Cynthia hastened in one direction towards the hospital, and Andrew towards home; but he paused for a minute, and looked thoughtfully up at the humming pile of Lloyd's. The battle was over and the strike was ended. He drew a great sigh, and went home to see to the kitchen fire.

Chapter LVIII

Lyman Risley was very seriously injured. There was, as the men had reported, danger for his eyes. When Robert was called into the reception-room of the hospital to see his aunt, he scarcely recognized her. Her soft, white hair was tossed about her temples, her cheeks were burning. She ran up to him like an eager child and clutched his arm.

"How is he?" she demanded. "Tell me quick!"

"They are doing everything they can for him. Why, don't, poor Aunt Cynthia!"

"His eyes, they said —"

"I hope he will come out all right. Don't, dear Aunt Cynthia." The young man put his arm around his aunt and spoke soothingly, blushing like a girl before this sudden revelation of an under-stratum of delicacy in a woman's heart.

Cynthia lost control of herself completely; or, rather, the true self of her rose uppermost, shattering the surface ice of her reserve. "Oh," she said — "oh, if he — if he is — blind, if he is — I — I — will lead him everywhere all the rest of his life; I will, Robert."

"Of course you will, dear Aunt Cynthia," replied Robert, soothingly.

Suddenly Cynthia's face took on a new expression. She looked at Robert, deadly pale, and her jaw dropped. "He will not — die," she said, with stiff lips. "It is not as bad as that?"

"Oh no, no; I am sure he will not," Robert cried, wonderingly and pityingly. "Don't, Aunt Cynthia."

"If he dies," she said — "if he dies — and he has loved me all this time, and I have never done anything for him — I cannot bear it; I will not bear it; I will not, Robert!"

"Oh, he isn't going to die, Aunt Cynthia."

"I want to go to him," she said. "I *will* go to him."

Robert looked helplessly from her to Fanny. "I am afraid you can't just now, Aunt Cynthia," he replied.

Fanny came resolutely to his assistance. "Of course you can't, Miss Lennox," she said. "The doctors won't let you see him now. You would do him more harm than good. You don't want to do him harm!"

"No, I don't want to do him harm," returned Cynthia, in a wailing, hysterical voice. She threw herself down upon a sofa and began sobbing like a child, with her face hidden.

A young doctor entered and stood looking at her.

Robert turned to him. "It is my aunt, and she is agitated over Mr. Risley's accident," he said, coloring a little.

Instantly the young physician's face lost its expression of astonishment and assumed the soothing gloss of his profession. "Oh, my dear Miss Lennox," he said, "there is no cause for agitation, I assure you. Everything is being done for Mr. Risley."

"Will he be blind?" gasped Cynthia, with a great vehemence of woe, which seemed to gainsay the fact of her years. It seemed as if such an outburst of emotion could come only from a child all unacquainted with grief and unable to control it.

The young doctor laughed blandly. "Blind? No, indeed," he replied. "He might have been blind had this happened twenty-five years ago, but with the resources of the present day it is a different matter. Pray don't alarm yourself, dear Miss Lennox."

"Can you call a carriage for my aunt?" asked Robert. He went close to Cynthia and laid a hand on her slender shoulder. "I am going to have a carriage come for you, and perhaps Mrs. Brewster will be willing to go home with you in it."

"Of course I will," replied Fanny.

"You hear what Dr. Payson says, that there is nothing to be alarmed about," Robert said, in a low voice, with his lips close to his aunt's ear.

Cynthia made no resistance, but when the carriage arrived, and she was being driven off, with Fanny by her side, she called out of the window with a fierce shamelessness of anxiety, "Robert, you must come and tell me how he is this afternoon, or I shall come back here and see him myself."

"Yes, I will, Aunt Cynthia," he replied, soothingly. He met the doctor's curious eyes when he turned. The young man had a gossiping mind, but he forbore to say what he thought, which was to the effect that — why under the heavens, if that woman cared as much as that for that man, she had not married him, instead of letting him dangle after her so many years? But he merely said:

"There is no use in saying anything to excite a woman further when she is in such a state of mind, but —" Then he paused significantly.

"You think the chances of his keeping his eyesight are poor?" said Robert.

"Mighty poor," replied the doctor.

Robert stood still, with his pale, shocked face bent upon the carpet. He could not seem to comprehend at once the enormity of it all; his mind was grasping at and trying to assimilate the horrible fact with an infinite pain.

"Have they got the man that did it?" asked the doctor.

"I don't know. I had to see to poor Risley," replied Robert. "I hope to God they have." Then all at once he thought, with keen anxiety, of Ellen. Who knew what new tragedy had happened? "I must go back to the factory," he said, hurriedly. "I will be back here in an hour or so, and see how he is getting on. For Heaven's sake, do all you can!"

Robert was desperately impatient to be back at the factory. He was full of vague anxiety about Ellen. He could not forget that the shot which had hit poor Risley had been meant for her, and he remembered the look on the man's face as he aimed. He found a carriage at the street corner, and jumped in, and bade the man drive fast.

When Robert entered the great building, and felt the old vibration of machinery, he had a curious sensation, one which he had never before had and which he had not expected. For the first time in his life he knew what it was to have a complete triumph of his own will over his fellow-men. He had gotten his own way. All this army of workmen, all this machinery of labor, was set in motion at his desire, in opposition to their own. He realized himself a leader and a conqueror. He went into the office, and Flynn and Dennison came forward, smiling, to greet him.

"Well," said Dennison, "we're off again." He spoke as if the factory were a ship which had been launched from a shoal.

"Yes," replied Robert, gravely.

Nellie Stone, at the desk, was glancing around, with a half-shy, half-coquettish look.

"How is Mr. Risley?" asked Flynn.

"He is badly hurt," replied Robert. "Have they found the man? Do you know what has been done about it?"

"They've got all the police force of the city out," replied Flynn, "but it's no use. They'll never catch Amos Lee. His mother was a gypsy, I've always heard. He knows about a thousand ways out of traps, and there's plenty to help him. They've got Dixon under arrest, and Tom Peel; but they didn't have any fire-arms on 'em, and they can't prove anything. Peel says he's ready to go back to work." Flynn had a somewhat seedy and downcast appearance, although he fought hard for his old jaunty manner. His impulsive good nature had gotten the better of his judgment and his own wishes, and he had gone to Mamie Brady and offered to marry her out of hand if she recovered from her attempted suicide. The night before he had watched, turn and turn about, with her mother. He gave a curious effect of shamefaced and melancholy virtue. He followed Robert to one side when he was hanging up his hat and coat. "I'm going to tell you, Mr. Lloyd," he said, rather awkwardly; "maybe you won't be interested in the midst of all this, but it all came from the strike. She's better this morning, and I'm going to marry her, poor girl."

Robert looked at him in a dazed fashion. For a moment he had not the slightest idea what he was talking about.

"I'm going to marry Mamie Brady," explained Flynn. "She took laudanum. It all happened on account of the strike. I'll own I'd been flirting some with her, but she'd never done it if she hadn't been out of work, too. She said so. Her mother made her life a hell. I'm going to marry her, and take her out of it."

"It's mighty good of you," Robert said, rather stupidly.

"There ain't no other way for me to do," replied Flynn. "She thinks the world of me, and I suppose I'm to blame."

"I hope she'll make you a good wife and you'll be happy," said Robert.

"She thinks all creation of me," replied Flynn, with the simplest vanity and acquiescence in the responsibility laid upon him in the world. "That shot wasn't meant for Mr. Risley," said Flynn, as Robert approached the office door. His eyes flashed. He himself would gladly have been shot for the sake of Ellen Brewster. He was going to marry, and try to fulfill his simple code of honor, but all his life he would be married to one woman, with another ideal in his heart; that was inevitable.

"I know it wasn't," Robert replied, grimly.

"Everything is quiet now," said Dennison, with his smooth smile. Robert made no reply, but entered the great work-room. "He's mighty stand-offish, now he's got his own way," Dennison remarked in a whisper to Nellie Stone. He leaned closely over her. Flynn had followed Robert. The girl glanced up at the foreman, who was unmarried, although years older than she, and her face quivered a little, but it seemed due to a surface sensitiveness.

"I want to know if you've heard that Ed is going to marry Mamie Brady, after all," she whispered.

Dennison nodded.

She knitted her forehead over a column of figures. Dennison leaned his face so close that his blond-bearded cheek touched hers. She made a little impatient motion.

"Oh, go long, Jim Dennison," she said, but her tone was half-hearted.

Dennison persisted, bending her head gently backward until he kissed her. She pushed him away, but she smiled weakly.

"You didn't want Ed Flynn. Why, he's a Roman Catholic, and you're Baptist, Nell," he said.

"Who said I did?" she retorted, angrily. "Why, I wouldn't marry Ed Flynn if he was the last man in the world."

"You'd 'nough sight better marry me," said Dennison.

"Go along; you're fooling."

"No, I ain't. I mean it, honest."

"I don't want to marry anybody yet awhile," said Nellie Stone; but when Dennison kissed her again she did not repulse him, and even nestled her head with a little caressing motion into the hollow of his shoulder.

Then they both started violently apart as Flynn entered.

"Say!" he proclaimed, "what do you think? The boss has just told the hands that he'll split the difference and reduce the wages five instead of ten percent."

Chapter LIX

*W*hen Robert Lloyd entered the factory that morning he experienced one of those revulsions which come to man in common with all creation. As the wind can swerve from south to east, and its swerving be a part of the universal scheme of things, so the inconsistency of a human soul can be an integral part of its consistency. Robert, entering Lloyd's, flushed with triumph over his workmen, filled also with rage whenever he thought of poor Risley, became suddenly, to all appearances, another man. However, he was the same man, only he had come under some hidden law of growth. All at once, as he stood there amidst those whirring and clamping machines, and surveyed those bowed and patient backs and swaying arms of labor, standing aside to allow a man bending before a heavy rack of boots to push it to another department, he realized that his triumph was gone.

Not a man or woman in the factory looked at him. All continued working with a sort of patient fierceness, as if storming a citadel — as, indeed, they were in one sense — and waging incessant and in the end hopeless warfare against the destructive forces of life. Robert stood in the midst of them, these fellow-beings who had bowed to his will, and saw, as if by some divine revelation, in his foes his brothers and sisters. He saw Ellen's fair head before her machine, and she seemed the keynote of a heart-breaking yet ineffable harmony of creation which he heard for the first time. He was a man whom triumph did not exalt as much as it humiliated. Who was he to make these men and women do his bidding? They were working as hard as they had worked for full pay. Without doubt he would not gain as much comparatively, but he was going to lose nothing actually, and he would not work as these men worked. He saw himself as he never could have seen himself had the strike continued; and yet, after all, he was not a woman, to be carried away by a sudden wave of generous sentiment and enthusiasm, for his business instincts were too strong, inherited and developed by the force of example. He could not forget that this had been his uncle's factory.

He shut his mouth hard, and stood looking at the scene of toil, then he resolved what to do.

He spoke to Flynn, who could not believe his ears, and asked him over.

"I beg your pardon, sir," he said.

"Go and speak to the engineer, and tell him to shut down," said Robert.

"You ain't going to turn them out, after all?" gasped Flynn. He was deadly white.

"No, I am not. I only want to speak to them," replied Robert, shortly.

When the roar of machinery had ceased, Robert stood before the employés, whose faces had taken on an expression of murder and menace. They anticipated the worst by this order.

"I want to say to you all," said Robert, in a loud, clear voice, "that I realize it will be hard for you to make both ends meet with the cut of ten percent. I will make it five instead of ten percent, although I shall actually lose by so doing unless business improves. I will, however, try it as long as possible. If the hard times continue, and it becomes a sheer impossibility for me to employ you on these terms without abandoning the plant altogether, I will approach you again, and trust that you will support me in any measures I am forced to take. And, on the contrary, should business improve, I promise that your wages shall be raise to the former standard at once."

The speech was so straightforward that it sounded almost boyish. Robert, indeed, looked very young as he stood there, for a generous and pitying impulse does tend to make a child of a man. The workmen stared at him a minute, then there was a queer little broken chorus of "Thank ye's," with two or three shrill crows of cheers.

Robert went from room to room, repeating his short speech, then work recommenced.

"He's the right sort, after all," said Granville Joy to John Sargent, and his tone had a quality of heroism in it. He was very thin and pale. He had suffered privations, and now came additional worry of mind. He could not help thinking that this might bring about an understanding between Robert and Ellen, and yet he paid his spiritual dues at any cost.

"It's no more than he ought to do," growled a man at Granville's right. "S'pose he does lose a little money?"

"It ain't many out of the New Testament that are going to lose a little for the sake of their fellow-men, I can tell you that," said John Sargent. He was cutting away deftly and swiftly, and thinking with satisfaction of the money which he would be able to send his sister, and also how the Atkins family would be no longer so pinched. He was a man who would never come under the grindstone of the pessimism of life for his own necessities, but lately the necessities of others had almost forced him there. Now and then he glanced across the room at Maria, whose narrow shoulders he could see bent painfully over her work. He was in love with Maria, but no one suspected it, least of all Maria herself.

"Lord! don't talk about the New Testament. Them days is past," growled the man on the other side of Joy.

"They ain't past for me," said John Sargent, stoutly. A dark flush rose to his cheek as if he were making a confession of love.

"Lord! don't preach," said the other man, with a sneer.

Ellen had stopped work with the rest when Robert addressed them. Then she recommenced her stitching without a word. Her thoughts were in confusion. She had so long held one attitude towards him that she could not readily adjust herself to another. She was cramped with the extreme narrowness of the enthusiasm of youth. At noontime she heard all the talk which went on about him. She heard some praise him, and some speak of him as simply doing his manifest duty, and some say openly that he should have put the wages back upon the former footing, and she did not know which was right. He did not come near her, and she was very glad of that. She felt that she could not bear it to have him speak to her before them all.

When she went home at night the news had preceded her. Fanny and Andrew looked up eagerly when she entered. "I hear he has compromised," said Andrew, with doubtful eyes on the girl's face.

"Yes; he has cut the wages five instead of ten percent," replied Ellen, and it was impossible to judge of her feelings by her voice. She took off her hat and smoothed her hair.

"Well, I am glad he has done that much," said Fanny, "but I won't say a word as long as you ain't hurt."

With that she went into the kitchen, and Ellen and Andrew heard the dishes rattle. "Your mother's been dreadful nervous," whispered Andrew. He looked at Ellen meaningly. Both of them thought of poor Eva Tenny. Lately the reports with regard to her had been more encouraging, but she was still in the asylum.

Suddenly, as they stood there, a swift shadow passed the window, and they heard a shrill scream from upstairs. It sounded like "Mamma, mamma!" "It's Amabel!" cried Ellen. She clutched her father by the arm. "Oh, what is it — who is it?" she whispered, fearfully.

Andrew was suddenly white and horror-stricken. He took hold of Ellen, and pushed her forcibly before him into the parlor. "You stay in there till I call you," he said, in a commanding voice, the like of which the girl had never heard from him before; then he shut the door, and she heard the key turn in the lock.

"Father, I can't stay in here," cried Ellen. She ran towards the other door into the front hall, but before she could reach it she heard the key turn in that also. Andrew was convinced that Eva had escaped from the asylum, and thus made sure of Ellen's safety in case she was violent. Then he rushed out into the kitchen, and there was Amabel clinging to her mother like a little wild thing, and Fanny weeping aloud.

When Andrew entered Fanny flew to him. "O Andrew — O Andrew!" she cried. "Eva's come out! She's well! she's cured! She's as well as anybody! She is! She says so, and I know she is! Only look at her!"

"Mamma, mamma!" gasped Amabel, in a strange, little, pent voice, which did not sound like a child's. There was something fairly inhuman about it. "Mamma," as she said it, did not sound like a word in any known language. It was like a cry of universal childhood for its parent. Amabel clung to her mother, not only with her slender little arms, but with her legs and breast and neck; all her slim body became as a vine with tendrils of love and growth around her mother.

As for Eva, she could not have enough of her. She was intoxicated with the possession of this little creature of her own flesh and blood.

"She's grown; she's grown so tall," she said, in a high, panting voice. It was all she could seem to realize — the fact that the child had grown so tall — and it filled her at once with ineffable pain and delight. She held the little thing so close to her that the two seemed fairly one. "Mamma, mamma!" said Amabel again.

"She has — grown so tall," panted Eva.

Fanny went up to her and tried gently to loosen her grasp of the little girl. In her heart she was not yet quite sure of her. This fierceness of delight began to alarm her. "Of course she has grown tall, Eva Tenny," she said. "It's quite a while since you were — taken sick."

"I ain't sick now," said Eva, in a steady voice. "I'm cured now. The doctors say so. You needn't be afraid, Fanny Brewster."

"Mamma, mamma!" said Amabel. Eva bent down and kissed the little, delicate face; then she looked at her sister and at Andrew, and her own countenance seemed fairly illuminated. "I ain't *told* you all," said she. Then she stopped and hesitated.

"What is it, Eva?" asked Fanny, looking at her with increasing courage. The tears were streaming openly down her cheeks. "Oh, you poor girl, what have you been through?" she said. "What is it?"

"I ain't got to go through anything more," said Eva, still with that rapt look over Amabel's little, fair head. "He's — come back."

"Eva Tenny!"

"Yes, he has," Eva went on, with such an air of inexpressible triumph that it had almost a religious quality in it. "He has. He left her a long time ago. He — he wanted to come back to me and Amabel, but he was ashamed, but finally he came to the asylum, and then it all rolled off, all the trouble. The doctors said I had been getting better, but they didn't know. It was — Jim's comin' back. He's took me home, and I've come for Amabel, and — he's got a job in Lloyd's, and he's bought me this new hat and cape." Eva flirted her free arm, and a sweep of jetted silk gleamed, then she tossed her head consciously to display a hat with a knot of pink roses. Then she kissed Amabel again. "Mamma's come back," she whispered.

"Mamma, mamma!" cried Amabel.

Andrew and Fanny looked at each other.

"Where is he?" asked Andrew, in a slow, halting voice.

Eva glanced from one to the other defiantly. "He's outside, waitin' in the road," said she; "but he ain't comin' in unless you treat him just the same as ever. I've set my veto on that." Eva's voice and manner as she said that were so unmistakably her own that all Fanny's doubt of her sanity vanished. She sobbed aloud.

"O God, I'm so thankful! She's come home, and she's all right! O God, I'm so thankful!"

"What about Jim?" asked Eva, with her old, proud, defiant look.

"Of course he's comin' in," sobbed Fanny. "Andrew, you go —"

But Andrew had already gone, unlocking the parlor door on his way. "It's your aunt Eva, Ellen," he said as he passed. "She's come home cured, and your uncle Jim is out in the yard, and I'm goin' to call him in. I guess you'd better go out and see her."

Chapter LX

*L*loyd's had been running for two months, and spring had fairly begun. It was a very forward season. The elms were leafed out, the cherry and peach blossoms had fallen, and the apple trees were in full flower. There were many orchards around Rowe. The little city was surrounded with bowing garlands of tenderest white and rose, the well-kept lawns in the city limits were like velvet, and golden-spiked bushes and pink trails of flowering almond were beside the gates. Lilacs also, flushed with rose, purpled the walls of old houses. One morning Ellen, on her way to the factory, had for the first time that year a realization of the full presence of the spring. All at once she knew the goddess to be there in her whole glory.

"Spring has really come," she said to Abby. As she spoke she jostled a great bush of white flowers, growing in a yard close to the sidewalk, and an overpowering fragrance, like a very retaliation of sweetness, came in her face.

"Yes," said Abby; "it seems more like spring than it did last night, somehow!" Abby had gained flesh, and there was a soft color on her cheeks, so that she was almost pretty, as she glanced abroad with a sort of bright gladness and a face ready with smiles. Maria also looked in better health than she had done in the winter. She walked with her arm through Ellen's.

Suddenly a carriage, driven rapidly, passed them, and Cynthia Lennox's graceful profile showed like a drooping white flower in a window.

Sadie Peel came up to them with a swift run. "Say!" she said, "know who that was?"

"We've got eyes," replied Abby Atkins, shortly.

"Who said you hadn't? You needn't be so up an' comin', Abby Atkins; I didn't know as you knew they were married, that's all. I just heard it from Lottie Snell, whose sister works at the dressmaker's that made the wedding fix. Weddin' fix! My land! Think of a weddin' without a white dress and a veil! All she had was a grey silk and a black velvet, and a black lace, and a travelin'-dress!"

Abby Atkins eyed the other girl sharply, her curiosity getting the better of her dislike. "Who did she marry?" said she, shortly. "I suppose she didn't marry the black velvet, or the lace, or the traveling-dress. That's all you seem to think about."

"I *thought* you didn't know," replied Sadie Peel, in a tone of triumph. "They've kept it mighty still, and he's been goin' there so long, ever since anybody can remember, that they didn't think it was anything more now than it had been right along. Lyman Risley and Cynthia Lennox have just got married, and they've gone down to Old Point Comfort. My land, it's nice to have money, if you be half blind!"

Ellen looked after the retreating carriage, and made no comment.

She was pale and thin, and moved with a certain languor, although she held up her head proudly, and when people asked if she were not well, answered quickly that she had never been better. Robert had not been to see her yet. She had furtively watched for him a long time, then she had given it up. She would not acknowledge to herself or anyone else that she was not well or was troubled in spirit. Her courage was quite equal to the demand upon it, yet always she was aware of a peculiar sensitiveness to all happenings, whether directly concerned with herself or not, which made life an agony to her, and she knew that her physical strength was not what it had been. Only that morning she had looked at her face in the glass, and had seen how it was altered. The lovely color was gone from her cheeks, there were little, faint, downward lines about her mouth, and, more than that, out of her blue eyes looked the eternal, unanswerable question of humanity, "Where is my happiness?"

It seemed to her when she first set out that she could not walk to the factory. That sense of the full presence of the spring seemed to overpower her. All the revelation of beauty and sweetness seemed a refinement of torture worse to bear than the sight of death and misery would have been. Every blooming apple-bough seemed to strike her full on the heart.

"Only look at that bush of red flowers in that yard," Maria said once, and Ellen looked and was stung by the sight as by the contact of a red flaming torch of spring. "What ails you, dear; don't you like those flowers?" Maria said, anxiously.

"Yes, of course I do; I think they are lovely," replied Ellen, looking.

She looked after the carriage which contained the bridal party; she thought how the bridegroom had almost lost his eyesight to save her, and her old adoration of Cynthia seemed to rise to a flood-tide. Then came the thought of Robert, how he must have ceased to love her — how some day he would be starting off on a bridal trip of his own. Maud Hemingway, with whom she had often coupled him in her thoughts, seemed to start up before her, all dressed in bridal white. It seemed to her that she could not bear it all. She continued walking, but she did not feel the ground beneath her feet, nor even Maria's little, clinging fingers of tenderness on her arm. She became to her own understanding like an instrument which is played upon with such results of harmonies and discords that all sense of the mechanism is lost.

"Well, Ellen Brewster," said Sadie Peel, in her loud, strident voice, "I guess you wouldn't have been walkin' along here quite so fine this mornin' if it hadn't been for Mr. Risley. You'd ought to send him a weddin'-present — a spoon, or something."

"Shut up," said Abby Atkins; "Ellen has worried herself sick over him as it is." She eyed Ellen anxiously as she spoke. Maria clung more closely to her.

"Shut up yourself, Abby Atkins," returned Sadie Peel. "He's got a wife to lead him around, and I don't see much to worry about. A great weddin'! My goodness, if I don't get married when I'm young enough to wear a white dress and veil, catch me gettin' married at all!"

Sadie Peel sped on with her news to a group of girls ahead, and the wheels of the carriage flashed out of sight in the spring sunlight. It was quite true that Risley and Cynthia had been married that morning. He had not entirely lost his vision, although it would always be poor, and he would live happily, although in a measure disappointedly, feeling that his partial helplessness was his chief claim upon his wife's affection. He had gotten what he had longed for for so many years, but by means which tended to his humiliation instead of his pride. But Cynthia was radiant. In caring for her half-blind husband she attained the spiritual mountain height of her life. She possessed love in the one guise in which he appealed to her, and she held him fast to the illumination of her very soul.

After the carriage had passed out of sight Abby came close on the other side of Ellen and slid her arm through hers. "Say!" she began.

"What is it?" asked Ellen.

Abby blushed. "Oh, nothing much," she replied, in a tone unusual for her. She took her arm away from Ellen's, and laughed a little foolishly.

Ellen stared at her with grave wonder. She had not the least idea what she meant.

Abby changed the subject. "Going to the park opening tonight, Ellen?" she asked.

"No, I guess not."

"You'd better. Do go, Ellen."

"Yes, do go, Ellen; it will do you good," said Maria. She looked into Ellen's face with the inexpressibly pure love of one innocent girl for another.

The park was a large grove of oaks and birch trees which had recently been purchased by the street railway company of Rowe, and it was to be used for the free entertainment of the people, with an undercurrent of consideration for the financial profit of the company.

"I'm afraid I can't go," said Ellen.

"Yes, you can; it will do you good; you look like a ghost this morning," said Abby.

"Do go, Ellen," pleaded Maria.

However, Ellen would not have gone had it not been for a whisper of Abby's as they came out of the factory that night.

"Look here, Ellen, you'd better go," said she, "just to show folks. That Sadie Peel asked me this noon if it was true that you had something on your mind, and was worrying about — well, you know what — that made you look so."

Ellen flushed an angry red. "I'll stop for you and Maria tonight," she answered, quickly.

"All right," Abby replied, heartily; "we'll go on the eight-o'clock car."

Ellen hurried home, and changed her dress after supper, putting on her new green silk waist and her spring hat, which was trimmed with roses. When she went downstairs, and told her mother where she was going, she started up.

"I declare, I'd go too if your father had come home," she said. "I don't know when I've been anywhere; and Eva was in this afternoon and said that she and Jim were going."

"I wonder where father is?" said Ellen, uneasily. "I don't know as I ought to go till he comes home."

"Oh, stuff!" replied Fanny. "He's stopped to talk at the store. Oh, here he is now. Andrew Brewster, where in the world have you been?" she began as he entered; but his mother was following him, and something in their faces stopped her. Fanny Brewster had lived for years with this man, but never before had she seen his face with just that expression of utter, unreserved joy; although joy was scarcely the word for it, for it was more than that. It was the look of a man who has advanced to his true measure of growth, and regained self-respect which he had lost. All the abject bend of his aging back, all the apologetic patience of his outlook, was gone. She stared at him, hardly believing her eyes. She was as frightened as if he had looked despairing instead of joyful. "Andrew Brewster, what is it?" she asked. She tried to smile, to echo the foolish width of grimace on his face, but her lips were too stiff.

Ellen looked at him, trembling, and very white under her knot of roses. Andrew held out a paper and tried to speak, but he could not.

"For God's sake, what is it?" gasped Fanny.

Then Mrs. Zelotes spoke. "That old mining-stock has come up," said she, in a harsh voice. "He'd never ought to have bought it. I should have told him better if he had asked me, but it's come up, and it's worth considerable more than he paid for it. I've just been down to Mrs. Pointdexter's, and Lawyer Samson was in there seeing her about a bond she's got that's run out, and he says the mine's going to pay dividends, and for Andrew to hold on to part of it, anyhow. I bought this paper, and it's in it. He never ought to have bought it, but it's come up. I hope it will learn him a lesson. He's had enough trouble over it."

Nothing could exceed the mixture of recrimination and exultation with which the old woman spoke. She eyed Fanny accusingly; she looked at Andrew with grudging triumph. "Lawyer Samson says it will make him rich, he guesses; at any rate, he'll come out whole," said she. "I hope it will learn you a lesson."

Andrew dropped into a chair. His face was distended with a foolish smile like a baby's. He seemed to smile at all creation. He looked at his wife and Ellen; then his face again took on its expression of joyful vacuity.

Fanny went close to him and laid a firm hand on his shoulder. "You ain't had a mite of supper, Andrew Brewster," said she; "come right out and have something to eat."

Andrew shook his head, still smiling. His wife and daughter looked at him alarmedly, then at each other. Then his mother went behind him, laid a hard, old hand on each shoulder, and shook him.

"If you *have* got a streak of luck, there's no need of your actin' like a fool about it, Andrew Brewster," said she. "Go out and eat your supper, and behave yourself, and let it be a lesson to you. There you had worked and saved that little money you had in the bank, and you bought an old mine with it, and it might have turned out there wasn't a thing in it, no mine at all, and there was. Just let it be a lesson to you, that's all; and go out and eat your supper, and don't be too set up over it."

Andrew looked at his wife and mother and daughter, still with that expression of joy, so unreserved that it was almost idiotic. They had all stood by him loyally; he had their fullest sympathy; but had one of them fully understood? Not one of them could certainly understand what was then passing in his mind, which had been straitened by grief and self-reproach, and was now expanding to hold its full measure of joy. That poor little sum in the bank, that accumulation of his hard earnings, which he had lost through his own bad judgment, had meant much more than itself to him, both in its loss and its recovery. It was more than money; it was the value of money in the current coin of his own self-respect.

His mother shook him again, but rather gently. "Get up this minute, and go out and eat your supper," said she; "and then I don't see why you can't go with Fanny and me to the park opening. They say lots of folks are goin', and there's goin' to be fireworks. It'll distract your mind. It ain't safe for anybody to dwell too much on good luck anymore than on misfortune. Go right out and eat your supper; it's most time for the car."

Andrew obeyed.

Chapter LXI

*T*he new park, which had been named, in honor of the president of the street railway company, Clemens Park, was composed of a light growth of oak and birch trees. With the light of the full moon, like a broadside of silvery arrows, and the frequent electric-lights filtering through the young, delicate foliage, it was much more effective than a grove of pine or hemlock would have been.

When the people streamed into it from the crowded electric-cars, there were exclamations of rapture. Women and girls fairly shrieked with delight. The ground, which had been entirely cleared of undergrowth, was like an etching in clearest black and white, of the tender dancing foliage of the oaks and birches. The birches stood together in leaning, white-limbed groups like maidens, and the rustling spread of the oaks shed broad flashes of silver from the moon. In the midst of the grove the Hungarian orchestra played in a pavilion, and dancing was going on there. Many of the people outside moved with dancing steps. Children in swings flew through the airs with squeals of delight. There was a stand for the sale of ice-cream and soda, and pretty girls blossomed like flowers behind the counters. There were various rustic adornments, such as seats and grottos, and at one end of the grove was a small collection of wild animals in cages, and a little artificial pond with swans. Now and then, above the chatter of the people and the music of the orchestra, sounded the growl of a bear or the shrill screech of a parakeet, and the people all stopped and listened and laughed. This little titillation of the unusual in the midst of their sober walk of life affected them like champagne. Most of them were of the poorer and middle classes, the employés of the factories of Rowe. They moved back and forth with dancing steps of exultation.

"My, ain't it beautiful!" Fanny said, squeezing Andrew's arm. He had his wife on one arm, his mother on the other. For him the whole scene appeared more than it really was, since it reflected the joy of his own soul. There was for him a light greater than that of the moon or electricity upon it — that extreme light of the world — the happiness of a human being who blesses in a moment of prosperity the hour he was born. He knew for the first time in his life that happiness is as true as misery, and no mere creation of a fairy tale. No trees of the Garden of Eden could have outshone for him those oaks and birches. No gold or precious stones of any mines on earth can equal the light of the little star of happiness in one human soul.

Fanny, as they walked along, kept looking at her husband, and her own face was transfigured. Mrs. Zelotes, also, seemed to radiate with a sort of harsh and prickly delight. She descanted upon the hard-earned savings which Andrew had risked, but she held her old head very high with reluctant joy, and her bonnet had a rakish cant.

Ellen, with Abby and Maria, walked behind them.

Presently Andrew met another man who had also purchased stock in the mine, and stopped to exchange congratulations. The man's face was flushed, as if he had been drinking, but he had not. On his arm hung his wife, a young woman with a showy red waist and some pink ribbon bows on her hat. She was teetering a little in time to the music, while a little girl clung to her skirts and teetered also.

"Well, old man," said the newcomer, with a hoarse sound in his throat, "they needn't talk to us anymore, need they?"

"That's so," replied Andrew, but his joy in prosperity was not like the other man's. It placed him heights above him, although from the same cause. Prosperity means one thing to one man, and another to his brother.

Presently they met Jim Tenny and Eva and Amabel. They were walking three abreast, Amabel in the middle. Jim Tenny looked hesitatingly at them, although his face was widened with irrepressible smiles. Eva gazed at them with defiant radiance. "Well," said she, "so luck has turned?"

Amabel laughed out, and her laugh trilled high with a note of silver, above the chatter of the crowd and the blare and rhythmic trill of the orchestra. "I've had an ice-cream, and I'm going to have a new doll and a doll-carriage," said she. "Oh, Ellen!" She left her father and mother for a second and clung to Ellen, kissing her; then she was back.

"Well, Andrew?" said Jim. He had a shamed face, yet there was something brave in it struggling for expression.

"Well, Jim?" said Andrew.

The two shook hands solemnly. Then they walked on together, and the sisters behind, with Amabel clinging to her mother's hand. "Jim's goin' to work if he *has* had a little windfall," said Eva, proudly. "Oh, Fanny, only think what it means!"

"I hope it will be a lesson to both of them," said Mrs. Zelotes, stalking along after, but she smiled harshly.

"Oh, land, don't croak, if you've got a chance to laugh! There's few enough chances in this world," cried Eva, with boisterous good humor. "As for me, I've come out of deep waters, and I'm goin' to take what comfort I can in the feel of the solid ground under my feet." She began to force Amabel into a dance in time with the music, and the child shrieked with laughter.

"S'pose she's all right?" whispered Mrs. Zelotes to Fanny.

"Land, yes," replied Fanny; "it's just like her, just the way she used to do. It makes me surer than anything else that she's cured."

The girls behind were loitering. Abby turned to Ellen and pointed to a rustic seat under a clump of birches.

"Let's sit down there a minute, Ellen," said she.

"All right," replied Ellen. When she and Abby seated themselves, Maria withdrew, standing aloof under an oak, looking up at the illumined spread of branches with the rapt, innocent expression of a saint.

"Why don't you come and sit down with us, Maria?" Ellen called.

"In a minute," replied Maria, in her weak, sweet voice. Then John Sargent came up and joined her.

"She'll come in a minute," Abby said to Ellen. "She — she — knows I want to tell you something."

Abby hesitated. Ellen regarded her with wonder.

"Look here, Ellen," said Abby; "I don't know what you're going to think of me after all I've said, but — I'm going to get married to Willy Jones. His mother has had a little money left her, and she owns the house clear now, and I'm going to keep right on working; and — I never thought I would, Ellen, you know; but I've come to think lately that all you can get out of labor in this world is the happiness it brings you, and — the love. That's more than the money, and — he wants me pretty bad. I suppose you think I'm awful, Ellen Brewster." Abby spoke with triumph, yet with shame. She dug her little toe into the shadow-mottled ground.

"Oh, Abby, I hope you'll be real happy," said Ellen. Then she choked a little.

"I've made up my mind not to work for nothing," said Abby; "I've made up my mind to get whatever work is worth in this world if I can, and — to get it for him too."

"I hope you will be very happy," said Ellen again.

"There he is now," whispered Abby. She rose as Willy Jones approached, laughing confusedly. "I've been telling Ellen Brewster," said Abby, with her perfunctory air.

Ellen held out her hand, and Willy Jones grasped it, then let it drop and muttered something. He looked with helpless adoration at Abby, who put her hand through his arm reassuringly.

"Let's go and see the animals," said she; "I haven't seen the animals."

"I guess I'll go and see if I can find my father and mother," returned Ellen. "I want to see my mother about something."

"Oh, come with us." Abby grasped Ellen firmly around the waist and kissed her. "I don't love him a mite better than I do you," she whispered; "so there! You needn't think you're left out, Ellen Brewster."

"I don't," replied Ellen. She tried to laugh, but she felt her lips stiff. And unconquerable feeling of desolation was coming over her, and in spite of herself her tone was somewhat like that of a child who sees another with all the cake.

"I suppose you know Floretta got married last night," said Abby, moving off with Willy Jones. John Sargent and Maria had long since disappeared from under the oak.

Ellen, left alone, looked for a minute after Abby and Willy, and noted the tender lean of the girl's head towards the young man's shoulder; then she started off to find her father and mother. She could not rid herself of the sense of desolation. She felt blindly that if she could not get under the shelter of her own loves of life she could not bear it any longer. She had borne up bravely under Robert's neglect, but now all at once, with the sight of the happiness of these others before her eyes, it seemed to crush her. All the spirit in her seemed to flag and faint. She was only a young girl, who would fall to the ground and be slain by the awful law of gravitation of the spirit without love. "Anyway, I've got father and mother," she said to herself.

She rushed on alone through the merry crowd. The orchestra was playing a medley. The violins seemed to fairly pierce thought. A Roman-candle burst forth on the right with a great spluttering, and the people, shrieking with delight, rushed in that direction. Then a rocket shot high in the air with a splendid curve, and there was a sea of faces watching with speechless admiration the dropping stars of violet and gold and rose.

Ellen kept on, moving as nearly as she could in the direction in which her party had gone. Then suddenly she came face to face with Robert Lloyd.

She would have passed him without a word, but he stood before her.

"Won't you speak to me?" he asked.

"Good-evening, Mr. Lloyd," returned Ellen.

Then she tried to move on again, but Robert still stood before her.

"I want to say something to you," he said, in a low voice. "I was coming to your house tonight, but I saw you on the car. Please come to that seat over there. There is nobody in that direction. They will all go towards the fireworks now."

Ellen looked at him hesitatingly. At that moment she seemed to throw out protecting antennæ of maidenliness; and, besides, there was always the memory of the cut in wages, for which she still judged him; and then there was the long neglect.

"Please come," said Robert. He looked at her at once like a conqueror and a pleading child. Ellen placed her hand on his arm, and they went to the seat under the clump of birches. They were quite alone, for the whole great company was streaming towards the fireworks. A fiery wheel was revolving in the distance, and rockets shot up, dropping showers of stars. Ellen gazed at them without seeing them at all.

Robert, seated beside her, looked at her earnestly. "I am going to put back the wages on the old basis tomorrow," he said.

Ellen made no reply.

"Business has so improved that I feel justified in doing so," said Robert. His tone was almost apologetic. Never as long as he lived would he be able to look at such matters from quite the same standpoint as that of the girl beside him. She knew that, and yet she loved him. She never would get his point of view, and yet he loved her. "I have waited until I was able to do that before speaking to you again," said Robert. "I knew how you felt about the wage-cutting. I thought when matters were back on the old basis that you might feel differently towards me. God knows I have been sorry enough for it all, and I am glad enough to be able to pay them full wages again. And now, dear?"

"It has been a long time," said Ellen, looking at her little hands, clasped in her lap.

"I have loved you all the time, and I have only waited for that," said Robert.

*L*ater on Robert and Ellen joined Fanny and the others. It was scarcely the place to make an announcement. After a few words of greeting the young couple walked off together, and left the Brewsters and Tennys and Mrs. Zelotes standing on the outskirts of the crowd watching the fireworks. Granville Joy stood near them. He had looked at Robert and Ellen with a white face, then he turned again towards the fireworks with a gentle, heroic expression. He caught up Amabel that she might see the set piece which was just being put up. "Now you can see, Sissy," he said.

Eva looked away from the fireworks after the retreating pair, then meaningly at Fanny and Andrew. "That's settled," said she.

Andrew's face quivered a little, and took on something of the same look which Granville Joy's wore. All love is at the expense of love, and calls for heroes.

"It'll be a great thing for her," said Fanny, in his ear; "it'll be a splendid thing for her, you know that, Andrew."

Andrew gazed after the nodding roses on Ellen's hat vanishing towards the right. Another rocket shot up, and the people cried out, and watched the shower of stars with breathless enjoyment. Andrew saw their upturned faces, in which for the while toil and trial were blotted out by that delight in beauty and innocent pleasure of the passing moment which is, for human souls, akin to the refreshing showers for flowers of spring; and to him, since his own vision was made clear by his happiness, came a mighty realization of it all, which was beyond it all. Another rocket described a wonderful golden curve of grace, then a red light lit all the watching people. Andrew looked for Ellen and Robert, and saw the girl's beautiful face turning backward over her lover's shoulder. All his life Andrew had been a reader of the Bible, as had his father and mother before him. Today, ever since he had heard of his good fortune, his mind had dwelt upon certain verses of Ecclesiastes. Now he quoted from them. "Live joyfully with the wife whom thou lovest all the days of the life of thy vanity, which He hath given thee under the sun, all the days of thy vanity, for that is thy portion in this life and in thy labor which thou takest under the sun."

Ellen saw her father, and smiled and nodded, then she and her lover passed out of sight. Another rocket trailed its golden parabola along the sky, and dropped with stars; there was an ineffably sweet strain from the orchestra; the illuminated oaks tossed silver and golden boughs in a gust of fragrant wind. Andrew quoted again from the old King of Wisdom — "I withheld not my heart from any joy, for my heart rejoiced in all my labor, and that was my portion of labor." Then Andrew thought of the hard winter which had passed, as all hard things must pass, of the toilsome lives of those beside him, of all the work which they had done with their poor, knotted hands, of the tracks which they had worn on the earth towards their graves, with their weary feet, and suddenly he seemed to grasp a new and further meaning for that verse of Ecclesiastes.

He seemed to see that labor is not alone for itself, not for what it accomplishes of the tasks of the world, not for its equivalent in silver and gold, not even for the end of human happiness and love, but for the growth in character of the laborer.

"That is the portion of labor," he said. He spoke in a strained, solemn voice, as he had done before. Nobody heard him except his wife and mother. His mother gave a sidewise glance at him, then she folded her cape tightly around her and stared at the fireworks, but Fanny put her hand through his arm and leaned her cheek against his shoulder.

THE END

www.ingramcontent.com/pod-product-compliance
Lightning Source LLC
Chambersburg PA
CBHW030356030726
47497CB00002B/367